Alamo Dawn

Copyright © 2012 by Brian Henderson

Library of Congress Cataloging-in Publication Data
   Henderson, Brian "Alamo Dawn"Brian Henderson

Includes references and index

ISBN: 13: 978-1-934947-70-8

First Printing, Asta Publications, LLC, trade paperback edition, January 2013

1. Fiction. Title

Printed in the United States of America.

Alamo Dawn

Brian Henderson

Acknowledgements:

Giving thanks first and foremost to God. I'd like to thank my mother, brothers, and posthumously my father, and everyone who believed in me... that I could defeat the circumstances of a lengthy prison stay to achieve my goals. Love to my wife and beautiful children Karissa, Trinity, and Destin. Much appreciation to Assuanta.

Thank you

Chapter 1

It was a hot and muggy day: typical of an August afternoon in the southwestern plains region of San Antonio, Texas. The light blue sky was strewn with cumulous clouds because of a light breeze in the troposphere, which shifted across the sky and momentarily obscured the sun.

The traffic whizzed along busy Broadway Avenue past the ancient mission, The Alamo. The cars below and one in particular, a white late model Acura, passed by as the drivers momentarily observed the structure on their way to and from other subdivisions, which encompassed this bustling south Texas city. As the highlighted vehicle sped through intersections, the topography changed from the monolithic building structures, to business outlets, to the degenerative and dilapidated communities of the Eastside, which was predominately African American, and as in most U.S. cities, a setting for the debasement of the inhabitants by law enforcement officers and tension from an assortment of other antagonizing agents.

The white Acura was now in the heart of the Eastside, idling down Nevada St. before coming to a stop in front of a stylishly decorated white and green house with a fence encompassing it. In its front lawn were a variety of flowers and plants, giving the residence a rather floral serenity and quaintness, evidence of the presence of an elderly lady being at the head of this humble abode.

The occupant of the white Acura was a slim, light skinned brother named Devonté whose attention was directed in the same direction as the two boys standing in the yard behind the fence. There appeared to be a situation transpiring directly across the busy Avenue. Several white and grey unmarked agent cars aligned on the street in front of a convenience store where narcotics agents, dressed in dark blue jackets with the letters A.T.F. superimposed across the backs, were interceding. They donned black semi-automatics at their sides as they cautioned would-be store patrons that the business was closed. Devonté walked around the front of the car and glanced back at the narcotics agents as they entered into the convenience store, which was owned by Pakistanis. As Devonté entered through the front gate, his friends greeted him. One commented on the brand new Rocawear T-shirt and jeans he wore low slung over a pair of white Dada sneakers.

"Devonte', what's goin on, main? Rocawear? Dada?" stated a slim kid with a short haircut. His name was Braun.

Devonte's cousin Phil stated, "My aunt's car. You must be on your way to see Cameisha up in Live Oak?" He smiled, revealing three gold teeth. His name was Phil. He was nineteen years old, slightly older than both of them. His attire was suggestive of his involvement in narcotics sales. Devonte' shook his head.

"Cameisha? Main that's playin' it real close, huh? Don't Sharon stay in Live Oak, too?" Braun asked.

"Come on, main. I'm a playa. Anyway, what's goin' on wit dat?" he inquired nodding his head in the direction of the store. At that moment the narcotics agents appeared with their suspects in custody: two Pakistanis, one middle aged man with dark hair and heavyset and the other man looked to be in his mid-twenties, sporting expensive looking wire rimmed glasses. Both were dressed conservatively, with dress slacks. They wore expressions of non-complacency as they were escorted in handcuffs by the burly officers.

This was a scene that was beginning to happen with frequency within their community. Foreign entities such as these Pakistanis had begun to envelope the African American community. Free enterprising. Many of them were conglomerating to create large enterprises to the dissatisfaction of the denizens within the community, not on the pretense of racism, but rather a mutual sense of free enterprise disenfranchisement within their own community.

These foreign entities for the most part were hard laboring, business minded, blue collar citizens whom emigrated to the western hemisphere from Vietnam, Korea, Japan, Saudi Arabia, and in this case, Pakistan. They came in search of better market opportunities to effectuate their business ventures. However, as in all ethnicities, there remains a certain element of criminal mentality. Such is the case of this father and son team.

Phil took a sip of his cherry cola as he looked over in the direction of the narcotics agents then smiled at Devonte's naïveté.

"Main, you know what happenin' wit dat. Ery'body knows you can get what you want out Zak's; the works, and the product," Phil commented.

"Prob'ly been under investigation," Braun added.

"Gotta respect they hustle." Devonte' commented.

Braun shook his head in disagreement. "I'ont respect it. Nothin' bout'em. I mean, ones that legit." Phil took another sip of his cola and proceeded to hop up on the porch. Reaching for the door's handle he turned and said, "Main, you startin' ta be like dem Muslims. Come on main. Let's play some John Madden. Shoot! It's hot out here," Phil finished as he opened the door.

Devonte's face ignited at hearing the statement. Excited about playing his favorite video game, he blurted, "You got Madden? Which one? 04?" Devonte' inquired as he reached into his front pocket to turn on his car's alarm system. Braun yelled, "03. I got it from Marquis. Know, he 'bout some Madden. But my grandma sleep, so ya'll hold all dat noise down."

As the boys entered the house, the narcotics agents pulled away from the scene with their suspects in custody.

✶✶✶✶✶✶✶✶

Tariq Galla, CEO of a telecommunications company located in downtown San Antonio, is in complete thought as he taps on the keys of his computer. The office is buzzing with business-clad employees sitting at their cubicles typing away or walking around the office. The company provided marketing opportunities to international web marketers allowing them to expand their global reach. Tariq's company translated marketing products from English to various other languages, which was essential considering that 35.8% of the global online population speaks English. His work consumed a lot of his time and financial resources. For him to remain competitive, he converted his web site and marketing projects into more than one language to include: Spanish, Chinese, Hindi, Russian, and French.

Tariq reclined back in his swivel chair, took a sip of his coffee, shut off his computer, and yelled to his receptionist, "Mrs. Williams, check on that shipment we are expecting; the money exchange software. I am going home." Tariq grabbed his portfolio and headed out the door.

Tariq gripped the leather stearing wheel of his Lincoln Continental as he sped down the 410 expressway. Observing the sights of the city and other motorists as they whizzed by, he looked down at his speedometer. "70 mph. Humph." He chuckled to himself. "Everybody's in a hurry these days," he thought to himself. Then he glanced down at his watch; it was 5:45 p.m.

He was now cruising past moderate wood frame houses in his former eastside neighborhood: liquor stores, churches, low income housing projects, wood frame and brick homes, children at play, gang members congregating on corners, drug dealers passing by in hot new cars thumping, and gold teeth exposed. As he wheels the Lincoln onto Wyoming Street he slows down a block from the corner right in front of several youths who represented the neighborhood street gang.

Tariq Galla's name is a self-appointed Nubian name. He was originally given the name Lemone' Fields by two blue collar working parents who'd been born and raised in a small cow town in south Texas. It wasn't until after his sophomore year at University of Texas San Antonio that he became enthralled with the religious concepts and ideologies of Nubia.

Later, his Nubian mentor bestowed him the rite to membership within the Nubian Order. This was a group that had been formed during the radical 1960's.

He was now a professed descendent of Nubia and even more of a zealot for the advancement of his people, the African American people, whom he fought to liberate from the mental and socioeconomic deterioration of their current situation. He was an educator, an activist within the community, and a reactionary on the front lines of his people's never ending struggle against oppression.

He changed his surname to Galla, Tariq learned the Cushitic language and was now a member of the Organization for Black Unity (O.B.U.). He was highly educated, having earned a Bachelor of Arts in business and a Masters of Science in Sociology. His credentials, in sociology of course, enabled him to interact with the denizens of the community. He personally evaluated their problems, be it social or economic, and assessed the necessary measures he or she needed to take. He offered solutions, and whenever there was tension from whatever source, he had the rational approach. Whenever there were food drives, rallies, demonstrations etc., he was on the front lines. If there were political issues that needed to be addressed in front of a national forum, he was the voice of the community and everyone respected his opinions.

As Tariq's Lincoln rolled to a halt, the youth gang members were startled. A small framed, baby faced kid who couldn't have been more than fourteen, continued to inhale a marijuana joint until it was jerked from his fingertips. An older, more muscular youth snatched it and hid it behind his back as the fourteen year old coughed. With a perplexed expression he coughed out, "Hey Main!" The other members, most of them with their shirts off and low slung jeans conspicuously lowered their 40 oz. bottles of beer from their lips and respectfully gathered themselves for the brother Tariq. A dark skinned heavy-set kid with a bald head and scar on his face did his best to conceal what was obviously a hand gun.

"Hum, Brother Tariq. What brangs you by, main?" A brown skinned, baby faced kid asked as he smiled, showing his missing front tooth which clashed with his straight, white dental work. His eyes reddened from the effects of alcohol as he folded his arms before him. His body tattoos were evidence of his trek through the Texas Department of Corrections.

"Wild Bill, how's it going? Been reading any of the pamphlets I gave you at the center?" Tariq inquired. Wild Bill's eyes momentarily diverted from his. Then his smile widened as he looked back at Tariq.

"Yeah, yeah, main…I uh, was really into the one dealin' wit' community and socio…how you say? R-e-pree-sion?" he replied while gesturing with his hands, his black bandanna wavering with each movement as it was tied loosely around his fist.

"Repression. Socioeconomic repression." Tariq enlightened. "Bull, changed your mind about going back to Vo-tech school? Pretty lucrative trade in welding," Tariq inquired while concentrating on the burly kid with the bald head.

"Ah, yeah. I been givin' it some thought, Brother Tariq," Bull responded.

"Yeah, he like makin' sparks fly," stated the youngest kid in humor. There were snickers to his statement.

Tariq smiled. He then focused in on this wayward youth. It was apparent that the kid was a "wanna be." Tariq knew his mother and father well. Middle class, hardworking citizens who were doing their best to support and educate their only son in the proper routes in life, but he was enthralled with the gangster persona.

"Christopher, what…" His words were interjected as the kid cautioned him amidst laughs.

"Lil Gun. Dey call me Lil Gun," he responded as he tried to make his voice sound more masculine.

"Excuse me. Lil Gun. Why haven't you been going to school? You were making decent grades," Tariq stated. Lil Gun's expression was of embarrassment. In his misguided, adolescent frame of mind, to be given accolades for exceptional academic performance was debasing to his "thug image."

"Oh, main…I ain't got time for school. Ain't teachin' me nuttin' I can use. 'Sides, the set needs me. Gotta hold down the fort. Lotta desperados round here," Lil Gun responded.

"Like dem cholovattos. Or them rag head mafuckas dere," stated the fourth youth who was very light skinned and sporting a du-rag. As he commented he pointed in the direction of a middle aged Pakistani man getting out of a sedan in front of his business establishment. Tariq looked over into the direction the kid had motioned and then shook his head in disagreement.

"Nah, I don't think the Mexicans or the Pakistani are the desperados that you need to worry about, Red Dog. Definitely not Mr. Hamburani. But, they may be a problem," Tariq stated while motioning with a pointed finger towards an approaching police cruiser. The gang members dispersed. First walking briskly until the police cruiser's horn squawked and then they all ran separate ways as the cruiser sped past Tariq, whom remained idling on the corner. Tariq shook his head as he watched the gang disappear through building establishments while the cruiser crept down the boulevard.

✶✶✶✶✶✶✶✶

Tariq was greeted with a welcoming kiss by his wife of sixteen years, Ursula, when he walked through their modest brick home in Live Oak. After a brief embrace, Ursula returned to the kitchen to finish cooking and Tariq unbuttoned his dress shirt and released a sigh of fatigue. As Ursula opened the top of the crock-pot, steam released and a tantalizing aroma of specially spiced baked chicken caused Tariq to inhale deeply.

"Smells good. What's this you're cooking?" he inquired as he peeked over her shoulder into the pot. Ursula smiled.

"Stewed chicken. I was browsing through the recipe book and just thought I'd prepare a little gourmet meal," she stated while mimicking the dialect of some French chef.

Tariq smiled and nodded as he began to take off his tie. "You haven't lost your touch. You're still the best gourmet chef I know," Tariq stated.

"How were things down at the office?" she inquired as she began stirring the other entrées.

"Headaches, which is why I left early. Translating web sites for hours," he laughed. At that moment his fifteen-year-old daughter, Ikara, appeared. She kissed him on the cheek. She was the image of her mother with permed hair flowing onto her shoulders.

"Hi Dad," she chimed.

"Ikara, how'd you do on your exams today?" he asked as he proceeded out of the kitchen.

"I got an A," she replied as she flounced onto the couch and crossed her legs Indian style.

"That's good, baby girl. I'm proud of you," Tariq replied.

"Caleb, dinner is almost ready, go ahead and wash your hands," Ursula yelled to their twelve year old son who was playing with his PlayStation inside of his room.

Little did she know that Caleb's senses were tantalized by the aroma of the stewed chicken and he was waiting for his mother to let him know that dinner was ready.

"O.K., mom," he yelled back. Then he shot out of his room without even shutting off the game.

The Nubian family was now settled around their green clothed dining room table. Ursula set the table with the main course as the centerpiece. The sides of salad, bread, peas, and blueberry muffins encircled it. Coming from a culinarily rich and extremely diet conscious family, Ursula not only took pride in the preparation of the meal, but also in the table setting itself.

In the Galla family household, healthy diets of the basic food groups were essential and Ursula made sure that they got their share of daily vitamins. They consumed green salads and fruits daily in addition to fish and poultry. The family found the consumption of pork or pork products unacceptable, for health purposes.

Tariq motioned for all the members of his family to bow their heads in prayer. With his hands in customary prayer and salutation, he incanted the opening prayer of the Cushitic religious rites. After a moment of silent prayer, he ended the dedication by recanting the opening acknowledgement.

The family began passing around different entrees with each allotting the proportion they so desired. Typical with most siblings, little Caleb was playfully teasing his older sister over something that only the two knew about and this prompted Ikara to feint hitting him.

"Okay you two. We're at the dinner table," Ursula cautioned. Tariq smiled as he began cutting into his chicken breast. After sampling the first bite, his eyes registered his pleasure at the gourmet prepared chicken entrée, and he nodded in approval. The children however, simply tore into the dishes and gulped down large quantities of Kool Aid.

"Slow down Caleb. What's the hurry? That PlayStation isn't going anywhere," Ursula smiled. Caleb smiled and lowered his head attempting to take his time. Tariq chewed his food and observed his young son. In him he saw himself at that young age. Growing up in the 1970's, he remembered how he'd idolized his father for his strength, spirituality, and devotion to his mother. But perhaps the most compelling part of his father's character was his determination and hard work. His father was an entrepreneur and this was a motivating factor when he started his own business. He was proud of his father and he did his best to be a role model for his own children.

"Caleb, have you thought about what we discussed the other day, son?" Tariq inquired as he wiped the remnants of food from his mouth. Caleb fidgeted around with his peas before responding.

"Yeah, I thought about it. But kinda wanna just do what other kids do over their summer breaks," he responded dryly.

Tariq nodded and continued his meal as he stared at his son. "Caleb, I'm surprised at you. God has blessed us in ways that are far greater than children who are underprivileged and it's not like this is an everyday thing. It is only on the weekends," Ursula rationalized.

Tariq cautioned Ursula and said, "We're not forcing him. I'll let it be a call of his own conscience. I feel that he'll see that helping in these food drives for these underprivileged children is the right thing to do." Tariq moved on to Ikara as he let his son think about what he just said. "Ikara, I hear you're planning to switch to Roosevelt High School next semester. Any particular reason why? What's wrong with Judson?" Tariq inquired.

Ikara's eyebrows rose as she sipped her beverage. Setting her glass down she smiled and released a slight giggle.

"Well, there's nothing wrong with Judson. I just want a change of scenery. That's all," she replied looking down.

"A change in scenery?" Tariq offered.

"Yeah, well, I've been there two years. Plus, Roosevelt is interesting," she continued.

Tariq smiled, "Hmm. Roosevelt is interesting? Well, as long as your reasoning is along the lines of academics, I don't see any reason why you shouldn't switch."

Ursula smiled and the two exchanged meaningful glances. "It's not because of a certain Braun Erickson, is it?" Ursula smiled.

"Mom," Ikara stated as she hid her face in embarrassment.

Minutes had passed and the family was now finished with their meals. Tariq wiped the last remnants of sauce from his mouth as Ursula and Ikara gathered up the trays.

"Here, my servant," Caleb stated as he handed Ikara his tray. Ikara pinched his arm causing him to squeal. Caleb quickly moved away and caught sight of his friends outside of the kitchen window. He jumped up from the table and headed towards the front door.

"Off to the races already? Did you finish your homework, Caleb? 'Cause you've been in that room all afternoon on that game," Ursula shouted behind him. He responded that he'd completed his homework and then disappeared out the front door. Shaking her head, Ursula smiled, but her eyes registered concern. She proceeded back into the kitchen to wash the dishes.

Ursula entered the living room where Tariq was reclined back in his leather chair flipping through the newspaper. Tariq looked up and noticed the concerned expression on his wife's face. Before he could speak, a glass shattered in the kitchen.

"Oops. Sorry, mom," Ikara replied.

Ursula shook her head and smiled.

"Well, that leaves seven of my crystal glasses. I wondered if it was a good omen when Ikara started helping with the dishes," she laughed.

Tariq laughed. After a brief pause, he stared at his wife again and inquired, "Something troubling you, honey?"

Ursula sighed and then looked away. After a brief silence, she responded, "I don't know. Maybe I'm being a little over protective. But, I'm worried about Caleb."

Tariq set the newspaper upon his knee and meditated over her assertion. "Worried about Caleb?" he asked looking into his wife's eyes.

Ursula smiled. After a pause she arose from her seat and looked out of the window at her son as the boys laughed.

"Well, his grades aren't nearly as good and I just don't feel he's with the right peers," she remarked.

"We moved from the eastside. These are middle class kids. Are you now suggesting we send him off to boarding school?" he laughed.

"I'm serious Tariq. Just because this is Live Oak doesn't mean there still can't be bad influences. Remember the big drug raid? Negative influences are out here, too," Ursula stated.

"I know, I know, honey. And I wasn't trying to mock you. Look, Caleb's ok, so he's not making straight A's anymore, but the school curriculum has become more difficult at the junior high level. His grades are still good and his grade point average is high. Meaning he's still applying himself," Tariq assured her.

"I'm just beginning to notice little changes. I've overheard some of their conversations. Those boys are so caught up in the rapture of the street life and the images that they see on those rap videos. They are impressionable and Caleb associates with them. Who knows what kind of peer pressure they have him under when they're together, away from here," Ursula sighed.

Tariq smiled, but perhaps out of respect for his wife's melodrama remained serious. "They're pre-teens. Caleb will be thirteen next month. It's the generational gap with this rap and drug culture thing. Look, we're raising him right. Teaching him values," Tariq reasoned.

"You're making light of this, Tariq," Ursula stated.

"Look, Caleb's friends are good kids. They come from good homes. Jerry's father's a lawyer. And Chris is already making plans to be an engineer," Tariq stated in an attempt to trivialize his wife's apprehensiveness.

"You seem to know a lot about them," Ursula stated.

"Well, yes. I talk to them. I talk to all of the black youth. Remember that is what we do at O.B.U.," Tariq stated.

"Well, what does Caleb plan to do? What are his endeavors? Has he ever experimented with drugs? I know you know whether or not those other boys you mentor have tried drugs. What about our son? I know we have an obligation to the O.B.U. to talk to and mentor other black youth, but try to take out some time to talk to our son," she stressed as she walked away.

Chapter 2

Dressed in formal attire, which consisted of a tan shirt, slacks, loafers and a white Kufi, and an Islamic knit cap, Tariq stood outside of a small building off East Houston. A spectacled middle-aged man, small in stature with dark brown hair by the name of Mr. Nawaz Jinnah, joined him. His eyes were sincere and the warm smile that creased his Indian visage was reflective of his good nature and genuine spirituality. He was a Pakistani, from Islamabad and a devout follower of the Islamic faith.

Nawaz spoke English fluently, as well as his daughter and wife of twenty-one years, whom he met at an Islamic extravaganza thirteen years after his arrival in America. They met in 1971, the year that the civil war had broken out in his native Pakistan. The civil war resulted in East Pakistan declaring itself an independent nation called Bangladesh. In December 1971, India joined Bangladesh against West Pakistan. Two weeks after India's interjection, Pakistan surrendered. More than a million people died in this bloody war and President Yahya Khan resigned. With this resignation, Jinnah family immigrated to the United States.

Tariq and Nawaz had met under rather dubious circumstances. It was during a period of ethnic tensions arising after the September 11th terrorist attacks. Many citizens, black and white because of their ignorance about different ethnicities, enacted reprisals against anyone resembling Arabs, Indians, Iranians, and in one incident, even a Columbian was assaulted. His store was pelted with bricks. Nawaz had nearly become a victim when he attempted to leave his car and was met with bottles and bricks being thrown at him by four African American young men. Tariq happened to be driving near the store and saw what was going on and jumped out of his vehicle to provide assistance. Recognizing Tariq, the boys tossed their weapons and fled. Nawaz aptly thanked him, and invited him over to have dinner with him, his wife, and young daughter. Three years had passed and the relationship between Nawaz and Tariq had developed spiritually and socially. Both being from opposing sides of the ethnic strife had helped ease the tension, somewhat. The tension between the African American community and those of Middle Eastern descent were strong. Even though Tariq and Nawaz's friendship developed through the community city, their joint venture, there was still a little distrust between them, because of their different backgrounds.

The two stood before their joint venture in the community; a non-profit organization sponsored community center. They created a curriculum that had been well received and accredited. Imposing tutors, life skills teachers, health instructors, and perhaps most important, spiritual counselors were on hand to advise the children about the importance of believing in a higher power.

News cameras and reporters from San Antonio newspapers and television broadcasts were in position and gave the two sponsors their queue for the live broadcast. Cars passed by on the busy avenue with some slowing to observe the camera crews as the camera flashed and denizens passed by.

The nation of Pakistan itself was a product of a governmental split of the country of India. After, however, riots and religious conflicts incurred between the Hindus and Muslims. The new nation of Pakistan (an Urdu word meaning 'land of the pure') had its name proposed by the president of the Muslim League, Muhammad Ali Jinnah, became an independent dominion in the Commonwealth of Nations.

The country was annexed from the northwestern and northeastern parts of India, where followers of the Islamic faith make up the majority of the population. More than 1000 miles of the Indian terrain lay between the two sections, which were called Pakistan and East Pakistan. Muhammad Ali Jinnah became the first head of government. Conflicts between Hindus and Muslims continued even after the Partition of India, and approximately 10 million people fled from one country to the other. Hindus and Sikhs fled to India while Muslims left Pakistan. Thousands would die in this migration.

Disputes of independent Kashmir in 1948 resulted in war between India and Pakistan. Pakistan claimed Kashmir due to its peoples being primarily Muslim. But after Pakistani troops invaded Kashmir, the region's Hindu ruler annexed it to India. Indian and Pakistani troops fought until 1949, when the United Nations arranged a cease-fire. Pakistan became a republic in 1956, appointing Major General Iskander Mirza as its President. Military leaders were in control of the government throughout the late 1950's and 60's. The ongoing dispute over Kashmir led to renewed fighting between India and Pakistan in 1965. The United Nations was called once again to arrange a cease-fire.

In the late 1960's a different conflict of interest arose in the region of Paki-

stan, not related to the religious conflict or territorial disputes with India of the past, but within its very own borders. Since the partition of India in 1947, Pakistan had been divided both geographically and culturally into west and east. They only shared one major characteristic---Islam.

Most of the peoples of East Pakistan have different physical traits, cultural backgrounds, and traditions than the West Pakistanis. And many East Pakistanis were in opposition to the West Pakistani control over the nation's government, economy, and military. Thus, in 1971, these differences compounded by the East Pakistani peoples objections to West Pakistani domination, led to civil war.

✶✶✶✶✶✶✶✶

"We're standing here live on the 800 block of New Braunfel Avenue in front of the Galla-Community Center. We are joined with us two prominent activists within the community, Mr. Galla and Mr. Jinnah. Can you give us some insight into exactly what the community center's functions are in the community?" the news reporter inquired. Tariq began to explain while Nawaz stood looking very serious and distinguished in grey silk shirt, black slacks, with his arms behind his back.

"Ah, we've drafted up a curriculum for the community center which we feel is essential to the development of the children academically, socially, as well as spiritually," Tariq enlightened.

"Can you provide details about the curriculum?" the reporter inquired further.

Nawaz took the liberty of providing the details. "Yes, we have several volunteers who have been certified in each subject matter that is taught to the children. Our tutors are professors from universities, graduate students, and high school teachers. In addition to providing academics, we provide a foundation that develops strong values and work ethics. This ensures that they will be able to succeed within our society. We have theologians working with us to instill and encourage the concept of God, which is vital to the overall development of our children," Nawaz explained.

"O.K. So, what types of recreation will be available for the children in the community?" the reporter asked, extending his microphone before Tariq. He rocked on his heels as he momentarily looked up, and then locked eyes with the reporter before speaking.

"There will be the basics. Ah, there's a basketball court behind the building, and we've implemented Pushball tables and pool tables within a recreational room. And there will be sponsored inter-community basketball tournaments," Tariq enlightened.

"So, there will be life instructors, spiritual advisors, tutors for the children who might have trouble with academics, and forms of recreation. It sounds like a very promising curriculum. I understand that you are of the Islamic faith, Nawaz? I presume you are of Arabic descent?" the reporter stated as he held the microphone before Nawaz's face.

"I'm a native of Pakistan," Nawaz corrected.

"Oh, excuse me. Pakistan. And you, Mr. Galla, you are African American," the reporter confirmed.

Tariq smiled and nodded. His mind racing with inquiries as to exactly what direction the reporter was headed. "That's interesting, considering the escalating tension between the African American community and the Middle Easterners across the Nation.

Tell us, exactly what this unification has done to improve relations between your respective ethnic groups?" the reporter asked.

Nawaz motioned with a wave of the hand for Tariq to take the liberty of responding to the question.

"I've known Nawaz for over three years and our meeting was under very unusual circumstances," he said smiling widely. "It was during the 9-11 attacks and while I was driving by his establishment, I noticed some African American youths in the commission of vandalizing Nawaz's business. I immediately jumped out of my car to provide assistance and Nawaz thanked me by inviting me to dinner with his family, and it was a very appetizing meal," Tariq laughed. He continued, "His wife's a good cook and we've been spiritual brothers ever since. I'll say our relationship has eased some of the tensions in the community. Many who had a negative outlook on Middle Easterners now have a better view of them as people. Nawaz's work in the community has helped tremendously to break down some of the barriers."

"Hopefully in the near future, tensions will no longer exist and the two communities can embrace each other. Gentlemen, it's been a pleasure meeting you both. I salute you. Continue the good work. Two socially conscious men working together despite ethnic differences and tensions between their respective communities. Reporting live from the Galla-Jinnah Community Center on the 800 block of East Houston St., I'm Tom Bartholomew."

✱✱✱✱✱✱✱✱

Ikara was dressed in a peach shirt, white jeans, and sandals. Her long hair flowed to her shoulders, which she had to ever so often push away from her beautiful brown face as she walked alongside her two friends on the Judson

Senior High School campus. They were discussing their upcoming junior year, among other things.

Ikara had been a student at the interracially mixed school for two years and associated with people from all cultures and ethnicities regardless of social status. But, her closest friends were Sharon, a dark skinned African American girl of curvaceous proportions, and Swathi a giddy, talkative, and attractive Pakistani girl with glasses and long flowing brown hair. Swathi was the sixteen year old daughter of Mr. Nawaz Jinnah.

The campus was abuzz; different groups of students were socializing and conversing about academics and endeavors. Some were walking past holding hands as boyfriend and girlfriend, the jocks with their power lifting shirts or baseball shirts were laughing boisterously as they commandeered in groups about the campus, and the degenerates hung in whatever enclave they saw fit. A high percentage of the school's population, like most schools in San Antonio, were Mexican American.

The three friends stopped just short of the school lobby acknowledging certain students who passed. They focused primarily on the boys with emphasized "hello's" and alluring smiles. "So, with these two correspondence courses I'll graduate next year," stated Swathi. Only a sophomore, Swathi would graduate the following year due to the extra courses she'd been taking since her freshmen year. Her credits earned were enough that she was considered a senior. She was an honor student with a 4.0 average and had prospects for academic scholarships to prestigious universities.

"Some people can't even graduate after four years," Sharon commented. The two laughed. Ikara added, "Or like in his case, six years," she laughed as she pointed towards a young Caucasian boy who had a young girl pinned up against the wall.

The three laughed and then Swathi switched the subject.

"So, do you still plan on switching to Roosevelt next semester?" she inquired of Ikara.

Ikara smiled as she reflected. "I don't know. I have given it much thought. Braun wants me to and I really wanna be with him," she laughed with a bright and wide smile.

"You're really serious about him," Swathi stated.

"Is he still planning to go to college? Or is he tryin' to become the next 2Pac?" Sharon grinned.

"O.K. 2Pac. No, Braun is going to college. I told you he wants to become a lawyer," she responded.

"I think that's great. I mean, there are so many negative types. It's good to

15

see someone positive," Swathi offered. Just at that moment another of their associates, a Caucasian girl of diminutive stature wearing eyeglasses walks by with a Mexican girl. Both were carrying books and discussing an upcoming exam.

"Hi Swathi, Sharon, and Ikara. Got exams today? Hope you're ready," Kimberly, an honor student stated. She was with Maria, also an honor student.

"Yeah, I really need to do some more studying. I tried to cram last night. Shoot, I still have a headache," Sharon stated. At that moment the bell rang for school session.

"Oh well, no time now. That's what happens when we stay up talking on the phone to Devonte' until one o' clock and then cram until two in the morning," Ikara laughed as she picked up her books. Both Sharon and Swathi laughed. Then they proceeded to class.

✶✶✶✶✶✶✶✶

Ursula conversed with a client inside of her store. Ursula owns an interior decorating company and was showing her client where the Persian rugs were located. The client, an attractive Hispanic woman who appeared to be of middle class nodded in approval as she examined the fabric before touching it. As she felt the fabric she looked Ursula in the eye with an approving smile. The sales lady that she was, Ursula introduced herself and directed her to some wall interior, which would complement the Persian rug.

Ursula had earned her degree in interior design at the University of Texas, San Antonio, where she had met her husband. She immediately began using her expertise in the field by attending certain design shows in order to grow her clientele. She also designed a few of her friend's homes. Ursula had a sharp eye for color coordination and impeccable taste in selecting the appropriate fabrics. Her friends were pleased and recommended her to other people and this increased her customer base. After working for conglomerate interior decorating companies, she decided to branch out on her own and became a sole proprietor of Fabulous Interiors. Ten years in business for herself had proven to be very lucrative; she made well into six figures. In the prior year she cleared over $200,000 in retail sales and nearly $150,000 in design revenues. Fabulous Interiors sold fabrics and upholsteries for the interior and exterior of the home. Her clients included celebrities and other notables, which earned her accolades globally.

"Thanks Ursula, my name is Mrs. Gonzalez and I find that the items in your store are of high quality. My husband and I just bought a Victorian home and it has beautiful wood and floors, so this would go perfectly," she stated. At that moment one of Ursula's consultants dressed in a conservative tan suit eased over to speak to her.

"The Chief Marketing Officer of Home Decorators is on the chat line, Mrs. Galla," she informed. Ursula nodded and informed her that she would take the call in a moment. Ursula turned back to Mrs. Gonzalez and stated, "Excuse me for the interruption, I think it is precisely the color compatible with the architectural design you described. Take a look at the bright color patterns in this couch; this will also compliment it. While you think about it, I must step a way for a moment, and will be right back."

When she entered her office, the consultant stood in front of the computer and was jotting down information from the screen. Ursula quickly grabbed a seat next to her and began communicating with the Chief Marketing Officer, who was located in London, England.

Ursula smiled as she read the Chief Marketing Officer's message to her. She looked at her consultant and said, "Catrina, revenues will increase considerably with this deal. I think I'll extend our contract with Home Decorators and place an order for a shipment of Colefax and Fowler."

Catrina stopped jotting down notes and replied, "They're becoming pretty popular. Of course, they are being boosted by their home redesign shows."

Ursula typed another entry then logged off with the Chief Marketing Officer.

"Catrina, I want you to take inventory of the Brunschwig and Fils and find out if the deal has been reached on the new shipment," Ursula ordered. She then glanced down at her watch and exited the office.

More clients were coming into the interior design shop. Most of these clients comprised of the upper echelon of society, which is, of course, whom Ursula primarily catered to. These were clients who could afford to relinquish thousands of dollars to refurbish their six figure homes. Ursula courteously greeted the clients as they entered. Those visiting for the first time were astounded at the elegant arrays of leathers and exotic rugs and ceiling decor.

Mrs. Gonzalez continued to browse and examine the Italian designed furniture displayed in the showroom against the picture she had of the inside of her house. As Ursula approached her she inquired, "I was thinking of maybe extracting these leather sofas and redoing the living room with something more renaissance, like these. Would they clash with the rugs and wall designs?" Mrs. Gonzalez asked.

Ursula looked at the photo. Her expression, though disguised with a smile, evidenced her opinion of the lady's lack of interior coordination skills.

"Definitely, but they're an excellent complementary piece with this room. You want to keep color patterns as well as the actual fabric well coordinated," Ursula informed. Mrs. Gonzalez nodded in agreement.

As Ursula and the lady continued talking, a Caucasian couple approached them and said, "Excuse us."

"One moment, Mrs. Gonzalez," Ursula stated and approached the couple.

"We have some pictures of the interior of our home and…" The gentleman began to explain, Ursula directed them to one of her assistants.

"Okay, if you will go to that office right on this aisle one of my consultants will help you," she directed. The couple followed her directions and then she went back to assist Mrs. Gonzalez. "Sorry, Mrs. Gonzalez. As I was saying, these pieces will go excellent in this room along with these color patterns…"

Ursula loved what she did. Working with clients to make their home fantabolous not only provided her with a comfortable lifestyle; it made her feel good about helping her clients to transform their living space into something beautiful.

✶✶✶✶✶✶✶

Ikara sat down Indian style on her heart shaped bed. Around her decorated room were stuffed teddy bears. On her walls were a variety of posters. Some of them were her favorite pop icons. Some were pictures of herself and her best friends, Swathi and Sharon. The photos had them dressed in their cheerleading outfits. Ikara was engrossed in a conversation on her Razor cellular phone when the doorbell rang. Standing outside observing the beautifully manicured lawn hedges and the architectural design of this ranch styled home was Braun. His posture was awkward giving evidence to his self-consciousness about his attire. He adorned a simple white T-shirt with a red, black, and green Africa symbol; low slung jeans, which he consciously pulled up on his waist, and white Asics Gel cross trainer sneakers. He was as nervous as he had been the first few times he'd donned these doorsteps. Although it was obvious that the Galla family received him well, he could not shake the thought that he wasn't quite good enough for their daughter.

After a brief moment Mrs. Ursula Galla answered the door. Braun cleared his throat and smiled nervously inquired, "Good evenin' Mrs. Galla. Uh, is Ikara home?"

"Hello Braun, she's here. You can come in and have a seat. She's on the phone with her friends. So I'll have to go pry her away," Ursula laughed.

Braun laughed and then proceeded into the house closing the door behind him.

Ursula heard her daughter's loud laughter as she approached her bedroom door.

"Ikara, Braun is here to see you baby," she informed.

Ikara's face ignited as soon as her mother mentioned Braun's name. She informed her friend, hung up the phone, and quickly ran out of her room to greet him.

Braun fidgeted with his hands as he looked around the elegantly decorated living room, which of course, was designed by none other than Ursula. He observed many of the culturally conscious statuettes and Islamic based pictures. Some were of Malcolm X and Elijah Muhammad in places where in most African American homes would be pictures of a very Caucasian looking Jesus, like in his grandmother's home. His grandmother happened to be a devout Baptist who would often catch the 'Holy Ghost' every Sunday. As he reflected over his beloved grandmother he smiled. Shortly after, Ikara appeared wearing a yellow shirt which fell just above her thigh and over her well fitted white jeans.

Braun's smile broadened as he arose from the couch. Ikara approached him and the two held hands. "Hi, Braun," she said. She then took a quick peek to see if her mother was looking and kissed him. After the short engaged kiss, the two lovingly appraised the other then eased down on the leather sofa. "I wasn't expecting you. You should have called first," she stated softly. Braun looked confused.

"You...was expectin' somebody?" he asked.

Ikara smiled and said, "No, Braun. But I was about to go over to Swathi's house," she said.

Braun nodded then rubbed his hands together as he looked into her eyes and thought to himself, "Beautiful, in every aspect of the word." Braun found her personality underlined by her principles and morals to be ideal, and he romanticized about taking her hand in marriage someday.

"You look beautiful, Ikara," he complimented as he continued to clutch her soft delicate hands.

Ikara blushed as she averted eye contact.

"I don't even have on any make up on and my hair isn't even done," she replied.

"That's the beauty in itself. You don't even need make up. Your beauty is natural," he stated. He praised her beautifully manicured nails as she looked down at her hands. He then inquired, "Would you...like to go to the senior prom with me?"

Ikara was ecstatic. "Yes. Yes, I'd love to go. But, I don't know what mom will say about it. You know I have a ten o' clock curfew," she laughed while looking down at her hands. Since Braun is a year older than her, she was afraid that the restrictions placed upon her, compounded by her chastity, would eventually push him away.

"Yeah, I know. I hope they can make an exception because I really want you to go. You know what I'm sayin'?" he stated.

"Well, if I can't, I still want you to go. It's your prom," Ikara responded.

Braun shook his head. "I am not going without you. It will have no significance. No meaning. Know what I'm saying?" Braun stated softly.

Ikara looked at him. Sensing the sincerity in his voice, she was flattered that he would consider missing his senior prom on her account, a girl whom he had briefly known for three months.

"You would miss your prom for me?" Ikara asked

"Yeah, I only want you there with me. I mean, I know it might be kind of hard to believe. Bein' that we have only been together three months but, but I really got these feelings for you. You are ideal to me. You make me feel special and sometimes I be feelin' like I ain't good enough for you," Braun confessed and looked away.

Ikara stared lovingly at his handsome face and reached out to rub the side of his cheeck delicately. As he turned to face her, she leaned forward to kiss him, but was prevented by her mother's voice, which startled them both.

"Braun, would you like some dinner?" Ursula offered.

Braun flinched and responded, "Uh, no ma'am. Thanks anyway."

Ursula smiled. She briefly observed the interaction between them and knew that she had interrupted their brief kiss. After Braun declined, she retreated back into her bedroom.

Braun and Ikara looked at each other and laughed.

"Wanna watch T.V.?" Ikara asked.

"Yeah, before we get in trouble," he responded.

Ikara reached for the remote control and flicked the television on. She began to channel surf as she leaned back onto the couch and snuggled up to Braun as he placed an arm around her shoulder.

Chapter 3

The Garvey House was filled to its capacity. The men of the Organization for Black Unity were dressed in dashikis and kufis, while some of the women were dressed in colorful native African garb and headwear. This was not the typical O.B.U. meeting. The New World Learning Center and educational program sponsored by the O.B.U. was holding its Hitmu (Moving Up) ceremony tonight for a young brother who had recently graduated.

Tariq conversed with the man beside him. His name was Somali, who is middle aged with a dark brown complexion and muscular built. Much like Tariq, he had changed his 'slave name' to a Nubian one after becoming conscious. Somali was an original member of the southern based radical group 'Republic of New Africa' (R.N.A.). He had served time in prison as a result of the F.B.I. Cointelpro, (Counter Intelligence Program) who in the 1960's and 70's, under J. Edgar Hoover's diabolical covert operation, dismantled most of the Pro-Black radical organizations. Somali was railroaded on trumped up charges of conspiracy and shifted around the United States to prisons such as Lompoc, Marion, and Lewisburg. But his trek through the system did not waiver him. It was there behind the concrete walls of these institutions that his drive for political activism and radicalism grew. He developed an intransigent hatred for the imperialistic system of oppression, which he felt held his people down. This intransient hatred and motivation towards activism and nationalism would grow two folds upon his release from prison in 1987, after serving more than sixteen years.

Somali had garnered the sympathy and financial backing of prominent African American business gurus, politicians and liberalists from all over the globe who were anti-repression activists. They were against the systemic genocide and imprisonment of African Americans. Upon his release, these were the people who would reinstitute Somali back into a prominent role in activism. Because of his degree in business, they placed him in a high-level position within a successful corporation. Through the efforts and support of others, Somali was granted full amnesty from the government.

Rather than returning to his hometown of Jackson, Mississippi, Somali opted to venture overseas and live in various countries, such as France, Holland, and England. Each country was a home to several of the activists and political figures that supported him during those sixteen years. He lived quite lavishly and rubbed elbows with the upper echelon of black suburbia in these countries. He attended galas and appeared on talk shows. But he felt he had lost contact with the struggle. He decided to go to the country where he had traced his ancestral origin, Sudan.

It was in 1989, during a period when rebels in southern Sudan, which was populated by black Christians and followers of tribal religions, took up arms against the government's domination of northern Sudan, whose people were predominantly Arab Muslims. The war and famine had ravished the land. As a result, there were 1.3 million casualties and 3 million southerners displaced. During this time Somali was newly married and had a one-year-old son, whom he named Piye. He named him after a Nubian king of the 22nd dynasty in 747 B.C. Somali was living a firsthand account of his people's struggle— a struggle which had escalated considerably since his arrival there in the 60's when he'd been on the lam. Although he contributed to the aid of political activists and the United Nations sponsored health care initiatives, Somali knew that his indigenous country was not the atmosphere he wanted for his young wife and son. Thus, in 1993, the year Amnesty International cited Arab-Muslim dominated Sudan with ethnic cleansing against the Nubian people, he uprooted his small family and returned to the United States. Somali decided to resettle his small family in San Antonio, Texas, which was home to one of his primary sympathizers, a young brother named Tariq. He had started writing Tariq during his sophomore year at the University of Texas in San Antonio. Two years prior to Somali receiving amnesty, he notified Tariq about his decision to leave Sudan. Tariq immediately welcomed Somali. During that time Tariq was an assistant manager of an upstart restaurant, which foreclosed after six years, due to mismanagement.

It was then that Tariq and Somali, who through his R.N.A. affiliation in high places, began working at a black owned business corporation, decided that it was time to flex their business minds and crash the Internet marketing arena. In 2000, the two had come up with the idea for the company, Global Reach, which was finally created in 2002.

Somali had also been a catalyst in Tariq's joint venture with Nawaz and was one of the volunteer tutors. Along with Tariq, they continued to be activists within the community and served on special committees and were voices in the political forum. On numerous occasions both appeared on radio talk shows that catered to the ever-present crises that occurred within the black community and strove to come up with logical as well as legal solutions to curtail these crises.

As Tariq continued to converse with Somali, the O.B.U. chairman called the meeting to order, causing both Tariq and Somali to pay attention.

"Good evening brothers and sisters," the chairman stated in Sudanese. "It is a pleasure to be standing here before the congregation on this momentous occasion. As you all know, this night has been reserved for an award presentation. We are giving congratulations where it is due. This young man seated before you has achieved academic excellence. He has risen above obstacles and disproved the stereotype that continues to be placed upon our people in modern day America. So, to get this special presentation started, I'd like to call to the podium Brother Somali Qusta." The speaker motioned with the wave of a hand towards Somali. His dark face a mask of elation as he arose to his feet amidst applauds.

Somali neared the podium and touched some sisters on the shoulders in acknowledgement as he shook others hands. He then reached the podium and embraced the small speaker and accepted the microphone.

"Thank you Brother Kali. As the Brother informed, tonight we'll be presenting an award to this outstanding young brother here who achieved academic excellence in his chosen field. He aspires to become a community activist. He is diligently involved in politics. In short, down with the struggle…" As he spoke the constituents listened attentively, including his lovely wife Khadija and his seventeen-year-old son, Piye. Both wore expressions of pride. After a brief pause Somali looked up from his notes and continued. "But first, I'd like to raise some pertinent issues. Issues that I feel relate tremendously with each other. That is the condition in the Sudan in comparison to what's happening right here." For the next half hour Somali would compare and contrast the two regions and inform the constituency of the current crisis going on in Sudan.

His basis of the comparison was the influx of Arabs in the community, whom he felt was like when the Arabs invaded Nubia in 600 A.D., that resulted in 'ethnic cleansing'. This ethnic cleansing in their community would not be the extermination of people, but rather the complete takeover of business entities within their communities.

Ancient Nubia's civilization lasted from around 3800 B.C.E. until approximately 652 A.C.E. During this period, kingdoms, Dynasties, many cities, temples, roads and even pyramids were established. It was even suggested that there were more pyramids constructed in Nubia than in Kemet.

23

But after nearly 5,000 years, Nubia was finally overthrown by the Arabs who first invaded around 632 A.D.

The spread of Islam to the region would enhance over the course of the next several centuries by these Arab invaders. The Egyptians in antiquity converted the region to Coptic Christianity in the sixth century. The incessant Arab conquests eventually over ran all ancient Nubian and Egyptian power and by the 15th century Islam became the dominant religion.

More conquests from invading nations would continue over the next three centuries. The ancient Nubian system far displaced even the remnant of empires that arose after the earlier Arab conquests crumbled. Revolutions brought an end to the last of these empires such as the Fung, which were led by Muhammad Ahmed who called himself the Mahdi, leader of the faithful and his followers, the Dervishes.

Egypt, in conjunction with Anglo forces would crush the Mahdi's successors at the turn of the century. In 1951 the Egyptian parliament would abolish its 1899 and 1936 treaties with Great Britain eventually amended its constitution to provide for a separate Sudanese constitution.

In the 1980's, economic problems would plague the nation. This was aggravated by civil wars and the inundation of refugees from neighboring countries. These problems of civil unrest would continue to escalate over the course of the next two decades, including Arab militias carrying out acts of ethnic cleansing and killing indigenous Nubians.

As of May 2005, the ethnic cleansing in the Sudan had reached alarming statistics. In Darfur, the death toll had reached over 400,000. Many of these were Nubians murdered by the Sudanese armed forces and their accomplices, the brutal Arab Janjaweed. There was a shocking average of 500 deaths reported every day. More than 2 million are now destitute after being driven from their homes and villages.

After Somali paused for the effect, he continued to explain his comparison scenarios in reference to the Arabs. "In the Sudan, there is ethnic cleansing of the indigenous Nubian peoples. Our people, by these invaders, I'm speaking about the Arabs. Yes, the Arabs. I refer to them as invaders. True, these Arabs have been in Africa for over a thousand years, but this does not negate the fact that they are invaders. And, they are brutalizing, raping, and executing every native Sudanese African they encounter," Somali stated. The constituents were at full attention. "According to a watch group coalition for international justice, almost 500 people are murdered every single day. Our people are dying at the hands of these Arab militias and the Janjaweed. Over here there is a different type of cleansing going on, though by the same

Arab invaders. The Saudis move in and scout prospects and then corner the market on our black owned businesses. In essence they are destabilizing our economic stability. They are making us impotent and powerless. After our people are forced to make their business flourish, they abuse us, psychologically as well as physically. Just the other day a nine year old was verbally accosted by one of these Arabs. Why, because the nine-year old's bicycle accidentally scarred the man's car!"

For the next half hour Somali's speech would become more impassioned and angrier. His words were dripping venom with each mention of the Arabs. As Somali went on in his tyrannical speech, Tariq's expression began to register concern. It was apparent that Somali had become racist against Arabs. Not just the Arabians occupying the Sudan, but all Arabs. He began to stereotype them all as evil because of a few isolated incidents. His rhetoric to Tariq began to mirror the types of speeches he presumed took place in Ku Klux Klan meetings.

"And as I bring these issues to a close my brothers and sisters, I'd like to emphasize how imperative it is for us as a people, Nubians, to drive these invaders out of our communities. Not in a physical sense, unless it comes to protecting ourselves of course, but in an economic sense. Buy black. Thank you." He saluted with the Black Power sign. There was applause for their beliefs in his nationalism. But those people who thought like Tariq clapped listlessly and exchanged looks of concern with one another.

"That was a very educational and impassioned speech by Brother Qusta. Now at this time I would like to call to the podium Sister Assata Kali. As we prepare to credit those who have put forth extra efforts in this daily battle against oppression and socioeconomic repression in our communities, let's give Sister Assata a round of applause," the speaker announced. As the constituents clapped, a light skinned woman in her early 50's approached. She had strong features serious eyes and flowing dreadlocks.

"Good evening brothers and sisters of the struggle. My opinion mirrors that of Brother Somali. I am a Nationalist first and foremost. But, I would like to address other issues before I begin calling those to receive their awards. First, I'd like to address the issue of job discrimination among the African American. I feel…"

★★★★★★

The elderly fanned themselves on porches under the intense Texas sun as children played a variety of games. They were shouting, laughing, and basically enjoying themselves this weekend. Unwavering in the tropical heat as sweat poured down their brown faces.

Braun, Piye, Phil, and Devonte' walked along a busy avenue while sipping Twisters, observing their surroundings and discussing various topics from sports to current affairs. Ahead of them a teenage boy in tank top and shorts struggles to walk a grey pit bull. His stringy muscles rippling as he fights to contain the dog.

Braun gulps down a large portion of his Twister but never takes his eyes off of the boy and his Herculean grey pit bull. As he and his friends reached the intersection, a thumping SUV passes. Its fresh dark blue paint job and Spreewell rims glistened in the sun. All four boys observed the SUV as it paused for a stop sign. The boy with the pit bull stops and turns around completely to appraise the vehicle. He smiles and nods his head. His three gold teeth sparkling as he shields his eyes from the immense sun. Then Braun speaks out in almost a shout so as to be heard over the rumbling of the SUV's stereo sound system and the growling of the dog.

"Cocaine is growlin' and pretty vicious. You thank he is ready for Phil's pit?" Braun instigated. He eyes on the vicious pit bull, whose muscular chest flexed as he barked.

"Terror? Main, Cocaine's eat'em up. Phil knows dat. Whatever you thank, Terror is ready. We can get it on, man. Are you confident? Bet dem rangs you got. And yo rims," he laughed in a braggadocio manner.

Braun laughed. "Cocaine ain't ready fo Terror, Keith," Phil replied.

"Hey, any time you ready, man," Keith stated and smiled as he continued up the street. The boys then proceeded on their walk.

The four were now approaching a service station. Each looked around the vicinity before entering. Inside the store the Mexican owner took inventory of the merchandise in this family owned business, which consisted of his wife, son and daughter. They were well-mannered, pleasant and quiet people. Their family name was Gonzales. They were migrants from Mexico City, Mexico and usually wore traditional garments. They were Mestizos, which means they were of both Caucasian and Mexican blood. The children chose to wear American clothing.

Outside of the store on the busy avenue the voices of the four boys could be heard. Phil's voice was the loudest. He raised it so as to be heard over Devonte', who was in deep discussion about professional basketball. A daily subject this time of year; especially the San Antonio Spurs and their success in the playoffs year after year.

"Main, Tim Duncan got off last night! You see that dunk he did over ole boy?" Phil stated with his gold teeth glistening in the bright afternoon sun.

Main, we are going to sweep'em. They ain't ready for the Spurs, man. What you thank about the Spurs and Lakers series?" Braun inquired.

"I thank we are gon beat'em in six. We got the squad, man. And experience," Phil replied.

Devonte' shook his head to the contrary.

"I'ont know man. Big Shaq's got experience," Devonte' responded. There were sarcastic sneers and blows.

"Main, you just riding with Shaq because he went to Cole and you be out dere in L.A., Man. Spurs gon' smash them people," Phil retorted. At that moment each boy's attention was gripped by two red and black 1500 Ninja engines revving to a stop in front of a tan wooden house. But their attention was gripped even more by the occupants who had gotten off of the bikes.

"Ooh, man! Check dat out! Umm!" Phil stated while smiling from ear to ear as he looked lustfully at the young girls walking away from the motorbikes. Both girls were lavishly attired in the latest fashions with gold jewelry glistening, well-oiled curvaceous thighs exposed, hair freshly styled and permed with manicured nails. It was evident that they both were enveloped in the materialistic drug culture.

As the girls walked around the motorcycles, they sashayed causing their ample buttocks to become exposed and appeared to move spasmodically with each step. This caused more lustful jeers from Devonte' and Phil.

"Umm, umm, umm! Dat's how it's goin' down. Main, dem hoes fine as a motha!"

"Huh, bra. I'd like to work wit both dem hoes!" Devonte' and Phil stated while staring in the girls' vicinity.

Piye shook his head. "Man, regardless of dey reputation, they black sistas. Why cain't you refer to them as that?" Braun stated. Devonte' cracked a smile. Then as they entered the store, Phil responded, "Aiight, main. But damn! You gotta admit dem ho...I mean, dem gals was fine as a motha!"

He squeezed Piye's shoulders, but Piye shrugged away.

"That's all they were; faces and sex appeal. Dope man prostitutes who'll never get a good husband. That's part of the social problem in the black community," Piye stated. Devonte' and Phil exchanged glances. Phil rolled his eyes and faked a yawn that went unnoticed by Piye.

"How are you doing Mr. and Mrs. Gonzales?" Braun greeted courteously. The storeowners smiled and returned their greetings. But Mr. Gonzales' eyes turned nearly snake-like as he exchanged glances with Piye who never tried to mask his disdain for the man and his family.

Phil went to the last aisle where the cold drink freezer boxes were located. He retrieved his favorite cherry 16 oz. cola and asked Devonte', "What kind do you want?" In the meantime, Devonte' was grabbing Bear claws and Twinkies off of the shelf.

"Grape, man," he responded. Piye and Braun scanned the shelves for their snacks when Piye began speaking.

"We had an award presentation at Garvey House the otha night. Pops gave a fire speech. Wish you coulda been there to hear it," Piye stated as he grabbed a Yoo-Hoo drink and two Bear claws.

"Oh yeah?" Braun responded while grabbing a bag of potato chips and ham-n-cheese Hot Pocket.

"I got you a Tropical Punch, B," Phil stated.

"Aiight Mr. Gonzales, I need to stick this in the microwave," Braun requested. He motioned for him to do so and opened up the cash register as Phil reached the counter with the cold drinks and snacks. Piye followed Phil while continuing to look at Mr. Gonzales.

"Yep. Pop was bringing the message raw. He was talkin 'bout how them invaders is killin our people in the Sudan. Ethnic cleansin is what dey call it. Arabs. Towel wearin suckas. He talked about 'em over here takin' our business. The cholovattos ain't no different. Wet backs comin' over here knockin' brothas from jobs 'cause they'll work for crumbs. White man know dat, cain't stand them or them Pakistani and Arab bastards," Piye exclaimed.

"That'll be seven dollars and fifty three centz," Mr. Gonzales stated.

Mrs. Gonzales was confused as to why this young man seemed to hate her family so much. Whenever he came into their store he stared at them with discontent and hatred. Her family never said a harsh word to anyone in the community and she feared that one day the tension would escalate to violence.

Phil noticed the look of concern on Mrs. Gonzales' face and observed the way Piye was menacing Mr. Gonzales. He shook his head and silently whispered, "Cool out, man." Mr. Gonzales began placing the items into a bag and his hands were visibly shaking. The boys left the store and proceeded to walk along the busy boulevard while eating, drinking and observing their surroundings.

"You saw the fear in that suckas eyes, huh?" Piye stated as he bit into his Bear claw.

Braun looked away.

"Main, you need to chill with all that Black Panther stuff. Ain't nobody living like that now. Dis 2004, man. Besides, Mr. Gonzales and his family treat ery'body in the hood good," Phil stated and gulped down a large portion of his cherry 16 oz. cola.

"Main, all of them suckas are the same. They don't really like us. Just don't want us burnin' they store down," Piye retorted. There was a momentary silence. "Like pops said, we as a community need to band together and run all dem and dem camel riding suckers back where dey came from," he finished.

"Listen at you, man. Those are good people. You are being racist, Piye. You preach everyday about racial oppression by the white man, but you are acting just like the Klan," Devonte' stated nonchalantly.

Piye's eyes turned fierce. Then he dropped his half eaten Bear claw and half full Yoo-Hoo and lunged at Devonte'. But, he was stopped by Phil and Braun.

"Don't neva compare me to them devils! I'll knock you out here!" Piye shouted as he tussled to break loose from his two friends who nearly couldn't contain him. Devonte', with fear in his eye, nevertheless put on an act suggesting his preparedness to fight. He clenched his fists as he bounced in place. As Piye calmed down Phil and Braun released their hold on him. Devonte' backed a considerable distance away. He never took his eyes off of Piye who was still breathing hard and approached him saying, "Don't neva say nothin' like that outta yo mouth again!" Piye pointed his finger in Devonte's face. Devonte' remained silent.

"Come on, Piye. We boys. You Nubian. Now you wanna fight your brotha? Come on," Braun pled. Piye continued to stare down the petrified Devonte'. At 5'11 and 240 pounds, Piye was a fear-some opponent for anyone. As the boys continued to plead with Piye, a police cruiser crept to a halt. Its occupants, a salt and pepper team looked the boys over with a cynical eye. Phil looked away and sipped his cola fearfully.

"Some sort of problem here?" inquired the police officer. He was a very dark complexioned man with piercing eyes.

"No sir...officer. We are just on our way home," replied Braun.

"You all ain't no gang members are ya? Don't lie ta us," the Caucasian officer stated. Before any of them could respond the black officer snapped his fingers at Piye who with a scowl, was looking away.

"Hey! What's your problem? You didn't hear my partner ask you a question? And what's that on your arm?" the black officer asked.

"It says Uhuru. It's African and means freedom," Piye enlightened.

The officers smiled, "Freedom, huh? Well, you won't have freedom when we catch you sellin' them crack rocks," the Caucasian officer smirked.

"Not every black brotha deals drugs. And not every black man is a brotha," Piye stated defiantly. The black officer recognizing the insult felt compelled to retaliate and put the car in park. He emerged with one hand on his semi-automatic handgun.

"Just what the hell was that supposed to mean!? Huh! Get up against the car!" He barked as his partner exited the vehicle. He reached for Piye's shoulder and attempted to shove him. But Piye was braced and immovable. This enraged the cop who withdrew his weapon then twisted Piye's arm behind his back. He shoved him full force onto the side of the car as he placed his pistol to the back of his head.

The Caucasian officer who had motioned for the other three to place their hands on the hood of the car bore an expression of nervousness as he patted and searched Braun.

"You want me to put a bullet in your head, huh?" The black officer shouted as Piye grimaced in pain. Meanwhile, pedestrians were beginning to stop and stare. Some were muttering insults of police brutality causing the Caucasian officer to glance around nervously.

"Jackson! Jackson! Let's go. Jackson, let's go. These kids ain't got nothin' on'em. You kids get on outta here. Go on," the officer ordered. Phil, Devonte', and Braun began backing away from the police cruiser. Each nervously watching what was transpiring between the black cop and Piye. Then Officer Jackson released his grip and backed away from him, however, continuing to train his semi-automatic at his back. With tears of anger in his eyes, Piye backed up a few steps as the officers got back into their vehicle.

"I don't wanna see none of ya'll faces no more this week. And you, I'm on to ya, boy, Mr. Dope man," Officer Jackson stated while looking fiercely at Phil. Phil remained silent. The cop then removed the car from park and began coasting away from the curb while giving Piye one last glare.

As the police cruiser disappeared around the corner Braun spoke out. He looked in the direction of Piye who was staring down at the concrete.

"Devonte' ain't your enemy. Mr. Gonzales ain't the enemy either. That was the enemy," he stated. Piye looked up at him and averted eye contact. His mind was reflecting on the incident that had just transpired as sweat poured down his brown face from the hot, afternoon Texas sun.

Chapter 4

T ariq was accompanied by Mr. Nawaz Jinnah. Both were clad in casual attire and sipping coffee as they inspected the students' progress at the community center. There were approximately twenty-five students present in varying age groups from middle school and high school. The tutors present, including Somali, were diligently counseling students. In the black community where the problems range from many different sources, the children are at the core of the problem. Children are the roots and much the same as a tree and flower: in order for the children to grow they have to be nurtured properly.

The nurturing of a plant calls for proper watering, sunlight and nutrients. Without these essential elements, the plant cannot grow. If the plants do not grow, they cannot bear fruit. The same is with children. Proper nurturing of the children calls for proper education, spiritual guidance and work ethics. Without these essential elements, the children cannot grow in a physical sense. It is also essential in order to become leaders in the community; activists; entrepreneurs or be productive. When addressing the problem of children in a community's future, most do not sit down and take the time out to arrive at solutions. We know the problem already. There are too many negative images on the screen and on the radio and inadequate real world job preparedness. There are dysfunctional family structures, systemic repression by the government, and perhaps the biggest problem, peer pressure. They want to be accepted in the sub-culture of drugs and violence.

We know the problems. What are the solutions? Let's dissect each problem aforementioned and come up with a logical solution. There are negative images on screen and on the radio. Being realistic, there is no way to de-sensitize the harmful imagery that our children listen to or watch on television. We can only educate them to the cold, hard facts in reference to these negative images portrayed and provide them with as many positive alternatives. As for inadequate "real world" job preparedness, our black youths have a high percentage of dropping out of school due to a biased school curriculum.

Students lose the motivation to excel in a curriculum where history tends to demean, misinform or is misleading when dealing with African Americans. Subjects such as algebra are where many feel it is not essential to the 'real job' world and seem frivolous. The solution would be to implement a specific course into the curriculum that enlightens African American youths to the many job fields available to them upon graduation, thus, motivating them to stay in school. Because it is no secret among the youth that many people go to college and are still systemically held back from achieving the level of success in corporate America that their chosen major commanded, this often plays a vital role in a child's motivation or lack thereof, in obtaining goals. These African American youths are the ones who need the community centers above all others. Being raised in such a home setting could prevent any potential that the child may have. They are most likely to lose interest in school, objectives in life and moral values. And lastly, there is peer pressure. This generation of black youths is similar to their predecessors. In every generation, a very high percentage of youths succumb to peer pressure and the need to belong. They want to be accepted as a part of the "in crowd" and with so much negativity in music videos, and the growing sub-culture of drugs and violence in the average black community, there is a neo-culture of our youths blatantly disregarding all rationale from positive motivators because they want to be sociably accepted. The drug dealer and gangster profile is deemed "cool." The flagrant disregard and exploitation of the black female is "real." This counterproductive ideology has to be crushed. This is why it is imperative for the implementation of life and social skill instructors into community centers. Having young motivational speakers to come in and lecture the youths and to show them what's really "cool" is important. Cool is becoming a doctor, or lawyer, or entrepreneur. Having enough assets and income to retire at forty is also cool. By showing them how drug activity can only lead to death or incarceration will help them make the right choices. If these instructors showed "shock" film footages of slain dealers, or confessions of dealers doing life in federal prisons, it could help provide an image that these students do not want to choose that way of life.

These are the primary sources of self-oppression and systemic repression of the youth in the community. Several suggested solutions to rectify this alarming trend of our youths falling victim, were considered and then implemented at the Galla-Jinnah Community Center.

"How's everything going?" Tariq inquired of Somali. Somali glanced back over his shoulder at the row of youths he had just given tutelage.

"They all seem to be grasping the concepts. Most of them just really need the information administered to them in a more understandable way," Somali responded as he extended his hand to Tariq. He then nodded in acknowledgement towards Nawaz. He was hesitant to extend a hand until Nawaz himself extended his.

"It's good to see that you are getting through to the children," Nawaz stated in his heavy accented English. His eyes were honest and his smile was sincere. Somali shook his hand, but the smile on his face and the look in his eyes were not of the same sincerity. Similar to his son, Piye, whom he had indoctrinated with consciousness towards the oppression of his people by Arabs, Somali was untrusting of Nawaz. Though he stated to Tariq on many occasions that he respected Nawaz's contributions to the black community, Somali also frequently confessed his distrust for him.

"Yeah, well, it's good that you two brothers made all of this possible for the youths. I'm just proud to be a part of it," Somali responded. The three began walking through the vast main room of the community center.

As the three men walked through various corridors of the center, they had the opportunity to greet the tutors and mentors. They shook the hands and gave accolades to these men and women volunteers who took time out of their busy schedules to provide support to these children on their academic, social and spiritual needs. As the three exited out onto the buildings front steps, Tariq bore an expression of great pride.

"Yeah, these children are the future. If we are ever to make advancements, on any level, it has to start now," Tariq stated as he looked out onto the busy traffic. The air was still humid even though the sun had set and was casting a purplish haze over the sky in this twilight hour.

"I certainly agree. It is maybe incorrect to say that teachers are not doing their jobs, but certainly the schools' curriculums have to be altered," Nawaz stated. As he spoke, the lights of passing cars illuminated his face.

"Altered? Perhaps that's kind of an understatement. The curriculum needs to be changed altogether. It's biased. And I still believe that making algebra mandatory was a scheme that targeted minorities and escalated the dropout rate," Somali stated. Tariq shook his head in disagreement.

"No, my brother. To accept this as theory is to buy into the stereotype that minorities are not as smart as our European counterparts," Tariq corrected. Nawaz began nodding to this assertion indicating that his assessment mirrored that of Tariq.

"No. No, that's not what I was implying. We know we're just as intelligent. What I meant was algebra and all of its mechanics holds no tangible significance to most of our youth in relation to the real job world. It doesn't hold their interest. We need a life skills class incorporated into the school's curriculum. Teaching them the many different trades available at technical institutes after they graduate and reserve algebra as an elective," Somali corrected.

"I understand now, my brother. You simply feel that algebra is over-emphasized and you presume that the youth look at it as such," Tariq responded.

"Well, yes. I feel that the youth identify it as insignificant. We are not talking about accounting or geometry. These are subjects that can actually be useful in the job market," Somali further explained.

"But it 'is' a major. That's the way it is. And if the children don't make the grade, they can't graduate," Tariq responded.

"That's a good point. While we're on the subject of graduation, that's another point I stress. How many young brothers and sisters go off to college and major in highly technological fields only to still be discriminated against in corporate America. Let's face it, our youths are not ignorant to this fact," Somali retorted. Tariq nodded along with Nawaz.

"This is a very valuable assertion. Look, I really need to be going as I have urgent business," Nawaz stated as he glanced down at his Rolex watch. He patted Tariq on the shoulder and gave Somali an assuring smile. They watched on momentarily as Nawaz boarded his grey Lexus before and departing back inside of the building.

✷✷✷✷✷✷✷✷

The sunlight shined in beams through the blinds of the French window curtains, which enhanced the colors of forest green tropical plants strewn around Ursula's living room. The coordination of tans and earth colors from the sofas and couches that were designed by Colefax and Fowler was one of Ursula's favorite interior decorating sources.

Ursula was dressed conservatively in a yellow blouse, tan long skirt, and sandals. Sitting beside her was one of her closest friends, Catrina, who also happened to be one of her best consultants. The two were looking through a home decorating magazine making suggestions on the furniture or other interior or exterior accessories that would enhance their perspective homes.

Catrina was much younger than Ursula at twenty-five years old. It hasn't been that long since she graduated. She was a very attractive and intelligent woman with caramel complexion, Asian eyes, and long hair. She graduated at the top of her class from the magnet high school in which she attended. In college, Catrina continued to hold a high GPA at the University of Texas where she majored in sociology.

Catrina was still single and recently moved from her mother's home. Her mother was very successful and incidentally was a high school teacher and volunteered as a tutor at the community center. Catrina purchased a three-bedroom home in Kirby for $125,000. It was a very nice home. Considering that Catrina was single, Ursula was confused that her friend would think about buying a house as a single woman without children.

Ursula flipped a page in the magazine as she shook her head. "I just don't understand why you didn't just rent an apartment? It would have been cheaper. You're single. Why would you buy a three bedroom house, Catrina?" Ursula asked

"Well, apartments you can live there ten years and never own it. I wanted to own my own home," she explained.

"True. But Catrina, a three bedroom home for $125,000? You could have purchased a home for far less. Your car note is $400 a month and now with your mortgage you are spending $900. What about the other expenses that come with owning a home like light and gas, food, and maintenance?"

Catrina laughed, "You're sounding like my mother again. Next you'll be telling me, Catrina, you need to find a good husband before owning a home."

"That would be logical," Ursula affirmed.

Catrina shook her head smiling. "I'm independent, Ursula. I've always wanted to have my own home and don't want to depend on any man," she stated with conviction.

There was no sense lecturing her. She was firm in her convictions as only young people in post-adolescent stages can be.

"I like these beautiful soft tone patterns. I think it would look great in my living room," Catrina stated. Ursula examined the elegant furniture on the page.

"George Smith is rather expensive. These are all handmade furniture and fabrics. It is elegant, though. I like the color patterns too. Ooh, look at this rug. That would look good in here. I'm thinking of taking up this carpet," Ursula stated.

"Amritzar. Beautiful," Catrina acknowledged as she stared at the antique multi-colored rug. She then flipped the page. "Ursula," she started and hinting that a question was forthcoming. Ursula anticipated the question as she examined a photo of some outside furniture.

"Yes?" she inquired, but never taking her eyes off the page.

"When you and Tariq got married, how did you know that it was right? That he was the right one?" Catrina asked earnestly. Her expression gave evidence to the fact that she was in search of someone. Someone special yet captivated with creating the illusions of self-sufficiency and adopting the 'independent and I don't need a man' complex. But, Ursula had seen through it.

"Well, when Tariq and I had been together, oh maybe a few months, everything just seemed so natural between us. We had so much in common. He was sensitive, yet strong. And his spirituality was of his essence. I guess that was probably the defining factor. I knew he loved me. I knew it. And I fell more in love with him," Ursula stated euphorically. Her eyes were glazed over as if in reverie about the love they shared. Catrina looked down after she finished. A smile creased her face as she raised her head and looked away as she spoke.

"You are so fortunate. It's so difficult to find that right someone. They wear these disguises at first," she laughed. "When you fall for them, the masks come off. I went through so much dealing with these illusionists. Why can't men just be real? Why the games? I don't have time for it. I'm a professional and I just can't allow anymore distractions to hinder me from achieving my goals," Catrina stated dejectedly.

Ursula sensed her friend was hurting.

"Is this why you consume yourself with work? Sister, look at me. You spend ninety percent of your day consumed with interior decorating and the rest exalting yourself in this 'super woman,' professional persona, while badgering all black men. There are good black men out there. You can't keep building these walls. If you do, the right one may get locked out. You just have to follow certain rules and you will recognize him," Ursula enlightened.

"Rules? What kind of rules?" Catrina inquired with a curious expression.

"Rules such as, does he have spirituality? Most women only seek what's apparent, like his looks, his savior faire and his financial status. But, if he's not for God, he can't be for you," Ursula further educated her on the importance of seeking out spirituality in a mate. Catrina nodded and smiled. Her eyes searching deep into Ursula's as she absorbed her wisdom. The two stared back down at the pages of the magazine.

"This is nice. Edwardian. I'd love to do my kitchen like this."

✷✷✷✷✷✷✷✷

Tariq's charcoal grey Lincoln whipped into the driveway of a modest bricked home. It was one of several on this checkered neighborhood block in a rather quiet community which is unlike most eastside neighborhoods where crack dealing and gunfire were of the norm.

He got out of his car and looked around. Everything was typical on this sulky and hot day in May. Children were at play with their super soakers, young girls were strolling down the street laughing and talking, and young kids riding bicycles or tearing around corners on 4 wheelers while the older ones washed and polished vehicles. Yes, it was quite a typical day in this well-manicured middle class suburb.

Tariq walked up to the house and knocked on the large oak door. Moments later a teenage boy wearing a black T-shirt with a picture of Bob Marley appeared. It was Piye.

"Mr. Galla," Piye greeted with his mouth still partially stuffed with the beef burrito he was eating. "Pop! Mr. Galla out here ta see ya," Piye shouted back over his shoulder as he moved to the side. He allowed for Tariq to enter. The house permeated with the aroma of well-seasoned tacos and burritos. On the dining room table to his left as he closed the door were several bags from Taco Bell. "Wanna burrito or chicken fajita?" Piye offered.

"No, no thanks Piye. Boy you've put on some bulk, haven't you? You look like you're auditioning for Mr. Olympia," Tariq inquired.

"Naturally, I'm Nubian," Piye retorted in confidence that superseded his humor. At that moment Somali appeared down the hall wearing an orange and black dashiki calling out a phrase in Nubian to greet his fellow Nubian brother. The two embraced as Piye disappeared into another room.

"Brother Galla," greeted Somali's wife as she passed to go into the kitchen. She was radiant even at the age of forty-three years. She had a dark brown-complexion with unusual colored eyes and brown hair. Her smile showed her pearly white teeth. Tariq returned her greeting in kind and the two proceeded into the living room.

Tariq took his seat on one of the leather black sofas with his fingers interlocked as he glanced around the room. Images of profound African American scholars, such as Dr. Niem Akbar and Chiek Anta Diops leaped out at him. Also, there were blown up photos of Somali shaking hands with President Joseph Mobuto in Zaire in the 1970's, before trumped up charges from a corrupt police department would dispatch him off the streets for sixteen years.

"Would you like some lemonade or ice tea, my brother?" Somali offered.

"Yes, yes. I will have some tea, thanks. It is hot out there, I'll tell ya," Tariq replied. Somali laughed and retrieved the cold glass of iced tea for him.

After Somali returned with the tea, Tariq observed his longtime friend as he sat down in silence. He quickly discerned that Somali hadn't just called him over for a casual visit. Something was troubling him deeply.

"Is something troubling you, my brother? What's on your mind?" Tariq inquired. His facial expression showed his concern as he leaned forward. Somali released a sigh as he clasped his hands together and without exactly holding eye contact with Tariq he began to speak.

"I can never deceive you. Yes, there's something. Something is troubling and agitating me. I just found out yesterday, which was days after it happened, that Piye was assaulted by the police," Somali stated.

"What?" Tariq stated with a more concerned expression.

"Yeah. He was with his friends and apparently this 'negro' cop got out and harassed him. And you know Piye, he takes after me, I guess. And, the cop laid into him. It's as if they have nothing else to do other than antagonize the blacks in their own community. You never hear about the police involved in brutality cases in one of those white neighborhoods," Somali stated in disgust. "We're just fortunate Piye wasn't seriously injured. This has become a frequent occurrence. Just last week the police roughed up an unarmed thirteen-year-old boy because they said he fit the description," Tariq stated emphatically. It was clear his feelings towards what had become a crises and something needed to be done.

Year after year in the United States, police departments from big cities to small towns come under fire on allegations of police brutality. This is a reality that has been forced into the consciousness of unaffected white America by the brutal videotaping of Los Angeles motorist Rodney King. No longer were they able to say that racial injustice from the police department against minorities was a figment of an imagination. The videotape was shocking and conclusive evidence.

However sad as it is, the amount of police assaults on minority victims have not declined. In fact, since the Rodney King brutal beating in 1991, there has been countless other more heinous attacks upon minorities by corrupt police departments across the United States. For example, Amadu Diallo, the Haitian brother was gunned down outside of his home in Brooklyn, New York. Summarily executed after being racked with nineteen rounds from police weapons, of which over 40 rounds were fired. Over kill? Excessive force? Take your pick.

Currently nothing is being done to prevent these malicious attacks upon minorities. The people rally, march, and even riot, but still the attacks occur. There are no ramifications suffered by the police assailants. Only in isolated incidents do the victims or family members receive any form of reprieve. Most often this only happens as a result of government intervention.

Somali shook his head as he reflected on Tariq's statement pertaining to the thirteen-year-old boy.

"When is it going to cease? Our people and other minorities are target practice for these corrupt cops. Their creed is supposed to be to preserve and to protect. But who is this aimed towards? Not our communities," Somali stated. Tariq nodded his head. He himself had often pondered over this declaration.

What are the police preserving? What are they protecting? The community continues to degenerate. The citizens are still victims of crimes. When one becomes conscious, it is then that he will ascertain what the police's job really is in the black community. It's not to preserve or protect, but rather to 'control,' much like prison guards and administratively controlled institutions. This is what our communities have relegated to: controlled environments that are actuated by the 'cry' for a need to beef up law enforcement.

"Certainly not. They preserve and protect white communities. If you're a black motorist who's lost his way in a white community, within minutes a patrol unit will appear. You will be frisked, vehicle searched, and you will be escorted out of their community. That's preserving and protecting," Tariq stated emphatically.

"But gunshots ring out in black communities and no patrols come. This problem needs to be addressed. We need to have a forum on this. We just can't sit by idle while our children are beaten and murdered on the streets," Somali stated. Tariq nodded and pondered over the crisis that had just been addressed.

★★★★★★★★

The moon was in its full stage appearing as a giant light in the dark blue void of space with only the twinkling stars stealing some of its magnificence. Inside of his grandmother's home, Braun lay across his bed with his shirt off. He was smiling as he talked on the phone. He whispered so as not to disturb the still of this night at 2 a.m. and awaken his grandmother.

"Yeah. If you want to put it that way, come on, you know you mean more to me than that," he stated softly.

On the other end of the phone was Ikara who was wearing a long T-shirt with pink bunnies on the front.

"Um, hmm. You'll tell me anything, Braun. I'll see. I'll see. When? Ah, I don't know…you know how my mom is. No. Boy, you so crazy," she whispered.

"You done got all quiet on me. What chu thankin' about?" he inquired.

"Just some things. Us. Our relationship," she responded.

"I've been thinking a lot about us too. All I can thank about lately is you," Braun stated. "Thinking about how beautiful you are and how it'll be the first time we make love," he continued.

"You know, I've never really been involved with anyone. I've always been so caught up in school. Ya know, cheerleading and the organizations." There was a brief pause. "I really like you, Braun. You're so different and I'm just afraid I'll push you away," she stated.

"Push me away? Ikara, I told you. I ain't in no rush. I ain't rushin' you. You supposed to be about your academics. That's your future. Do you know what I'm saying? We got time," he assured her. This made Ikara feel secure. Before she responded, Braun's light switch turned on. Squinting, he looked in the direction of his bedroom door. It was his grandmother. A full figured woman of sixty years old with graying hair in spots in her otherwise jet black hair stood there. She was extremely dark skinned, pie faced and her eyes always appeared saddened, even when she smiled.

"Braun, boy you still up? How you gon' get up for school in the mornin'? You been on that phone five hours," she stated as she turned off the light. Braun smiled and then yawned.

"Ikara look, I gotta go, aiight. Yeah. Know how Ma mah is. I'll call you tomorrow, ok? You know I do. Bye," Braun stated and hung up the phone. On the other end Ikara lay back on her bed with a smile etched on her face as she clutched her teddy bear.

Chapter 5

It was another scorching hot day in May. The bright sun was glistening off of the glass buildings and cars. Children scampered, tumbled, and ran about in yards and through lawn hose sprinklers to keep cool. They were just having fun.

Braun held a booksack strap in one hand while he sipped his grape soda with the other. Piye accompanied him and he wore a red, black, and green tank top with Bob Marley's face across the front.

As the two boys walked they discussed various topics, mostly pertaining to school and their prospects for senior year. Some topics centered on Piye's exploits with his steel weight bench set. When he wasn't in a tirade over the current dilemma in the community or giving commentary about second hand rhetorical speeches from the 60s, he spoke about being physically fit. He had heard time and time again these stories from his father and this seemed to be a topic that he liked to talk about.

"Pops went through a lot with the cops on the streets and the sixteen years he spent in prison. Pops is always speakin' 'bout how the system is designed to reincorporate slavery and put us back in shackles. The only thing now is that instead of whips they got shot guns and rifles. He is speakin' 'bout somethin' called the prison industrial complex," Piye informed. Braun nodded and looked off into the distance as he continued to walk.

"Yeah, I heard of that. Prisons are makin' money off of prisoners. There's a prison out west that is usin' prisoners to make clothin' lines to sell at businesses," Braun offered.

"Exactly, but it's much more than that," Piye stated while hitting his fist into his palm.

As he was about to further give his own personal insight into this prison industrial complex, two little boys approached. One was walking and the other was on a bicycle. The two stopped walking as the two little boys approached them. "Deshon, are you tryin' out fa lil league football this year?" Braun asked the kid as he rubbed his head.

"Yeah. I'mma win trophies too," the little boy replied. Piye smiled and shook his head.

"If you gon' play football, you gotta get muscles like his," the other little boy stated. Piye flexed his muscles. Two other children, who had been bouncing a ball, came over to inspect.

"Ooh! Look at his muscles!" the two boys stated in enthusiasm. Then one leaped up to hold onto Piye's arm. This seemed to amuse both Piye and Braun.

"Ah, dat ain't nothin'. Look." The eight year old stated while flexing his small muscles. Everyone laughed. Piye rubbed the boy's head and the two continued on down the street leaving the three boys behind to carry on with their play.

"All they wanna do is harass kids on the corners. They know that turban wearin' sucka sell paraphernalia out of his store. And they know that's a crack house," Piye stated indignantly. "Kids ain't safe nowhere. This neighborhood is all messed up," he finished.

"It's like that when they are on a payroll," Braun responded. He finished the remainder of his cola and threw the bottle into a trashcan beside the Pakistani's store. The two proceeded across the avenue and approached the neighborhood street gang members who were posted up on the sidewalk in front of a dilapidated house that was encompassed by a fence.

The gang members were engrossed in an apparent comical conversation as the four laughed loudly. Two of them were brandishing 40 oz. bottles of beer and taking sips every so often. A red complexioned kid with a black do rag sat upon a plastic bucket as the fourth kid, about fourteen years of age, narrated the comical episode. It was Red Dawg, Bull, Wild Bill, and Lil Gun.

"Too hoo! Man, Piye, you din got big as a mafucka!" Lil Gun stated. Placing a fist to his mouth as he appraised him. Piye smiled.

"Lil Gun. What's up Wild Bill?" Piye called out. Wild Bill responded with a wide smile exposing his missing tooth.

"What's up, man? Ya'll been out there in your backyard hitting them weights, huh?" he inquired.

"Nah, jis kicking' it about the revolution," Piye responded. Wild Bill nodded as the two boys approached. Each acknowledged each other with daps before turning to continue on up the street.

"Lil Dred. Kick some lyrics for' us Lil Dred." Wild Bill coaxed. He was referring to Braun, who rapped using the name Dred. Braun laughed and shook his head, but the other boys coaxed on and compelling him to stop walking.

"Ok. Ok. Check it out," Braun stated while placing his fist to his mouth as if holding the microphone for testing.

"Give'em a beat, Red Dawg," Bull requested. Red Dawg then began making rhythmic sounds with his mouth as he tapped on the plastic bucket.

"Cmmph! Aiight…check it…Corruption, destruction…all I see, imperials enactin' their ideologies…the government is shakin' us down, holdin' us down, terrorists in they own right, ya hearin' me now? But you don't wanna hear this, because it's realness, aimed at informin' the blind…you can appeal this…but yo writ will get shut down…cause ain't no gettin' in on frivolous grounds…ya barred, mentally scarred, the system is hard, without probable cause, the cops bogart…they way in yo crib at night…batons and they fo ones up in they hands tight." Braun recited a brief bar for the gang members. He rocked from side to side as if on stage, and then pretended to place the microphone into the holder. "That's all, main. That's just off the top of my head," he stated.

"Come on, Lil Dred. Kick some mo'."

"Yeah, main. That was tight. Kick some mo', main," Bill and Lil Gun stated. Braun shook his head and continued walking as Piye raised up a 'Black Power' fist towards the boys.

"You gon' rap for the Juneteenth celebration next month, huh?" Red Dawg inquired.

"Fa sho," Braun replied as he walked backwards. The boys then nodded, each bearing expressions of anticipation. Then as Braun and Piye distanced themselves, the gang members continued on with their conversation.

✶✶✶✶✶✶✶✶

An Avia (San Antonio bus line) turned through a maze of brick dwellings and trees passing up many Caucasians, Hispanics, Pakistanis, and African Americans children at play. Some were playing together. Some were playing in small groups with their own ethnic group. The entire community seemed to be abuzz; yet, there was serenity in this bricked community. A serenity that was not felt or seen in the gang infested region of the east, west, and south sides where drug activities carried on day and night and gunshots rang out in the wee hours. The south and west sides were notorious for their Mexican gang wars. This was Fort Sam Houston, one of San Antonio's military bases.

The Avia finally wound to a stop at a corner. As it came to a stop, two Hispanic girls ran by in front of the bus laughing giddily as one chased the other who held a colorful ball. The Avia's doors opened up and unloaded several passengers. The last one to get off the bus was Ikara's friend, Sharon. She was sporting sexy summer apparel: a yellow T-top and shorts with sandals. Her beautiful dark skin was shining in the sunlight, her hair done in stacks, and her eyes hidden behind a pair of fashionable sunshades.

Inside of his mother's military home, Devonte' sat on the sofa talking silently on the phone. He raised the remote control to the home entertainment center and began turning down the volume.

"Yeah, you know that, babe. I'm all about you. What do you want? Look, meet me at the Hacienda tonight…right? Afterwards I got a lil somethin special for ya. Aiight… I love you too, Kim," Devonte' smiled mischievously as he rubbed his bare chest. He then immediately began dialing another number. "Hey, what chu doin', Lashon? Yeah. I'm thankin' about you. Dat's why I called."

At that moment Sharon was approaching the walkway up to the front doorstep and looking around the vicinity as she fanned herself.

"Yeah, remember that outfit you'se talkin' about? Right. I'mma take ya out to Rollin Oaks Mall tommar and hook ya up on a lil something something'… Hey look, mom 'bout ta go so why don't you ease on over so we can pick up where we left off. Imam caress, and finesse that…" As he talked sex talk, Sharon was peering through the front window observing the expression on his face. Judging by his erotic chest rubbing she discerned him to be talking to a female. Her facial expression turned menacing that she rapped loudly at the door which startled Devonte'.

"Who is it?" he called out as he placed his hand over the receiver.

"Who you want it to be?!" Sharon responded back.

Devonte's expression registered worry.

"Hey, Lash on, boo. Look I'mma have ta call you back. I gotta to go, my boy just had a car wreck. Yeah. I hope he alright too. I'mma get back at ya. Bye. I'm comin', baby," he called out to Sharon while quickly dialing Braun's number so that in the event Sharon pressed redial, he would answer.

With a guilty expression on his face, Devonte' answered the door. Seeing Sharon's puzzled look, he placed on a fake smile. "Hey, baby," he greeted while tempting to kiss and caress her. But, he was cautioned with a defiant hand as Sharon rolled her eyes before pushing past him into the house.

"Don't hey baby me. Who you was on the phone wit?" she inquired. Devonte' closed the door behind her. Before he could respond, Sharon had picked up the telephone.

"Girl, what you doing?" he asked as he attempted to grab the phone from her hand. But she had already pushed redial. "What, you don't trust me?"

He further pleaded while feinting as if he was really trying to wrest the phone from her grasp. Of course he wanted the number to go through and he masked his amusement as her expression changed once Braun answered the phone.

"Oh, hi Braun. Look, did Devonte' just call there?" she inquired. Devonte' hadn't been expecting this maneuver. He had to think fast.

"So you don't trust me? You trippin," he shouted so that Braun on the other line could hear. Braun was then on cue to deceive her and responded that he and Devonte' did indeed just speak.

"Ohum, hmm. I know your lil sneaky butt be lyin' fo his ass. I thought you were my little friend, Braun. Dats alright, I'm ma catch him. Um, hmm. bye," she stated with a half-smile as she hung up the phone. Devonte' struggled to contain his laughter. A few seconds later after he sat down next to her attempting to snuggle, which she resisted as his mother walked in.

Technical Sergeant was Yavonne Johnson's rank in the military. She was petite, but had a very nice figure with caramel skin and reddish hair. Yavonne was thirty-nine years old and had been enlisted in the United States Air Force for seventeen years. She attended four years at Texas Tech University before entering the Air Force as an officer.

Yavonne traveled the globe and experienced Europe, Asia, and Hawaii, all courtesy of the military. Incidentally, she met Devonte's father, who is of Hawaiian descent, and found him to be a very handsome, sensitive man. The two courted during her brief military station there. They wined, dined, walked the sandy beaches, and swam in the beautiful bluish green waters under the bright sun. She totally consumed herself with his debonairness and cultural charm that she became pregnant with Devonte'.

Barely in the military a year, Yavonne was twenty three years old and pregnant. Nevertheless, she remained focused. Shortly after the pregnancy the romance ended when her Hawaiian beau's other girlfriend became the focal point. When Yavonne's tour was up she slipped away on a 747 plane back to the United States another location. It would be nearly a year before she would contact Devonte's father.

Yavonne learned from her experience, which was essential. She would be stationed at many exotic countries and meet many more men with savoir-faire in the future. But, she would only meet one man worth marrying while stationed in Okinawa. This time she met an African American who she entertained the thought of marrying. But things didn't work out. He was a retired military man and had a complicated and emotional past, which conflicted with their future.

Yavonne would eventually settle back in her native San Antonio, though periodically she would put in requests for some overseas destination. At this time Devonte' was coming into his adolescent stage and didn't want to leave his friends. Devonte' would reside with Yavonne's mother while she was away. Piye, Braun, and his cousin Phil happened to live a block from Yavonne's mother's home, which was perfect. Devonte' spent some time with his father in Hawaii during the summer. At thirty-nine, Yavonne was still very attractive, and would be flattered at Devonte's associates on Fort Sam Houston mistaking her for his sister. She walked into the living room adjusting her uniform coat, which adorned a blue Airmen hat, and jacket and blue pants, which gave hint to her curves as she walked. Her superbly polished black boots squeaked on the linoleum floor.

Devonte' quickly removed his arm from around Sharon who adjusted her tight yellow shorts and tried to look innocent as his mother approached. Yavonne had observed the action and smiled.

"Hey Mrs. Johnson," Sharon greeted. Yavonne smiled.

"Hello, Sharon. At least now I don't have to worry about the M.P.'s rushing over here," Mrs. Johnson laughed. Sharon and Devonte' laughed, too. "If you decide to leave, you call me on that expensive cell phone you bugged me for a month to buy, okay?" Yavonne continued. Sharon observed the many medals and pennants she had pinned on her jacket, which represented various honors that had been bestowed upon her over the seventeen years of her service.

"Aiight, ma." Devonte' responded with an assuring glance. She proceeded out of the door walking gracefully in a military mannerism as she opened up the door to her new Acura. After the car backed out of the driveway, Devonte' resumed his attempts at caressing and kissing Sharon, but was thwarted once more.

"Uh, uh. I ain't through with you, yet. I know you been on the phone with some wench. But let me find out and the M.P.'s will be rushin' over here. Move na" she stated as Devonte' laughed and kissed her neck. She began smiling as her emotions gave into his sensuous touches and kisses. "You make me sick," she said. After a brief stare into each other's eyes, they began passionately kissing and groping each other.

✶✶✶✶✶✶✶✶

Cellular phones rang and the sounds of rapid fire reverberated the tapping on computer keyboards in the large office space at Global Reach Telecommunications Services. Business suit clad men and women walked around with folders and portfolios in hand as they sipped coffee and discussed the latest in their marketing ventures and collaborations on new ideas.

Tariq, wearing his spectacles, sat before his computer. His eyes scanning the blue screen as his fingers diligently tapped away at the computer keys. He was conversing online with a marketing client in France who was interested in investing a lot of money in pharmaceuticals. As Tariq continued tapping on the keys, Somali approached holding a typed document in one hand and a cup of coffee in the other.

"Take a look at this," Somali stated as he extended the document before Tariq's face. Tariq's peripheral vision caught sight of it and he held up a cautioning finger.

"One minute," Tariq replied continuing to tap on the keys without taking his eyes off of the screen. After he finished with the e-mail, he received the document from Somali's fingertips. "Okay. What is this?" Tariq inquired. His eyebrows furrowed as he squinted his eyes to read the small print on the document.

"It's a text printout from Global Online Financial Service Company," Somali explained.

"So, what exactly are the functions of this Global Online Financial Service?" Tariq asked further.

Somali took a sip of his coffee.

"Well, it provides easy and secure online money transfers anywhere and at any time," Somali explained.

Tariq nodded his head and looked back down at the print out.

"Hmm. So this Global Online Service caters to website searchers in foreign languages?" Tariq inquired.

"Several different languages," Somali confirmed and asked Tariq what he was working on.

Tariq twiddled his thumbs and swayed slightly in his swivel chair as he looked at the screen on the computer, before responding.

"A French nutritional surplus center was interested in ordering a large shipment of pharmaceutical plastic bottles," he informed. He logged off of the computer and glanced at his watch. He took a sip of his coffee and rose from his chair and grabbed his briefcase. "Get on that as soon as possible. I have to make a run," he stated. Somali nodded, and turned on his heels. Tariq tossed his cup into a plastic wastebasket and hurried out of the office to go home.

At home Tariq sat at a desk in a very quaint room on the eastern most side of his five bedroom home. There was row after row of books ranging from novels to encyclopedias to books of law. As he read, he jotted down notes and points of reference that would be significant for his next business meeting. At that moment the atmosphere of his serenity was broken as he felt a soft kiss to the side of his face. It was Ursula. She was in her nightgown and scented by the body lotions that perforated her beautiful brown skin.

"I thought you had turned in when I took my shower. Don't strain your eyes too much, honey," she stated as she turned to walk out of the room. Tariq smiled and removed his glasses, while rubbing his sore eyes.

"I was just about to wrap it up. I'll be there shortly. I'm gonna catch a little bit of the news first and see what's going on out there," he stated. As the screen came into focus a very serious expression on the face of a Caucasian man sitting behind the newsroom counter was visible. Tariq adjusted the volume so that the news reporter's words could be audible. He swiveled his chair to better view the television as his expression registered intense interest.

"At the top of the news at this hour another bank robbery on the city's west side has resulted in a homicide. The perpetrator of the robbery as you can see in the footage appears to be of Hispanic descent."

As the reporter verbalized the details of the robber, the bank's black and white video recording showed what appeared to be a Hispanic male in his late twenties possibly thirties, entering the bank foyer. He was dressed in all black, but no mask. The perpetrator then reached into his pocket and produced a small caliber revolver. He aimed it in the direction of the guard. Suddenly, there was a bright muzzle flash. Though not audible, the panicked expression of the tellers and patrons were evident as the robber yelled waving his gun back and forth. After a period of approximately forty seconds, the perpetrator gathered up several bags with indiscernible amounts of cash and fled the bank.

Tariq shook his head, but continued looking seriously at the screen. Meanwhile Ursula had turned on Caleb's light and peered in at him as he slept. She flicked back off his light switch and continued on down the hallway to Ikara's room. There she found Ikara semi-awake with textbooks before her and pink headphones in her ears. Ursula looked quizzically at her daughter who after a considerable time, finally noticed her mother. Startled, she turned off the radio and fumbled with her pencil. She looked down at her note pad and feinted a smile as she looked up at her mother.

"Ikara, it's almost twelve o'clock," she stated. Ikara smiled and ran a hand through her hair.

"Yeah, I have to study for this final exam," she informed. Ursula folded her arms.

"Um, hmm. Well, you can't get any studying done like that. You're barely awake. I told you about staying up half the night on the phone with Braun. It's amazing how he makes passing grades," Ursula stated.

"I'm awake. I'm okay, I'm just going to go over these notes from this chapter once more," she smiled, while masking her fatigue. Ursula smiled as she shook her head then left her to her studies.

"The security guard was pronounced dead on the scene. The robber made off with an undisclosed amount of cash and according to eyewitness accounts there was an accomplice in a getaway vehicle. It has been described as a black Durango. The perpetrator has been described as being between 5'9" to 6'0 tall, weighing between 170 and 180 pounds. Anyone with any information contact…"

Tariq stared at the screen replaying the scene that he'd just witnessed. He'd seen it time and time again. Different suspects, different ethnicities, even different genders, but the same scenario. As the news man finished off the details of the bank robbery, another scene showed up on the screen. It was that of a crime scene taped off with yellow police tape. Beyond it lying on the grass of a dilapidated house, was a victim, wrapped in a white sheet.

"In other headline news tonight, a gang fight between two rival Hispanic gangs leaves one man dead and two others injured. Witnesses on the scene claim a grey car with four occupants sped to a stop in front of this residence on Crestfield Drive. The occupants got out and threats were issued. A fight ensued in which one man pulled a knife and stabbed two of the rival gang members, before a gun was produced from the rival gang's vehicle. Gunshots were reported, which struck one of the men in the lower torso, after which, the four re-boarded the vehicle and fled the scene." The images on the screen were grim and emotional, which Tariq had also grown accustomed to seeing. Police lights flashed and onlookers were pushed back from the scene as an emotionally distraught mother wailed for her dead son. Tariq shook his head as he thought about the violence, crime, racism, and oppression that consumed his city. It was eating away at it like a cancerous growth and he wondered if there was any cure.

Chapter 6

Windsor Park Mall was literally crawling with shoppers. This vast mall was one of the largest in San Antonio. There were hundreds of stores that catered to all fashion tastes for the old generation as well as the new, and all age ranges were in full bloom on this Saturday afternoon.

Phil, Devonte', and Braun were accompanied by two female companions as they strolled through the mall. These females were Devonte' and Braun's girlfriends, Sharon and Ikara, respectively. The five had vindicated themselves with various clothing items from different stores in their two hours either through exchange of gifts or personal purchases of their own fashion critique.

They were now approaching the escalators laughing and talking about trivialities. The two couples were dressed in compliment of each other. Ikara and Braun adorned matching white T-shirts with each other's name air brushed in blue writing and blue jean shorts. Devonte' and Sharon, both were dressed in all black outfits with matching white sneakers.

Phil, who was lavishly dressed in colorful gear and jewelry, as usual, was hawking nearly every attractive female he saw. Ethnicity was irrelevant, whether African American, Caucasian, Asian, or Hispanic, it didn't matter. If it were not for his inappropriate pickup lines, he probably would have collected a considerable amount of phone numbers, but inappropriate was Phil's forte'.

To refer to Phil as unethical would be an understatement. Brash, flirtatious, and emotionally unattached to the feelings or emotions of females was a better description of him. He was a drug dealer by trade and a womanizer by nature. With his boyish looks, he was notorious among the females much the same as his cousin, Devonte'. Girls who were involved with him either hated him or held a love-hate fixation for him. And, the females who were familiar with his status, for some reason adored him.

Growing up in a single parent household, Phil had become somewhat of a derelict at a young age. His father had gone to prison for a drug related murder when he was only eight years old. He was still in prison despite not being the triggerman. His mother, who had three other children, at the time of his incarceration, was forced into welfare and into prostitution in order to support them.

From a young age, Phil had been introduced to psychological, as well as physical abuse, from his mother as well as her beaus, and even Johns. He saw his mother doing drugs like marijuana, crack, and prescription medicine as she tried to escape from the realities of her perilous situation. He saw men come and go. Many were only around when bills were due. These ghostly figures would manifest in the middle of the night and disappear into his mother's room. Hours would pass before these ghostly figures would slip out just as silently as they had manifested.

There were however, periods when Phil's mother would regain stability. She fought her drug addiction, found good jobs, and retained meaningful relationships with decent men. These were the periods when young Phil would develop a semblance of respect for his mother. He loved his father and respected him, but he preferred for his mother to be in a committed relationship rather than being a prostitute. He even developed a strong relationship with one particular brother.

This man whom he had grown to respect had been an honest, blue-collar worker. He was a lot younger than his mother and had no children of his own. This man had taken on the responsibility of helping to raise her remaining three children while still treating his mother with dignity and respect. Phil had two other siblings that no longer resided at home during this time. His older sister, Kiesha moved to the Caribbean with her new husband, and his older brother, Patrick was locked up. Over time the relationship began to deteriorate as his devotion and hard work towards developing the relationship on a spiritual and moralistic foundation was disrupted by her setback into drug addiction and promiscuity. When he was away at work in the chemical plant, the ghostly figures would again manifest. After putting up with the addiction and flagrant disrespect for two years, the relationship dissolved. Phil also lost respect for his mother and black women in general.

When Phil was in the ninth grade his interest in school began to decline. His mental perspective of a future was slowly giving way to his visual perspectives of the drug dealers with all of their extravagance and street fame. His mother's live-in companion made strides in keeping him focused and when he left, that was the final ingredient that propelled Phil into his present state of mind.

Phil was about two years in the drug game. He started off small by peddling for neighborhood marijuana dealers, but after a few short months he graduated to selling his own from half ounces to ounces and then quarter pounds. But, his financial status never escalated to the proportions he so desired due to his extravagance.

Phil took his salesmanship to his high school campus until the police were tipped off by fellow students. He was arrested and received probation, which caused him to slow down a bit. While he was slowing down he met a serious minded and conscious sister who attempted to redirect him. The repercussions of getting arrested and her reasoning were outweighed by his need for materialism and the need to provide for his family. Thus, his dealing escalated to crack cocaine. With the implementation of the 'war on drugs' in 1986, and the changes in laws concerning minimum mandatory sentences on distribution of crack, the amount of drug offenders clogged the system. This began the era of the "incorporation of prisons", a rise in informants, as well as an increase in police and federal surveillance of high crime drug areas. By 2005, it had reached an apex.

Being on the police's most wanted files wasn't Phil's only worry. His primary problem was that he dealt drugs for a major stakeholder in a drug ring. This ring consisted of colorful characters who were both informants and killers at the same time, including some who were infiltrators for the F.B.I. Phil was oblivious to his ring affiliates modus operandi, with the exception of the murders.

Phil, Devonte', Braun, Sharon, and Ikara ascended on the escalator and pointed to different department stores they wanted to shop in. In the meantime, Phil became preoccupied with three attractive African American females who appeared older than him. Their mannerism and conservative attire suggested their level of maturity. Phil in his unorthodox manner said to them, "Which one of ya'll distinguished gals wanna thug in ya life?" The young ladies' looked at Phil and halfheartedly acknowledged his approach. Two of the women instantly turned their heads as they continued to descend past him. The last one humored him with a smile and prolonged look. She did not give a look of interest, but rather one of sympathy. She showed sympathy for her young African American brother who was en route to an early death or incarceration, further adding to the statistics. These statistics were disproportionate in death and incarceration rates for blacks and whites. Blacks only make up approximately 17% of the U.S. population compared to their white counterparts.

Seeing that he captured one of the ladies attention, but, of course he misconstrued her reason for this attention, Phil began holding onto the rail and hopped back down the escalators to meet them on their way down and he talked as he went.

"Say, say baby. I'm sayin...what's yo name? I'm distinguished too. We might can coagulate, know what I'm sayin'?" he stated. His friends were all staring back at him in amusement. The young lady smiled, belying her sympathetic eyes.

"No, I don't think so. I make it a point never to date anyone younger than me, under twenty five. Besides, I'm engaged," she responded while twisting her hand to expose her engagement ring. The diamond ring sparkled. Phil stopped and began to ascend as he stared at the attractive young woman.

"So, what that mean? I caint get them digits?" he laughed. The young woman smiled and turned around towards her friends as they shook their heads.

"Dats aiight. I bet I clock ten times mo din yo fiancé, baby," he stated, while waving a wad of money.

Devonte' and Braun shook their heads.

"Come on here, main. Fo you get us all jacked up," Devonte' yelled.
Phil then ran back up the escalator steps to catch up to his friends.

The next hour and a half the group of friends continued to browse through various stores, whether men's and women's and conservative and expensive. The boys bought several sports jerseys and Hip-Hop Wear, while Ikara and Sharon carried bags with racy purses and the latest in perfumes and summer outfits.

Most of the stores they ventured into they found themselves being scrutinized by the watchful eyes of the sales people, who happened to be Caucasians. They tried to maneuver inconspicuously, but when observed, feinted a deceptive smile. The group saw through the fake pleasantries and exchanged meaningful glances with each other. Several times Phil flashed his money before their faces defiantly. He assured them that he had no intentions or need to steal any of their merchandise.

After their shopping spree, they had gotten a bite to eat at the delicatessen. They ordered taco salads, Fajitas, chili dogs, and nachos. They occasionally spoke with their friends from school and respective neighborhoods as they passed by. They made plans for upcoming events, such as the upcoming Juneteenth celebration, which everyone was excited about.

As they left the delicatessen, Devonte' and Phil conversed about their favorite sport, basketball. The Spurs were in game three against the Los Angeles Lakers.

"Main, I'm tellin' ya, two games to nuthin'. They might steal this game in LA and if not this one, fa sho the next one. That'll put they backs against the wall," Devonte' stated confidently as he gulped down the remainder of his cola before throwing it into the wastebasket.

"I know the Spurs gon steal one in the Staples Center, but they gon fight, though. Shh. It's a must win situation fa big Shaq' nem tonight," Phil responded.

"Uh, why every time Phil comes along I feel like we watchin' ESPN?" Sharon stated. Braun and Ikara both laughed.

"What chu tawkin 'bout? I don't say nuttin' when you go tawkin 'bout Shemeeka and Noctuneesha or somebody hatin' on yo hair. Oh dey hatin' on my hair, dey hatin' on my outfit, hatin' on my eyes…ery'body hatin on you? Please!" Phil shot back.

"Well, it's the truth," Sharon responded.

"Ya'll two are always arguing," Ikara smiled.

At that moment Phil took notice of two Mexican girls who were talking in front of a set of wooden benches and a floral centerpiece. Rubbing his hand on his chin with a devilish grin, he practically undressed them with his eyes. The two were gorgeous in form. They adorned outfits that were accentuating their voluptuous curves.

"Te ves sexy. ¿Puedo llevarte a casa conmigo?" (You look sexy. Can I take you home with me?) Phil called out to them. The girls stopped talking to look in his direction. Instantly their expressions beamed as both smiled and whispered to one another. Phil then made a lewd comment in reference to having sex with them, which caused them to laugh.

Several feet away five Mexican boys were conversing. One of the boys, a kid with Indian features, a stocky build, and piercing eyes caught sight of what was transpiring between Phil and the Mexican girls. The girls happened to know two of the Mexican boys: one was a boyfriend and the other was a brother. Nodding his head in their direction, the kid directed the boy in front of him to turn around.

With a black du-rag tied down to just above his eyes, the kid turned around slowly. His expression turned to a menacing leer as he observed. His chest heaved and accentuated his bulk that emanated underneath the silk black T-shirt he wore with khaki pants and black Nikes. It was obvious that he was gang affiliated, much the same as the others. Some bore elaborate tattoos and wore basic or stripped shirts and sagging jeans.

As the group walked past the Mexican girls, Phil continued talking perversely to them as the gang members converged. They stopped abruptly in front of Phil. One of the gang members, the one wearing the du-rag and silk shirt, held up a cautioning hand. Braun examined each of the gang member's expressions. Two of the biggest boys looked like they stood over six feet tall, at least 6'1" or 6'3". They folded their massive arms as they grinned devilishly, while the other three ranging from medium to small build put on their most intimidating looks.

"What's going on here Vatu? Are you making passes at my girlfriend ESSE'?" he inquired. His hand was underneath his shirt. Phil noticed the gesture and began taking a few steps back. Braun and Devonte' both bore expressions of weariness.

The two Mexican girls intervened, "Stop it, Eduardo. He didn't mean anything."

Eduardo glared at the two girls. He then returned to intimidating Phil.

"Say main, I ain't know they was wit ya'll. I," Phil nervously answered. His rebuttal was interrupted by another small-framed gang member with the tattoo "El Gatos" on his neck.

"Shut the fuck up, Puto!" he yelled.

Phil recognized the derogatory remark in Spanish and yelled, "Fuck you, you lil bitch!" Phil clinched his fist and setup in a boxing stance. Braun and Devonte' moved their girlfriends behind them.

Phil's remark seemed to ignite the gang bangers into a tirade. They flexed up into a fight mode and shouted obscenities. The two Mexican girls tried to get in between them to stop the melee. The shouting attracted attention, primarily from the Mall Police who broke into jogs towards them as they communicated over their radios. Seeing the approaching police, the gang members began to ease away as some pointed and issued threats.

"What's going on here? Is there a problem? You bangers? Gang bangers! Come here! Turn around!" One police ordered Eduardo, as he turned him around to be frisked. Eduardo slowly raised his arms as he shot Phil a fierce look. At this time more officers arrived on the scene. The officers began pat searching each of them as the other mall goers observed and whispered comments amongst each other as they passed.

It was a scene, a spectacle. The edgy officers thoroughly frisked everyone. The gang protested this frisk as they cited harassment. All the while Eduardo and "El Gatos" issued threats over the shoulders of the police officers to Phil and Devonte', who in turn entertained the insults and threats with racial epithets.

"Alright! Alright! You shut that up! I want you right here to go that way. And you, that way. I want you out of this mall, right now. And if there's any incident, everybody's going to jail. Comprende?" one of the officers ordered.

The two factions began moving in opposite directions while observing the seven officers as they glared at each other.

"Puto! Maricone!" The gang sneered. The tall officer shoved them away.

"I gotcho Maricone. You chili eatin' motherfucka!" Phil responded.

"Hey! Keep moving!" A black officer ordered. Eduardo mouthed off and gestured for them to meet him outside.

Braun's expression registered his leeriness about this, because of they were outnumbered.

"You ain't said nothin'! Whatever, Taco!" Phil shot back in response to the gesture.

Braun grabbed his arm and stared him in the eye with a cautioning look.

"Let's just go home, Phil," Braun stated.

Ikara looked between them both.

"Yeah, let's just go," she agreed.

Phil looked off with an irritated expression.

Sharon pulled at his shirt and he began walking in the opposite direction. Devonte' bore an expression of worry and stared back once more at the gang members as they walked towards the mall's exit.

The sun was beginning to set on the horizon and the clear bright sky turned to a purplish hue as the twilight hour set in. The sounds of dogs barking and the eerie shrieking sounds of crickets reverberated around the vicinity. The three were joined by Piye and were now standing in front of Phil's mother's house. Each wore disgruntled expressions, which were obviously a result of the day's confrontation with the Mexicans.

Phil took a sip of cherry cola and stared out into the distance towards one of the Pakistani owned liquor stores. He was in a crouched position on the steps while Devonte' stood beside him. Devonte' stared down at the ground as Piye stood with his arms folded in deep contemplation. His massive arms accentuated under the luminance of the front porch light. Every so often he looked at Braun as if in anticipation of his giving rationale into how the confrontation could have been avoided.

A black four door Chevy Impala's lights swept the faces of the boys and they squinted. The car rounded the corner and stopped in front of the house. As the boys watched, a rather curvaceous middle-aged woman of caramel complexion with long hair emerged from the house. Her face was drawn and eyes were sunken. Her very eminence was evidence of self-defeat and a lack of self-confidence. It was Phil's mother.

"Hey you all. Braun, you look like you into some shit," she stated with a devilish smile. Her eyes were reddened and her clothes reeked of cigarette smoke and alcohol.

"Ain't nobody in nothing," Phil stated indignantly as he looked past his intoxicated mother.

"Better not be. Devonte', keep his ass out the jailhouse," she stated as she sashayed down the steps past Phil.

"I don't need anybody to keep me out of nothing. Why are you on me? Look at you. What do you do?" he remarked.

His mother paused and said,"Whatever the hell I want to do because I'm grown." She placed hand on her hips.

The other three boys looked away embarrassed for their friend. They could not fathom having a mother who flagrantly prostituted herself for money or drugs. After her remark, she climbed into the passenger's seat and closed the door behind her as the boys continued to stare into the car, trying to gain recognition of the driver. Then the Impala crept away as silently as it had come. Phil released a sigh of anguish and shook his head as he stared off into the distance.

"I gotta get away from here and from her. This, this situation all fu...," his sentence was interrupted by a loud noise that couldn't have been more than a few blocks away. Then there came several more gun shots behind it. It sounded like a large caliber semi-automatic, possibly a 45 caliber Glock. The hollow metallic sounds of each gun shot, echoed in the vicinity. Then there was silence.

"Shhh. Man, shit fucked up. I have to go. Man, I'm sick of this shit. I'm sick of the police harassing and shit. Them burrito-eating motherfuckers. This shit every night," he finished exasperatedly. He waved his hand in the vicinity that the gunshots had come from. Seconds later there were the sounds of sirens.

"Where are you going to go? Where are you running to?" Piye asked, as he stared out into the approximate location the sirens were approaching from.

Phil sipped another portion of his cola and rose to his feet.

"Anywhere from here. This town, man. Florida maybe. Do you know what I'm saying? Beaches and hoes. Beautiful scenery. Not this shit," he stated and turned up his bottle.

Piye and Braun both shook their heads.

"You think Florida does not have all this? Any hood anywhere that has poverty, is messed up, Phil. Police brutality, shootings and dope. Even with all those palm trees and sunshine, Florida still has problems with police brutalilty, shootings, and dope," Piye stated. Braun nodded in agreement.

Phil looked up into the now nearly dark sky and his expression evidencing frustration.

"Man, so much is building up if I don't leave here. I may end up with a murder charge. Man, if I had my nine today, I would be in central booking right now for popping one of them cholovattos," Phil stated.

"And what good would that do? Shooting up the mall is not going to solve anything, Phil. 'Sides, I keep telling you main, the enemy is bigger than the Mexicans and the Pakistanis. You have to be able to see an unseen hand, know what I'm saying?" Braun replied.

Devonte' arose from the porch and looked at his watch.

"Man, let me get this car back before mom be tripping. Holla at ya'll. Ya'll coming over to watch the game Sunday, huh?" he inquired. The boys' half enthusiastically responded in kind, before Devonte' boarded the car.

"Hold on Devonte'. Let me catch that ride?" Piye asked. He turned to face Phil once more. "Cool out, Phil. Braun talk to'em," Piye said. He trotted to the passenger's side door. After the car pulled away from the curb, Braun walked up the steps and sat next to a very disgruntled Phil.

Chapter 7

A 2004 grey Mercedes Benz rounds a corner with the sunlight glistening off of its glass windows. Children of many ethnicities played outside with balls or frisbees or slid down water slides that had been placed on front lawns. These lawns were quite expansive with stylish driveways snaking up to the front of posh brick homes, each having well-manicured shrubbery. This was Universal City, a quaint, racially mixed subdivision northeast of downtown San Antonio.

Ikara was sitting inside of a very decorative den area with expensive 19th century furniture, including an Aubuson rug, paintings, and vases. Perhaps what gave the quaint little room its flavor was all of the cultural mosaics, pictures of elaborate mosques, the green and white Pakistani coat of arms with Arabic writing, a Pakistani flag, artifacts, and a large Pakistani carpet, which was elaborately designed.

Ikara was intrigued by this cultural display, but at the moment, wasn't inventorying these mosaics that she had long been familiar with. She was laughing as she watched a television program. Her white teeth were complimentary of her impeccable, smooth caramel skin. Her long silky black hair flowed down over her shoulders, which exposed her tan tank top. She placed a hand underneath her chin and crossed her legs and kicked them back and forth. The sunlight beamed through the curtain accentuating her legs all the way down to her sandaled feet.

"What's so funny?" Swathi inquired as she entered the den area carrying a large plastic bowl. The bowl was covered in a thin wax paper. As she sat down she removed the paper, allowing the aroma from the entrée within to entice Ikara.

"What is that? It smells good," Ikara inquired as she moved closer to Swathi.

"Pilau," Swathi informed.

Pilau is a dish served throughout Pakistan. Pilau consists of rice, mixed meats, vegetables, raisins, or nuts. In this case, Swathi prepared the dish by mixing ground meat with the rice and seasoned with onions and peppers.

"Want some?" she offered.

"Yeah, I love pilau. You know I want some. Why didn't you bring a bowl for me?" Ikara grinned.

Swathi laughed and rolled her eyes. After taking a bite of the savory dish, she set the bowl on the table and rose to her feet.

"You told me you had just eaten. You won't be able to fit into that dance line outfit next semester if you keep eating like this," Swathi laughed.

Swathi nearly bumped into her parents as she left the den to get Ikara a dish of pilau. She excused herself and asked them where they were going. She noticed that they were formally dressed.

"We're going to an event at the museum. We'll be back in awhile," her mother responded in Urdu, their native language. Her mother is a beautiful woman with long flowing black hair, just like Swathi. It was evident where Swathi inherited her enchanting beauty. Her parents warmly acknowledged Ikara before leaving.

"Good evening, Ikara. Tell your father that I will inform him about the proposal tomorrow," Mr. Nawaz Jinnah stated.

Ikara told him okay and waved good-bye to them as they closed the door behind them. After her parents left, Swathi returned to the den with Ikara's meal.

"I brought you some Chapati," Swathi stated.

Chapati is a form of processed bread.

Ikara made herself at home as she smiled and crossed her legs Indian style on the sofa, now that Swathi's parents left.

"You're trying to get me fat, aren't you?" Ikara giggled.

Swathi laughed and sat down as she poured the pilau into Ikara's bowl.

As the two watched television they dined, laughed and commented on certain issues. As the episode began, Ikara's eyes seemed to glaze over as she ate her last scoop of well-seasoned rice and meat.

"You know, I wonder sometimes if people are ever going to put aside their differences, whatever they are," Ikara stated.

"You mean from a color standpoint?" Swathi inquired.

Ikara released a sigh as she looked down.

"Primarily, I mean, even in certain religions, race is an issue. And, it shouldn't be that way. God created all of us the same. We may speak different languages, but we're all people," she responded.

Swathi nodded in agreement.

Devout Christians who consume the scriptures of the Holy Bible's text into their psyche on a daily basis, believe that the Israelites are the 'Chosen People' and that Palestine is the 'Holy Land'. People of all nationalities, African American, Asians, Irish, Indian, Caucasian, etc. Every Christian follower has a concept of this theology. How can this be? Perhaps in some genealogical misconception, these people actually believe that they are descendants of the ancient Israelites. Why would the creator of the galaxies and all human beings, have a chosen people? This is the question which intellectual Christians might want to take into consideration.

"I agree and I don't know why people feel that their particular race is exalted above another. But, it seems like there is more that you're not telling me." Swathi insisted.

She knew that something beyond hypothetical contemplation over race issues and religion was troubling her friend. Ikara paused briefly as she reflected and recalled the scenes that had transpired the other day in the mall and responded.

For the next few minutes Ikara went over the incident and explained to her the intense hatred that had nearly boiled over because of racism. She described the misguided hostilities that spewed forth racial epithets and obscenities between the Mexicans and her friends. She expressed sincere sympathy as she spoke and her voice had a saddened undertone.

Swathi listened to the rendition of Ikara's day, she recalled the many times in her young life that she found herself in a similar situation. She was bombarded with racial slurs and made to feel like a second class human being. She never encountered physical ethnic strife along the lines in which her parents had experienced while growing up in Pakistan in the 1970's.

Swathi heard countless accounts of atrocities surrounding the civil war. The hatred and horrors of the war, including the human suffrage inflicted upon the innocent simply because of ethnicity and religion. She didn't experience racial strife up close and personal until the September 11th attacks in 2001 when everyone with Arabic features were targeted as terrorist. This ignorance was displayed by both whites and blacks.

After Ikara had finished explaining the circumstances surrounding the incident, she stared at the television screen and was oblivious to her friend's sympathetic look.

"Well, it's just good that things didn't develop into something more seri-ous. And, I'm glad Braun did the levelheaded thing by preventing it. He's re-ally mature for his age," Swathi stated.

At the mentioning of Braun's name, Ikara began to smile and the stress of the moment dissipated.

"Yes, he's sweet. I didn't know at first if I was making a mistake allowing my feelings to get involved with him, but then I got to know him," Ikara stated. Her smile widened as she looked at her friend, but her eyes still hinted of worry. She knew that the intense ethnic strife between her and Braun's community still simmered and she feared for him. "I just fear for him. In his environment, there's so much agitation. He has plans to go to Texas A & M University, though I don't want to go to A & M. It will be a good move for him to get away," she stated.

"So, where do you plan to go?" Swathi inquired.

Ikara paused as she pondered. She had not given any serious thought to universities.

"I don't know. I have a whole year to decide. And, depending on where he and I are at that point in our relationship will determine whether or not I decide on A & M," she responded.

"I just hope you will still be able to keep that GPA up when you're around him," Swathi smiled.

Ikara laughed and dropped her head. Swathi walked to the den's door, looked at her friend and smiled. Staring at her friend she said, "There's no racial boundaries between us. You are my sister." Ikara smiled and watched Swathi disappear into one of the rooms in the back.

✶✶✶✶✶✶✶✶

Inside of their den, Tariq and his wife Ursula entertained their guests; their fellow Nubian brethren, Somali and his wife Khadija. The four were in the middle of a rather serious discussion concerning political matters, social standings, and the current issue revolving around gentrification. Tariq wore a white shirt and grey slacks while adorning a tan kufi atop his head. His expression as he spoke was sincere. His eyes expressed deep concern for the social problems at hand.

"And, I feel that it is an issue that really needs to be addressed at the next meeting. We need to get more people in the community involved with this," Tariq stated.

"I agree. I feel that the people should get involved more with this issue of subsidizing. There are always government plans of displacing the black masses from their communities," Khadija commented. Somali looked over at his wife as she spoke. He contemplated while she spoke. After her point had been made, he offered his assertion.

"Displacing is right. These government contractors come in and they make promises of revitalization. They sell our people a dream and promise to revamp this project or these housing areas, but when the bulldozers roll. Huh, there's something different," Somali stated.

For years, public housing in the urban black communities was downsized by government contractors. The ramification of this government downsizing is the displacement of the urban blacks from their homes. It was under the guise of the government's interests in curbing distressed housing, or what they term "blighted public housing," that lead the citizens of the black communities to believe that units destroyed will be replaced by more adequate units. Most often this does not transpire. Instead, the tenants of the units are driven out of their homes and become displaced with promises of relocation. Meanwhile the unit continues to dilapidate with the government having no intentions of revitalizing. This is known as gentrification, a covert strategy by the government to further repress the black community.

In most large cities, cutbacks from government funding to the housing developments in urban communities has contributed greatly to this dilemma. In certain situations, other contributing factors may be an underlined initiative for the demolition of these units. These initiatives, in most cases, have to do with the facilitation of commercial enterprise, whether it be banks, malls, or sports arenas. It has become a nationwide method for blacks to be pushed out of their communities.

"The government simply wants to push the minorities away from the center city for enterprising. They don't care about the people," Ursula added. She rose from her seat and offered, "Would anyone like some more lemonade?" Everyone seemed to be in favor of this motion. As she disappeared, Tariq switched gears to another issue that was less tenuous and more along the lines of cultural awareness within the community.

"We've got the Juneteenth celebration coming up in the next three weeks. All funding is in order, so there are no problems with that," he stated.

"Fortunately, I think it's been a real success as far as giving the community a semblance of knowledge on the emancipation, even if it were primarily on paper. Hell, we are still not free, hmph!" Somali shouted. At that moment Ursula returned with a tray holding the four beverages. Everyone collected their glasses and acknowledged their appreciation. Ursula sat down with her own glass.

"I agree. But it's good for other reasons too. The youth can really come out and enjoy themselves," Tariq commented.

"Yeah, provided that none of the gang members start actin' like fools," Khadija responded.

"That's a whole issue in itself. Their presence in the community helps the government's cause in relation to all this relocating and proposed remodeling. With the shootings and robberies, it's easier for the media to demonize the area. But their presence will persist. I talk to them every chance I get. But words of encouragement are no deterrent," Tariq stated.

"Exactly. As long as they are repressed, discriminated against and harassed by the police, they will continue to exist as a social enigma. They will continue to vent out their frustrations in the wrong direction because they really can't lash out at the unseen hand responsible for their situation," Somali emphasized.

Over the next half hour or so, the conversation would cover various issues that were centered on changes in the community. Most were suggested or proposed as a part of the city council's meeting agenda, such as funding for urban academic programs and certain laws pursuant to the state guidelines. Each gave their own perspective and insights into possible solutions. Soon the sun began to set beyond the horizon, signaling for some of the neighborhood children to discontinue their play outside and head inside, including Caleb and his friends.

As Somali looked down at his watch, Caleb came bolting through the door drenched in sweat and holding a basketball in his hands.

"Caleb, looks like you've been trying out for the Spurs, son," Somali laughed. Caleb smiled and acknowledged him Somali and his wife. Before his mother could get a word out to caution him, Caleb began bouncing the basketball through the house into the kitchen.

"Caleb! Boy, how many times do I have to tell you about bouncing that ball in this house?" Ursula yelled. Everyone smiled as she shook her head. Somali rose to his feet and beckoned his wife to do the same.

"Boys will be boys. But, look at it this way, we'd much rather have him bouncing a basketball, then smuggling a gun." Somali responded. Everyone agreed on this assertion. As he placed his hand upon his wife's shoulder, Tariq and Ursula arose from their respective seats and escorted their houseguests to the door.

Inside of his grandmother's home, Braun was seated at his desk with his Algebra II book open before him. He was not exactly enthused with Algebra, but nevertheless excelled. He managed to have a 3.8 average, which is exceptional. He was a particularly gifted student and with his academic prowess it was almost certain that he be granted an academic scholarship to a university. His room was besieged with his ideological mentors whom he admired, from influential speakers like Stokely Carmichael who was the head representative of the S.N.C.C., and coined the 1960's radical phrase "power to the people" to brothers such as George Jackson, founder of the revolutionary "People's Army" and a Black Panther affiliate. George was assassinated inside of San Quinton prison in September of 1971 for his militant stance against an oppressive security staff. Braun also had posters of his favorite rap groups. Of course as a rapper himself, his wall would not be complete without them. His ideological stances in his raps were reflective of the poster groups. Groups such as X Clan, Brand Nubian, Dead Prez, and Public Enemy were groups whose lyrical content covered diverse and radical issues, which incited government attention. They addressed issues that dealt with the need for black unity, the eradicating of black-on-black crime, the opposition to drug abuse and drug dealing, and exposing government corruption. As he finished the last of set of logarithm formulas, he placed his pencil onto his desk then released a sigh and pinched his tired eyes. For a moment he simply sat there and reflected over the upcoming agenda for the following day. It was the final week of school and he was cramming for his final exams. After two and a half hours, he was completely exhausted.

Picking up his pencil, Braun closed the Algebra textbook and opened up another notepad. Inside were bars of his political and Afro-centric laced raps. Looking down at the pad he began tapping his fingers and pencil on the desktop as he nodded his head and simulated a beat.

"They don't know, they don't know, they don't know. I envision a scene where my people are kings, no violence, no stereotypes, narcotic fiends, blissful, this realm that I wish for…conscious minds enlighten all of those who oppressed for…" His rap was interrupted by the presence of his grandmother. She was standing there in his doorway with a proud smile enmeshed across her ebony face. She was indeed proud of him. Proud that her grandson had developed into the type of young man his mother and father would surely have been proud of, an honor student in school, who volunteered in his community. He was respected by everyone, especially the elders of the community who considered him a credit among a generation they had otherwise been written off as unconscious.

Braun never knew his mother who was only twenty at the time of his birth. She was a sickly girl and suffered from epilepsy. She developed complications during her pregnancy and as a result died after giving birth.

Her mother, Agnes, was understandably distraught. Her only daughter died at such a young age and was never allowed to experience much more in life. She was determined to see to it that Braun would live a full life and obtain the successes that she had not been able to. She raised him on her own. His biological father, was three years older than his mother, was killed by the police. His father's name was Eddie and he attended Texas A & M and was an activist. He was home for the summer when he was killed. While he was alive, he helped Agnes care for his young son. The circumstances were unclear to exactly what transpired that fateful day. According to the accounts in the San Antonio Express News, he reached for a weapon and the police were forced to use precautionary resistance. However, this weapon was never recovered from the vehicle. In his hands he clutched his student identification card from Texas A & M University. Their reason for arresting him was that he fit the description of a bank robbery suspect. Conversely, this suspect had been geared in all black, and Eddie had adorned traditional O.B.U. garb.

The incident had sparked outrage in the black community. There had been talk of rioting. Eddie had been vocal in the community and stood up in the face of oppression. He was an advocate of African American civil rights and reputed as anti-establishment, and was well embraced by the black community. He was a student, a father, and an activist. They mourned. Meanwhile, the police officers were acquitted on all charges.

Agnes had told Braun many accounts about his father's valor. In his short time, he was a very good father to him and if it were not for his untimely death at the hands of racist cops, his academic excellence in college and his ambitions would have certainly propelled him to prominence in political activism. Although Braun never knew his father, he held him as his biggest hero and biggest mentor. His father's picture was the largest photo at the top center of his room. Braun paused his rap and looked up into his grandmother's face as she stood there in the doorway appraising him.

"Baby, I thought you were in bed by now. You not gonna want to get up in the mo'nin'," she stated with a warm smile and a hand on her ample hips.

"Yeah. I'm 'bout to turn in, ma mah. I just had to finish studyin' fo this final exam. Gotta keep my chances up fo a academic scholarship next year," he explained. Agnes folded her arms and propped up against his doorframe.

"Don't worry too much, baby. You will. Your momma and daddy would be so proud of you baby. So proud. Just like grandmamma's proud, baby," she stated as she rubbed his face affectionately. For the next several minutes she reflected over his mother and father and thought about their dreams. She remembered in their young reveries, they had high expectations for their unborn son. Also, she thought about how Eddie had proudly branded him the second coming of Malcolm X, his own personal mentor. "Now, you go on and get some sleep so you won't fall asleep in class takin' that test," she laughed and went back into her room.

Braun smiled, "O.K., Ma mah," he replied as he returned to looking back down at his rap bars. Agnes looked once more back at her grandson with a loving smile then eased away from his room.

Chapter 8

It was another hot and muggy summer day in south Texas. The sweltering heat had driven most inside this afternoon. But, the children nevertheless were at play and glad to be finally out of school on vacation, which had been in effect for the past couple days.

On Phil's mother's front porch, the four boys sat perched talking about issues from the latest in rap, sports and girls, to plans for summer vacation, which was an incredibly broad subject in itself. Each of the boys had their own perspectives of what exactly to do over the summer. Some wanted a hiatus from their environment. In recent weeks there had been an increase in police harrassement and tensions between the various street gangs. There was also an incident that had fingers pointed at several possible suspects in a heist of a supply of cocaine belonging to Phil's cocaine ringleader— a topic that would later become a strong focal point.

"Main, they put that crack on Toady. He don't even sell crack," Phil stated while sipping a 40 oz. beer. They all nodded in unison as he was speaking in reference to a close neighborhood friend who had fallen victim to one of the police's covert schemes, which involved targeting and setting up innocnent people with drugs.

"Main, that was cold, main. They just beat his cousin down last month. He got lawsuits and ery'thang on'em. Prob'ly why they set Toady up. Rotten suckas." Piye stated.

Phil feinted handing Braun the 40 oz. bottle knowing what Braun's reaction would be.

"Main, I'ont want that. I'ont see how ya'll drank dat," Braun responded with a half-smile as he pushed the bottle away. Phil laughed and turned the bottle up. There was a pause of silence as Devonte' switched subjects.

"Man, Spurs shot bad, man. Lakers played defense, though," Devonte' said.

"Gotta come with they game next time." Braun replied.

"Yeah, gotta come wit a different scheme. And they gotta contain big

Shaq." Devonte stated.

Turning up the bottle. Phil feinted a jump shot.

"Main, I feel like I can walk on for the Spurs. Be like Tony Parker. Rain J's and, and puttin' niggas on highlight films," Phil bragged. At that moment a black Lincoln Navigator pulled up at the stop sign across the street. The boy's attention was gripped as a low rhythmic thumping sound emitted from the interior, and the sun glistened off of the chrome rims, which continued spinning. As they watched, a teenage boy in latest fashionable gear and jewelry ran up to the driver's side door.

"That's 'Chatter' and Dorele nem?" Devonte' inquired while holding the bottle before his lips as he stared in the direction of the SUV.

Phil remained silent and stared as well. The kid seemed to be explaining something with deep emotions as his hand gestured. The flash of a chrome weapon was visible from a hand reaching from the back seat and pointed squarely at the kid as he was collard by the driver, Dorele, who is also Phil's supplier.

"Main, that dere 'bout dat jack play. Boy's masked up and got ole boy right dere for a quarter key. But shit ain't right. And Dorele know it," Phil educated.

"Ain't he wit Wild Bill-n-nem?" Devonte' asked.

Phil nodded and at that precise time, from their vantage point a block away, members of Wild Bill's street gang began making their way towards the SUV. As the boys watched, the gang of four walked briskly, with their low slung jeans and khaki pants. Their faces masks of caution as they passed words amongst each other as they came upon the SUV.

Bull, who was the largest of the gang, stood in the background. His hand rested on the lining of his pocket just beneath the handle of his .45 caliber Glock. It had been intentionally exposed. Red Dawg and Lil Gun both flanked on each side of the SUV's door as Wild Bill brushed the kid, whose name was "Rocco," aside in order to peer into the vehicle. Instantly, he forced the passenger in the back to withdraw his weapon.

Minutes passed as the boys watched with intense interest. They observed the suggestive hand gestures by Wild Bill as he appeared to be explaining something to the dealers in defense of Rocco. After a few minutes the gang members backed away from the SUV and the dealers pulled silently away from the curb.

"Man, that's gonna turn out bad. Tension is in the air," Piye stated as he watched the gang members stroll up the street.

"Wild Bill-n-nem don't want no war wit us," Phil stated as he accepted the beer bottle back from Devonte'.

Braun looked puzzled and said, "Us? You mean, you and, and this 'Chatter' character? And flunky 'Johnny Black?' We grew up with Bill and them. You don't even know these dudes. 'Sides that, I believe you in over your head. I mean, it's bad enough that you dealing."

"Hold on, hold on. In over my head? Main, I can handle anythang and any situation, B. Yeah, yeah I understand ya'll wit the positive anti-drug campaign and shit, but main, I'm out ta get paid. Money, real money, main and what Bill-nem pulled off affected me too. 'Cause I roll wit dem boys, main," Phil slurred.

Piye shook his head in disgust and stared with scrutiny at his friend as if in disbelief. The drug dealer lifestyle had completely consumed him and transformed him from the friend he once knew.

"You way off course, Phil. Them fools is cross throwin', cut throat killers that don't give a damn about you," Piye stated.

"You thank Wild Bill nem gives a fuck about me? About you? Or anyone of ya'll? What makes demniggas any different? They killas! Jack artists! And, and dey ain't nevabroke me off shit! I'm makin' paper hand over fist, main. And what make you so righteous, Piye? Kill the white man this! Kill the white man that! You ain't no betta than me. What, what 'cause you don't sell drugs? Yo people got it like that. We don't. Raise up off me, main!" Phil yelled as he beat a hand to his chest as he walked away from Piye.

The escalation of his voice and the look on Piye's face alarmed Braun. He verbally mediated by calling out to Phil in a cautioning manner. At that moment, Phil's mother--who was wearing only a night gown and her hair was in disarray came to the door, with a cigarette in one hand and a glass of whiskey in the other.

"What is all dis goin on out here? Aint no shit startin' front my house. I din told ya'll. Nuff of dat shit goin' on round here every day. Oh…hey, Braun. I didn't even see you, baby." His mother stated as she flicked ashes from her cigarette and smiled at him. Braun smiled and acknowledged her.

Phil nervously finished the beer then tossed the bottle across the street in front of an abandoned building.

"Boy, what the hell wrong wit you? Piye, what's' goin' on out here?" she further inquired. Piye shook his head.

"Nothin'. Me and Braun was just leavin'," Piye responded. He proceeded to open the gate and Braun attempted to touch Phil consolingly, but was rejected. Phil's mood turned completely somber while Braun expressed concern for his friend. Braun realized the change in Phil's temperment was primarily due to the alcohol, and felt it best if he left him alone. Proceeding behind Piye through the gate, Phil's mother retreated back inside and left an alcohol induced Phil there with his cousin, Devonte'.

✳✳✳✳✳✳✳✳

Tariq's Lincoln pulled up into the small parking lot of a cleaning business. Above the small building was a sign with white letters imposed over the green top façade. It read: Jinnah's Cleaners. Tariq stared up at the sign as he cut off the engine and then opened the driver's side door.

He stepped into the cool air-conditioned building, which was a complete contrast from the humid temperature outside. Tariq made a sigh of relief, since it was a muggy day. The heat index added with an evening shower, which made it all the more uncomfortable.

Inside of the building the sounds of high tech sewing machines could be heard in the pressrooms. Several employers in uniform maneuvered about, coming to and fro from the back where all of the machines were located. There was a customer at the counter with several articles of clothing to be altered and was given an estimate by a rather extroverted African American man in his twenties. Spotting Tariq he acknowledged him.

"Excuse me. Mr. Galla," the young man chimed.

"How are you, Kevin? Where's Mr. Jinnah?" he inquired.

"Oh, he's back there in his office. You can go right in," Kevin said. Tariq smiled and proceeded to the back. He waved and acknowledged the employees who were diligently at work on the steam press machines and the electric sewing machines. He reached Nawaz's office and rapped lightly on the door as he peered into the glass window at Nawaz. Nawaz looked up as he was talking on the phone.

Tariq walked into the small office and closed the door behind him. After Nawaz hung up the telephone, he rose to his feet and extended his hand. His eyes looked enthused as a wide smile creased his lips. He motioned for Tariq to have a seat.

"Brother Tariq. What brings you by my office today? I wasn't expecting you. It's a pleasant surprise. How have you been doing?" Nawaz asked.

"Oh, I'm doing okay, taking it one day at a time. My daughter informed me that some sort of ordeal had transpired in your homeland. She says Swathi was very distraught today. I couldn't wait until you came home, so I decided to come here to see how things were," Tariq responded. He looked Nawaz in the eyes. Nawaz averted eye contact as he reflected over the ordeal, which had just transpired in his homeland of Pakistan.

The incident in question was one that mirrored other violence that had become synonymous to the Middle East. This was a region where ethnic conflict and political dissention rivals only that with the continent of Africa; where terrorist bombings, assassinations, and coups were a daily occurrence. In Nawaz's homeland, one such incident had taken the lives of thirteen Pakistani's, mainly women and children, including some close relatives. It explained why Swathi had been distraught.

In the wake of the United States war on terrorism and the "Operation Iraqi Freedom," U.S. presence throughout the Middle East had become rebuffed and despised in the eyes of many of the Muslim people. It was believed that the U.S. was having a covert war against Muslims under the guise of a war on terrorism. Many cited the mistreatment of Islamic prisoners at Guantanamo Bay as proof to their allegations. U.S. troops were not responsible for the bombing incident which left two of Nawaz's family members dead, but there were still anti-U.S. protests throughout Islamabad. The denizens carrying signs with President Bush's face on it and chanted, "Down with U.S.A.!" had become a slogan in the Middle East.

After the brief pause of reflection, Nawaz explained to him what transpired. "It was a very unfortunate situation. Some Islamic extremists for whatever reason set off a car bomb outside of a church in Islamabad, which killed thirteen people, including two of our relatives who were there visiting from the United States," Nawaz informed.

"I'm sorry to hear that. Is there any way I can be of some assistance? Anything, I can do?" His consoling proposal was interceded by Nawaz's cautioning hand and assuring smile.

"No need. Tragedies happen in a world of so much hatred. So much political and ethnic dissention that there may always be fighting. There will always be the deaths of the innocent, women, and children, just like in Islamabad and just like right here," Nawaz stated. As he spoke his eyes told of many memories of dissention, ethnic strife, and the bloodshed he had witnessed. After he finished speaking, Tariq looked away. He was thinking about the statement and envisioned the horrible images of screaming women and children running through the streets in the wake of the blast that killed over a dozen people. The buildings engulfed in flames and bloody carnage strewn about. He shook his head in disgust.

"I can only imagine the volatile environment over there. You experienced it over here in the United States, but there are only instances of ethnic violence or government protest. And the ramifications of a coup would be tremendous, so that's not even entertained. But I have to be honest, I look at the situation in our communities here and I wonder if the malice that's present will ever escalate to the proportions of your country," Tariq stated with concern.

"Let's hope that it doesn't," Nawaz responded.

There was a pause of silence before Tariq continued, "I feel the community center has been a success on many grounds, especially in terms of bringing nationalities together. I thoroughly enjoyed the last turnout. It was spiritually uplifting. No one really thought that we could bring them together." Tariq was referring to the enrollment of Pakistani and Mexican youths into the tutoring program offered by the community center.

"Yes, it truly was quite an accomplishment. Maybe one day throughout the world people, regardless of race or religion, will come together also," Nawaz smiled.

"Maybe so, but look, I don't want to hold you up any longer. I know you're a busy man. I just wanted to stop by and see if everything was okay," Tariq stated before leaving the office. Tariq headed back to the office.

The midnight bluish sky rapidly changed hues from dark to the opaque blue that arrives with the coming of dawn. And with its rapid change the luminous lighting of San Antonio high-rise buildings began to simultaneously flicker off. The headlights of the cars that whizzed along the 410 highway and other main thoroughfares remained on. Some were coming from work aiming to go to their homes with the prospect of relaxing. Others such as Ursula, whose white Lexus passed the Alamo mission as the pinkish hued sky set in the background, were sped to work.

It was the dawning of another day in the bustling San Antonio region. Tariq could be seen maneuvering through his office building. His looked serious as he sipped his coffee with one hand and clutched a cellular phone in the other hand up to his ear.

Across town as the hours pass and the flow of traffic speeds along through the downtown area on New Braunfels, other scenes were taking place in the eastside neighborhood between Wyoming and Sanders streets. Youths scampered about in the bright afternoon sun and SUV's with stylish 24" inch rims thumped past dilapidated houses. As the hours passed and the cumulous clouds overhead rapidly changed forms with the steadily ascending sun, the scenes changed, as was the case with the coming of night each day.

As Ursula made her last entries into her computer; and Tariq diligently filed paperwork into a cabinet, the 5 o' clock traffic all around the 410 expressway began to get congested. It's rush hour and with it there were several accidents that had to be attended to by local police. They direct traffic around car accidents during the busy rush hour, the only instance where San Antonio's finest were making their presence known. On the south side of town where tensions flared between rival Mexican gangs, the police were doing routine frisks. Several squad cars aligned a street of modest homes with well-manicured lawns and palmetto trees. Their guns drawn and barked out orders to Eduardo, "El Gatos," and several of their gang affiliates who simultaneously knelt down beside the curb as they interlock their fingers behind their heads. All of them were dressed in what police discerned as "gang wear," black bandannas that came down to their eyes, khaki shorts, sneakers, and tank tops exposing tattooed bodies. As one officer with a semi-automatic pistol pointed at them does the frisking, the other officers either shouted at them or rummaged through a purple 57 Chevy pickup and gold low rider 95 Impala. At the same time, the gang members were agitated and scowled at them.

Across town as the sun steadily dropped below the horizon, Wild Bill and his gang stood outside on a corner. They periodically peered down the block in alert, aware of the presence and impending dangers of the police. Bull sat on the front end of the Impala sipping a 40 oz. beer, Lil Gun knelt down by the curb, Rocco walked back and forth rapping, and Red Dawg was a block away with shotgun in the bushes giving signals while Wild Bill conducted a drug transaction with a crack addict. All dispersed after Red Dawg whistled down the block, alerting the gang of an approaching police cruiser that flashed its blue lights at seeing the scampering gang members. The officers jumped out of their vehicle with semi-autos drawn and in full sprints after them.

These scenes, which seemed to swing as much as a pendulum, began to be displaced in time and space. The scene now was that of the high-rise buildings downtown. The traffic lights below zoomed by and the neon lights of the social scene was a backdrop to sirens as the twilight hour slowly turned to dusk. In the economically repressed communities, all was not so quiet. As night fell on this particular evening, gun blasts from a car window driven by Mexican gangsters on the south side could be heard and a fatal stabbing on the west side was occurring. Both were a result of more gang violence that was being observed by the police whose sirens and lights illuminated the area. As officers jotted down information, on East Houston, a masked gunman fled a liquor store and on Wyoming St., Braun and his friends bore curious expressions as they walked slowly towards a crime scene and more violence. Police forensic units in white gloves prepared to enter a house for a domestic violence case. An abused woman, her nightgown splattered in blood, was escorted in handcuffs across the front lawn by police. Her facial expression deadpanned. Her hair frayed. Moments later, ambulance attendants would wheel out a medical gurney with a white sheet placed over the victim. This unfortunate display of yet more genocidal violence within the urban black and Hispanic communities was being viewed by Tariq.

In all neighborhoods, from poverty stricken to middle class or to the upper class, most residents such as the Jinnah's prepared for bed. Mr. Nawaz Jinnah and his wife snuggled under their sheets. Hitting the night light in her room, Swathi hung up her cellular phone and snuggled in bed too. All is quiet. In the Galla household much was the same, where Ursula lay underneath satin sheets sound asleep while Tariq diligently browsed through legal books. In their respective rooms, Caleb and Ikara both prepared for bed as well. Tariq closed the books he was reading and opted to watch television before retiring to bed. He liked to keep abreast of what was going on in the world. In this case, he watched the news to see the current self-destructive trends within the community. He stared blankly at the images of his old neighborhood on his television screen. The news reporter began to give accounts of precisely the occurrence.

"In the wake of a drive-by shooting from rival gangs on the south side that left two men critically wounded and another in serious condition, an unrelated stabbing death of a Hispanic youth occurred shortly after 7 p.m. in front of his home on the west side. In an apparent domestic dispute in the 800 block of Wyoming, a thirty six year old black female whose name is being withheld pending investigation, is being charged with fatally stabbing her forty three year old live-in boyfriend. The two stabbings brings the death toll this year to 43 thus far, for the month of June. In yet another incident…" As the news reporter continued to report, Tariq removed his glasses, he shook his head.

✲✲✲✲✲✲✲✲

The red nosed pit bull pulled and choked at his rusted chain. He barked and pawed at the dirt as droplets of spittle fell from his mouth. He was hungry in anxious anticipation of Phil placing his bowl of scrap meats before him. Phil set the bowl down and talked to the dog he'd named Terror. He stood and watched him hungrily devour the meat in the bowl before him and smiled proudly.

"There ya go, Terror. Gotta getchu ready fo tomorrow," Phil stated while wiping his hands together and backing away from the dog's kennel. Piye stood a considerable distance back observing the pit bull with reverence. He didn't care too much for dogs, especially not uncontrollable, vicious killers such as pit bulls. The two walked along the backside of the house towards the front and assessed an old 93' Impala in which the rims had been removed.

"Man, that dog is vicious," Piye stated.

Phil laughed, "That's how I raised'em. Destroy anythang come befo'em. You gon see tommar. Leroy thank his pit Jody can mess wit Terror. Ain't no way, main."

He was speaking in reference to a sport which is quite prevalent in the south. Dog fighting, which had been targeted by the federal government under the cruelty to animal's law and was punishable by fines and/or time in jail.

"Yeah. Man, you gotta be careful. Feds is pickin'em up on a regular on that dog fightin'. Man, what you gon do with this car?" Piye asked looking inside of the Impala. Phil shrugged his shoulders.

"I don't know, main. All kinds of shit wrong wit it. I paid mo fo da rims than I did the car. Mexicans tried to steal my shit! Remember that?" Piye laughed as they sat down together on the front porch.

"Man, you was way outta bounds anyway on the south side. And you were with one of the finest chics in the hood? Lucky you even made it out of there," Piye laughed.

At that moment a police cruiser passed by slowly. The occupants being the salt and pepper team of Jackson and Hutchinson stared over in the boys' direction momentarily until a call of a robbery in progress at a convenience store on Rigsby Street came over their radio. This call sent them in pursuit with their sirens flashing. The boys watched as the police vehicle whipped around the curb.

Piye shook his head in disgust as he looked down at the ground. Then in the process of making a comment on the police pursuit, Phil interjected.

"Say main, the otha day…I's really messed up wit myself fo the thangs I said. Main, you know I'm down wit ya'll. We like family. It's jis…main you don't understand how it is in the game. Cain't trust nobody. But it's like I'm trapped. With no way out."

"You have a way out, P. You—"

"No, I don't, main. My mom ain't workin' or doin' shit. I'm payin' the rent and electricity and puttin' food on the table. Everythang she tricks fo she smokin' it up. Peoples' tawkin 'bout puttin' us the fuck out on the streets. Main, I gotta thank about my lil baby brotha and sister," Phil stated nodding his head in the direction of his nine year old brother. At the moment his brother was playing with other neighborhood children across the street.

"You are not thankin' about them right now. Who is gonna be there for them if you catch a charge? Or get gunned down out there when you slangin' rocks? You got choices. Look, one of the O.B.U. brothers are gettin' me set up to do roofin' work wit'em this summer as a favor for my pops. I'll get 'em to hook ya up." Once again Phil interjected.

"Ain't that simple, Piye. Ain't that simple," Phil retorted.

At that moment a low and rhythmic thumping sound could be heard approaching. Moments later the black Lincoln Navigator belonging to Dorele whipped around the corner and stopped in front of Phil's house. Piye stared at the vehicle then looked over at Phil. Phil could sense the concern in Piye's gaze and averted eye contact. As the window of the Lincoln rolled down, the smiling, gold-toothed visage of Dorele was visible.

"Phil, come on, main. Gotta make a run," he stated as he gulped down a large portion of the Michelob Lite he was holding. Phil rose slowly from the porch. As he prepared to make a statement, his little sister Jalena came running into the front yard and up the steps. She stopped before Piye to acknowledge him in her innocent seven year old way. Piye smiled and fidgeted at her pigtails.

"You can catch a ride if you want, Piye," Phil stated. Piye rose from the porch and placed a hand on Jalena's shoulder.

"Nah, man, I can't make it," he responded.

Jalena ran on into the house calling out to her mother while Piye walked out of the gate past Phil and the Lincoln Navigator. Phil watched his friend as his muscular figure strode in silence up the street and past dilapidated houses and run down cars. He begrudgingly climbed into the backseat of the Navigator.

Chapter 9

It was another typical hot and humid day in San Antonio. This being the usual scorching temperatures, the agendas of the natives were unaffected as many enjoyed various festivities centralized to this urban multi-cultured Texas city. In April there were many sponsored fiestas in the predominately Mexican communities. In February, cowboys rode broncos and roped calves at the annual rodeo. But, on this day, a large percentage of the African American community attended the annual Juneteenth celebration.

At the vast grounds of Martin Luther King, Jr. Park on the eastside, thousands had gathered in celebration of a historical event which had first taken place in Texas on the 18th day of June, 1865. This was the day the slaves received the news of the Emancipation Proclamation, nearly two years after it had been enacted. It was also made known that battles were still being fought in Texas two years after the Civil War had ended.

To spice up this heralded African American celebration of freedom that had been sponsored by black organizations and the Mayor, various musical artists had been invited. There were several local R&B groups who performed their own songs as well as renditions of songs popularized by some of Motown's greatest artists.

There were also local rap groups there who were prepped prior to the event by the sponsors and cautioned about their lyrical content. Stipulations had to be made in this regard so as not to incite violence between rival factions. Since there was anticipation of the large park being inundated with drugs and street gangs from various neighborhoods, the police were commissioned in and around certain points in the park.

One local rapper whom was scheduled to perform at this African American celebration was Braun, who used the rap moniker "Lil Dred". He spent hours rehearsing his usual political, and Afro-centric laced lyrics all week in preparation for his presentation for the large crowd. Considering the expected presence of San Antonio's finest, he had to tone it down a bit, especially because brutality claims were at the root of Braun's heated lyrical contents. The acres of park land were teaming with young black youths from various neighborhoods and regions dressed in the latest of hip-hop cultured fashions, such as Fubu, Sean John, Rocawear, Mecca, and Jerseys shorts with colorful and expensive foot wear and jewelry. The young brothers were sporting razor lined cuts or braids while the sisters were revealing curvaceous thighs and cleavage in their fashionable exotic, colorful outfits. Their hair dos were in impeccable styles of many different tints.

The celebration goers were being directed through traffic into the park by police. Many who, for the most part, bore expressions of uneasiness about the job they'd been required to do this day. As Braun rode in the passenger's side in Devonte's mother's white Acura and looked out of the window observing the crowd, he could understand why.

Growing up in his environment, Braun could identify with it, although he was not directly involved in or linked to the drug and gang sub-culture. He knew the drug dealers and the status of each respective player in the game. They were also known as the "Big Timers" to the street lieutenants. He knew their "beefs" and who was skimming, who was living on borrowed time, who was a threat with weaponry, and who was a threat through covert operations in conjunction with the Feds. As their vehicle passed them, many had smiles revealing gold teeth and necklaces glistening from the sun. His mind processed this data. While he observed their rambunctious flamboyancy, overly intrigued young girls flocked amongst them. Braun recognized those involved with gang cultures regardless of whether or not they wore colors or just by their mannerisms. Many of them, even the ones from other neighborhoods, he knew personally. He knew their real names, status and gang affiliations. His eyes swept the mass gathering at the park and he took inventory of the presence of several rival gangs. He observed their movements.

Although music was playing the rhythmic tunes of many flavors of music simultaneously, people were dancing, females were laughing, brothers were sipping their beverages, and the overall atmosphere seemed conducive to black people coming together to celebrate a real holiday—one pertinent to us as a people—there was still a strong element of tension. Braun hoped that it did not escalate to violence as it had done so numerous times at many events in the past.

Devonte' parked his mother's car alongside a group of youths who congregated around a late model, smoke grey Taurus. The car was accessorized with dazzling spinning rims. Its doors were open exposing Burberry interior and a high-tech sound system that reverberated a rhythmic thump that vibrated throughout the vicinity. Braun knew the owner of the car, a twenty year old former classmate who'd dropped out of school. This former classmate traded in prospects of attending a university for a life of dodging surveillance, informants, and bullets. His name was Chris. He was part of a web of petty drug peddlers who worked for a big time dealer in competition with Dorele's clique.

Braun closed the passenger side door behind him and acknowledged several of the females in Chris's entourage as he sipped on a cherry cola. Devonte' walked around the front of the car and exchanged daps with Chris who smiled widely and nodded at Braun. His eyes were reddened and his speech was slurred, which were probably the effects of cough syrup and marijuana. Braun nodded back with a complacent smile. He made it a point never to be condescending, have a malicious character, or be judgmental, although it was widely known his political and moral stances against drug dealers.

Piye was the last to de-board and stood next to Braun. His black and white tank top exposed his muscular physique, which caught the attention of the girls standing around the Taurus and ignited smiles and acknowledgements. He returned their greetings with a smile. The three boys began to move on through a gauntlet of congregating groups of dealers, gang members, "ordinary Joes," and females, who by their demeanors and enthusiasm, were fans of the individuals representing "the game."

The three boys walked past several of these types of sisters adorned in fashionable and revealing outfits with elaborately done hairdos. Devonte' made lewd remarks to many of them as they passed, while Braun and Piye simply acknowledged them. They sipped on their colas as they further took inventory of the mass gathering.

Nearly fifty yards away, in the mid-ground of the park was a stage with band equipment, speakers, equalizers and microphones set up. Atop the constructed bandstand was a red banner with the words "Juneteenth Celebration" imposed in black, green, and yellow writing. There were droves of celebration goers now emerging on the bandstand at the moment as a local rap group dressed in hip-hop gear prepared to take center stage.

Piye tapped Braun on the shoulder as they walked. He pointed in the direction of the bandstand. Braun focused in and observed whom he presumed to be one of the many sponsors doing a mic check as the man tested the equipment.

"Braun. Piye. What's goin' on wit ya'll, man?" Came a voice from their left as Piye made eyes with some passing females on their right. The two turned to the direction of the voice, which had been projected from a youth wearing circled spectacles. He looked studious. His black T-shirt had pictures of prominent African American leaders, such as Paul Robeson, Malcolm X, and Stokely Carmichael super imposed on the front. His level of conscious awareness was obvious. He was accompanied by three others: two girls and a boy.

"Marquis. What's goin' on wit ya?"

"Peace be. What's goin' on, Marquis?' Braun and Piye greeted.

Devonte' approached the small group after just being given the cold shoulder by an attractive young sister with gold tinted hair.

Giving his acknowledgements, he said, "Looks like things are about to start up in a minute. You gon do yo thang today, huh? Give everybody a sample of MC Lil Dred's perspectives?" Marquis inquired with a smile. Pushing up his wire rimmed glasses as he patted Braun on the shoulder.

"Fa sho. I know I got competition. But you know they are going to pretty much kick the basics and cater to the club crowd. I'm still going to bring that positive and hit hard with it. They are going to feel it," Braun informed.

"How'd you come up with the name MC Lil Dred? You don't have any dredlocks," stated a pie faced, red skinned girl. She was petite and conservatively dressed in loose fitting blue jean shorts, sandals and a T-shirt with the words "Africa Unite" superimposed. Each laughed at her declaration, including Braun.

"So, did he win his case?" inquired the second girl. She was a heavy set, brown skinned sister with braided hair.

"No, he didn't. It was dismissed as frivolous on the grounds that he was considered property," Braun further educated. The youth's expressions now registered empathy, disgust, and confusion.

How could the judiciary system, under the Constitution's 7th Article, allow this injustice? Was it not written under this Article that "an accused shall not be compelled in any criminal case to be a witness against himself, nor be deprived of life, liberty, or property, without due process of law?" The injustice in Dred Scotts' case only served to prove that the Constitution was not written with the dark man in mind.

"So much for the 7th Article of the Bill of Rights," Marquis stated sarcastically. At that moment the sponsor of the Juneteenth celebration called the event to order. The group began moving towards the bandstand. Kicking around various topics or commenting on the appearance or presence of others they had observed.

The sponsor, a middle aged African American with rugged features, and sporting a red, black and green baseball cap began acknowledging the people who had made the function possible. He commended the primarily youth filled attendees for their consciousness to black history because it is essential that people have conscious awareness of their history and significance if they are to elevate themselves and reach high levels of self-sustenance and eventual power.

The sponsor for the next twenty minutes or so delivered a firebrand speech on the topic of slavery. He stated how it was imperative that the youths of this generation and generations to come know the truth instead of the misinformation offered in public school curriculum: half-truths printed with the intentions of lowering the morale of any African American with racial pride and causing them to feel an inferiority complex due to the debilitating occurrence of slavery. He also explained about the psychological chain of inhumane treatment inflicted by the white slave master upon the broken slave. He enlightened them to the fact that contrary to the history found in their school textbooks, our African forefathers did not in many instances, come peacefully to this land. They were not submissive, but rather in many cases, fought to the death on the African shores. In other instances cast themselves into the ocean rather than subject themselves to the inhumane treatment from obviously cruel people.

There were the mutinies in which the slaves took over the ships on the seas. These rebellious African captives came together as one to overthrow these imperialists upon the vessels en route to America. There are many documented accounts of these insurgencies. However, they elude the American school textbooks much as the slave revolts, which were numbered over 130 during the period of the 1640's to the 1830's. The only one being mentioned in text is of course that of Nat Turner. He was a preacher and house slave who led an uprising in Virginia on the date of August 21, 1831, that resulted in the murders of 57 whites.

The sponsor wrapped up his firebrand rhetoric by covering the importance for the youths to stay positive. He encouraged them to fight for their socio-economic and political liberation as their forefathers had fought and died for their physical liberation from the bondage of slavery.

"So you see, people, it is possible to revert backwards into slavery if you submit to a lifestyle of drug dealing or other crimes and land in these institutions which are systemically designed for you. It will re-shackle you and impose an existence upon you, reminiscent of our African forefathers in slavery," he stated. Most of the youths, whether drug dealers, gang members, or positive youths, listened intently. "Now, to kick off this celebration, we have with us here live, a local hip-hop group ready to pump it up for you all. I know you all are anxious to get crunked up. So give it up for the Eastsidaz."

The sponsor made way for the young hip-hop group of three to emerge. They were dressed in their Spurs jerseys, hats turned backwards, and low slung black jean shorts. All three had to hold their shorts up with one hand as they paraded around the stage.

Most of the youths were really into the hip-hop performance. Everyone gyrated to the thumping percussion of the huge speakers and some pumped their fists to the lyrical content, which had been cleaned up of its strong, street basis of drug dealing and violence. However, the music still possessed glorified references to thug life and sipping "Syrup."

Though Braun did not approve of even the watered down version of the group's song, he nevertheless nodded his head in an attempt to look enthused. As the youth around him became more into the performance, the sponsor appeared to his left and informed him to get ready to perform.

The Eastsidaz performance was over. The three boys looked exhausted. Their chests heaving and dripping with sweat. The group exited the stage among claps and cheers and acknowledged certain onlookers by pointing in their directions before raising their fists. The sponsor began giving accolades for the group's performance before introducing Braun.

"At this time we have one more performance before phase two of this Juneteenth festivity. So, while you're getting your barbeque eat on and enjoying your refreshments, take notice of this positive young brother. He has something educational and Pro Black for you and we definitely need plenty of that. Give it up for Lil Dred," the sponsor introduced enthusiastically. Braun entered amidst claps and calls of his name.

Braun appeared nervous at first as the track began to play. He nodded his head and tried not to focus on individuals in the crowd. He gripped the microphone in his right hand tightly and pulled up his slowly sagging black jean shorts with his left hand as he walked.

"They say Africa's the cradle of all man...that everythang's centered around knowledge incepted by the black man...truth be told, it unfolds...read between lies in school texts...don't keep ya eyes closed. Cause if you do, they will distort yo whole concept of black pride... and then destroy you... with false pretense of self-worth...no education means no hope, no prospect fo you ta land work... and no work leads ta bad thangs... totin Glocks robbin ya brother...and sellin drugs jis ta maintain. Poisonin' the community...police is violatin our civil rights, and granted with immu–

nity..." As Braun rapped, he paced back and forth before the crowd who were listening attentively to his every syllable. He began gaining energy from the electricity that coursed through the afro-centrically receptive crowd.

As the culturally and politically laced rap went on, Piye made observation of the youths in his immediate vicinity. He knew that even though everyone was listening to the contents of the lyrics, only a few would apply it to their lives. Some were bangers who personally believed there were no alternatives. They felt trapped in the destitute confines of their impoverished community and forced to commit crimes or unleash violence as an outlet. How be it genocidal.

There were the dealers who were perhaps the scourge of the community right on up there with the law enforcement's primary target of Braun's heated rap. Most of them were nodding along with everyone else and Piye perceived them to be simply enthralled by the track and the hype of the moment. Surely they weren't receiving the message? Or could they?

Braun continued pacing the stage only to emphasize a highlighted point for thought during the "break down." As the track systemically depreciated, each musical instrument one by one, Braun began bringing the climax of the rap.

"...cause ignorance is not bliss...so black man free yo mind and resist... they gunnin' fo ya, stand yo ground and dismiss... don't let them take yo strive, jis persist...cause economic prowess allows us to run thangs...instead of bein corporate slaves inside the mainstream. Or locked down in hell, or subject to bein shot down for retails from a crack sell. So put yo guns down now and come together, so we can finally grow in this land, and not wither." The crowd erupted in cheers for Braun's empowered rap. With a proud smile, he raised both hands in victory and made his way from the stage.

The small entourage of Braun and his friends were accompanied by Marquis and the others. As they walked and conversed, they observed the celebration goers. There were conscious African Americans of many age groups. Old men played quiet games of chess (if that were really possible considering there were automobiles playing music at high volumes) or played poker while the teenagers and adolescents meandered about socializing. The young children played their games or slid down water slides that were set-up for them.

There were also barbeque and fish fries in progress. The air was filled with the tantalizing aroma of seasoned fish, chicken, ribs, and hamburgers cooking over open flames. Everyone seemed to be thoroughly enjoying the festivities, communicating, socializing, and bonding with one another. The scene truly demonstrated the meaning of the word unity, even with the few incidents where rivals gave each other non-complacent exchanges.

"You really brought it, man. That was tight," Marquis stated as they reached a picnic table. Braun was modest about the compliment. As he sat down, Marquis removed a set of dominoes from a box and began shuffling them around.

"Devonte', are you going to play?" he yelled out. Devonte' who was involved in an obvious romantically inclined conversation with one of the girls who was with Marquis, declined the offer with a wave of his hand. Marquis smiled and shook his head.

"He looks like he is feeling her. Who is she anyway?" Braun inquired as he picked up seven dominoes and held them before him.

"She is my cousin Crystal. She is from Alexandria, Louisiana," he informed. The two began to play the game of dominoes.

"That's fifteen. Start this off right," Marquis stated. Braun smiled.

"Yeah, you still got that luck," Marquis said.

"No luck. Heh! That's ten. Come on. Mark my money, man," Braun smiled and shook his head. Minutes passed as onlookers became participants, boys and girls alike. They laughed, braggadocio, and of course slammed the dominoes. Then Piye and another boy came to the table with several trays. The females who had crowded around the domino table jumped to their feet anxiously.

"Hey. Hold up. Hold up. There is enough here for everybody. Anyway, Shell, you all just ate. Get on back. Get on back," the boy played with the trays. There were laughs and protests from the girls who tugged at his arm.

"Stop playing, Joseph," they pleaded.

"Alright, alright, but this is for my boy, Dre. Look, you see how skinny he is?" he stated in humor as another rather frail boy approached.

"Oh, you decided to come eat, huh? You aren't so in love for some ribs," Marquis laughed.

As the small group moved down away from the dominoes to eat, a black Lincoln Navigator pulled up just a few yards away, but was unnoticed by Piye and the others as they hungrily ate their fill of barbeque, fish and corn.

"Do you all celebrate Juneteenth in Alexandria?" Braun inquired of Crystal as he carved his fish. A middle aged man with specks of grey in his mustache and sporting a red, black and green knit cap passed out culturally conscious pamphlets. He extended one to Crystal and several others as he explained to them their contents. Crystal smiled and accepted the pamphlets, then answered Braun's inquiry.

"Yes, for about the past ten years. And, it's about the same as this," she explained. As she talked, Joseph studied her quizzically while chewing on a piece of barbeque ribs.

"That's where you are from? Louisiana? I got cousins who stay in New Orleans. Mardi Gras-and-all that. Fele gumbo and what you all call it? Second lining. The Cajun state," Joseph stated. Like most whose knowledge of Louisiana was limited, Joseph wasn't aware of the cultural diversity of the state. It was a state with multi-dialects and ethnicities.

"Well, actually, we don't second line in Alexandria. And I have never met a Cajun. But, we make good gumbo and boudin ballsm" she laughed.

"Boudin balls?" Piye inquired.

"Yeah, boudin balls is dirty rice, you know, spicy rice and ground meat, stuffed inside a pork skin," she informed as she delicately ate a slice of fish. Piye's expression initially was of savory intrigue until the mentioning of pork.

"I have to try that. I know Piye would love that," Devonte' smiled. Piye laughed as he wiped his mouth. Braun meanwhile was seriously reading a page in one of the pamphlets, which dealt with an African American inventor named Otis Boykin.

"Piye, are you familiar with Otis Boykin?" Braun asked. With Piye's facial expression it was obvious he was not familiar with him. He nodded his head to indicate so. "Anybody?" Braun further inquired. No one was familiar.

"Any chance he is where the legal term derived from? I know you are up on the legal spectrum," Marquis offered as he continued to eat his fish. At that moment Phil and his drug cronies were weaving through the crowd enroute towards them.

"No. According to this article, he was an inventor. Hey, Jerry, you passed this year in school?" Braun inquired of a small child of approximately nine years of age. He rubbed the boy's head as he passed. The boy acknowledged that he did with a wide smile that exposed a missing baby tooth.

"So, what did he invent?" Michelle asked.

"More than 25 electronic devices used in computers and guided missiles. Humph. I didn't know that. This was way in the fifties, too. He was from Texas. Dallas. It says he also created a mechanism for regulating the first pacemaker," Braun concluded.

"More hidden information about a prominent black man that was excluded from the history books in school," Piye responded. At that moment Phil and his crew had approached behind him. They were acknowledged by Braun and the others.

"What's going on, Piye?" Phil asked as he patted Piye's shoulder.

Piye smiled and glanced into the faces of the young dealers. Phil discerned his dislike for the other dealers and briefly observed Piye who returned to eating. He left his back exposed to them.

"Y'all gettin' yawls grub on!" stated an extremely dark brown skinned, twenty something kid to Phil while exposing a mouth full of gold
teeth. His street name was Johnny Black and he was renowned as the "trigger man" of the drug crew. As they stood around the table hungrily eyeing the cuisines, several passers-by acknowledged them. The other dealer, a small framed kid of twenty one whose street named was Chatter was called to come along with Dorele who'd sensed they were unwelcome by the conscious group. Johnny Black continued trying to coax Michelle into giving him food from her tray. She seemed to be uncomfortable with him as he reeked of the alcoholic beverage he clutched in his hand. After discerning he was wasting his time, he laughed, gulped down a swallow of beer, and arose from the table to follow Dorele and Chatter. He left Phil there with his friends.

"I don't know why they drank that stuff. All it does is make their breath funky," Michelle stated. She waved her hand before her contorted face as if still able to smell the scent of alcohol that had been present on Johnny Black's breath. Everyone chuckled.

"Sup, B?" Phil inquired as he sat down. His expression was pleading. Although he places on a smile it was apparent that he sensed something. He sensed the cynicism of his friends.

"What's up with you?" Braun asked as he wiped his mouth. His tone showed his feelings towards Phil's continued involvement with the dealers.

"Hold on. I'm catching vibes. Look, I know you all are not feeling Chatter nem. But I'm still your boy," Phil stated. Looking back and forth between his three friends, Braun diverted eye contact so as not to show his expression of empathy. Meanwhile Devonte' turned his head. Piye slid a plate of ribs towards him and examined him as he got up and motioned for Joseph.

"Thanks, man, I'm starving," Phil stated as he tore at the ribs. His eyes were bloodshot and his tenacious appetite proved his marijuana inducement.

"What are you going to do, Phil? Why didn't you bring your little sister and brother out to the celebration? See all these kids? They need you, Phil." Braun stated with concerned.

"You are blowing my high, man," Phil responded.

"You are blowing your life," Braun shot back.

Phil shook his head.

"I got me, alright. Come on, man. I thought we were not going to get into that no more. I told you man…I going to get it right. I have time to go to college and all that. Right now, I have to stack ends, man and make sure my family is straight. You go ahead and eat that right there?" Phil pointed at Michelle's plate. She responded to the contrary just as Dorele called out for him. He waved him in his direction as he stood beside another dealer. Phil snatched the piece of fish Michelle had on her tray and rose to his feet. "I have to go, man," he stated with a rib at his mouth. As he jogged away Braun observed him and exchanged meaningful glances with Marquis. Both shook their heads as Phil weaved between the steady flow of festive goers.

The music played, the people laughed and socialized, and the children soaked up the fun loving atmosphere that emanated through the air like electricity on this Juneteenth celebration day.

Chapter 10

Children of various ages were provided with a hot meal on this early morning. The outreach program in which Tariq and Ursula sponsored had been established to assure that the children of the community were taken care of. They along with their children and other sponsors, were diligently at work preparing and passing out trays of nutritional meals as the children eagerly accepted the food.

Tariq and the other sponsors were conscious of the fact that many of these children hailed from impoverished or low-income single parent households. They were deprived of the luxuries of a middle class family, such as waking up in the morning and being able to go to the refrigerator and actually find sustenance. In some cases, these children's refrigerators were empty because their mothers spent their money on drug habits and expensive clothing.

Tariq empathized with these children who were often products of derelict fathers. These were fathers who abandoned them at birth or were vanquished off to state prisons as a result of their particular illegal trade. They often left the young black mother to take on all of the responsibility of raising the child. These were the children who were being served.

Perspiring slightly, Tariq opened four buttons from the top of his white shirt as he moved expediently, passing out a tray to a small boy of kindergarten age. He smiled courteously as the child thanked him. His son Caleb, who happened to be the youngest participant at age twelve, was making his rounds through the cafeteria passing out orange juice while Braun helped distribute milk.

Behind the cafeteria steam line, Ikara, Ursula, and several other concerned women of the community prepared trays with a variety of nutritional breakfast foods, such as scrambled eggs, grits, and buttermilk biscuits with jelly. The bakers behind the scenes, most of them actual school cooks, took the real liberty of preparing the meals. They took into consideration preparing pork and non-pork meat to the breakfast entrée. The line was getting shorter now and it appeared that the last of the children were making their way down the steam line, which compelled the steam line workers to begin breaking the line down. Tariq removed his plastic gloves and hair net and began making his way towards the main dining area where two suit clad sponsors and another forty something appearing African American woman, were supervising. Tariq was making his way over to the woman when he stopped short of her to observe the children. He was proud to see the satisfied faces of the children. He smiled as he reached to rub the head of one of the boys.

"Mr. Galla, Mrs. Washington," acknowledged Braun as he passed holding a crate that had contained milk. The woman smiled as she greeted him and Tariq patted his arm. After he disappeared behind the steam line, Tariq made reference to him.

"It's good that the community has some young people who are concerned. In this day and age and with this generation, it's really special to see that," he stated. Mrs. Washington agreed.

"These children in here are the next generation. They are the future and we cannot allow them to degenerate further. That is why I commend you Mr. Galla, on your efforts with the community center. I look forward to viewing your progress this upcoming week," Mrs. Washington stated. She walked expediently towards the cafeteria's exit while smiling and acknowledging the other volunteers.

Tariq walked around to each table and spoke to the children, briefly inquiring into the stability of certain ones whom he had a personal knowledge of. He counseled them in certain areas in a fatherly like manner and patted them on their heads or shoulders before moving on to the next child. His demeanor was evident of his passion for the children.

The economical, emotional, and physical well being of each child was his concern. His duty as a black man compelled him and all of the others to reach out to these children in the community. He was overjoyed that he could actually make a difference in their lives.

✳✳✳✳✳✳✳✳

The sky turned from an opaque blue to completely dark. The only interjection in the dark void of space was the brilliance of the stars and the luminance of the moon. The area surrounding Ikara's bricked home was brightly lit by streetlights as she and Braun sat on her mother's Janus outdoor furniture. They enjoyed each other's company and the light breeze that blew periodically.

"Beautiful setting that's nothing like my hood. I wish that one day it could be like this. So much would be happening. Everybody would be tripping. I can't wait to go off to college. Leave it all behind," Braun stated. Ikara looked at him quizzically as if not fully comprehending the declaration made by the young man whom she had often heard profess devotion to the struggle of his people.

"You don't really mean that. I know you, Braun. I've watched you with the children. I hear the passion in your raps. You love your community. And when you love something, you just don't abandon it. Leave it all behind," Ikara stated. She looked compassionately into his eyes. He diverted eye contact and dropped his head.

He smiled as he spoke, "Yeah, yeah, I do love my community. The hard working citizens and the children. But, you just don't understand. You live here. You watch the news and you know what time it is where I'm from. Don't get me wrong, I'll always give back. But my hood has lots of bad elements in it and anything can happen. I don't want to get trapped up in there and die before I can make things happen like my father did," Braun explained.

Braun began confiding in her about things he'd never before revealed about his parents. He told her about how his mother died during childbirth. Her having epilepsy and how she envisioned her unborn son becoming a leader, a prominent figure within the community. He felt obligated to fulfill his mother's dream. Braun described his father and how he had been told of his valor. He proudly told her of his father's scholastic achievements and strides within the community at such a young age. He explained how he refused to depart from the community. He returned after obtaining a degree at Texas A & M University only to be brutally murdered at the hands of the police. This incident escalated the tension filled between the black community and the police.

Braun's rendition was impassioned and Ikara leaned on his every syllable. She studied him and envisioned the past scenarios that he had spoken of. She'd never experienced growing up in an environment where derelict street gangs roamed the streets committing robberies and murder and where there was so much ethnic tension and oppression by the police who swore to preserve and protect. She was sheltered from this type of perilous existence, where even the innocent can become victims. She sympathized with Braun and admired his strength and resilience. She realized that in such a negative environment, it was easy for a youth to conform to negativity. Most often this is the case with urban black youth. They witness homicide and drug dealing in their community on such frequency that their morals and perception of life is distorted.

"Your father sounded like a strong and intelligent man. He reminds me of someone I know," Ikara stated softly as she looked up into his eyes. Braun recognized her hint towards him by the smile that had creased her lips. Her eyes told the story of the empathy she felt for him. After a brief pause, she rested her head onto his shoulder and looked up at the stars. She made reference to them in their splendor, theorizing their significance to the universe.

For the next few minutes the two hit on small talk making each other laugh over various scenarios and playfully petting each other in the manner that teenage youths do. Ikara raised her head from his chest and stared into his eyes. She was fascinated with him. *Or was it merely fascination? Was she experiencing love for the first time in her life?* He was so different from the two boys she dated before. He was so strong spirited and positive.

"Braun, how do you feel about me? About us? Where do you see us in the future?" she inquired. The questions took him aback. They were unexpected coming from a girl who was serious about her abstinence for the past five months in their relationship. Several possibilities crossed his mind.

"Where do I see us in the future? Uh, that's kind of deep, real deep," he responded. Then his eyes locked with her and the sincerity was revealing. "Where's all this coming from? I mean, I care a lot about you. You are special to me and I, I don't..." His rambling was interjected by a less opaque question this time.

"Do you love me?" she asked. The clarity in the inquiry and the look in her eyes were compelling. He knew the way Ikara made him feel. He could only equate it with love even though he never formally expressed it. He knew for many in his peer group they would express this confession of love to girls without an inkling of sincerity only to achieve sexual gratification. He felt this was morally wrong and he vowed never to express this sentiment unless it was undeniably true.

After a brief pause, he responded, "Ye...yeah. Yeah, I love you Ikara. You know that." He finally found the words to express himself. Ikara's face ignited and her eyes seemed to sparkle. She confided that the feeling was mutual. The romance was almost electric in the atmosphere compounded by the serenity and therapeutically soothing sounds of the night and the moon's luminance illuminating Ikara's beautiful Asiatic face. He rubbed his hand through her silky black hair as she rubbed a gentle hand on his chest, and the two engaged in a romantic kiss.

✶✶✶✶✶✶✶✶

A car passed by a section of stores, houses and a barbershop. It was a late model Sentra painted in a pastel color driven by a middle aged, light complexioned sister with her hair done in Shirley Temple curls. Moments later, Devonte' and Braun reached for the barbershop door. Both dressed in shorts and tank top. Braun wore white with green and red stripes and Devonte' sported grey with a bold black stripe which had the words "Mecca" emblazoned across the front.

The barbershop wasn't crowded this particular afternoon as it would often be. There were three people in the barber chairs, and only two waiting to get their fresh cuts. The two were youths who couldn't have been more than nine and eleven respectively. They appeared to be brothers. Devonte' and Braun acknowledged the two boys from their neighborhood and the barbers before taking their seats.

Braun glanced around the small barbershop and observed the pictures posted about. Some of them displayed the latest styles while others, which were turning yellow at the ends, appeared to be from the 70's and 80's. There were other pictures that he always focused on each time he visited the barbershop. They were one of several black cowboys including "Cherokee Bill," Nat Love, and Jackson Sundown. There were pictures of the 10th Calvary or better known as the "Buffalo Soldiers."

The Buffalo Soldiers were perhaps the most effective troops on the western frontier. They were dispatched as Company H of the 10th Calvary. This troop of black pistoleers in the 1860's and 70's earned reputed respect from the Native Americans of whom they battled. Their dark skin and kinky hair resembled that of the buffalo, the Native Americans primary food source. Thus, the name Buffalo Soldier derived. During the Civil War (1861-1865), an estimated 200,000 African Americans had borne arms for the Union Army filling out regiments, divisions, and even entire corps. One of these corps, as documented in the annals of the Civil War, were the 25th, who a portion of which occupied Richmond, Virginia during the closing days of the war. These units were all volunteers that were established for the duration of the war, since there were no companies in the standing regular army open to African American recruits.

However, this stance by the United States military would change. On July 28, 1866, Congress would provide for four regular army infantry to consist of black infantry men, the 38th , 39th , 40th, and 41st. Also, two Cavalries (the 9th and 10th) consisted exclusively of blacks.

For eight years, the 9th Calvary fought battles between Lipons, Kickapoos, Kiowas, Comanches, and what could have been considered their arch enemies—the Apaches. Warriors who didn't like the aforementioned Native American tribes, had long since mastered skills in mountain guerrilla warfare. These Apache warriors would often strike out with raids off of the reservations. They knew how to lay meticulous ambushes in the steep cliffs lining the valleys of the southwest. In 1879, the Buffalo Soldiers would find themselves engaged in what was perhaps the deadliest war against the Apaches since their inception.

With the tension building, the Indian Affairs bureau attempted to evacuate a band of Apaches to the San Carlos reservation in Arizona, Victorio, chief of this band, led an uprising. Fleeing their reservation in New Mexico with 60 members. Their numbers increased to over 300 and the U.S. Calvary troops, including the Buffalo Soldiers were ambushed. They suffered eight casualties after a well-planned ambush by Victorio in the canyon of the Los Animos River. This was one of their biggest in their eight year campaign on the American western frontier.

The war between the U. S. Calvary intensified and lasted throughout 1880. The Apaches posted guerrilla tactical warfare on the Mexican borders slipped and away into Mexico. This tactic was applied because the 9th Calvary were unable to follow pursuit. Head on attacks against entrenched opposition was not a part of the Apache protocol.

After months of indecisive attacks by Victorio and his band of Apaches, a unit of Native American scouts ripped Victorio's camp. This sent him in flight to Mexico with Calvary troops at his heels setting the stage for the final phase of the campaign in which the Buffalo Soldiers would play a key factor in the defeat of Victorio.

The 10th Calvary was dispatched to the Rio Grande, led by Lt. Henry O Flipper, the first black graduate of West Point. The Apaches had been seen crossing the river into Texas. Responding to the dispatch, Lt. Flipper rode 98 miles in 22 hours through country where the Native Americans were expected to be heavily aggressive.

Over the next five months Victorio's warriors would wage guerilla warfare on the U.S. Calvary. They ambushed from cliffs; sudden charges of dozens of screaming, rifle toting warriors encircled unsuspecting Calvary men. But their attacks were most often repelled by the riflemen ship from the sharp shooting Buffalo Soldiers. By October 1888, Victorio's warriors were greatly decreased and weakened. It was in this month that perhaps a decisive victory by the Buffalo Soldiers, set the stage for Victorio's demise. After an intense firefight in which the Apaches sniped at Calvary men from their position holed up in the rocks, a line of wagons rounded a mountain near Rattlesnake Springs in Texas. This drew a party of warriors to emerge from the rocks in anticipation of an easy target. But they were deceived.

As the Apaches pulled up to the wagon train, suddenly out poured the Buffalo Soldiers from the 24th infantry. They were escorted for this particular supply train for the 10th Calvary. They unleashed a torrid of fire across the valley floor. The Buffalo Soldiers repelled the Native Americans causing them to flee. Within a few days of fighting, the decimated band of Apaches fell back to Mexico on October 14, 1880, Victorio was trapped by Mexican troops and killed.

The Buffalo Soldiers over the remaining years of the frontier era would engage in several battles with the Native American foes. A couple of battles included the 10th Calvary's role in the Geronimo campaign of 1885-86; and the 9th and 25th infantry's joint campaign against the Sioux in 1890-91.

As for Lt. Flipper, the only African American line officer in the 10th infantry, he faced racism, hatred and envy from his fellow officers. This led to his court martial on trumped up charges, which resulted in his being expelled from the military. He never cleared his name while he was alive, but on December 13, 1976, the Army's Board of Corrections exonerated him. It was 36 years after his death when they issued him an honorable discharge.

The barbers, who were all middle aged African American men, were engaged in a conversation centered on the San Antonio Spurs, who incidentally had lost a pivotal game five and subsequently the series to the Los Angeles Lakers. The barbers were disgruntled and Braun would get a kick out of the zany barbers. They would often have outlandish stories to tell about their growing up in the 1960's and all three of them would claim to have had personal encounters with radical or civil rights leaders.

As the conversation carried on, one of the youths pointed a finger and inquired about one of the pictures on the wall.

"Man I'm telling you, that was poor decision making on that boy Duncan. He made some big plays, but towards the end..." when one of the youths interrupted Joe, the barber who was speaking.

"Who is that?" the kid inquired earnestly. The barbers paused to look in the direction the kid was pointing.

"That right there is one of our African American heroes, son. He was the first black to graduate West Point. That's a military school, son. Lieutenant Henry O' Flipper was a line officer of the 10th Calvary," Joe enlightened proudly.

"Buffalo Soldiers," added the barber named McKay, a red skinned man with thinning curly black hair and spectacles. He was the calm intellectual of the crew and was reputed as the best barber. He was the one most youngsters would wait for hours to get his professional styles.

"Buffalo Soldiers? They hunted buffaloes?" the kid asked. Everyone in the shop chuckled at his obvious lack of knowledge, which was quite common.

"No, they were called Buffalo Soldiers by the Native Americans because of their dark skin and kinky hair. The Native Americans said they reminded them of the buffaloes." Braun enlightened with a smile. He rubbed his hand across the boy's hair and stated, "kinky hair."

"You are a Buffalo Soldier, Jared. You are dark and your hair sure is kinky," stated his brother beside him while trying to control his laughter. The boy acted like he had two revolvers shooting at Native Americans.

"So, what are the boys going to do tomorrow night, Mr. Green?" one of the barbers stationed at the back of the shop asked.

Jared observed himself in the mirror approvingly then got up as another boy approached the chair for his turn. Jared handed the barber his money and dapped Braun and Devonte' on his way out.

"Oh, we are going to pull this game off. Everybody is going to handle their business. Everything is on the line now, Joe. Put up or shut up time," Mr. Green replied.

"I sure hope you are right. I have already put up," Joe responded. As they continued their in depth point of views into what tactical approach was imperative and who had to perform well for the Spurs, the time seemed to whiz by. Braun and Devonte' exchanged meaningful glances at each other while both got their haircuts. Mckay unsheathed the apron from around Braun's neck.

"Alrighty. What do you think?" Mckay asked Braun as he examined the fresh haircut. Braun nodded approvingly and reached into his pocket to retrieve the necessary amount of money to pay for the hair cut. Devonte' who had merely gotten a line up, had long been finished and was waiting at the door as Braun conversed with the barbers.

"Yeah Tim has got to step up for this one. He must play his game. Parker and Big Shot Rob have to be a factor too, then we got this," Braun stated as he picked at his Spurs jersey in confidence. The three barbers agreed and each nodded with wide smiles. Mr. Green looked at Braun underneath his spectacles as he pointed his finger in the form of a pistol at him.

Braun smiled exposing a gold tooth and stated, "You all take it easy Mr. Green, Joe and McKay."

✶✶✶✶✶✶✶✶

The bright sunlight on this hot day glistened off of the concertina wire and glass from correctional administrator's vehicles outside. The view was desolate with acres upon acres of dull-bricked buildings that made up the prison complex at Huntsville State Penitentiary. This maximum security prison was deemed virtually inescapable due to natural hazards such as swamps.

On Thanksgiving Day in 1998, seven men who were condemned to the Ellis -1 Unit, which is death row, sought to make history and defy what most deemed insurmountable odds. They faced with towering wired fences, armed correctional officers in gun towers, and the rough terrain of woods and swamps surrounding the vast prison complex. But desperate men, in desperate situations, will make desperate moves.

Meticulous in their thoroughly planned escape from the "row," the seven desperados made dummies from extra blankets and clothing to put in their bunks and used felt pens and carbon paper to dye their long underwear black for camouflage.

After effectuating this phase, the escapees enacted phase two. They cut through an interior fence using a hacksaw blade and scaled up to the roof. Under the guise of the dark night and a dense fog, the seven desperate escapees moved quickly across the roofs of the prison's buildings to the chapel where they slid down to the ground.

Once the escapees had reached the ground, it was a frantic, mad dash for the two outer fences that were 75 yards away. This action was spotted by the guards in the gun towers who then fired 18 shots in the general direction of the escapees. Whether it was the thunderous reports of the search team, or simply exhaustion, six of the men hit the ground in surrender. Only one of the escapees, Martin Gurule 29, continued the mission.

Gurule prepared himself for the immense task of scaling the fence, which was reinforced with rolls of barbed wire He wrapped his body in cardboard for protection. With this added armor, Gurule then scurried over the two fences barely dodging the barrage of bullets and vanished into the swampy woods of east Texas. The last successful escape was by the Bonnie and Clyde gang member, Raymond Hamilton in 1934.

National attention was immediately called to the escape, due to the notoriety of the prison and the Ellis -1 death row unit. An army of 500 law enforcement officers equipped with jeeps, boats, helicopters, tracking dogs, horses, and military heat seeking and night vision equipment patrolled the woods around the prison for seven days and nights.

Desperate, the army of police had turned up nothing. There were no signs of Gurule. The prison administration continued to sweat bullets and face ridicule for having allowed a dangerous death row inmate to escape from a prison that had been deemed inescapable. The despair ended for the Texas prison officials on the seventh day of the intense search. Two off duty prison guards discovered Gurule's floating body in Harmon Creek bayou while fishing. It was located about two miles from the prison. Apparently the extra armor of cardboard had taken him under.

It is debatable what is deemed worse: a death sentence, or a life in prison. But the debate is primarily focused on the evaluated opinion of politicians, judiciaries, and common citizens. They are the ones who attempt to weigh in the balance of the two sentences, which in essence, parallel to each other. This was made self-evident by the statistics of condemned men who lobby for a speedier death. They dropped their appeals and chose to die rather than to languish 20, 30, or more years. They would rather not die a slow death on top of humiliation, deprivation, and dehumanization that accompanies a life in prison.

✴✴✴✴✴✴✴✴

Abiding by gang laws. Separatism and tension among ethnicities as shown on the faces of the Mexicans working out on the yard. Tattoos identified their affiliations. Muscles bulging. Eyes studying the vicinity and security as they stretch between sets. This was the scene in the yard. Inside, a man in an orange jumpsuit makes his way towards the visiting chamber to see his son. His demeanor is solemn. Stress and fatigue are now permanently engraved into the natural lines of his face. Worn there by the constant psychological abuse, and deprivation of his life. The separation from his family due to mistakes he'd made as a young, unconscious man. Maybe it was all of the above. Whatever the case, Phil's father shuffled along to the chair set before a glass. His chains rattled and clanged against the chair as he sat down. The burly correctional officer that escorted him to the chamber stood post by the door. The prisoner eyed his son as he walked silently and sat on the chair on the other side of the glass partition.

Phil was adorned in all black, gold chain, and a diamond pendent in his left ear. He looked like the drug dealer he was. The expression on his father's face was of mixed emotions. He wanted to show the loving side, the bond of a father glad to see his son, even though he had a feeling of disdain and anxiety for the degenerative person his son had become. He felt powerless and weak.

Seconds passed with the two simply staring through the glass partition at each other. Phil's eyes glazed over and showed signs of humility as he recognized his father's disapproving facial expression.

Phil spoke out, "How's it going, Pop? Why, why do they still have you in chains and stuff?" he inquired.

His father glanced down at his shackled wrists and shook his head as he looked away. He started to respond as he turned back to make eye contact with his son.

"It's just a part of the process. They are trying to break my spirit. It's not necessary, but in this society it's practical," he responded as he stared deeply into his son's eyes. Phil looked away. Then his father asked, "How's your mother?" Phil shook his head and his father instinctively knew what the gesture meant.

"Not good, Pop. Shh. I don't know what to say about Momma, Pop," Phil stated disgustedly. His father looked guilty when he said this.

"Well, if there's nothing good to say, just leave it. Remember, she still is your mother. And everything she is going through or has done, it's my fault," his father stated solemnly. He reflected over how he made Phil's mother into a co-conspirator into his drug dealings as well as abused her physically and psychologically. He introduced her to cocaine inhalation and virtually transformed what had been a good black woman, into the immoral, drug abusing, subservient to men, type of black woman she had become. " How are your brothers and sisters?" he inquired.

"Kiesha sent us a postcard from the Caribbean. She is really happy. I went to see Patrick last week. He is stable, I guess. Jalena and Gary are doing good in school. I'm keeping my eyes on them. They are going to be straight," Phil smiled. His eyes were in reverie as he thought of his little brother and sister. His father examined him.

"Are you really? Are you really keeping an eye on your little brother and sister?" his father inquired.

The smile slowly vanished from Phil's face and he stared deeply into his father's sincere and concerned eyes.

"How can you be sure they'll be straight? You're not straight, Phil. You're perpetuating what I did and what your brother Patrick did. You will end up in a cell next to one of us. You're too smart, son. You could be somebody. That material stuff is just for the moment. The cars, the jewelry and those little hot girls are all temporary. You could make a future for yourself, son. Right now, you've got none," his father chastised.

Phil shook his head and his eyes saddened.

"Pop, what am I supposed to do, huh? I'm not just in it for me. I can't get a good job, Pop. I quit school. Who is going to hire me? I have to think about my little brother and sister and keep my eye on their best interest. Mom isn't doing anything. People are talking about kicking us out, Pop. What am I go–

ing to do?" Phil explained.

His father listened with empathetic eyes.

"There are trade schools, son. You should enroll in one. You say you're keeping an eye on your little brother and sister, but who's got their eyes on you? It's a cold game, son. I don't want you to end up dead or in here with me." Phil's father's enlightening speech left him in a meditative posture. He looked his father in the eyes and mentally wanted to make a change, but not knowing exactly how or if it could be done. After a moment of silence his father placed a hand to the glass partition and stared soulfully at his discontented son. Phil placed his hand to the glass as tears formed in his eyes. The two shared a very reflective and emotional moment.

Chapter 11

T he rotary blades of the police task force helicopter was deafening as it soared over the speeding traffic on Highway 410. The task force in conjunction with several San Antonio police cruisers, Bexar County Sheriffs and Highway Patrol officers, were in hot pursuit of a grey Aerostar van that was recklessly maneuvering through traffic. It side swiped several vehicles, went over medians, and sped through intersections as the flashing lights of police cruisers stayed close.

The chase commenced at Broadway Avenue where three men dressed in black clothing and apparently wearing body armor, robbed a bank with automatic weapons. The men exited the back with an undetermined amount of cash and boarded the grey van.

"As you can see, the bank robbers are pulling out all the stops and this is getting really dangerous. Their speed has reached up to 100 mph now. These are desperate, desperate men," informed a reporter from a news team helicopter that was broadcasting live, the high-speed chase.

The chase carried on for over ten minutes with the desperados exceeding 100 mph through the traffic as the police cruisers and helicopters followed. Several times the van nearly lost control and side swiped a red Tacoma. It lost one of its hubcaps when the van swayed and ran off the shoulder of the highway. The driver of the Tacoma lost control and spun the vehicle in circles. A police cruiser, who was too close, smashed into the back of it. The crash sent metal and shards of glass splattering onto the highway as other vehicles swerved to miss the accident. The parade of speeding police cruisers could barely maintain control of their vehicles. Several motorists were unable to avoid the vehicles and a small pile up ensued until oncoming traffic began screeching to a halt and completely shut down that stretch of highway.

"Whoa! As you can see below, there are several collisions in progress. We have just lost a State Trooper. Traffic is shut down from that point and it looks like one of the vans tires is smoking. They are dropping speed drastically. Is that smoke coming from the engine? Whoa! There it goes! The van crashed into a guard rail!" the reporter accounted.

After the smoking van came to a halt, it was cordoned off by the State Troopers, Highway Patrol, and San Antonio police cruisers, who screeched to a halt. The driver, who was Caucasian, frantically got out of the vehicle and attempted to flee as shouting police officers chased after him.

The other two bank robbers exited the vehicle with their hands held high as the officers inched forward with semi-automatic weapons pointed in their direction. They were ordered onto their knees and to place both hands behind their heads with their fingers interlocked. The police aggressively hustled them to the concrete.

Meanwhile, the fleeing suspect was thrown to the concrete by a hurled baton that had caused him to stumble long enough for two officers to collar him. With a knee in the perpetrators back, an officer placed handcuffs onto his wrists. He twisted his arms behind his back and caused him to grimace in pain as several other officers kept their weapons carefully trained on him.

"All three suspects have been subdued and it appears that the danger is over. They are being led to the awaiting police vehicles," the reporter informed as the helicopter hovered over the scene. The thirteen minute car chase had been filmed nearly in its entirety and would be re-aired on a segment of "Dangerous Police Chases." At that very moment, San Antonio residents who happened to be in front of their television sets, had their programs interrupted and viewed the gun wielding, shouting police as they escorted the desperados into the back seat of police vehicles. Many viewers, primarily minorities, no doubt had questions. Though guns were trained and there were audible shouts of indignant officers, the suspects were not handled with "excessive force." Minorities have had to contend with this during routine traffic stops from police all across the nation.

One particular incident that could be defined as excessive force involved a black male motorist in Compton, California who endured a barrage of gunfire from police without provocation. The police surrounded and opened up with over one hundred rounds. The vehicle was riddled with bullets and the windows were shot out of cars and homes in the neighborhood. The driver of the vehicle miraculously suffered only minor injuries.

The video footage of what could only be termed as an ambush brought outcries for justice. The African American community of Compton, as well as the rest of the United States, was appalled and outraged at the blatant use of excessive force on an unarmed black motorist. After being shot and bleeding, he was violently jerked from the vehicle. *If the motorist had been white and in a white suburban neighborhood, would this guerrilla style police ambush have occurred? I think not.*

✶✶✶✶✶✶✶✶

In the video footage, the Caucasian bank robbers, who flagrantly endangered the lives of motorists as well as police, were casually escorted to police vehicles. Certainly the African American community was left wondering of the bias of the police force in using excessive force when apprehending whites in comparison to blacks.

Braun, in his uniform, punched the clock at Taco Bell. He had been working there for the past month. It was a summer job to help take some of the burden away from his grandmother, who purchased his school clothes and supplies. After punching the clock, he bid farewell to his fellow co-workers then walked out of the building where he would await an Avias bus to take him back to the eastside.

The Avias bus dropped him off a block away from his home where he happened to see his friend Piye walking towards him. They dapped each other in greeting and began walking. Both made suggestions to get colas to quench their thirst on this hot and humid day.

They walked to a Stop-n-Go. It was owned and operated by the Gonzales', the Mexican family who treated everyone fairly, but were spitefully persecuted by many African American youth, in particular, Piye. He was relentless in antagonizing them.

"Yeah, I was watching some videos when they broadcast it. I just knew it was going to end with police cutting loose," Braun stated as he wiped sweat from his brow and squinted from the sun.

Piye's expression turned sarcastic as he said, "Me too, until that white boy got out and ran. I knew they were going to shoot him. See if that had been me or you, we would have been tagged and bagged," Piye stated matter-of-factly. "We are targets even when we aren't doing anything. Imagine putting innocent civilians and police lives in danger in a high speed chase like that? There wouldn't have been anything left of that van after the cops finished unloading. Believe that," Piye added, as he opened the glass door. He nearly bumped into Mr. Gonzales' daughter, Maria, which caused her to blush.

"Oh, excuse me. I didn't even see you," she stated laughing. Her eyes lit up, but dimmed slightly, when she made eye contact with Piye. It was as if she could sense his covert racism towards her and her family.

"That's okay. You didn't do any harm," Braun responded. She smiled and proceeded out of the store and into the parking lot. Braun discretely observed her beauty as she climbed behind the wheel of a 2003 Jetta. Her bright complexion, grey eyes, and light brown flowing hair, showed her multi-racial mixture.

The Gonzales family had their deep-rooted heritage planted firmly in old Mexico. They were descendants of Indians and whites, their ethnicity was called Mestizo. Mr. Gonzales had grown up in the town of Taxco near Mexico City where his parents, grandparents, and great grandparents had grown up, all having the distinction of Mestizo.

The Mestizos played a significant role in Mexico's war for independence in year 1810. It began with Miguel Hidalgo y Costillo, a creole priest, who rose to liberate its people from the reign of its Spanish conquerors. The Spanish had dominion over the region for over 300 years after the conquistadors defeated the Aztecs in 1519-21. After the fall of the great Mayan civilization, a civilization which constructed cities complete with temples, courts, and pyramids. In A.D. 900, another great civilization arose. The Aztecs came from a the northern land called Aztlan. They conquered the Toltecs in A.D. 900. They later founded Tenochitlan, now Mexico City, in A.D. 1325.

Nearly 200 years later the Aztecs would remain in power constructing large buildings, bridges, and roads. But the invasion of the conquistadors would end their reign. The Aztec weaponry of spears, bows, and arrows and proved to be no match for the conquistador's horses and rifles. Their immune system was no match for the diseases the conquistadors brought either.

When Miguel Hidalgo y Castillo rose 300 years later to liberate his people from the Spaniards rule, he recruited untrained Indians and Mestizos. Almost all of them were captured and killed. Because of this uprising, the Spanish king was greatly displeased and severely taxed the creoles.

The king also organized a large army in Mexico in response to the uprising. Because of oppression and harsh taxation, the creoles turned against the Spanish king and joined alliance with an army officer, Agustin de Iturbide. By 1821, Mexico had won their independence and it was during this period in the 19th century that the Apaches, Wichita and Comanche arrived in Mexico. Their arrival added to the Indian population that already existed and consisted of the Coaltuitecan, Karwnkanwa, Caddo, Jumano, and Tonkawa people. These inundations of Indian tribes were not the only invasion of Mexico as Americans themselves moved into the region also occupying Texas. After Mexico had liberated itself from Spanish rule under the military leadership of Agustin de Iturbide, Mexico would fight many more wars against Texas and the United States. These wars were now under the leadership of Antonio Lopez de Santa Anna, who became dictator in 1835.

Texas, which was a Mexico province, rebelled. The Americans who flooded the region, wanted to be liberated themselves from the military dominated government of Santa Anna's dictatorship. Many battles presumed with such men as Jim Bowie and Davey Crockett losing their lives for the liberation of Texas. In what is perhaps the most noted battle of Texas' wars for liberation, Santa Anna wiped out American defenders at the Alamo in 1836. Under the helm of Sam Houston, the Texans would later defeat Santa Anna at San Jacinto. That same year, independence was proclaimed.

The state was then recognized as the Republic of Texas with Sam Houston as its President. The Lone Star flag replaced the Mexican Flag, which replaced the flag of Spain. Texas would function as a nation until 1845 when it would be admitted to the Union.

The battle at the Alamo had long been fought and displaced in time behind many other battles fought on American soil for liberation, re-admission, civil rights, and now judiciary and ethnic differences. A new wave of hostilities in the urban black communities derived from mistrust of foreign entities that they felt had taken over their businesses. This was one of Piye's main reasons for his hatred towards the Gonzales family and other ethnic groups, such as the Koreans and Pakistani.

Braun and Piye walked into the store. The owner's expression registered a mixed emotional reception. He was pleased to see the courteous and respectable Braun, yet discomforted at the presence of the hostile Piye.

"How's it going, Mr. Gonzales and Manuel," Braun stated, acknowledging the owner and his young son. Manuel was a shade darker than his father and sister. Their bright skin could sometimes easily cause people to mistake them for whites, but Manuel was unmistakably of strong Indian descent. Much like his sister, whom had been dressed in westernized attire, Manuel was adorned in the latest hip-hop fashion gear with a Spurs hat turned to the back and all.

"What's happening, Braun? Going down tonight, huh man?" Manuel stated as he clasped hands with Braun. He was referring to the pivotal game six of the Spurs and Lakers series. As he spoke, his eyes momentarily glanced at Piye who turned down one of the aisles.

"Yeah, it's going down. We are going to pull it off, believe that," Manuel stated.

Minutes passed and the two boys returned holding the items they intended to purchase. Braun carried a cola, chips, and Bear claws while Piye placed his powdered donuts and chocolate milk onto the counter. He eyed Mr. Gonzales disdainfully.

"Ring it up, Juan Valdez. I ain't got all day, and give me a discount while you're at it," Piye stated.

"A discount for what?" Mr. Gonzales inquired.

Piye smiled.

"A discount for us letting you even have this store. You would be still working for slave labor in some camp if it wasn't for the blind brothers that let you take the place," Piye replied.

"What have we ever done to you, son?" Mr. Gonzales responded. His eyes were woeful.

Manuel who heard the remark seethed as he returned from the back.

"We never worked for any slave labor! Our people fought for liberation! What did you do?!" Manuel retorted. Manuel was partially right, but under the Bracero Program in the 1940's, Mexican laborers were brought into the U.S. for seasonal harvests. They worked for rock bottom wages and deported back to Mexico after the contract expired.

"What you mean, what did I do?! You are talking about my people, gringo?! That's what you are implying you wet back sucka! Come on outside!" Piye barked. Braun held him back.

"Please, just take your items and go. Please," Mr. Gonzales pleaded. Braun finally maneuvered Piye away from the counter and to the door. He retrieved their purchase and gave Mr. Gonzales and his son an apologetic look before he exited himself. He left a hyper Manuel and a nervous Mr. Gonzales staring at each other perplexed. His wife came from the back stockroom and had a startled look on her face.

"Es todo aceptable?" (Is everything okay?) she inquired. Manuel shook his head and returned to the back while flinging off his apron. His mother eyed him, then turned her attention to Mr. Gonzales who released a sigh of frustration as he ran both hands through his dark hair.

Outside Piye was still infuriated by the remark made by Manuel. He frowned and jerked away from Braun. He stared before proceeding to walk down the busy avenue.

"Piye, man you have to chill with all that. Come on man, this stuff is going to turn out bad one day. You can't keep harboring all this hatred for other races. It's eating you up inside. Piye, yeah we as a people had to deal with a lot of oppression and racism. Most of what you are getting fed up by happened to your Pops decades ago. And these people that you hate have done nothing to you, P. They have never done anything to our people. Nothing.

Come on, P." Braun pleaded.

Piye shook his head. "You heard what he said, huh? He was talking about slavery and all," Piye retorted.

"Yeah but that was just a natural defensive response because you was on his people," Braun replied.

Piye smirked.

"Man, I don't know how you can't see through them suckers. Anyway, it doesn't matter. I am going to stop even going in their damn store and giving them my money. Everybody should boycott all these sucker stores. Them, those rag head suckers and those Koreans. We need to take back our own businesses," he stated matter-of-factly. Braun was silent. A few meters behind them was the sound of low, rhythmic thumps from the high tech woofers inside of a rust colored Lexus. The loud musical beats caused both boys to turn in the direction of the approaching car. As the Lexus pulled to a stop, the boys stared inside to see if they recognized the driver. They saw sparkling gold teeth and gold rings on a hand that clutched a customized steering wheel. It was Phil. He turned down the music as he began to speak. Braun listened, but Piye cautiously glanced around the vicinity for cops or surveillance and was not paying attention.

"What's going on, my niggas? Where are you all headed to?" Phil in-quired. Braun informed him that they were headed home. "Jump in, man, I'm just cruising the hood, know what I'm sayin? Might go scoop a few freaks…lil drankin,' herb blowin'…then hit the mo' T. Know that's all they want, ya heard. Let's ride, main," Phil offered as he wolfishly examined some teenage girls crossing the street a few yards up the street. He sipped on a wine cooler bottle. Braun felt compelled to decline the offer. Recently he had been uneasy about being in Phil's presence with the conspiracy sur-rounding Rocco's heist and the circulating rumors of Chatter and his crew working with the Feds. He was even more skeptical, but he and Phil had been childhood friends. It was awkward to disassociate himself without feeling he had turned his back on his friend.

This is most often the case in peer pressure situations when youths who had the same mindset as kids begin to grow in different directions. Each will pretend to condone or promote one another's actions so as to create a delusion. To keep down suspicion that the friendship is still the same. To be congenial. Or in some cases, to not appear square. This is a dangerous practiced psychology. As Confucius is quoted as saying, 'One should never retain friends with people who are not of your same mindset.' But youths in many cases worldwide, never adhere to this wise connotation. And their unequivocal friendships most often end in jail time or death.

Braun looked away and contemplated as to what to do. He was torn between what would be the rational move or the move predicated by street ethics, which he held.

He inquired, "Alright, you don't have dope or nothing in here, huh?" Feinting a humorous smile that belied his eyes, Phil gestured with a sarcastic expression. Braun opened up the passenger's side door and got in the car. Piye continued to look down the avenue and slowly backed away from the car before turning to give Braun a meaningful look.

"What's up, P? Are you riding or what?" Phil asked once more. The smile still engraved on his face, but his eyes were uncertain. Piye had not been in his presence in over a weekend and was avoiding him.

"Nah. Nah, I'm going on in to take me a shower. I have a speech to give at the Center. I'll call you," Piye responded. His tone was deadpanned and his eyes were empathetic. After giving one last meaningful look at Braun, whose expression was of recognition, he walked away from the car. After a brief moment Phil looked over at Braun and stared briefly as Piye crossed the street.

A suspicious looking grey Taurus rolls up on the 700 block of Nevada Street. The twilight is beginning to set in and the crack dealers are setting up position. Seeing the Taurus approach, signals are given and movements are made. The driver of course sees this and eyes are hidden behing his dark shades. It obscures his smiling face. He knew the dealers, all of them. The smile was due to his inside
knowledge of their warrants.

The Taurus turned the block and its night lights swept across a familiar sight on this particular block. A police cruiser with flashing lights was parked in a vacant lot. Its two officers were conducting a procedural search on several gang members, namely Wild Bill, Red Dawg, Lil Gun, Rocco, and Bull. They were with three other youthful looking members who were obscured from the gang files, until now. The seven were on their knees with fingers interlocked behind their heads as the officers with semi-automatics drawn conducted the frisk and interrogation.

The driver of the Taurus passed the scene and acknowledged another white cop who firmly gripped his weapon as he aimed it at the gang members. The Taurus then continued on up the block.

Several blocks away from this almost too common sight of police harassment, was yet another sign of the millennium covert war against urban communities. This agent of covert political warfare was not as visible as the police sirens and pistol wielding police officers. In fact, most denizens, respectable or miscreant, were totally oblivious to these new devices. The officers in the cruising Taurus were well aware of this agent. After all, they erected these surveillance cameras.

On this particular block, dealers moved swiftly in the dark under the guises of raggedy attire. They cautiously scan the vicinity as they produced white rocks of cocaine to addicts who appear from the alleyways or in a fume emitting, descript vehicle. Frequently their customers were black females whose crack habits were like taking food from the mouths of their children. Their emaciated bodies and sunken faces were evident of the death to come. These dealers would pump their poison into these sisters' system without even the slightest concern for the indirect crime of murder or deprivation of food from their children.

A crack addict in a white T-shirt, cut off brown jeans and black All Stars vanished inside of a crack house while a light skinned sister of voluptuous, yet petite proportions, propositions a youthful looking dealer. The dealer's gold teeth glistened under an illuminated street light. He lustfully appraised this unkempt and dingy clothed misguided sister, as his hand groped and squeezed her ample buttocks. Another dealer trots down the street as a dispute over a bad batch of crack is conducted between three men took place. Men clad in black were spotted ducking between houses as they ran. The grey Taurus cruised and continued to observe what was going on, while the hidden cameras located on a utility pole filmed the entire vicinity.

Further down the street was more evidence of a community that was disintegrating. Jumping out at anyone who for whatever reason darkened this particular area on the eastside. There were broken bottle glass and spent shell casings untouched and unnoticed by ballistics detectives. Dried up blood, stained the front of a tan wooden framed house that had yellow police tape aligned from a front yard tree to a telephone pole. The house itself was riddled with bullet holes. The windows were shot out and glass sprayed across the porch and lawn due to the high velocity bullets that had penetrated it. It was obvious by the two un-retrieved shell casings on the street that a .223 Mini 14 carbine weapon was used.

What had transpired here was a scene played out across perhaps every urban community in America, whether in metropolitan areas, such as here in San Antonio or small town USA. Wherever socio-economic repression or misdirected hatred was present, quests for monotonous materialism was obvious and these images were common. As a result, there remains an extremely high statistical death rate of blacks between the ages of eighteen and twenty-five. They succumbed to their destitute and oppressive environments through drug inducement, homicide, or suicide.

But there is another element that looms as an obstacle for the African American male, the corporate business of prison. Incidentally, Texas leads the nation in incarceration rates of minorities, next to Louisiana. Both states rank number 2 and number 1 respectively, in total incarceration rates. Both average over 700 lock ups per 100,000 residents. To state that this is an alarming incarceration rate would be an understatement. Texas' rank at number 2 in the nation for incarceration rates may be underscored by its notoriety for leading the nation in executions.

Harris County, District Attorney John Holmes in 1998, the same year of the execution of Karla Fay Tucker. The articulate Caucasian woman, whose Christian conversion in prison after her conviction of a pickaxe killing in Texas, garnered considerable Christian hardliners support was the nation's leading death penalty prosecutor. Also, in 1998, Texas held a whopping 458 inmates on death row and executed 35. Many of these prisoners were executed due to the rising exoneration of wrongfully convicted death row inmates. Questions surfaced afterwards of their actual innocence. Many questions have been taken into consideration in relation to prison executions as well as hiked incarceration rates. *In relation to executions, are these inhumane vehicles of "justice" or a deterrent to homicide? And is "truth in sentencing incentive grant programs" really depreciating the amounts of crime in our nation? Or is it all propaganda? A scheme devised by republican politicians to re-enslave the black populous and create the mass market of the prison industrial complex?* Whatever the case, we as a people still have to deal with the issue of the vanishing black male. An issue that in the eyes of the driver of the grey Taurus, was gratifying apparently. A smile etched across his face as he watched the scampering dealers, heard reports of gunshots. and watched the hidden camera focus in as the vehicle idled at a stop sign. He fidgeted with his dark shades and turned off onto a busy avenue. He blended in with the other traffic until his vehicle was no longer visible amidst the oncoming headlights and red brake lights.

Chapter 12

Several youths of approximate middle school age walked down the street talking in postmortem about the shocker that had happened in game six. Some dribbled an imaginary basketball and pulling up for imaginary shots at a basket. They were dismayed and they had reason to be. The San Antonio Spurs had lost Game six to the Los Angeles Lakers the previous night. They lost their bid for a third national championship.

Braun, Phil, and Devonte' were posted up outside of Braun's grandmother's home and engaged in a similar mournful review of the pivotal sixth game. Their attention was gripped by the look of dejection on the faces of the youths.

"Braun, man, I caint believe that. Man, we were up two to nothing on the Lakers, man. Shh," stated one of the youths. His frail, bare chest heaved as he stopped dribbling the basketball long enough to attract the older boys' attention. After a moment of brief sports analysis, the boys continued on up the street.

"Yeah, that was cold blooded. Tim came through, but shoot man," Devonte' stated while shaking his head in dismay.

"Man, that loss with four tenths of a second was the momentum changer. Plus Parker was contained and I just don't think the Spurs were mentally in it. You can't blame Popavich. It's over," Braun stated. The others agreed.

"It all came down to the Lakers making the clutch shots and key defensive plays at the end. I give them credit, you know. The Lakers won the game. All the pressure was on the Spurs. We just didn't respond well last night in the clutch," Phil stated as he made an imaginary jump shot. At that moment a lime green colored Montero Sport SUV passed with glistening rims. Inside the vehicle were a group of females smiling, laughing, and talking above the sound system. Each took inventory of the three boys, and was enthralled by the captivated and lustful expressions of both Phil and Devonte'.

"Damn she looks good! Do you know her, Devonte'?" Phil asked as he sipped on his cola, never taking his eyes off of the red skinned driver of the

SUV. Her gold teeth sparkled and her eyes were afire as their reflection was caught in the rearview. She was looking back at them or at least at one of them.

"Yeah, I know her. That's Cantina and Rene-n-nem out of the apartments on South Cross. One of them is Chris' girl. Stone freaks. Paper chasers," Devonte' informed. He looked down at his watch. "I would flag them down for you all, but Braun, I know you in love and Phil does not have a stick," Devonte' laughed as he walked towards the front lawn gate.

"Stick? I don't need a stick for those type of hoes. I have a thousand dollar smile, nigga," Phil responded.

Braun smiled and shook his head. Devonte' laughed then opened up the gate.

"Besides, I have to get Sharon at seven and it's almost six fifty. Catch you all later," Devonte' stated as he jostled with the keys.

Phil laughed and turned up the bottle of cherry cola as Devonte' climbed into the driver's seat.

"Yeah, I know. Sharon has you whipped. Sprung like Braun, nigga," Phil stated. Braun smiled but his eyes showed his uncomfortable disposition with the reference. Devonte' laughed and then closed the door.

"No man, how is Braun going to be sprung? You have to hit to be sprung, Devonte' laughed at his own humor then pulled away from the curb in his mother's Acura and turned up the volume on the radio. Phil watched the Acura reach the stop sign, then turned to face Braun who held his head down. He bore a strained smile, but his eyes revealed his meditation over the statement Devonte' had made.

"He is just kidding, huh? I mean, you have done hit, right?" Phil tried to pry with a smile. Braun playfully nudged him as he urged him to change the subject.

"Go on, man, I don't want to get into all that," Braun laughed. Phil smiled and drank the rest of his cola. He decided not to pry further into the situation as he was well aware that Braun and Ikara had not been intimate.

After finishing his bottle of cola, Phil remained silent and surveyed the neighborhood. He took inventory of the dilapidation of his community. Over the years he watched it change from moderately manicured lawns and homes to slowly decaying lawns and neglected homes. The "Broken Window Theory" seemed to become a reality. The theory being that if one window is broken in the community it will lead to larger criminal acts.

This theory was proposed by James Q. Wilson and George Killing. It was endorsed by law enforcement officials across the nation who cracked down on crimes of vandalism in an attempt to preserve the "quality of life" in urban crime ridden areas. In theory, believing that if vandalism and other disorderly behavior in urban communities are reduced, over time serious crimes will slowly decline.

But Wilson, the theorist behind the "Broken Window Theory," admitted that the theory lacked substantive scientific evidence that it actually worked. He was quoted as saying, "I still to this day do not know if improving order will or will not reduce crime. People have not understood that this was a speculation." In urban cities such as San Antonio, the "Broken Window Theory" may be considered by most to be a fallacy because it merely makes arrests for vagrancy, graffiti scrawling, youths breaking abandoned building windows, or shooting out street lights. Does it actually help decrease or deter major violence? The violence that stems from gang warfare and drug beefs, which have become ingrained as a part of big city culture. There needs to be more evidence to substantiate this theory if it is going to make an impact in reducing drug and gang related violence that plagues urban America.

Reconstruction or revitalization of these urban communities will take more than outside intervention. This outside intervention involves the law enforcement. More importantly, it will take "inside" intervention from the concerned citizens themselves. They must organize and develop support groups to include the implementation of after-school programs such as what Tariq and Nawaz have created.

Many urban Latino and African American neighborhoods across the country, do not have activist voices and determined working class citizens to organize such programs. They have left the fate of their crime ridden communities to a racially biased, corrupt law enforcement agency, who simply profile every young black male rather than help to preserve and to protect the community from the criminal elements. In essence, they too have become the terrorists.

Phil and Braun both could attest to this. Police brutality had become increasingly a part of everyday life. It was commonplace to witness a youth being manhandled and thrown to the pavement. It is not out of the ordinary for a young black male to be pulled over simply because he happened to be driving a nice car. Their community, much the same as other urban black and Latino communities across the country, were becoming tense.

In that brief moment of reflection over his community, Phil's mind drifted to simpler times. These were times that he and Braun and the others had shared. "I used to talk to my Pops and you know he is like thirty something. So, he grew up in the seventies. He talked about how it was then. How he and his friends used to have fun. He told me one time how he and his friends were crossing a cow pasture and one got stuck on the fence. He was scared to death because a bull was charging at them and they had to pull him over. They ripped him clean out of his pants, man. Yeah, he talked about the days in the early seventies where there would shoot marbles and fight with their hands. How rare it was for somebody to even shoot somebody. Kids could play outside and they never had to worry about getting hit with a stray one. Cops were their biggest enemy. Now, we are," Phil stated.

The sun was now beginning to set and the sky was beginning to take on the beautiful pastel colors of twilight as crickets serenaded with piercing music prevalent to the country. Braun, who had been smiling initially at Phil's rendition of his father's stories, was now somber after hearing his grim realities of the oppressive environment.

After a brief pause, he responded, "Yeah, things are all messed up now. But there are going to be some changes. O.B.U. and other activist groups are working. The community must work together, though," Braun asserted.

Phil's eyes remained sordid, though a smirk creased his lips.

"Work together and do what? Man, straightening all this up is a pipe dream. I deal with reality, B. I know you aren't feeling me, though. Piye isn't feeling me either. It's why he has been avoiding me. But I have to do me, B., because there is no getting out of this shit now," Phil sresponded.

Braun examined him and it was in that moment he looked deep into Phil's distressed eyes that he realized just how deep his friend was involved in the cesspool of narcotics dealings. He could almost look into the perilous future that awaited him.

"You can. You have to. Your little brother and sister are depending on you," Braun said.

"Same thing my Pops told me when I went to see him up at Huntsville. But he doesn't understand either. Mom isn't doing anything, but smoking up everything. How is my little sister and brother and her going to eat if I don't get this money?" Phil replied. He released a sigh as he paused while looking out over the serene block as the street lights popped on.

Before Braun could elaborate, Phil's cell phone rang. He removed the cell phone and talked briefly in code to the calling party before putting it back into his pocket.

"I have to make a run, B. I'mma holla tommar." Phil dapped Braun. He left Braun to stare sympathetically at him and wonder exactly what future was in store for him.

✶✶✶✶✶✶✶✶

The sound of tapping on computer keys could be heard as employees worked diligently and responded to Global Marketing customers or downloaded other business information. Tariq, who was getting a cup of coffee, was now receiving a pamphlet from a secretary who came up just behind his shoulders. He sipped the cup of coffee as he read over some documents and was nearly startled by her sudden appearance.

"I think you should read these, Mr. Galla," the secretary stated as she held the papers before him. She was beautiful in form with a light complexion, mysterious eyes, and close cropped hair. "Spector Spyware. Pretty interesting," she stated as Tariq received the paperwork. He smiled as he expressed his appreciation, though his eyes behind his wire rims remained scrutinizing. Sipping his coffee he began walking back towards his cubicle as he read the paper.

"Hmm. Easy to track the computer use of employees? Unwanted users of your computer? Hmm. This could really come in handy," he stated silently to himself. Beside him, talking business over the phone was his longtime friend, Nubian brother, and business associate Somali. As he read with enthusiasm, Somali's large shadow appeared above him and he looked down at the paperwork. His curiosity compelled him to inquire.

Tariq explained to him the specifications and functions of the Spector Spyware, which was the latest technology for computer owners. This software would protect their system against misuse or damage. It featured a full picture recording and playback of the computers daily activity. The recording feature takes pictures of the desktop as the users work.

Somali nodded as he listened. He was impressed with the technology of the latest in system security. He presented Tariq the paperwork he held in his hand. Setting down the Spector Spyware papers, Tariq took another sip of his coffee before retrieving the papers from Somali.

"There were some complications with the marketing of the product from our website, so I came up with a different strategy," Somali stated. Tariq continued to read and nodded in agreement to Somali's new stratagem. Somali sat on the edge of Tariq's desk and asked, "So, have you figured out where you are going take the wife on your anniversary?" Tariq raised an eyebrow as he placed the folder back into Somali's hand, then reclined back in his swivel chair.

"I don't know yet. I want to do something a little different this year. We usually just go to a quaint restaurant and order our favorite dishes. I think

I'll set a different tone this year," Tariq replied.

"A cruise, maybe?" Somali pried.

"Nah, we just went on a cruise for vacation. I was thinking more of a high scale restaurant and a little romance, you know. Kind of re-ignite our relationship, to keep the fire alive," Tariq replied. His eyes revealed his reverie of romancing the woman he loved.

Somali sipped his coffee and smiled, "You're talking like this is your Golden Anniversary. You're still young." He patted Tariq on the shoulder with the folder and turned to walk away. He stopped suddenly short of his cubicle and turned to face Tariq. "Do you have the points of the presentation prepared for the meeting Friday, I hope?" Somali inquired.

"I almost forgot. Thanks for reminding me," Tariq stated. His agenda was so congested that he totally forgot the business meeting that he had scheduled. Somali smiled and shook his head as Tariq began fumbling through his portfolios before he sat down behind his desk and began typing.

The five star restaurant was filled with people of the upscale bourgeoning class, or they were at least dressed to the image, and were enjoying their entrées. They were commenting on either the menu, the entrée they had chosen or the exquisite atmosphere of the restaurant as the tuxedo clad waiters in white gloves pranced to and fro with silver platters. Soft opera styled music perforated the air waves.

Tariq dressed in a grey suit and tie and held before him a menu. His eyes behind his wire rim glasses darted as he scanned the different exotic and expensive entrees. Ursula who was sporting a very stylish purple ensemble, was radiant in all her splendor. She was wearing only a hint of makeup and her silky black hair flowing to the nape of her neck. She began pointing to the menu as she held it just before her signifying that she had decided on her entrée.

"This sounds good. Broiled poussin," she stated. Tariq's raised his eyebrows. "What exactly is that?" he asked. She explained to him that broiled poussin was cornish hen in a mustard crust. He nodded and agreed the Poussin indeed sounded appetizing.

"Have you decided?" she asked. At that moment a waiter passed and stopped at the table to their left. This caused Ursula to glance in the direction of the table. A well to do Caucasian couple in their late forties were seated there. Tariq sighed and stared back at the menu. A few seconds later the waiter briskly appeared at their table. His rigid, but friendly visage beamed with etiquette, and a hint of debonairness. His pride was evidenced in his very posture and greeting.

"Good evening, Sir and Madame. Have you decided what you will be dining on tonight?" he inquired while removing a pencil and small notepad. Tariq smiled awkwardly as he greeted the waiter and looked once more over his menu. Ursula sensed that he had not decided, and then informed the waiter of her choice.

"Yes, umm…I'll have the broiled poussin, celery root, Duchesse potatoes, and for desert I'll have the strawberry chiffon," Ursula read out.

"Will that be all, Madame? Excellent. And you Sir?" the waiter inquired.

"Yes, I'll have thee turkey scaloppini; peas a la francaise; Duchesse potatoes also, and let's see, for dessert I will have the apple crisp," he said. The waiter suggested some wines that would compliment their meal.

Tariq scanned the wine section even though he already knew what he wanted to drink.

"Martini on the rocks," he responded.

"I'll have the same," Ursula responded seconds afterwards before the waiter could inquire.

"Very good. Would you like hors d' oeuvres while you wait?" he politely offered. The two agreed with an appreciation in advance before the waiter pranced away with the same dignified gate in which he had come.

As they waited for their appetizers, Tariq and his wife conversed about their marriage bliss, respective jobs, and prospects of the evening to come. Mellow music played in the background while the waiters pranced by periodically to attend to other patrons. With the lights dimmed, there was a romantic aura that could be felt throughout the restaurant.

"It is really romantic in here. I like the touch of the place," Ursula commented as she looked around approvingly. Tariq agreed as he finished a bite of his hors d' oeuvres and dabbed a napkin to his mouth.

"It is, and kind of reminds me of our first real dinner date. Of course the entrées weren't this expensive. Then again, the menu wasn't anything like this either. I don't know, but it's the lighting I guess, and the atmosphere. I guess it is romantic because I'm staring across at the most beautiful woman I've ever known," Tariq stated.

With an endearing smile that coincided with the loving gaze in his eyes, Ursula blushed as she dropped her head. With an effervescent expression and entranced gaze, she reached for his hands at the moment the waiter appeared.

"Here you go, sir. Your turkey scaloppini, peas a la Françoise, duchess potatoes and apple crisp. And here you are madam. Your broiled poussin, celery root, Duchess potatoes, and strawberry chiffon. Bon Appetite," the waiter stated before he briskly sped away.

The two conversed softly and commented on their entrees. "This poussin is delicious. Care to try a piece?" Ursula offered. Tariq smiled as he looked at the very appetizing mustard crusted cornish hen and sliced and diced into his turkey.

"Maybe just a little piece," he answered. "I'll have my hands full with this. The scaloppini looks good, too," he commented. He finally finished cutting his turkey and when he sampled a piece the poussin, he expressed delight.

"Good?" Ursula inquired as she chewed heartily at her poussin. Tariq nodded to her inquiry then sampled a portion of his potato as the waiter returned with their martinis.

After extending the gratitude for their beverages and receiving a smile from the waiter for their acknowledgement of the restaurants great atmosphere, the two continued with their conversation.

"This martini is just right," Tariq commented. Looking at his glass his mind reflected over their long and fruitful marriage and a smile emerged from his lips. "I was just thinking back to that first night and how you looked. You were so beautiful and so timid. It was awkward at first, for both of us," Tariq stated. His expression was one of endearing love as he stared across the table at his wife. Ursula smiled.

"It was. I think back to that night many times. It was magical and I find myself getting nostalgic," she commented.

"It was magical. It still is magical and I don't think the magic will ever end." The two stared into each other's eyes, then Tariq continued. "At that time, did you see us still together after eighteen years? And two kids?" he inquired.

Ursula smiled, "I knew I loved you and that you loved me. I didn't even want to consider the possiblilty that we wouldn't be together eighteen years later," she stated.

Tariq wiped his mouth with his napkin and stared at Ursula as she finished up the last portion of her strawberry chiffon leaving a smidge of whipped cream on the side of her mouth.

"You're saving that for later?" he winked. Ursula looked puzzled when Tariq informed her.

She laughed and dabbed a napkin to her mouth.

"It must have been good," Tariq added. There was a pause of silence when Tariq leaned across the table to hold Ursula's dainty hands. "You're still beautiful and I will always love you," he said.

"And I will always love you," Ursula responded. her husband's eyes.

After a brief pause, Tariq's expression turned devilish when he posed another question.

"Do you remember what happened after the dinner date?" he asked slyly. His voice was of a deep whisper.

Ursula looked away shyly and smiled as her chest heaved slightly. Becoming aroused as she reflected over the way they'd made love that night for the first time.

"Um, hmm," she responded. Her eyes showed thoughts of sensual consented sex with the one man that completely stimulated her.

"Was it everything you expected? Oh? Well, it'll be a lot better tonight," Tariq smiled.

"Waiter," Ursula shouted out as if in anxious anticipation of returning to their boudoir so that Tariq could hold true to his promise. Tariq laughed at her humor as she pretended to fan herself. The two engaged in a passionate kiss, despite being observed by the other patrons and as the waiter made his way over to their table.

9:47 PM, North New Braunfels and Wyoming St.

The flow of traffic down the busy boulevard had slowed. The dark side streets however, seemed to be abuzz with the movement of denizens. White sneakers or T-shirts could be seen shuttling back and forth across the streets. Jogging across lawns or running down alleyways, or backing away from cars after completing transactions. This was a "hot zone" where drug activity was prevalent and being observed by surveillance cameras.

Most of the dealers on this block were well known by the police and had been on the police crime files for quite some time, whether gang members or dealers. One such object of scrutiny was a young dealer who had moments earlier sold drugs to an undercover agent. He was wearing all black and en route to a rust colored LeMans as he counted his money.

Another kid, wearing bright colored clothing and having a distinctive studious mannerism was pushing buttons on a cellular phone as he walked out of a corner house. He kept looking around the area as if paranoid. To his right, the young dealer appeared nudging his shoulder and almost startling him.

"Little Jamie, what are you doing this time of night? And in this hood? Boy, you know your mom is going to be hitting your cell up because the street lights are on," the dealer stated as he placed his money back into his pocket. The kid looked around the vicinity at the drug dealers as he placed the phone back into his pocket.

"I got caught up in the moment. I didn't know it was this late. Man, I have to study for a test tomorrow. Shh," Jamie replied. At that moment a girl appeared at the door of the house he just left and called out his name.

"Jamie you forgot something," the girl called out.

The dealer looked back in her direction. Then Jamie jogged back to the door to retrieve what it was she had for him. He began walking back down the driveway still looking around cautiously as the smiling dealer examined him.

"Man, I see now why you are on this end. Hoo! She tight!" the dealer shouted.

Jamie smiled bashfully.

"You hitting? Huh? It's good, Little Jamie?" the dealer heckled. The dealer whistled across the street at another dealer. "Pete! Hit me man if that deal go through, business is moving man. I have to go replenish, you hear," he shouted.

"Holla at you, Little D," Jamie stated as he began walking down the street. But, he was halted by the dealer.

"Hold on, you can ride wit me. Man, you about twenty blocks away. Come on ride, man," the dealer offered as he retrieved his car keys. Looking down as he approached the LeMans, Jamie looked unsure. After some consideration, Jamie complied. He paused at the door, before inquiring," You aren't holding are you?" Jamie smirked.

"Come on Little Jamie. You just heard me say I'm out. Boy, you are green as hell. It's good to be that way though. Still playing that B-ball? the dealer asked.

"Yeah, I am going to get that scholarship," Jamie responded.

The dealer stated, "This street life is not what's happening. I'm just stuck out here. Door open."

 Jamie proceeded to climb into the passenger's side.

Meanwhile, the black and white patrol car was rounding the block. Its headlights illuminating the faces of citizens standing outside in yards and sent crack dealers in motion to stash their drugs as whistles came from up the block.

Inside of the patrol car the driver, a Caucasian man with brown hair talked over his radio, as his partner, a Hispanic man with mean features and a military haircut, sipped on a cup of coffee then bit into a donut. The driver's eyes scanned the derelicts encompassing the street and his eyes were primarily trained on the two pulling off in the rust colored Lamanz with 20" inch rims.

The LeMans' pulled away from the curb. The dealer was visible in every detail from the vantage point of the officers. His eyes checked cautiously the rearview mirror as the cruiser turned off on the street to follow them.

"Damn!" the dealer exclaimed. Jamie looked over in his direction with an expression of fear and confusion. His eyes pleaded for an explanation, but the dealer remained silent. His eyes stared back at the black and white with his hand firmly gripped to the steering wheel.

"Don't look back at them, man. They can see that shit," the dealer panicked. But Jamie wasn't listening. "You aren't dealing, so why are you panicking?" the dealer demanded. Jamies' expression was nervous as his eyes darted.

"Why are they chasing you? Wha…what's going on, man?" Jamie asked neurotically.

"Man, I don't know. I didn't do a mother fucking thing, man. Shit! I am trying to lose them. Fuck!" he stated while whipping the LeMans around a corner. Jamie was edgy and jittery as he continued to look back at the sirens. the dealer hit a curb causing the glove compartment to open. It revealed packets of pills and a loaded .32 caliber semi-automatic pistol.

"Oh, man! You have dope and a gun?! Shit!" Jamie exclaimed as he slumped in the seat. At that moment the patrol car's light flashed and caused the dealer to curse aloud and stomp on the accelerator.

"Suspect is fleeing on Wyoming, due East! He is presumed armed and dangerous!" the driver of the cruiser shouted into his police radio as he hit his own accelerator. This caused his partner to spill the remainder of his coffee as he attempted to brace himself.

The high-speed chase was all of twenty five seconds. The panicked dealer swerved to elude side swiping parked cars before turning sharply to another street. The tires screeched and the car's rear end nearly fish tailed. He stomped on the accelerator causing the LeMans to lurch forward and swipe a parked Volvo. Shards of glass scattered the concrete, as the police cruiser whipped in behind him. The dealer lost control of the car and swung into the back of another parked vehicle, which pinned his door, preventing from escaping.

The police car screeched to a halt and both officers withdrew their weapons. Inside of the LeMans, Jamie panicked and frantically pushed open the passenger's side door because he wanted to avoid a drug and weapons charge, or simply out of fear. All the while a terribly flustered dealer in the driver's seat looked back at the police lights and up at Jamie's fleeing shadow.

His sneakers pit patted through a puddle of water as he cleared the front of the car.

"Freeze!" shouted the Caucasian officer as he suddenly appeared at the front of the car. The dealer stared on shaking his head as the officer aimed his semi-auto in the direction Jamie ran. After a brief moment, the stocky built officer headed out in pursuit of Jamie as his Hispanic partner trained his weapon at the sulking dealer.

"Get your hands up where I can see them! Move, now!" the officer barked. The dealer disgustedly raised his hands in show of surrender. The Hispanic officer, armed with his weapon, back peddled to secure an observing view of the alley in which the kid and his fellow officer had run. Four reports of the officers' semi-automatic shattered the silence of the night.

There was an intense silence as lights from homes in the vicinity popped on and chained dogs in back yards began barking. The Caucasian officer casually walked back from the alleyway glancing at his confused partner as he began speaking into his radio in panted breaths.

"One of the suspects is down. I checked him and didn't feel any pulse, but send a mobile ambulance unit over anyway. Ten four." The officer then placed the radio back onto his hip and briefly locked eyes with his partner before averting.

"What happened in there, partner?" the Hispanic officer inquired while steadying his weapon at the dealer. His partner wiped sweat from his brow and began walking back towards the squad car. He continued to avoid eye contact as he held down his head. His weapon hung loosely at his side.

"He…he went for a weapon…it was dark in that alley. I had to open fire," the officer stated as he wiped a nervous hand across his face. His statement sounded deceptive and nervously premeditated. The expression on his partner's face as he watched him pass showed his recognition of this deceit as well.

Chapter 13

A late model Buick Le Sabre passed by. The sunlight on this hot and humid July day glistened off of the vehicles windows as a teenage youth dressed in baggy black jeans, sneakers, and white T-top entered into a pool hall. His hat, which was turned sideways, read: Lil Gun.

Inside of the pool room, several teenage boys congregated. The jukebox, which was juxtaposed with the door, was playing a rap song laced with lyrics pertaining to police brutality. The solemn expressions on the teenagers, as they related to the lyrics; especially with the recent murder of basketball standout James "Jamie" Smith at the hands of the police.

There were several who greeted Lil Gun as he entered. Each bore expressions of grief. Red Dawg, who sat quietly on a crate against the far wall, acknowledged him with a head nod. Bull leaned against the counter holding a 40 oz. bottle of beer and did the same. His expression was sordid.

Wild Bill wore a cast from a recent shooting incident and embraced Lil Gun with open arms. He took a sip off of his own 40 oz. then handed it to him.

"Lil Gun, what's up?" called out Braun. He held in his hand a pool stick. He was engaged in the game with Devonte' who also acknowledged the young gang member with a peace sign. At this moment Piye walked up and dapped him.

"How was New Orleans man? I know you were parleying with them creole girls," Wild Bill stated with a wide smile etched on his face.

He revealed the missing tooth that had become synonymous with Lil Gun's smile.

"Yeah man, the women were tight. They were tight. I love their accent." He mimicked the New Orleans slang and laughed. "They are about that gun play out there, though. Thought I was getting away from all that type of shit. Shiiit! It's worse, man," Lil Gun informed.

"No shit?" Bull stated as he sipped his beer.

"I thought you were staying all summer? Niggas ain't run ya, huh?" Red

Dawg stated jokingly. Everyone seemed to find humor in the statement.

"Run me?! Come on, main. Nobody runs Lil Gun, main. I came back because all this shit. I thought you all had let the fort fall. Niggas coming through busting at you all and shit. Busta ass nigga pop my boy Bill right here. I got them in a cast and shit. Damn. Then I heard about little Jamie, main, that's messed up. The little dude was probably going to college for that basketball."

"Yeah, that was messed up," Wild Bill retorted with his head down.

"So, you all handle that business with this busta ass nigga shot Bill?" Lil Gun inquired. He took another sip of beer before handing it back to Wild Bill. Devonte' glanced up into Bill's face before focusing on a shot.

"Main, that scary ass nigga probably left town. He did that shit out of fear, main," Bill replied.

"Who are the niggas that were coming through here blazing? You all handle that?" Lil Gun asked.

"That was Rider and Tre Dawg'nem. Niggas off Rigsby. They got into it with them niggas in the Park on Juneteenth. Bill flashed that chrome in Tre Dawg's face. Niggas come through that night. They didn't hit anybody though. We let them think shit was over for about two weeks rolled through on their ass," Red Dawg responded.

"How many did you all hit up, Red Dawg?" Lil Gun inquired with childlike enthusiasm. Red Dawg got up nonchalantly from his crate and strolled over to the pool table to retrieve the pool stick from Braun.

"I don't know. There were a lot of them out there. Fourth of July they are never going to forget. I had that Marsburg bucking," Red Dawg smiled, as he retrieved the pool stick. Braun expressed empathy at the callous conversation in reference to the genocide of his people. His heart was heavy at the thought of the mothers who no doubt wailed after receiving the news that their child had been murdered. The expression on Piye's face was evident that his feelings were mutual.

"Who got last ups? Alright, I'm next din. Say main, they say police shot little Jamie in the back, main," Little Gun stated. This comment caused nearly everyone in the pool room to speak and provide various scenarios of what might have happened.

"Yeah, main, those cops are out of control," stated Bull while folding his arms and sipping on his 40 oz.

Braun interjected, "That white cop and his partner are under investigation." Devonte' chuckled as he rubbed chalk over the tip end of his pool stick.

"Suspended with pay, huh? As usual," Devonte' retorted. "Combination six ball off the 'levin ball," he called his shot after a careful eye examination released. Everyone in that brief moment watched as the Q-Ball struck the six ball and pushed it into the eleven ball which fell into a side pocket.

"That's cold blooded. They gunned that little brother down and they get a paid vacation," Piye stated.

"What do you think they are going to do when they go to court?" Red Dawg inquired. There were negative sighs and comments bordering on sarcasm from the others when Piye spoke out.

"You know the answer to that, Red Dawg. The same thing always happens. The white cops who work in black neighborhoods that are crime ridden, they will always say they found guns and dope in the car. The D. A. will justify the need to shoot and will argue on behalf of the white cops and they will walk," Piye stated. The statistics of such scenarios were made obvious dozens of times during the course of the year throughout the United States. Being all too familiar with these statistics, none of the boys inside of the pool hall had any real confidence that justice would prevail in Jamie's favor.

Each nodded and reflected in silence before Devonte' positioned to take another shot and said, "Eight ball in the side pocket."

Inside of the confines of the Lodge, members of the O.B.U congregated. Dressed in their splendid African attire, the O.B.U. members were called to order for the purpose of addressing issues of concern, such as the current crisis in the Sudan, the politics relevant to their community, and the widespread of police brutality targeted at blacks in the community. One major issue of concern was the recent incident involving the shooting death of high school basketball standout, James "Jamie" Smith.

Jamie was a junior at Cole High School and star basketball player. It was known that he ran in panic from the police, but it did not justify their actions. They shot an unarmed youth under very questionable circumstances. The community was outraged and appealed for justice to the media and anyone who would listen. Most feared that the police would go unpunished for what was a case of excessive force. This has been the case in the past.

At the moment a middle-aged lady of caramel complexion and reddish hair was voicing her opinion emphatically about the recent incident and other issues. "Something has to be done. We cannot simply continue to sit idle while our youths are indiscriminately targeted by the police," she stated. Her voice was a high octave and her delivery eloquent and concise. Her comments drew nods of agreement to her implication of a unified effort of resistance.

"Yeah, they are supposed to be in the community to preserve and protect.

All these new laws were implemented simply as a way to harass our youths in the guise of cleaning up the community!" ranted Sadiq, a young brother in his middle thirties. His eyebrows furrowed and his delivery a fire brand as he arose to his feet. He looked around at the other constituents. The rank and file leaders who were seated behind the tables listened intently as they jotted down notes on legal pads.

"I believe everyone here tonight is appalled and outraged at the misconduct of the police. And, I know you are even more so at the miscarriage of justice when trying the police in a court of law, which has been displayed in the past. But what are the solutions? I mean, what can we do to prevent these types of situations from occurring in the future?" inquired the organization's president. His speckled grey hair, spectacles and dashiki gave him a dignitary appeal. Across from the president jotting down notes was Tariq. He looked up from his notes and took a sip of water before offering his own solutions.

"I think that we, as a community, should stop allowing law enforcement agencies to turn our neighborhoods into police states. We should stop allowing them to use vices like Sadiq mentioned to profile our youths. I believe that more intervention by the federal government is imperative in cases where excessive force is obviously an issue," Tariq concluded. The expressions on the faces of the constituents, including his wife Ursula was in direct agreement to his firm assessment.

A middle-aged man in a tan patterned shirt stood up and punched his fist in his open palm to stress emphasis.

"But what's it going to take for the federal government to bring investigations against these terrorist attacks? Because that's what they are, terrorists! It seems like every other week in this country, one of our black youths is gunned down by these predators! That legally blind boy in Denver, Paul Childs was an African American, fifteen year old male, was killed by Denver police on July 5, 2003. What about Timothy Thomas, the little high school kid in Cincinnati," he reported emphatically. His speech was momentarily interrupted by Somali's comment.

"And they took to the streets in 'Over the Rhine,'" Somali stated.

"That's right and I feel they had the right idea! A message has to be sent!" Sadiq shouted as he wielded a clinched fist and looked around the constituency. Only a few were in favor of what he was implying. As he sat down, Ursula spoke out against this irrational suggestion.

"Brother Sadiq, I feel, and I believe a lot of the others will agree, that rioting is never a solution to the problem. Now, I can understand your emo–

tions. All of us in here feel it when something like this happens. But, we have to be diplomatic with these matters," she stated assuredly. The man slouched in his seat. His body language showed his lack of support in her ideologies.

"So, what do we do? Take to the streets arm in arm singing we shall overcome?" another young man shouted.

"No. But we can't form militias and go killing officers either," Ursula shot back. Her remark to the man's reference towards the Dr. King Jr. inspired civil rights movement was being answered with her own self-evident disagreement with the later Pro-Black militant organizations that sprang up in the mid 1960's. These were organizations that had no political format to complement their militaristic practitioning.

Though the BPP (Black Panther Party) was perhaps the most visual radical group of the 60's, there were many more. Some mirrored what the Panther's objectives and initiatives were in its inception, while others were more clandestine or Afro-centric/Nationalistic in platform, such as the RNA. In the case of all these Pro-Black Radical factions, there were weaknesses in the infrastructure that caused their movement to be eliminated. These weaknesses varied with each organization. These weaknesses were pinpointed in a political science overview entitled: "Black Fighting Formations." Their strengths, weakness, and potential were detailed. In this constructive analysis of the radical 60's organizations, several factions were broken down and their strengths assessed. Also in this survey the BPP, BLA (Black Liberation Army), The Deacons for Defense and Justice, and RAM (Revolutionary American Movement) of the militant extremists to the more politically conservative groups such as S.N.C.C., and the NAACP were examined.

When analyzed, the Black Panthers and the Black Liberation Army were not adequately politicized. Each group was well equipped in terms of soldiers on the battlefield, but their lack of a real political formation lent them little stability to attack primary civil rights agendas, which was the initiative of the whole movement.

Even the Deacons who were a southern activist group and were well militarized, were lacking in the political formation. In reverse to this analysis of these militant formations, groups such as S.N.C.C., SCLC, and the NAACP were well politicized, but lacked the militaristic formation necessary to counter act violent resistance to their political agenda. And as a result, with the exception of the NAACP, these groups succumbed to the work and calculated blows of the FBI's Counter Intelligence Program.

Today, in this era of black advancement in the economical fields of the free enterprise system, there is still that same oppressive resistance and from the same sources. Although the days of the night riding Ku Klux Klansmen have seemingly vanished, the lynching of rural and urban youths continue through incessant new law enforcement aimed at the black community.

Much the same as the concerned denizens of the activist O.B.U., who were congregated on this day, concerned African American citizens around the nation were crying out for justice or formulating a feasible modus operandi to combat these malicious attacks. When the world witnessed the deadly rioting in South Central Los Angeles as a result of the Rodney King verdict, African Americans soon learned that this did not put an end to these attacks. In fact, they seemed to have heightened.

The ideological debate between the conservative Ursula and other members against the radical militant stances of others, continued on over the course of the next few minutes. Each argued their points to justify their reasoning and the debate became heated. The situation had tempers flaring among the constituents that the O.B.U. President decided it was proper for him to act as mediator and order the debate to cease.

"Okay. Okay. Let's keep things in perspective and not let our emotions overtake our good judgment. Let's just settle down and go over the facts. It is unclear as to the circumstances surrounding the shooting. It is obvious that the shooting is questionable because the two cops were relieved temporarily of their duties, pending an investigation. What we can do, instead of arguing, is show the media just how questionable this officer's judgment was. We must stress the fact that this studious, high school standout was unarmed, and hope that there will be a grand jury indictment," the president stated.

"What if there is no indictment? Or, if there is a trial what if they get acquitted?" inquired a very cynical Somali. There was a pause as the president interlocked his fingers and stared back at Somali.

"We will all just have to wait and see, Mr. Qusta."

✶✶✶✶✶✶✶✶

Braun stood before his mirror giving himself a once over. He was checking out his freshly trimmed haircut, Ecko outfit and tan Dada sneakers. It was Ikara's birthday and he had been granted permission to use his grandmother's brand new Mercury Grand Marquis to take her out.

As Braun swiped at the lint on his dark denim jeans, he was unaware that his grandmother, in a nurse's uniform, was at his bedroom doorway. She was doing some appraising herself. A smile etched across her brown face and her eyes revealed the love and pride she felt for the boy she raised as her own. As Braun began to leave, he was startled and laughed upon seeing his grandmother's visage. "Oh, hey Mah mah, I was just on my way out," he stated adjusting his baggy shirt once more. His grandmother patted him on the side of his face.

"You look more like your father every day. You even got his aura," she claimed as she adjusted his shirt. She ran her hand across his forehead. "It's almost six o' clock, baby. I have to be at work early to sort through all these charts. I'll ride home in the morning with Joanne, but I need you to take me. Remember, I trust you with my car, now. Please don't have any alcohol in my car and respect her and yourself tonight, okay?" she stated with concern.

"I know, Mah mah. I will always respect myself and others. You taught me that," he stated and kissed his grandmother on the side of her face. She smiled blushingly then fidgeted with her hands as she watched him disappear down the hallway.

Children of different ethnic groups scampered about at play. Little white girls sat side by side with little black and Hispanic girls. They played with their dolls outside and little boys enjoyed games of hoops from miniature portable basketball goals set up outside on the curb or raced their battery operated remote control cars down the long stretches of elaborate driveways.

As Braun turned onto the block to Ikara's cul de sac, he observed this cultural intervention. In his neighborhood, ethnic groups seldom interacted. Whites were seldom seen, which is ironic considering that San Antonio's eastside had at one time been populated by peoples of Germanic origin. Migrants from Europe during the World Wars had dominantly populated this area. Time and the push of African Americans into this section of the city forced these Germanic peoples to resettle north of the city in New Braunfels.

Braun slowed on the brakes to allow a blonde haired, Caucasian boy to retrieve his basketball. He watched for a few seconds as the kid resumed play with another white kid, a Hispanic, and two blacks. As he proceded on down the street to Ikara's, his mind entertained a reverie about his community one day being as utopian as this Live Oak setting. He imagined the gunshots and police harassment would cease and the racial resentment of inhabitants and business owners would discontinue.

He stood in front of the Galla family's large Africanized wood frame door and rang the bell with his right hand as his left held a tiny white Teddy Bear. He was slightly nervous as usual. They have been involved for over five months, but coming from his meager background he was intimidated and self-conscious by their wealth.

Ikara was putting on the finishing touches of her make up in the mirror when she heard the doorbell ring. She instinctively turned to the sound of the ringing doorbell and a smile etched her beautiful brown face. She was radiant and very womanly in appearance at her young age of sixteen. Her conservative, yet accentuating skirt ensemble and heeled boots gave her even more of a womanly appearance. She ran a hand through her silky black flowing hair then excitedly exited the room.

As Braun waited for someone to answer the door, he could hear movement and someone approaching the door. "Hey, boy you are early," Ikara greeted him in a soft sensual voice. Braun was taken aback by her stunning beauty and stood there for a brief second or two taking in her vibrant eyes, picturesque figure, glossed nails and her gorgeous smile. Finally he found the words to speak.

"Ikara, you look beautiful. Really, happy birthday," he stated nervously while extending the little white Teddy Bear. Ikara smiled graciously and retrieved the bear. She unexpectedly embraced him with a kiss, which was seen by her mother.

"Hello, Braun," Ikara's mom greeted after the two had disengaged from the brief, but passionate kiss. Ikara and Braun were embarrassed. They attempted to play it off, but it didn't detract from their neurotic movements.

"Oh, how are you doing, Mrs. Galla?" Braun responded.

Ursula couldn't contain her smile. She really liked Braun and felt that he was more suited to court her daughter than any of the others she had the misfortune of meeting.

"You can come in. I'll be ready in about five minutes, okay?" Ikara stated while glancing back at her mother as she spoke. She looked at Braun and laughed giddily. Braun accepted the invitation and proceeded into the air-conditioned large home.

"Would you like a piece of Church's chicken, Braun?" Ursula offered. The offer indeed sounded appetizing, but before he could respond Ikara's little brother Caleb came walking through the living room area where he was seated.

"Just don't give away the last drumstick. That's mine," he stated with a wide smile across his face. Braun smiled and dapped hands with the twelve year old.

"No thanks, Mrs. Galla," he responded.

"You sure?" she further offered while peeking her head around the kitchen wall at him. He assured her he did not.

"Let's go shoot some hoops, Braun," Caleb encouraged. He tugged at Braun's expensive pull over. Ikara appeared clutching a rather stylish Gucci purse as she placed a diamond stud into her earlobe. She also added a hint of sweet smelling perfume, which tantalized Braun's senses.

"Go play, Caleb. Braun doesn't have time to dribble a basketball. Smelly self. And go comb your hair," Ikara stated with a disgusted look at his un-kemptness.

"I have been playing ball all day. What do you expect? And how you know I am not growing dreadlocks? I'm a Rastafarian, Caleb stated in humor as he proceeded towards the door.

Ikara rolled her eyes and said, "Please. You can't even spell that. Let's go, Braun." Ikara placed a soft hand onto Braun's neck as he stood up. Caleb observed his big sister and the expression on his face showed that he was thinking of something sarcastic to say.

"She thinks she is grown now. Just because you are sixteen doesn't mean that you are grown. I bet you can't stay out past eleven," Caleb laughed.

"Caleb, leave Ikara and Braun alone. I thought you were going to go finish playing basketball," Ursula chastized from the kitchen.

"You always take her side," Caleb responded.

"And grow up," Ikara stated.

Caleb pretended to throw the basketball at her as they began to walk out the door.

"Good bye, Mr. Galla," Braun called out.

The hours would pass with the two enjoying each other's company. They went to the mall first, then a movie, and then onto eating at their favorite Taco Bell. It was not exactly a suave way to spend an evening, but they were teenage kids. They both were experiencing for the first time in their lives the sensation of being in love. They were totally consumed and enchanted with each other. It was euphoric and neither of the two "enchanted" lovers wanted the night to end. The night was still young. It was 9:20 p.m. to be exact, and both knew just how close it was to Ikara's 12 o' clock curfew. As the two sat in the front seat of the Grand Marquis a certain sense of urgency enveloped them. It was self-evident in each of their eyes.

What could this urgency be? Could it be that both had been experiencing strong sexual urges the entire evening and wanted to finally explore their secret fantasies of the other? For months they were sexually aroused only to have to restrain themselves. Ikara's nervous anxiety was due to her wanting to re-main chaste until she was certain she'd found the right guy. Braun's nervous-ness was due to his respect for her decision. But as they now sat in silence holding each other's hands and periodically staring into each other's eyes, emotions were overriding these reasons.

They were parked in a very secluded area around the city park and the sounds of the early night were coming in through the lowered windows. There was the periodic, unusual light wind blowing through that was sensual and the light from the moon, stars, and globes surrounding the park illuminated Ikara's Asiatic face. She gazed out at these beautiful constellations and was thinking to herself what a beautiful night it was. It was so ideal. She could sense Braun's fixation on her as he checked out her beauty and desired her sexually. The thought of them perhaps for the first time engaging in intercourse made her somewhat nervous. Her chest heaved slightly as she looked towards him.

"You're so beautiful, Ikara. And it's really special to be spending this time with you," Braun stated awkwardly.

Ikara smiled and turned to look away. She was fidgeting with her hands.

"I enjoy being with you too, Braun," she stated matter-of-factly, but still not making eye contact.

Braun reached into his pocket warranting her curiosity. As she examined what it was that he retrieved she began to breathe erratically. She smiled wider and her eyes became majestic. It was a small suede box. It wasn't open yet, but its content was obvious. Braun opened the box and retrieved the gold ring that was encased within. He held the ring out before Ikara's extended hand and slipped it onto her finger. Boys had offered her jewelry, outfits, etc. before, but even at her impressionable age she had good rationale. She refused their offers for the intent she knew was behind it. But Braun was different, and the sincerity of every gift he presented her made him all the more special to her.

"Happy Birthday Ikara," he whispered softly. Ikara smiled as she examined the ring and looked up into his loving eyes. In that instance she knew that he truly loved her and that they were soul mates.

"Thank you, Braun," she stated in an almost inaudible whisper that was controlled by emotion.

"I love you," Braun confessed as he leaned closer.

Ikara looked deep into his eyes and placed her dainty hand onto his face.

"I love you, too," she stated. The two began kissing passionately for a moment, then stopped. Both were breathing erratically as sexual impulses shot through their young bodies.

Braun was fully aroused and posed the question, "Do you want to go to my place?" His heart raced with high anticipation of her response. He had images of her soft, nude body being caressed by his hands as they made love extending his pulsating erection. After a pause, she responded with a nod. Her expression was timid as she nervously glanced down at his pants instinctively before looking away. Her chest heaved even more now. Braun caressed her face and forced her to look back at him. The two began kissing passionately once more.

The impassioned kisses which had begun in the front seat of the Grand Marquis continued on into Braun's room. The two were now seated side by side. Ikara's shirt was removed and Braun was kissing her shoulders softly. She seemed nervous and understandably so. The moonlight shown through Braun's bedroom window and highlighted her nervous expression and innocent doe-like eyes. He sensed her uneasiness. Braun stopped kissing her and stared at her. This caused her to glance briefly into his eyes before staring down at the floor.

"If you're uncomfortable with this, we can…" he whispered with a relaxing and assured tone, but was interrupted by Ikara.

"No…no, I'm okay. I'm ready. I want to," she confirmed. She stared into his eyes and undid her bra. She let it fall freely to the bedroom floor. Braun responded by removing his shirt. He gently reclined her back on the bed as the two began caressing and groping each other in ecstasy. They kissed passionately as Braun slipped off her panties and then pulled the sheets over their nude bodies.

Chapter 14

The houses on this particular block were adversely different from most sections. The shotgun style clapboard houses with sparse lawns and narrow yard space had given way to more spacious manicured lawns and well-kept homes. The drab visuals of junked out cars, dilapidated buildings and miscreants posted up with bottles of beer and weapons tucked under their shirts, had given way to stylishly decorated brick dwellings or colorful Spanish styled stucco. Braun decided to walk to his friend Piye's home. He was over two-dozen blocks away from his degenerative section, on Brice Street.

Braun walked through Piye's lawn and saw that he and Devonte' were lifting weights. Their shirts were off and both were exposing their physiques, which were dripping with sweat. You could see the effects of their strenuous workout the past thirty minutes on his steel weight bench set.

"Getting down, huh?" Braun asked Piye and Devonte'. Both gulped down bottles of Power Aid. Piye wiped the sweat from his brow and motioned with a hand towards the bench.

"What's up? I know you might use the walk up as a tired excuse, but come on get some of this," Piye stated. He slightly pushed Braun towards the bench. Braun smiled.

Piye was overly zealous about physical fitness.

"Let me cool off first. What's been goin on?" he asked as he took a seat on the bench.

Devonte' shook his head and released a sigh.

"Football coach got us out there with rigorous routines already. I'm straight, though. I have to make an impressive showing this year. You know that I switched to strong safety. I went up seventeen pounds and I got more hitting power now," Devonte' informed as he began curling the steel dumbbells.

"Are you all going to take state this year? Dallas Clark keeps a squad you know," Braun stated. Devonte' set down the weights.

"Too much speed and talent for them. Rocket fuel," he stated. Piye then patted Braun on the shoulder and motioned for him to get a set on the weight bench. After inquiring as to the amount (which was 185 lbs.) he laid back on the bench as Piye spotted him. He struggled to handle the weight at first but with a little gauging assistance from Piye he was able to bench press it three times. "You are getting a little strong there. You might hit two hundred. You always have to be ready. You never know when cops might come down on your head," Piye stated.

Braun got up shrugging his arms then felt his chest.

"I don't think muscles are going to do anything against police bullets. That's how they are coming. They aren't fighting. Shoot! I think I pulled something. How many sets you hit with that?" Braun asked looking back briefly at the barbell.

"That was my break down sets. I started out with everything on there, 310. Hit that ten times and start breaking it down. But I probably could hit that there forty times. That's paper to me, main," Piye stated after he continued back curling the dumbbells.

Braun sat there with a rather euphoric expression. It was obvious he was reflecting over something or someone and began to speak.

"I took Ikara out last night," he informed.

Piye continued curling.

"Yeah?" Piye responded as his face became contorted from the strain of curling the big 50 lbs. dumbbell. Devonte' smiled.

"Yeah, it was her birthday. We spent the whole day and night together practically."

They switched the subject to their friend Phil. Piye had been thinking about disassociating himself from him on several occasions.

"Man, Phil's playing the game more and more dangerous. Cartels? And Chatter? No doubt in my mind he got that name for more reasons than he talks fast. None of them dudes are straight. That's why I kind of disassociated myself from Phil," Piye stated.

Devonte' dropped his head. He knew that his cousin was in so deep that he could not turn back. In certain regards he empathized with the decisions Phil made. Although misdirected, Phil had confided in him that his primary reasoning for selling drugs was so that he could support his mother and siblings. He was their only source of income.

"We can't just disassociate ourselves from him. He is our friend, Piye. He is just not thinking straight right now," Braun stated. The other two remained silent. Braun began knocking on the hood of the car to simulate a beat, which caused Devonte' to begin nodding his head in anticipation of Braun's presentation of a fire brand rap. "Disease, misleads, police, cities under siege...we slang, we bang, genocidin' our communities...is all they see, medias out exploitin' me...but they can't see travesties from our poverties... its' more than just bling, it's more than just fame...cocaine to the otha main...put food on my table, main. Cause mom don't work...and sis need shoes...so I risk bein' a victim yellow taped on the evenin' news." Braun gave Piye insight into Phil's situation with a rhyme from the top of his head. "Are you feeling that?" Braun asked. Both Devonte' and Piye nodded their heads in agreement to the short but enlightening verse.

"Yeah, I'm feeling that. I mean don't get me wrong, I know how it is. We stayed down the street from you all, remember? I haven't been in the burbs that long, man. I come back every day. All I am saying is for the sake of his mom, for the sake of his little sister and brother, that he has to get out the game," Piye stated.

Devonte's eyebrows rose as he sipped on his Power Aid bottle and got up from the hood of the car.

"It might be kind of hard for me to ask him to do that. I mean, he is pulling down four to five G's a day. I can't get that working on roofs with you, Piye. And I sure can't get it working at Taco Bell with you, B. I have to get this car back before my mom starts tripping. Do you want a ride? I have to try not to lean back on the seat. It's kind of tart there, B," Devonte' laughed.

Braun pretended to take a swing at him causing him to recoil reflexively as he laughed.

"Nah, I'm going to stay here and run it with Piye," Braun replied. Devonte' climbed behind the steering wheel and closed the door leaving his two friends standing in the front yard. The streetlights began to pop on with the setting of twilight, which dissipated the effects of the scorching hot south Texas sun as a light breeze began to blow.

Tariq sat in his recliner chair with his feet propped, as he flipped through the newspapers as Ursula passed down the hallway. She commented about the spectacles he was wearing as he reads, to which he smiled aptly then stared at a headline caption which read: "Cocaine found in warehouse." Ursula continued down the hallway and stopped in front of Caleb's room. She peers in at him as he bobbed his head to music emitting from his headphones. He was oblivious to her presence. She smiled and proceeded down the hallway to Ikara's room. Inside the room sitting Indian style on her heart shaped bed, was Ikara wearing a long Mickey Mouse shirt. She was talking on the phone. A wide smile immersed across her lips. Leaning forward she brushes her long flowing black hair from her face as Ursula briefly observed. Sensing her mother's presence she turned, but she was gone.

On the other end of the phone were her two closest friends, Swathi and Sharon. Both were at their respective homes and dressed in similar bedtime attire at this late hour.

"We want to know everything now, Ikara. Come on."

"Yeah girl. Tell us the juicy details. Give us the real," Swathi and Sharon coaxed. Both were eager to hear the details of her night out with Braun. Ikara ran a hand through her hair again and repositioned herself on the bed. Her eyes mystified as she reflected back over the entire night. Her pulse quickening with arousal from the intimacy in which they had shared.

"Well, we had fun. He took me to the movies and we got a discount at Taco Bell," laughed. "And, we sat in the park and looked up at the stars," Ikara informed them, but tried to contain her hysterics at the vision of her two friends on the other end of the line. She knew they bore puzzled and sarcastic expressions. They weren't buying that being the only details of the night.

"It sounds like someone is holding back, again," Swathi stated. She pushed her glasses up on the bridge of her nose while shaking her silky hair.

"Girl, you know we are not buying that. You all did more than just star gaze. You might've seen some stars in that back seat," laughed Sharon. All three shared in laughter at her implied statement.

"You all are too much. And, no we didn't do anything in his grandmother's car," Ikara stated.

"Oh, so you all did do something? But, just not in the backseat of the car," Sharon heckled. Swathi struggled to contain her laughter. Ikara was silent for a moment as images of their love making session and the emotional ecstasy flashed in her mind. She experienced Braun's hands gently massaging and caressing her body and the thrill she had that night.

"Hellooo?" Sharon stated.

"I'm still here. God, I was doing something," she lied.

"Yeah, right. You were thinking about that night."

"I know Braun was working it. Shh. Six months too?" Sharon stated.

"So come on with the details. Gosh. This suspense," Swathi stated. At that precise moment Ikara's phone line buzzed and she had to excuse herself. Clicking over, she was greeted with the voice she could stand hearing twenty four hours a day. It was Braun. And her face ignited with glee at the sound of his voice and the thought of his handsome face.

"Oh, hi Braun. I wasn't expecting you to call back so soon," she said softly while curling up on the bed now and running her dainty hand the length of her leg before bringing it to rest on her feet.

"I was thinking about you, so I called," Braun stated. He was lying across his bed bare chest staring up at a picture of her. Upon hearing these sentimental words, Ikara blushed Meanwhile, on her other phone line, her two friends grew impatient. Sharon guessed who the caller might be.

"Braun, hold on one second, okay? I got Swathi and Sharon on the other line," she informed him. Braun smiled while his mind raced with case scenarios of just what conversation they might be having. Ikara clicked back over and said, "Hey, you all, look, that's Braun sooo... I will like, get back with you all much later."

"See, I told you it was Braun. You are going to be on that phone all night now," Sharon stated in frustration.

"Yeah and leave us in suspense," Swathi added.

Ikara laughed, "Bye, you all." A smile was etched on her beautiful face. She ran her hand through her hair as she reclined on the bed. Her expression changed instantly from one of giddiness to one of sensuality. In a soft seductive voice she spoke out to him, "Braun? Okay, I'm back."

✴✴✴✴✴✴✴✴

Traffic zoomed by on the avenue. A shadow loomed overhead on this picturesque mid-August day from the clouds, which had temporarily concealed the sun.

In an instant, the eclipse from the cumulous clouds had vanished and the sun was once again reflecting the glare from the glass and chrome of these vehicles passing the buildings downtown. One building in particular, which the sun reflected on, was the police headquarters. Through the glass doors of this modernized building, blue uniformed clad San Antonio Police scuttled to and fro. Some ushered in suspects whose modus ranged from DUI's to simple assault. Some suspects were hardcore looking Mexican gang members. Their expressions were non-complacent. Their chests, shoulders, and arms revealed some of the most elaborate tattoos. Their charges as the police officers corralled them would convey to shirt and tie clad detectives, ranging from gun possession, to intimidation, to vagrancy. Past this scene of stone faced bangers and other arrested miscreants who argued their innocence in vain to the contesting of police officers, were detectives and special agents diligently at work behind desks. The sound of computers and fingers tapping on keys playing rhythmically in accordance with the talking, shouting, and arguing reverberated around the precinct. The detectives and crime lab experts seemed to be oblivious to all the noise as they talked on cellular and office phones and sipped coffee and typed up paperwork.

Inside of their office, another branch of the precinct's law enforcers, the Drug Task Force, sat in silence as they carefully reviewed a surveillance tape. The tape which was extracted from a concealed enclosure and revealed incriminating drug transactions done from the vicinity of an eastside night club. This club was incidentally owned by one Dorele Jackson.

The surveillance camera recorded activities day and night of the vicinity; the suspects under surveillance were completely unaware that their incriminating activities were being monitored. Some scenes recorded were dealers callously running up to cars, counting money after consulting for several seconds with obvious crack addicts, holding pistols in their hands in plain view; and tossing plastic contained substances (presumably crack) into weed grown areas across the street at the sight of approaching patrols.

Occasionally, in such instances, the head agent would pause, rewind, and blow up the scene in slow motion as the other task force operatives looked intently. Most of the surveillance suspects were already in the crime files and warrants had already been typed up. Others were not familiar and their partially obscured faces on the semi-hazy black and white video were unrecognizable until tracked and blown up. One such dealer was Phil.

Dressed in a white T-shirt, black shorts, and white Nike Air Force Ones, Phil's smiling visage was shown standing next to Johnny Black. Both were exposing their gold teeth as they conversed as a slow moving silver SUV came into view and stopped in front of them. The vehicle obscured them from view. At this interval the task force agents with dead panned expressions intently observed the screen as other hip-hop clad, jewelry adorned dealers came into view, either crossing the street to the club or boarding expensive cars. The SUV pulled away.

As the officers examined further, Phil began walking away from the dark clad Johnny Black. He was counting bills as he walked up into the parking space area of the club where Dorele and some females now came into view. Inaudible words were exchanged and Phil began trotting to the edge of the parking space. There were several vagabond attired crack addicts who were being handled by a young dealer. The dealer was brandishing a bottle of beer and walked away as Phil approached. The task force agent zoomed in as Phil conversed with the two addicts. His face was now visible, especially after the headlights of a car turned the corner and illuminated his face. The vehicle sped down the dark street past row after row of dilapidated dwellings. Phil reached into his pocket and pulled out a packet and removed white rocks, one of which incidentally fell to the pavement. It was retrieved immediately.

The agents smiled haughtily as they exchanged meaningful glances, surprised that the dealers would be so reckless. The incriminating evidence was overwhelming. It would be difficult for Phil or any of the other dealers on film to argue the conspiracy case against them in a court of law.

"This is modern day surveillance technology, ladies and gentlemen. I'd love to see a defense attorney argue these cases," stated the head task force agent while sipping a cup of steaming coffee. The other agents laughed at his humor and continued viewing the video with the utmost concentration at the trafficking being done in plain view at the nightclub.

Tonight was parent's participation night at the community center. This gathering was recently implemented by the two founders, Tariq and Mr. Nawaz Jinnah. It was created in response to the escalating police assaults, drug dealing and gang activities. In a show of concern, the parents were asked to attend in order to for these issues to be presented to them.

Tariq and Nawaz did not anticipate this huge turnout of concerned parents. The main auditorium of the community center was filled to its capacity. As Tariq took to the podium, his eyes swept the room and observed the expressions of the interested parents. He was eager to learn the thoughts of the youths who ranged in ages from eight to eighteen.

Seating the constituency and facilitating them with refreshments were Somali, Ursula, Somali's wife, and other regular volunteer workers. Those in attendance ranged from junior high and high school teachers to instructors. Everyone took time out of their busy schedules once a week to reach these striving youths and to assure them there was a chance at academic excellence and a future in corporate America. They wanted to remind them of the dream that Dr. Martin Luther King, Jr. had and spoke so passionately about. Also, to remind them of what he died for as well as the many other activists, such as Medgar Evers, during the civil right movements.

Tariq tested the microphone he was gripping. This was a signal that the presentation was about to begin and to simmer down the murmurs which reverberated through the vast auditorium.

Tariq opened up his speech saying, "Ladies and gentlemen, concerned parents and students alike, I would like to first thank you all for coming. This presentation is only scheduled for an hour. The agenda will proceed as routine. So, without further a due, as I look at my watch it's a quarter till, I'd like to proceed." He looked out at the audience and saw their expressions were of great anticipation and interest. After a brief pause in which he sipped a glass of water, he began to speak.

From the start Tariq made it clear and self-evident that the community, the black community in the nation as a whole, was in a state of emergency. Academic literacy percentage among African Americans was down, drug influenced crimes among African Americans was up, anti-crime bills targeted at minorities was up, and police assaults and profiling of minorities, primarily blacks, was up as well.

As he spoke impassioned about the education and crime demographics, he studied the expressions on the faces of the audience. Most of them appeared to be hearing this information for the first time. Looks of surprise were displayed on their faces when Tariq made comparisons in ratio between blacks, Hispanics, whites, and others in the criminal justices spectrum. He informed them that African Americans, who comprise of only 13% of the overall U.S. consensus, account for 44% of the prison population. When carefully analyzed, this statistic is not necessarily a reflection of the percentage of crimes committed by African Americans in comparison to other ethnic groups. It is however, a reflection of indemnities incurred during judicial procedures involving white Americans who are charged with felonies. In these same judicial procedures with the same offenses charged to the African Americans, they receive stiff prison sentences. During his presentation he also covered the imperativeness for the African American people to put forth a unified effort to stop this trend. He encouraged them to curb this criminal tendencies of the black youths before they could place themselves in the position to receive disproportionate sentences for crimes in which their white counterparts would have received probation. Tariq believed that it was not effective to elect figures because there were more - partial towards minorities instead of condescending bias in favor of Caucasians.

He spoke with such passion and fervor that his speech was met with applauds and verbal shouts of agreement from males and females alike. Some rose to their feet and looked around for complacency as they clapped. Tariq brought his speech to a close by covering a topic, which as of recently, was very familiar to everyone: police brutality. He urged for the black community to come out in response to the recent shooting death of James "Jamie" Smith.

He disclosed the facts pertaining to James' scholastic achievements and appealed to the human emotion and nationalistic views of the constituency. He pointed out that an unarmed, black seventeen year old was shot four times. All the bullet wounds were to his back, arm, and lower torso. This evidence made it extremely difficult to pose any danger to the officer in pursuit even if he had been armed.

Tariq knew very well that during court procedures that the defense attorney would certainly play upon the drugs and weapon found inside of the vehicle the night of the shooting incident. The attorney will try to bias the jury's concept of James by creating a picture of him as a violent threat. Over the years he saw officers walk in cases where the victim, much like young James, was not only unarmed, but who had a clean record.

"In closing, before we continue on with our regularly scheduled agenda, and parents you can now actually see how our curriculum here works, I'd like to urge all of you to be more involved in the community. Let your voices be heard. Let it be known to the law enforcement, the government, the allies, whomever, that we will not, we cannot stand for any more profiling. Or worse, we will not accept our youths like young James Smith to be summarily executed at the hands of the entity that were sworn to protect us. Thank you." After Tariq's impassioned sign off, which registered an enthusiastic applause, the constituents rose and the volunteers began setting back up the auditorium to be more conducive to a tutelage forum.

Chapter 15

The room was dimly lit with only a beaming light from a lamp that had an ominous aura to it. The contorted expression on the face of the disgruntled detective made it even more ominous. His name was Detective Larusso. His furrowed brow, close cropped reddish brown hair and mean looking blue eyes gave him a fearsome look.

Clad in grey slacks, a white shirt and tie, Detective Larusso carefully interrogated the suspect who sat before him. His blue eyes were piercing and caused the suspect to avert eye contact and to shift slightly in his seat. The suspect appeared to be in his teens, although he could have been older. His platinum chain swayed as he moved. His hand, with a diamond ringed fingered, shook nervously as he wiped his hand across his face. This was all too familiar with the detective. The suspect's name was Anthony Pierce, a.k.a. "Chatter."

"Business seems to be booming on the block, Anthony," Detective Larusso smiled. His eyes registered a different emotions because he hated drug dealers. He had complete disdain for them and even more disdain for blacks.

Chatter remained silent and shrugged his shoulders. He stared the detective in the eyes. Chatter hated the detective's theatrics and he was beginning to experience anxiety.

"This can't be just routine reporting that he wants?" Chatter wondered to himself. He would be called in for information pertaining to drug sales, pick up times, and drug related homicides where there were no suspects. But this was something different, he figured. And, his anxiety continued to grow.

"What are you getting at detective? You are making me nervous with all the theatrics, main," Chatter stated, with fear in his fear in his eyes.

"No need to get nervous on me now, Mr. Pierce. I thought you were a thug. Ride or die. Isn't that what you people say?" the detective stated sarcastically.

Chatter remained silent as his mind raced with possible scenarios. The detective pulled a cigarette from his pack of Marlboros and offered him one.

He declined. After lighting the cigarette and blowing a funnel of smoke in Chatter's direction, he reclined back in his chair and carefully scrutinized him. He reached into a desk drawer and removed several surveillance photos. He tossed them onto the top of the desk.

Chatter eyed the first photo with great interest. He instantly realized now what the detective's urgency was at calling him down this time. The photos were that of a black tinted, black colored Mercedes Benz parked outside of a warehouse at an angle in front of a black Lincoln Navigator. The detective then flipped the photo and uncovered the second one, which featured a Mexican featured man getting out of the Mercedes. He wore dark shades, a light colored Versace shirt and black pants. In his hands he clutched something. Though the crime lab had blown it up, it was yet determined what the item was. In any event, the next several photos revealed him extending the device or packet to the driver of the Navigator, who happened to be Chatter before he got back into the Mercedes Benz. Both vehicles proceeded to pull away from the warehouse parking lot.

Chatter looked down at the pictures in astonishment and tried to figure out how the pictures could have been taken in this remote area without any of them noticing. But this pondering in its insignificance was far outweighed by the reality of what had been found inside of the warehouse by federal agents just hours later, which was over $3,000,000 worth of powder cocaine.

After a moment of Chatter staring at the pictures dumbfounded, the detective plucked ashes from his cigarette and stared quizzically at him before posing his next question.

"What do you know about these pictures?" he inquired with a cynical expression. He knew that Chatter knew everything about them and what was inside of the warehouse. Chatter's mind raced with possible deception to justify his association on film with a known drug lord from Mexico City in front of a warehouse that had been stuffed with kilos of cocaine. He could not find any and his only response was shaking his head as he envisioned going away to a federal penitentiary.

"Huh? I can't hear you," the detective stated sarcastically. He knew Chatter could not and would not answer. He decided to make Chatter a business proposition that he couldn't refuse.

The case would fall under the Racketeering Influenced and Corrupt Organization Act (R.I.C.O. Act), in which the violations include any act or threat involving murder, kidnapping, gambling, arson, robbery, bribery, extortion, dealing in obscene matter, or dealing in narcotic or other dangerous drugs. All of these violations are chargeable under the law and punishable by imprisonment for more than one year. In Chatter and the Mexican adjutant's case, it exceeded much more.

Under section 960 of the Criminal Code of Procedures, Prohibited Acts A-unlawful acts-any person who-contrary to section 952, 953, or 957 of this title, knowingly or intentionally imports or exports a control substance exceeding (in the warehouse case) 50 grams or more of a mixture or a substance (described in subparagraph B on the Criminal Code) which contains cocaine base, shall receive a sentence not less than 20 years, and not exceeding life.

Chatter was well aware of the R.I.C.O. statures and nervous beads of sweat began forming on his forehead.

"Federal agents found over $3,000,000 worth of cocaine. 50 grams could get you a life sentence and these pictures are evidence that you had knowledge of there being cocaine in that warehouse. It will be pretty goddamn tough to fight it in a federal court," the detective stated. His eyes were piercing into Chatter, who continued looking down at the floor. "Now, I know you're just a pusher. You're not the one importing the narcotics into the country. But, you have connections with the big man," the detective led. Though he is only considered an informant, Chatter feared for his own safety in doing what the detective was implying. He looked up with a timid expression and struggled to make eye contact. After starting to rebut, he ended up looking away.

"I don't know what you are talking about. The dude just wanted us to meet there." His deceptive rambling was interjected by the cynical detective.

"Cut the bullshit, Pierce! You're fucking looking at life in Lewisburg and you're all of a sudden applying some twisted street code to save this Mexican's ass! He's already got warrants pending and the federal government is prepared to indict his ass here and extradite him from Mexico on trafficking! He's no longer diplomatically immune! We've had him on file for a fucking decade! So keep playing this street code ethics bullshit and you'll find yourself in Marion!" The detective seethed as he pointed a finger in Chatter's face. The dealer was visibly shaken and unable to speak. After a brief moment he began to speak. His words were muffled and nearly inaudible prompting the detective to once again sarcastically ask him to speak up.

"What do you want me to do?" Chatter responded.

The detective nodded his head. His expression still of fury and disdain for the black drug dealer as he reclined once more in his chair.

"It's simple. All you have to do is testify in front of the Federal Grand Jury," the detective stated. He folded his hands behind his head as he scrutinized Chatter to read his reaction.

Chatter spoke up, "Where am I supposed to live? He has hit men-for-hire-n-shit. My mom is still living, main," Chatter pleaded. The detective, still with a cynical look, put out his Marlboro cigarette and leaned forward.

"The Feds will take care of everything."

✳✳✳✳✳✳✳✳

The twilight hour was on the verge of setting in. The sky above the grey concrete mission that is the Alamo, began to turn a pinkish hue as the bright orange globe of the sun sets below the horizon. Stratus clouds added a touch of picturesque beauty as various breeds of birds cut through the sky. All the while the lights on the steady flow of traffic began to beam on.

Blocks away on the eastside, the scene was usual for this time of the evening. Children of various age ranges played games or hung about in front of their homes soaking up the final minutes of daylight. They were dreading their guardian's arrival at the door with commands, which of course would be that the youths adjourned inside. Going indoors at this time would lessen their risk of being in the possible line of fire in the event rival gangs came rolling through. It was not uncommon for junked out cars to come by with windows rolled down and shotguns pumping, pistols firing, and automatic machine guns spraying indiscriminate missiles of death.

Adversely, those of this subculture existence and whose position placed them more directly in the line of fire were posted up at various junctures around the neighborhood. Gang members dressed primarily in all black with weapons either concealed or tucked away alongside buildings or cars. They were easily accessible in the event the enemy appeared. Their gang affiliation was only distinguishable by belts or the color of their hats. Their precise sects were self-evident by cryptic graffiti displayed on the sides of buildings and stores.

Phil's block was no exception to the rule. The four friends, which included Braun, Devonte', Piye, and Phil sat outside of Phil's front porch. The same scenes described were evident, but they were used to these sights. Their ears were always to the streets receiving inside knowledge of possible gang retaliation hits and almost having a sixth sense so to speak, of such occurrences. Tonight seemed calm and the boys were somewhat relaxed as they loosely conversed about the day's events, which incidentally included a dog fight exhibition.

Dog fighting was appalling and shocking to the senses of animal humane societies. They urged the enforcement of stiff federal penalties to owners of these animals who maliciously endangered their lives for gambling purposes.

Many times these animals would be severely injured, or even killed during these fights.

Phil, who was massaging the neck of his pit bull, Terror, had entered his dog into the competition. After minutes of vicious growling, lunging attacks, dirt flailing, blood and malicious locking by Terror, Phil felt compelled to stop the fight. The other dog was unable to continue due to serious wounds. This had not been looked at sympathetically by those who had gambled on the dog and lost. They were not concerned with the possibility that the dog could die from his serious injuries. Their arrogant and indifferent attitude appalled activists even more so.

"Jody was hurt bad," Braun commented.

Phil at rubbed the arm of Terror, as he glanced back over his shoulder with an unsympathetic expression.

"He's alright. He was like that the last fight they had. Shh. Terror was fucked up too from that fight," Phil stated as he turned his attention back to to Terror.

At that moment laughing could be heard down the street garnering the four boys' attention. The laugh came from Wild Bill. He and his gang had posted up in front of Red Dawg's house. Bill's smiling visage was highlighted by a thumping Escalade's headlights, which rounded the corner. To their left, four houses down, crack addicts were seen coming out of a boarded up crack house.

Braun's expression was of empathy as he reflected over the serious condition of the dog, Jody, and elaborated on his earlier assertion. "I don't know, man. He looked hurt, a lot worse than last time. He doesn't look like he is going to make it," he stated.

Phil looked quizzically at him then smiled as he climbed the steps to his front porch.

"Main, you sounding all sad and shit. You haven't turned into one of them animal rights activists, huh?" Phil laughed, as he took a seat on the porch. The others smiled at his humor, although Piye also held concern for the well being of the dog.

"What do you all have on the agenda for the night? Devonte', I know you got a lineup of hoes. I mean females for the night," Phil stated as he reached for the 40 oz. Devonte' held.

"Man, you are the one with the Lexus on Choppers and all the cheddar. I have got me thinking about trying my hand at the game. I have to work too hard to get the panties, know what I'm saying? This nigga doesn't have any game and got all the females, jewels and cars tawk," Devonte' stated. Both

Piye and Braun smiled as they looked away. Their eyes might have been suggestive of their mutual disagreement to Devonte's unconscious glorification and justification to sell drugs. Both gave him the benefit of the doubt that he'd never degenerate to that level.

"Main, you don't have to sell drugs. Auntie 'Vonne buy you everything you want. She's a what? Colonel? Shh. She has the cheddar," Phil stated matter-of-factly in rebuttal as he sipped on the 40 oz. beer. Meanwhile inside of the house, Phil's mother nervously placed a crack pipe into a purse. The twilight had now transformed to an opaque blue and the settling humidity seemed to give rise to huge mosquitoes which were dormant in the grass and thickets that periodically landed on the boys who'd frantically swiped at them.

"Damn, these are some big a mosquitos!" Devonte' stated.

Phil remained staring down the street. He caught a glimpse of Wild Bill and his gang members and a drug dealer posting up beside a building. He could see the drug dealers gold chain swaying, running down the street as he flagged down a couple riding in an old Chevy Impala. Two of the community's prime ailments in the disease of gentrification, which destroyed the neighborhood's cell structure, were that the immune system was already weakened by the plague of socio economic repression, and African American profiling by the police.

After a brief pause for reflection, Phil revealed exactly what had been on his mind. "Main, game isn't all it's cracked up to be, Devonte'. Man, Piye, I been understanding why you distant all of a sudden. And I am not messed up with you. Shit is serious. You know I like jewels, hot cars and females. But, it isn't all about that. I have to be out there. You feel where I'm at?" He pleaded while examining the expressions of his friends. The boys remained silent anticipating that he was going to speak further. "Shh. I wish I didn't have to. I wish I would have, like, had a scholarship. I would be going to college and make something out my life. But, the game has gotten fucked up. I don't know who to trust except you all," he stated emphatically. His eyes were full of regret. Before he could continue, his mother appeared at the door with her hair unkempt, appearance fatigued, and wearing a gown and slippers.

"Phil, I need you to take me to Sandra's. Shoot, I have to get me some… Oh, hey, Braun. I didn't know you all were out here. You all have to excuse how I look, you know," she stated while trying to smile. Braun looked at Phil's emaciated mother with her ashen dark skin and sunken eyes. It was obvious that she was under the influence of heavy narcotics and was seeking another hit. Phil's expression was of embarrassment. He knew that his mother was going to Sandra's to get high and to escape from her dismal reality by inhaling a toxicant that would eventually kill her.

"Momma, just go back inside. Why are you embarrassing me like this?" Phil stated as he rose to his feet.

"I need you to take me to Sandra's," she stated once more and looking neurotic as a wave of addiction creased her. "What do you all have? I know you have something. Give me something," she pleaded as she clutched at her purse. Phil was stricken with anger and grabbed her by her arms and shook her. Piye and the others intervened, but, not before he had wrested her purse away and shattered the crack pipe he extracted from within by slamming it on the concrete walk way. The splattering glass caused the dogs in the vicinity to bark and people to peer out of their windows.

In her addicted and delusional state of mind, Phil's mother stared at the broken glass. For a moment she made an advance down the steps before turning to swing at Phil. After deflecting her feeble punches, Phil had to corral her. She cursed while attempting to make a beeline for a young crack dealer who was walking by. This caused her to crumple down on the concrete steps and scar her knees. She clutched her knee in pain as Phil held her. A police cruiser rolled to a stop causing the dealer to flee through the adjacent houses as one of the officers flashed a light on them.

"Is there a problem here?" called out a detached voice.

Braun squinted his eyes and held up a hand before his face in an attempt to shield his eyes from the intense light.

"No, officer. She is sick. We are just trying to get her to the hospital," Braun deceived. The patrol car idled there for a brief second when the flashlight dimmed as the police cruiser slowly pulled away from the curb. The officers exchanged meaningful glances at each other before looking back cynically at Phil and his mother. As the cruiser advanced further on up the street, Braun dejectedly turned back to the embarrassing spectacle that his friend was enduring. He shook his head then released a sigh of anguish. He made eye contact with Piye while Devonte' joined his cousin in consolation of his aunt who was quivering and moaning as if in pain. She was moaning not from the injury, but from her anxiety and physiological craving for the narcotic she so desperately sought. Braun was emotionally stricken.

****

Tariq was cruising the traffic congested 410 after a day at the telecommunications service. Instead of heading to his rather posh home in his rather middle class neighborhood, he did what he most often, which was to take a less than scenic route to his O.B.U. brother's Somali's home. He had to drive through the degenerative section of the eastside where he had grown up.

Passing by stores and boarded up houses, his eyes were bombarded with the elements of gentrification, the disease that is present in most lower class African American communities. These people were injected there by the systemic modems of racial profiling and oppression by the government and made to spread by the unconscious, self-destructive activities of the inhabitants in the communities themselves. In these communities there were self-destructive activities such as drug sales, prostitution, black on black violence, and vandalism.

Turning on Montana Street, which was parallel to the avenue he took to Somali's home, he spotted what he deemed to being one of the elements of this gentrification, Wild Bill's gang. Rather than pass them up without acknowledging them, like so many other self-proclaimed black activists, did. Tariq slowed down to lecture them.

Upon seeing his approaching vehicle, the members of Wild Bill's gang began straightening themselves up. Bull pulled his large T-shirt down over his pants to better conceal the weapon he was carrying. Lil Gun passed the 40 oz. bottle of beer he was holding to Red Dawg who looked at him quizzically. Wild Bill, the gang's front man, began smiling and clasped his hands together as he approached Tariq's car. And Rocco, who sat on the hood of a car, hid the marijuana joint he was in the process of puffing.

As Tariq rolled down his electric window and turned off the air conditioning system, Wild Bill extended his hand. His face bore a warm smile that was superseded by the look of respect emanating from his eyes. Although he was considered a hardened gang member by the media and society, Wild Bill like many others involved in the subculture of street ethics, nevertheless held community activists in high esteem. He especially respected the ones such as Tariq who came back to the community and put forth political and economic efforts to uplift the neighborhoods they made an exodus from.

"Brother Tariq. How are things, man?" Wild Bill greeted while clasping hands with Tariq before folding his muscular arms. His bald head glistened in the intense desert like sun rays.

"Ah, I'm doing okay for a black man battling the odds with the system. I see you've got Christopher with you. Are you ready to go back to school, Christopher?" Tariq inquired. Intentionally agitating Lil Gun by referring to him by his real name. Lil Gun smiled as the others found humor in it. Repeating the name, Tariq would always do this.

"Lil Gun, Brother Tariq," Lil Gun corrected while bearing a wide smile as he shook his head. Tariq nodded as if he didn't know his gang moniker then returned his focus to the older Wild Bill.

"So, Bill, you still have no incentive to get out of this lifestyle? Every week young brothers are being carted off to jail or covered up in white sheets," Tariq stated.

Wild Bill looked away briefly as he changed his expression. He shook his head as he turned back to Tariq.

"I'm hard lined, Brother Tariq. Put in too much work. I could put my guns down and go into seclusion a year and come out preaching the gospel. I could get caught slipping in the wrong hood and some young fool is going to rip off downing me," Wild Bill stated. Each of the gang members nodded and commented in agreement. Tariq gripped the steering wheel and stared down the block. Wild Bill's response was typical, but also factual. Tariq grew up in the neighborhood and knew the gang culture. He also knew that certain gang members (O.G.'s) were hunted like Saddam Hussein because of their notoriety in connection to the slayings of rival gang members.

"Does that mean you have to continue riding? All of you? Selling drugs in the community and poisoning our own people? No, I understand that you have enemies and perhaps you feel uncomfortable not carrying a weapon. But, you can become a part of our organization and help in the community. You can receive a salary and still bear arms," Tariq stated.

"A dashiki is not going to stop them fools from trying to put a slug in my chest. Those fools don't want to hear about Africa uniting. You know that, Brother Tariq," Bull stated. His dark face was non-complacent but honest.

"A vest will not protect you either if you remain in the streets young brother. There are other alternatives," Tariq stated as he put the car in park.

"What alternative is that? There are no jobs and the cops are coming down on us every day. The fools are rolling through blasting," Red Dawg enlightened.

Tariq smiled, "You just further gave examples of why you should redirect your life, Red Dog. Opportunities are available. There are technical colleges or the job corps to help you get a job. If you go to one of these, you won't be in the constant position to be harassed by the police or visible for shooters coming through. Think about it. Throw what you were about to smoke away, Robert," Tariq directed Rocco startling the boy. He rolled up his car window and pulled away from the corner leaving the five gang members to ponder his words as they stared at his vehicle.

Tariq passed by Braun's home, who incidentally was outside practicing his raps as Devonte' listened. They waved as Tariq blew his horn. Tariq neared the stop sign at the end of the intersection directly across from Mr. Gonzales's store. He glanced over and spotted Mr. Gonzales outside conversing with a man whom looked familiar. Tariq was sure he had seen this man before. His mind raced to recall exactly where. Then it came to him. He was the Hispanic officer who was interviewed on the late night news the night his partner killed James Smith. Tariq made a mental note to question Mr. Gonzales.

Tariq now stood outside of Somali's front door observing, as he often did, the contrasting differences of this neighborhood in comparison to Braun and Phil's neighborhood. The neighborhood sections were clearly defined between lower class and middle class. After a few moments of waiting, the large African inspired designed oak wood door to Somali's brick home opened up. There stood Somali smiling. His black face was a welcome sight to Tariq. His dashiki and kufi displayed his strong cultural awareness. After a warm embrace, Tariq entered the house and took a seat on one of Somali's leather black sofas. Observing the African artifacts, he admired the tropical jungle coordination with elephant plants and leopard patterned rugs.

"What brings you over, my brother? I have some lemonade if you care for some," Somali offered as he was in the process of sitting down. After Tariq acknowledged his desire for the lemonade, Somali disappeared into the kitchen.

"Since when do we have to have special agendas to drop in on one another? We're brothers," Tariq called out. He continued to look around the artistically decorated living room.

Somali laughed as he poured the lemonade into a large glass.

"No, of course not, my brother. You never need an agenda. Here you go," Somali stated as he returned to the living room extending Tariq a glass of lemonade. Tariq thanked him and began sipping the beverage. He set the glass down onto a coaster on the coffee table when he began to speak. His eyes were reflective and his tone serious, although a smile creased his lips. All the while, Somali leaned forward with an intensely interested expression as he spoke.

"I was patrolling, so to speak, through the old neighborhood. I spoke to a few of the gang members and happened to recognize this Hispanic individual who was talking to Mr. Gonzales. He is the store owner over on Montana Street," Tariq explained.

Somali's eyebrows furrowed and he placed a hand underneath his chin. His eyes darted in their dark sockets as his mind grappled with the direction

Tariq was going. "And my mind raced with recollection of where I'd seen this individual. Then it dawned on me that he was the officer that interviewed the night the Smith boy was killed," Tariq finished.

"The officer who killed the boy under questionable circumstances. This was his partner?" Somali inquired. Tariq confirmed that he was correct. The two sat in silence reflecting over the newscast that had been aired that night. Both were reliving the images of the police cruisers' flashing sirens and onlookers who gathered outside of that alley. The onlookers stood around in hopes of catching a glimpse of yet another victim of the police's excessive force as the ambulance attendants removed the body. "So, what do you think their conference was about?" Somali finally continued. Tariq's eyebrows furrowed as he shook his head.

"I don't even have a clue to that. It looked casual. I don't know if they were discussing the indictment or not. My point is that we should consult now with Mr. Gonzales and see what kind of character the officer is," Tariq stated.

Somali's eyes darted as he pondered over Tariq's possible reasoning.

"Where do we go from there with what Gonzales gives us?" Somali inquired.

Tariq took another sip of the lemonade and stared off in space before looking Somali in the eyes and responded, "Well, provided Mr. Gonzales confirms him to be of morals and principles, we pay the officer a visit. He's the only real leverage the Smith boy's mother has for his defense. He's the only witness."

Somali's expression showed his lack of confidence in the Mexican officer doing what Tariq was implying.

"I don't know. You know what you're asking for? I mean that's a shot in the dark. Black kid gets killed by non-black officer and Hispanic partner testifies against him for breaking the law enforcement code? I don't know, Brother Tariq," Somali admitted.

Tariq nodded.

"I don't know either, but it's a shot we have to aim for if we expect some justice. We really have no other avenues," Tariq explained. Somali nodded in agreement and gulped down the remainder of his beverage before taking a long examining look at his friend and fellow O.B.U. member as he considered the proposition.

Chapter 16

There was a light drizzle falling outside on this mid-August night. A tempering wind brought relief to the denizens from the humidity that had been present most of the day, which had been a scorcher. The heat index reached 110 degrees. And most were inside the comfort of their homes enjoying central air conditioning. That is, for those who had the luxury. As the sky briefly lit up from a power surge of lightening, Tariq, who was lying next to his wife in bed, momentarily diverted his attention from the television set. He was holding the remote control and was in the process of flicking the set off. He was emotionally discouraged and upset with the story lines he had witnessed on the news. He was too anguished and tired to find refuge in satirical shows or a movie.

"Every day it's the same. Different places. Different ethnicities. Always turmoil," Tariq sighed. The bluish bright hue of the television set illuminated his distraught face as the news anchorman in the background announced a recent eastside shooting. A shooting that had been labeled drug related with no leads to a possible suspect.

"At the top of this hour, an eastside man has been shot and killed on the 800 block of Wyoming Street. Witness accounts were that of a dark skinned African American male in dark clothing, opening fire on the victim as he stood on the corner and fled on foot. The police are labeling the homicide drug related at the moment until further information becomes available."

Tariq shook his head in disgust at the newscast and aimed the remote control at the set flipping through the channels. On C-Span, officials were talking of Homeland Security; local news reputed of rival Mexican gangs shooting it out on the Westside; CNN covered live insurgent attacks in Iraq; paid television programming channels showed images of crying children. *When was there going to be any healing?* Tariq thought to himself and flicked off the television set.

Ursula stared up at the ceiling as Tariq repositioned himself under their satin sheets and snuggled up close to her. She too had seen about enough coverage of terrorism, black on black violence, and human suffrage throughout the world. These visuals had rendered her unable to sleep even though she felt exhausted from her activities and business at the interior decorating boutique.

Sensing that Tariq couldn't sleep either, perhaps due to his mental disturbance of the news coverage also. Ursula turned to face him. She studied the hard lines on his face as he stared up at the ceiling. His hands clasped behind his head as if in deep thought. She placed a gentle hand onto his chest and whispered softly to him, "Something troubling you besides the news coverage, honey?"

Tariq was broken from his mental train of thought now. He looked over into his wife's direction, but remained silent. He placed an arm around her and glanced out of the bedroom window at the raindrops trickling down the window pane.

"I was just thinking about our people here in America. The O.B.U. does so much. Other African American community activist groups do so much, but at times it seems as though the condition isn't changing. In some facets it seems worse. You begin to feel defeated," Tariq responded.

Ursula stared at her distraught husband. She could identify well with the emotions he was experiencing. Efforts being made for the advancement of the people in an economic, cultural, and educational aspect seemed to consciously or unconsciously be negatively countered through ignorance of a minority.

Even though the civil rights activists of the 1950's and 60's paved the way, and the windows of opportunities were wide open for African American today, there still seemed to be an ever increasing statistics of narcotic sales and self-hate among the youth in our urban cities, domestically and abroad.

After a brief moment of silent reflection, Ursula felt compelled to offer her husband some sanctity by reminding him and reassuring him that his works and the work of the O.B.U. were not being done in vain.

"I understand what you're feeling and many days I feel the same way. It's like a small minority is rebelling against the work we do. It's as if to defy us through continued ignorance. But we cannot focus on them, baby. We have to keep focusing on the ones who are positive and realize that it is our work, the work of O.B.U., and other black organizations. Many doors have been opened up. More importantly, it's evident, baby that everything we have done has not been in vain," Ursula consoled.

Tariq continued to have doubts and wondered if he or other black activists were putting forth enough effort to help in the struggle. Tariq remained silent and meditated over the assuring words his wife Ursula had just spoken. He shook his head as if in disagreement with her assertion and replied,

"You know, I was talking to the boys the other day. Some zany characters they are, Wild Bill, Bull, and the rest. I was reflecting on how these kids have actually only lived a short time. The reality is that they might not be around many more days and the thought is disheartening. As I was talking to them and lecturing to them about how imperative it was for them to get out of the gang life, I was hit with a powerful rebuttal. As I analyzed the situation, it was very real," Tariq informed his wife.

"What did they say?" she inquired.

Tariq's eyes darted in their sockets. Wild Bill's dark face and the powerful words he spoke.

"Bill said he couldn't get out. And the reason was that he had been a hard liner, excessively violent towards other gangs. He stated that he would be a target regardless of his getting out," Tariq explained exasperatedly and looked over to study Ursula's expression. She mentally grasped at the reasoning and tried to fathom Wild Bill and other gang members point of no return status and she sympathized.

"So, what did you tell him?" she asked.

Tariq's eyebrows rose and recalled how speechless he was the moment he heard Wild Bill's statement. He thought about how he really had no 'real' alternative for the ones in Bill's position. And thus diverted to his solution that would only at least, be applicable for young gang members who flew below the radar and were unknown amongst the hierarchy of the rival gangs. After a moment's pause, he responded, "I had to avert. I 'couldn't' answer him about his situation directly. I just directed my attention basically towards the younger ones who could slip out unnoticed. I told them about the opportunities at success in a life outside the gang culture, such as the technical schools and job corps. Wild Bill's statement made me realize we need to implement other programs." Tariq replied.

"Programs dealing with what?" she inquired.

"Job programs that are sponsored by non-profit organizations. Programs that are preferably outside of the 'red zones,'" he informed. He went on to explain to her the specifics and his idea in itself was not unique. In Los Angeles where the gang culture was more deeply rooted and the amount of gang related homicides far exceeded that of San Antonio, this very similar program structure had been organized. It afforded gang members the opportunity to escape their potential fates and become productive members of society.

This program, which catered to gang affiliates in South Central and

East L.A. was called 'Homeboy Industries' and was founded by Reverend Gregory Boyle. He was a Jesuit priest affectionately called 'Father Greg'. This non-profit program was affiliated with large companies such as American Apparel, the Iron Workers Union, Aramark Food Services, Conagra Foods, and the Community Mission Hospital which employed ex-gang members from the community. The program was a success on an indelible level. It salvaged the lives of gang members, uncovered talents and potential, and gave them a better spiritual perception of life. However, the program was hit with cynical reviews and ridicule, primarily from law enforcement agencies quoted as saying "they're being too soft on these gang members". This cynical statement by law enforcement had all the overtones of racism. It was self-evident that the problem of gang violence and some of the measures taken by law enforcement such as racial profiling and the lobbying for stiffer penalties.

After Tariq finished explaining his plan to Ursula, she nodded approvingly and offered her own opinion.

"I feel that a program like that will have a great impact because gang violence is definitely out of control and needs to stop," she stated. She continued rubbing her soft hand on his chest to further relax him. She then leaned over to kiss him on the cheek. He smiled as he looked down at his loving wife and gently ran his fingers through her flowing hair. He glanced once more out the window at the now ceasing rain and made his closing comment before closing his eyes.

"Yes, let's get some sleep. I'll need it, as it will be a long day tomorrow."

The following day, Tariq and Nawaz were both dressed formally, sporting kufis. They sat in a restaurant dining on entrees of cheese steak and enchiladas. The two founders of the community center would often meet to discuss the curriculum for upcoming content, reflect over prior meetings or just shoot the breeze about everything from political affairs to family-oriented conversations. However, today the primary topic was centered around the parent's night that took place the previous week at the community center.

Tariq cut a slice of his cheese steak with a knife while Nawaz sampled a hearty section of his enchilada. He reached hurriedly for his beverage to cool down the effects of this peppered Mexican treat and fanned himself afterwards. Tariq laughed as he sampled his steak.

"Wow, this is hot!"

Nawaz stated. Tariq joked, "You keep gulping down your wine after each bite like that and you will have to buy the whole cellar."

Nawaz laughed and began cutting another slice of the enchilada.

"You know, I believe the parent night was very beneficial. Many issues the parents needed to hear were addressed," Nawaz stated.

Tariq nodded his head as he chewed his food. He wiped sauce from his lips and began to respond.

"Indeed. We did address some pertinent issues. But, you know, I was talking to the wife the other night and I realized something." Nawaz looked puzzled as he chewed his enchilada and stared intently at Tariq.

"Realized something?" he responded with his mouth full.

"Yes. I realized that we've been focusing too much on the youth who come to us. We haven't really tried to come up with adequate solutions to reach out to the youth that haven't come to us. The youth who feel that we can't help them, like the gang members, the dealers or the robbers and other miscreant in the community," Tariq informed.

Nawaz wiped sauce from his mouth and sipped his wine.

"I see. Well, you said yourself that you lecture the gang members all the time. You're putting forth the effort to reach them as much as I put forth the effort to reach the Pakistani youth in my native country," Nawaz responded. However, Tariq shook his head slightly at Nawaz's assertion as if to suggest that he had missed the point.

"The problem with the gang culture and drug dealers goes deeper than just lectures, Nawaz. Redirecting, or should I say, attempting to redirect their way of thinking and living is lost if they can't or feel that they can't escape from their self-destructive lives. They have to be given alternatives. We as community leaders have to provide them with resources," Tariq stated.

Nawaz nodded in understanding. Tariq began to further explain the obligation of the activists to redirect and salvage the lives of those in the subculture. As he explained, he covered several important points so that Nawaz fully understood the situation in the black communities continued to deteriorate. He pointed out that there are people proclaiming to be activists who do not come up with working action plans to enable the race as a whole to advance. He condemned those in the streets with counterproductive cries for action by the police who are allied with the very same imperialist oppressors who've in the past and present, conspired to kill, cripple, make impotent, infest with disease, and incarcerate at alarming rates our people, instead of taking to the streets and putting forth the effort to get someone off the streets.

"Reclaiming communities and securing a better future for the children is the most important reason for being a servant." Grammy award-winning songstress Erykah Badu is quoted as saying at an awards ceremony at the Black Forest Theater in Dallas.

Her spoken words are indeed of great substance because advancement of our people is predicated on the level of consciousness and academics amongst the youth. Therefore, it is imperative that the elders in the community, activists and conscientious groups focus on the children in order to secure their perspective futures.

After Tariq finished explaining to Nawaz about the current state of the black community and what needs to be corrected within the political activist groups if these conditions are to change, there was a momentary silence as Nawaz reflected. He was mentally comparing and contrasting the situation between the African-American communities and the communities of his native Pakistan.

"In my country, drug abuse or violence as a result of drug peddling is not in an escalated scale as here in your communities. There is so much self-destructive behavior. It's genocide," Nawaz stated. Tariq diverted eye contact in shame. He felt embarrassed that even this foreigner who sat before him recognized what many black youths romanticize for what it really is—genocide, the systemic killing of our own people for such trivial material desires as a gold chain, or simply because "he was in my 'hood.' Yet, the police are always in everyone's 'hood'.

Tariq knew well that there was same-race killings and ethnic conflict going on overseas. He was also aware that the reasons behind these conflicts were quite different. These conflicts were often spurred by mutual feelings of oppression and discrimination of a particular ethnic group, frequently instigated by the government. This is the case for many countries in Africa and Asia. In Sri Lanka, the Sinhalese and Tamili warred because of political dissention in the 1980's. In Nawaz's native Pakistan, the Hindus and Muslims were at political odds. But among African-Americans, the motives were completely different.

After a brief moment of dejected reflection over the self-destructive peril of his people, Tariq was called to mind of a specific situation involving drug abuse. A youth approached him almost in tears over the drastically-declining mental state of his addicted mother. That youth was Phil.

"You know, I was talking to one of the youth in the old neighborhood the other day and he seemed real troubled for two reasons. First, he was involved in drugs, but wanted to get out. He had many reasons, including feeling that his associates were informants. He feared shootings and federal prison. It seemed to me that he had enough," Tariq explained as he relayed his encounter with Phil. Nawaz listened intently as Tariq spoke, his eyes darting as if envisioning this young African-American drug peddler who wanted to get out of that life.

"So, if he wants to get out, why doesn't he?" Nawaz inquired.

Tariq sipped his beverage, then looked around the patrons inside the restaurant briefly before responding.

"Well, he explained that too. He said it wasn't that easy. He couldn't just get out. He feared reprisals from the big man who oversees the operation," Tariq informed. Tariq's eyes glazed over as he reflected over the reason Phil had been so anguished: the pain he felt inside at seeing his sick mother enslaved by her addiction and being sexually exploited by other dealers. Tariq placed a clenched fist underneath his chin, then removed it and sighed before responding.

"His mother is addicted to crack. It's the very same poison that he himself pushes to other black children's mothers. It's eating him alive," Tariq stated in embarrassment. Nawaz nodded and looked away from Tariq. Tariq shook his head and popped the last piece of cheese steak into his mouth as he stood up. He wiped his mouth and gulped down the remainder of his beverage. "That was good. We have to come here more often. Maybe I'll get the enchilada next time," Tariq stated.

Nawaz smiled and wiped his mouth.

"Maybe next time the meal is on you, eh?" he stated as he got up. Tariq laughed and patted him on the back.

"I wouldn't have it any other way," he responded, placing his arm around Nawaz's shoulders. The two proceeded to head for the exit.

The intense Southern Texas heat could be seen rising in waves from the streets as the sunlight glistened off the chrome and glass of passing cars. Children sprayed each other with water hoses and laughed giddily as they ran around their sparse yards. The elderly sat in rocking chairs on porches fanning themselves and waving at pedestrians passing by.

Phil's little sister jumped rope with several other little girls. Her beautiful little shining brown face appeared happy. Her pigtails flopped with each jump. She was being affectionately watched by her big brother who sat perched on his front porch with his friend, Braun. Absent were his usual gold rings and chains. Phil was simply adorned in a white T-shirt, grey jogging pants, and Adidas shower slippers. He looked at his little sister jumping rope with love, adoration, and sadness. He was sad because of the uncertainty of his sister's future. Because of his and his mother's lifestyle, her future was in jeopardy.

His little brother dodged hitting their fence as he went to retrieve a football. It snagged his shirt in the process. Phil shook his head, but still managed a smile.

"Big head boy, I just bought you that shirt," Phil stated.

His little brother checked out the small tear and galloped off with the football as his playmates cheered him on. Braun smiled as he observed the boys in the intense game of catch. He reflected about the days when Phil, Piye, and he would take on any team of youth.

"Man, we don't even play football with each other no mo'," Braun asserted.

Phil nodded. His expression was evidence that he, too, was at that moment reflecting on their earlier childhood days.

"Yeah, I know, man. Seem like we jis be goin' in different directions, man. I wish it could be like the old days. I miss hearin' Devonte braggin and tauntin', ya know. Thangs done changed. Shoot, man, Piye actin' like he don't even wanna be 'round me. Can't blame 'em though. Main…I jis feel like shit comin' down on me, B." Phil stated as he sipped his cherry cola.

Braun studied his friend inquisitively. His eyes evidencing the empathy he felt for the turmoil Phil was experiencing.

"What do you mean, P?" Braun inquired.

Phil paused before answering. He was slightly embarrassed about what he was about to confide in his close friend. He remembered Braun's mentality and level of maturity for his mere seventeen years and felt relaxed.

"I mean…everythang's fallin' down on me at once. And I just want out. 'Times I wish I could just get away from all this shit. Pop's spirits get lower ery'time I go visit. I thank feds is watchin' me. Ery'time I look at my lil' brother and sister man…I jis don't know. What's in sto' for 'em? Shh. Mom's in bad shape, man. Other day I had to restrain myself from shootin' this nigga try'nna sell her some fuckin' crack. I had that iron…could've jis…I was this close, B." Phil stated as he dropped his head.

Braun's eyes were glazed over. He emphasized and feared for his friend. "You…you ever talk to Brother Tariq?" Braun offered.

Phil looked away. A smile emerged on his face that belied the pain in his eyes.

"Yeah. Talked to 'em other day. Told' em to help me get Mom in rehab. Said he would. Told 'em ery'thang, man. Told 'em I'm tired of this life. Wanna get out, away from all this shit. He told me I should start comin' to the meetin'-n-all. Get some spiritual guidance. Maybe I do. Maybe I'll start goin' ta church. Ain't been there in a long time," Phil said.

"You not thankin' 'bout becomin' a missionary and goin' to places like South America with the church, huh?" Braun laughed. Braun wanted to liven up Phil's spirit and he was pleased when Phil laughed.

"Yeah, might not be a bad idea, Braun. Way niggas is droppin' roun' here. Chris got blasted the other night. Man, look like we had jis seen Chris at the Juneteenth, man," Phil responded as he shook his head. Staring off into the thin air as he reflected about their classmate who'd been gunned down. He then took a sip of his cherry cola before returning his gaze to Braun. "I ain't dyin' in these streets. And I ain't goin' to no jail, neither, B. I's, I's kinda thankin' 'bout takin' Piye up on that offer." Phil stated. A smile etched across his face as he looked out of the corner of his eyes at Braun.

"Yeah? You? Workin' on roofs? Mr. 'I don't wanna get my hands dirty'?" Braun laughed.

"Yeah, I figure, if I keep goin' down this road, man, I be gettin' my hands dirty slavin' in some prison field." Phil responded.

Braun nodded. Though a smile remained etched across his face, his eyes evidenced his acknowledgement of just how accurate the remark was. Then, hitting Braun on the shoulder playfully, Phil redirected the subject. "So, man, where you headed to, all geared up? Know you ain't gonna break out the Air Force Ones and Pelle Pelles to come kick it wit me?" Phil inquired. His gold teeth glistened from the reflection of the setting sun that cast a brilliant glare off the windshield of Braun's recently-purchased Nissan. Braun smiled and looked away.

"Yeah, ah, me and Ikara goin' out to the Hacienda on Fort Sam with Devonte' and Sharon," he responded.

After a few seconds his cellular phone rang. The digits of the caller flashed on the screen. He glanced down at the screen and shook his head. Releasing a sigh which acknowledged his annoyance, he proceeded to ignore the ringing until it stopped.

"Some gal you met when you was drunk?" Braun laughed.

Phil smiled and shook his head, his eyes registered a distant, depressed gaze. It was like the look of a man imprisoned in a cell, looking out of his cell window at the rolling hills and green landscape of the freedom in which he sought beyond the walls.

"Nah, no gal I met when I was drunk, Braun. Niggas I met when I was sober. Look B, I ain't gon' holdja up, man I am not going to hold you up man. Go on out and enjoy yaself. Ain't got but two weeks left fo' school starts and all that rap writin' gon' change to essays and geography. Patogorytham Theroms-n-shit," Phil laughed as he patted Braun on the shoulder.

"That's Pythagorean Theorem and you know I ain't gon' never stop writin' my lyrics and brangin' that message," Braun responded as he got up.

Phil remained, looking at his friend in admiration. As Braun proceeded to walk down the porch steps, Phil swiped at his pant leg in order to catch his attention. Turning around slowly with a curious expression, Braun waited for Phil to speak. Instead, Phil simply extended his hand. Braun looked down at Phil's proffered hand for a moment, and then clasped it firmly while staring his friend in the eyes.

"Be cool, Lil Dred," Phil stated. There was a look of certain mourning in his eyes that belied his toothy grin. It was as if he somehow felt a bad omen or a karmatic vision that his future was in peril. Braun read his look and almost felt compelled to hug his friend. Instead, he returned the sentiment and continued down the steps towards his vehicle.

The word "hacienda" in Spanish means "large estate". However, on Fort Sam Houston it was a recreational center for teenagers, which was buzzing with youth of all different nationalities. African-Americans, whites, Hispanics, Asians, etc. were all enjoying themselves at this military base recreation center. The center provided entertainment and activities for these youth, such as, video games, pool tables, bowling and an assortment of other entertainment. It was a congenial alternative for the military kids and their friends or whomever they chose to invite in with a pass.

At the moment Devonte was engrossed in a serious game of Mortal Kombat. His facial expression was serious as he carefully maneuvered the controls. Braun, Sharon, and Ikara watched in awe at the game's characters. Raiden in white Kung Fu apparel and hat were flying through the air, only to be frozen by the character he was engaged in battle with, Sub Zero.

"None of that! Take that! Ah man! Shhh! Damn!" Devonte barked as he smashed the button necessary to combat a flurry from Sub Zero. But it was futile and his character now wobbled in a complete daze. "Finish him!" shouted the computerized voice of the game. His opponent proceeded to inflict the 'Death Blow' on his character, which was so graphic that parents criticized the manufacturers, claiming the game was "too gory" and "not suitable for children."

He shook his head and stared at the video screen in disbelief. Devonte reluctantly maneuvered away as his friends jeered at him. Sharon patted him on the shoulder and kissed him on the side of his face as she pulled him away.

"Man, that's sad. I coulda did betta' than that," Braun laughed as he and Ikara followed their friends. Devonte pretended to do a martial arts move on him, which caused him to flinch and recoil as Devonte laughed. "Alright, alright, Raiden," he stated. Ikara jumped into a fighting marital arts stance herself, meriting laughter from the group.

As they continued walking, Ikara recognized a classmate from her high school and greeted her. This merited a warm smile from the girl who proceeded over in their direction. She was Hispanic and gorgeous in form. Her name was Maria Gonzales. She was the daughter of the store owner, Mr. Felix Gonzales. Stopping short of the group, the girl opened with a bubbly greeting.

"Hello, Ikara. I didn't expect to see you here. Have you made your mind up about coming back to Judson?" she inquired. She gave each of Ikara's friends a cheerful smile which was lustfully admired by Devonte. In an instant he gave her a visual appraisal, before conspicuously looking away when Sharon gave him the eye.

"What?" Devonte pleaded, holding his arms at bay. Sharon rolled her eyes and smiled as she greeted their friend.

"Hi, Maria," Sharon greeted her, as Devonte and Braun exchanged glances. Braun held his laughter as he shook his head. "Yes, I've decided to go to Roosevelt," she informed confidently. Maria's expression lit up as she looked back and forth between Braun and Ikara.

"Oh, I see." Maria stated while folding her arms and posing a suggestive stance that complemented her mischievous look. Ikara recognized the body language and laughed.

"Come on, Maria," she giggled.

"Ya'll wanna get something to eat? I'll treat," Maria offered.

Devonte began rubbing his hands together, eager to take advantage of Maria's generosity.

"Yeah, but we'll pay this time. You paid last time," Sharon stated gripping Devonte's arm. His expression instantly changed.

"What?" he repeated. Braun and Ikara both laughed as the five proceeded to the restaurant section.

A half hour had passed and the five were now departing the restaurant. They were conversing and laughing amongst themselves until they got outside. Maria, who had been bashfully shunning boys' approaches all night, shyly waved at a rather handsome Hispanic teenager with a gentle smile. This prompted a remark from Sharon, who witnessed the exchange, as the boy continued looking back.

"Maria, what is wrong with you? He's been followin' you 'round all night. Why don't you go meet 'em?" Sharon coaxed.

"No. I don't think so. I mean, he's cute and everything, but nah," Maria responded.

"I thought you broke out of that shyness over the summer, Maria. We're gettin' ready to be juniors. Upperclassmen. You gotta get with it. I'll tell you what, I'mma hook you up with somebody nice," Sharon offered.

Maria folded her arms as she and Ikara exchanged meaningful glances, smiles broadening their faces and catching Devonte's attention.

"Sharon, stop being a matchmaker. Oh, hey, look," Ikara stated pointing in the direction of a crowd gathering around a stylized motorcycle. Her intentions however, were merely to divert attention away and hopefully distract them from the psychological effect she and Maria's meaningful glances had evoked in Devonte. The diversionary tactic didn't work.

"Hold on, hold on, what are all these looks s'pose ta mean? I caught that, Maria. What ya'll sayin? That Sharon ain't got good taste? Look at me," he plead. All three girls laughed as they continued to walk and left him standing there confused, until Braun playfully nudged him along.

The group was now separated. Braun and Ikara conversed and walked side by side towards Braun's vehicle while glancing around every so often at the scenes around them. They stopped periodically as other teenagers passed in front of them, laughing or conversing themselves. There appeared to be over three dozen youth from ages twelve to early twenties sporting the latest gear and boarding vehicles that most likely belonged to their parents. The vast majority of them were military kids and their parents were officers in the Air Force, Navy, or Army.

The two finally reached Braun's car. Ikara, whose complacent expression was highlighted by her radiance, folded her arms as she looked at Braun, who was still laughing over some humorous conversation the two had been engaged in. "That's not funny. She could have really hurt herself," Ikara stated. Braun continued laughing as he held down his head and glanced over in Maria's direction as she boarded her mother's gold Grand Prix. His gaze caught Ikara's attention.

"Maria is so reserved. I'm surprised that she's even out at the Hacienda," Ikara stated.

Braun agreed and changed the subject.

"You really comfortable with Roosevelt? I mean, I know Sharon, Maria, and Swathi are like your best friends. I don't wanna seem like I'm takin' you away from 'em, Braun stammered. He looked away from her periodically as if feeling guilt.

Ikara laughed and placed a gentle hand on his face before kissing him briefly.

"Braun, I want to go to Roosevelt. I wanna be with you," she stated sensually as her eyes followed his. He held her hand, but averted eye contact. This time the guilt stemmed from his subconscious belief that he was somehow unworthy. His insecurity of her upper-middle class status was compounded by his own his modest upbringing and her stunning beauty.

She studied his body language and looked deeply into his eyes as if examining his soul and smiled. "What?" she inquired.

He smiled and shook his head.

"Nothing. I was just thinking over some things," he responded in an attempt to distract her.

"Some things? What kind of things?" she pried further, sensing his attempt to mislead her.

"Come on. Don't do that. It ain't important. Quit probin'," Braun stated.

Ikara folded her arms and faked being offended.

"I am not probing, Braun," she stated.

Braun cleverly managed to get her stop probing by caressing her.

"Come on. Come on. You know I was just kidding. I's thankin' 'bout you. You know that," he stated.

She smiled and looked into his eyes. "You'd better be," she giggled.

Braun smiled and the two kissed as Sharon and Devonte popped up on the other side of the car. Both gestured and silently jeered at the two until their presence was detected, forcing the two to disengage. Braun looked away, embarrassed for a moment.

"Where ya'll been? We's waitin'on ya'll. You know I gotta get back. I got ta work tomorrow. Some of us got jobs, ya know," Braun stated as Sharon folded her arms and rolled her eyes.

"Mm hmm. Don't look like y'all's waitin on us, to me," she stated. She laughed and embraced Devonte, which caused Ikara to smile. Ikara shook her head while running her hand through her flowing black hair. Braun laughed and looked away before turning back to stare Ikara in the eye. Her stunning beauty prompted him to embrace her in a kiss once more, which they did briefly. He opened up the passenger's side door for her and closed it after she settled into her seat. He walked around the vehicle as his two friends hopped into the backseat. He made one last visual sweep of the parking lot before climbing in behind the steering wheel and closing the driver's side door.

Chapter 17

There were the lights of the motorists whizzing down the highways and interstates commuting to and from work; the brilliance of the lighted buildings of the downtown central business district; the backdrop of a pastel sky which was slowly changing to a pinkish hue with the quickly rising orange sphere of the sun; and the ominous but calm urban ghettoes of San Antonio's eastside. After a night of several police calls for shots fired, the ghettos were now peaceful. But, this calm was about to be disrupted.

A lone car passed down the 1800 block of Nevada Street with its lights still on, despite the high rate of visibility. A dog barks, initiating the barks of several other dogs chained behind the fences of these wooden clapboard houses. Several lights went on. These were probably people in preparation to commute to work. A black van and several other unmarked police vehicles crept silently to a halt adjacent to a yellow house with a dirt patch for a front lawn, and sparse shrubbery which only added to the dilapidated appearance of the neglected house.

The federal marshals, dressed in their black tactical uniforms and boots, with "U.S. Marshals" stenciled in yellow across the backs of their jackets, moved in precession across the lawn. Agents with submachine guns ready to bust through the door to serve a warrant to a well known drug dealer. The drug dealer was a twenty-two-year-old kid who owned several crack houses in the neighborhood. He also owned several expensive cars, including the silver Cadillac Seville which was parked outside the decrepit house. He had been under surveillance for over two years. He was caught on videotape on numerous occasions dealing crack out of his car, crack houses, and on street corners.

The agents proceeded to ram the front door violently. The first assaults were thunderous bangs on the fragile oak wood door, which nearly knocked it off of its hinges. The second assault managed to break it down. Six agents disappeared inside of the house while the other agents--some conversing on headsets, others carefully positioned with their assault weapons ready-- remained outside.

Moments after the agents disappeared into the dwelling, shouts and the sounds of combative tussling could be heard vibrating throughout the house. The commotion aroused neighbors, who began peering out of windows, and caused the submachine gun-wielding agents outside to become tense. An agent appeared at the doorway followed by the other agents who were manhandling the narcotics-dealing suspect. They were shouting and pushing the half-naked and handcuffed black man along the way. The pushing nearly caused him to fall to the ground before being aggressively yanked back upright. He grimaced in pain as his gold chain swayed back and forth. He appeared to be intoxicated and made a futile attempt to resist being placed into a waiting police vehicle. He placed a bare foot up to the window as a brace, but within seconds he was incapacitated, then yanked up and forced into the backseat.

This pre-dawn federal agents' searched the drug dealer's home as some of the neighbors observed them. Young and old alike, hardworking black men and women en route to blue collar jobs, as well as the minority criminal elements, and each reacted in various ways. Some community activists bore expressions of disdain for the excessive force administered on the young black man. They loudly expressed their objections.

This debilitating scene was one they had witnessed time and time again and which was reenacted with different young black males. It was being replayed at dozens of other locations throughout the entire eastside that morning as part of an ongoing tactical federal sweep. It was an operation funded by tax payers to build strong narcotics cases on dealers by means of surveillance and the issuance of federal warrants. The operation focused on targeting the minority communities. The cameras of news teams rolled. Some were in vans and others in helicopters. They covered different phases of this federal operation, which included live footage of agents bombarding houses in the same fashion as the yellow house. They captured agents exiting houses, apartment complexes, and housing projects with confiscated drugs and weapons. From Rigsby Street to the projects on Lamar, across Nevada, Wyoming, and Utah Streets, the news showed profiling of blacks and how they were 'abducted' from their residents by machine gun-toting federal agents. In some cases, their actions ignited protests from concerned denizens, such as in the apartment complex on South Cross. Several young black women had to be restrained as they violently protested the abductions of two teenage boys. On Lamar Street a middle aged black man in a welding uniform was maliciously subdued by police for practicing his First Amendment right to the Freedom of Speech. He was acknowledging his awareness of the government's systemic and clandestine war against the African-American man.

The cameras rolled and the images were shown throughout the day on various news broadcasts. Anchormen and women with blunt expressions gave detailed accounts of the operation as thousands of African-Americans in San Antonio watched. Some exhibited cheer for the downfall of the drug dealers while others, such as Tariq, exhibited outrage, especially when he saw the image of Phil being hauled from his mother's home. She violently protested his arrest. Tariq leaned forward towards the television set with his eyebrows furrowed and his eyes darting as a non-aggressive Phil appeared confused on the screen. He had a tired expression on his face while he was yanked and pushed across the lawn in his pajama bottoms before being ushered into the backseat of the police car. At this point, the scene switched to the broadcast panel.

Tariq stared bewildered at the screen. He only half-heard the words of the news reporters as he replayed the images he had just seen on the screen in his mind. Young black men, most of whom were in their teens and early twenties were virtually dragged from their homes by screaming, gun-toting federal agents and police from the drug taskforce. The crying and protesting mothers were restrained and shoved, while the middle aged activists and blue collar workers were hurled to the ground by police. The apartments on South Cross had dozens of people standing on the balconies taunting the police. Phil's emaciated and ill mother had tears streaming down her face as she pleaded with the officers.

Tariq released a sigh and leaned back in his chair, removing his wire-rimmed glasses. The images he'd seen were shocking to him. His people were being profiled and used as a symbolic emblem of the scourge of narcotics corruption in the United States of America. This was a tactic that had been used since the inception of the so-called 'War on Drugs' campaign in the 80's, during which people of the world saw news coverage of black dealers on their screens. They were disillusioned to the real facts that African-Americans neither flew, nor shipped these large quantities of opium, heroin, marijuana, or cocaine into this country, facts which mysteriously go undetected by our government's advanced drug taskforces. Yet the population of the prison industrial complex as Tariq knew very well, was over 40% African-American. After a moment's reflection, Tariq shook his head and rose from his leather sofa.

The blistering heat beamed off of the glass high-rise buildings and rose in waves from the streets as little black youth with bare chests sweated profusely. Their eyes squinted and their small hands wiped away sweat as they played basketball in the backyards or caught footballs in the street. One boy sailed the football over his intended receiver's head and into the hands of Braun, who feinted dodging defenders. He laughed before tossing the ball back to the boys.

After tapping and playfully rubbing several of the youths' heads, Braun and Piye continued on up the street. A block away, a Lincoln Continental pulled into the parking lot of Mr. Gonzales' convenience store as he swept the floor, causing him to stop and place a hand up to his brow in order to block the intense sun that beamed down over his head. It was noon.

As the occupants of the Lincoln exited the vehicle, Piye and Braun, who were rapping, passed by and acknowledged them with upraised fists.

Brothers Tariq and Somali greeted Braun and Piye. Their warm greetings were returned. The boys continued on as Tariq and Somali approached Mr. Gonzales' store with courteously extended hands. Both were casually dressed, sporting their kufis.

"Mr. Gonzales, how's everything going with the business?" Tariq greeted him.

Mr. Gonzales shook Tariq and Somali's hands. "Business is good. And yours?" he responded

"Oh, I'm above water. Paying the bills and eating okay," he responded as he patted Mr. Gonzales on the shoulder. Mr. Gonzales smiled and closely examined Tariq's eyes. It became evident to the man that their visit was not casual. These men were there with a purpose. He thought to himself, *but what?*

"Is something wrong?" Mr. Gonzales inquired, looking back and forth between Somali and Tariq.

Somali remained silent and looked over to Tariq, as if signaling his cue to inform Mr. Gonzales of the business at hand. His wife and daughter looked on curiously as they stood behind the counter.

"Well, Mr. Gonzales, first let me ask you, how do you know Officer Martinez with the San Antonio Police Department?" Tariq responded.

Mr. Gonzales' expression registered puzzlement at the inquiry. "You mean, Juan? I know him very well. He's a good man. Why do you ask?" Mr. Gonzales asked.

"As you know, he and his partner have been indicted and ordered to stand trial for the death of a young man a month ago. We just need some insight into the man's moral standings because we're almost certain that his partner used excessive force that night," Tariq stated.

Mr. Gonzales continued to look back and forth between the two Nubians.

"So, you are wondering if maybe Juan will testify against his fellow officer?" Mr. Gonzales inquired.

Somali exchanged a meaningful glance with Tariq. Catching the glance, Tariq reflected back over what Somali had stated at home. He asserted that there was only a very small chance that Martinez would go against the law enforcement code and testify to an excessive force claim against his partner.

"If he is a principled man and not biased against the ethnicity of the victim, he'll do the right thing. Right, Mr. Gonzales?" Somali stated.

"Juan is not a racist. I know him well. And, if there was indeed an issue of excessive force that night Mr. Qusta, I'm sure Juan will do the right thing," Mr. Gonzales stated defiantly in Officer Martinez's defense.

Somali's expression remained skeptical. Tariq nodded and folded his arms.

"That's what we are depending on, Mr. Gonzales. Do you have his address? My brother and I would like to consult with Juan ourselves," Somali stated, glancing over at Tariq.

Mr. Gonzales raised his eyebrow.

"Uh, yes, I know his address. If you're sure you want to pay him a visit," Mr. Gonzales informed. Somali recognized his reservations. "We're sure," Somali confirmed.

"128 Monticello Boulevard," Mr. Gonzales informed. Tariq and Somali exchanged meaningful glances once more. Tariq smiled warmly and extended his hand to Mr. Gonzales.

"Thank you, Mr. Gonzales. You've been a big help," he stated graciously as he patted the man's shoulder. Somali nodded his head as a gesture of thanks towards Mr. Gonzales as he and Tariq made their way back towards their vehicle. They left Mr. Gonzales standing there, leaning on his broom until the Lincoln backed out of the parking lot. He returned to his chore of sweeping, glancing once more at the slowly-vanishing Lincoln as it rounded the corner.

The following day…

A minivan pulled up to the drive-in window at Taco Bell and was greeted courteously by a caramel skin-toned black girl with enticing eyes and a beautiful smile. She accepted the cash payment from the Caucasian male driver and handed him several bags.

"Here you go, sir. Enjoy your meal and have a nice day," she chimed. The small family which consisted of the man's brunette wife and two small children began opening up their respective bags as the van lurched away from the drive-through window. Just beyond the girl at the window was Braun. He was dressed in a purple Taco Bell shirt and hat, working diligently over a grill preparing fajitas and tacos. Unbeknownst to him, Ikara pulled up in the parking lot in her mother's Range Rover with her friends Swathi and Sharon.

As Braun worked on the grill, he glanced up at the clock. It was nearly 4 o' clock, his knock-off time. After a busy day, he couldn't wait. As he methodically prepared a set of fajitas and placed them onto trays, it was then that he caught sight of Ikara through his peripheral vision. She was dressed in all white with her long flowing hair accentuating her Asiatic face.

Ikara spotted him and waved. Her face lit up with a wide smile, exposing her pearly white teeth. Braun held up a hand, acknowledging her, and whispered his greeting to Swathi and Sharon as he set the trays aside. He returned to the grill as Ikara prepared to order for herself and her friends.

"Hi, Ikara. What's up?" inquired another friendly African-American girl at the cash register. "Hey Tammy. I want a fajita, one beef burrito, an apple pie, and a coke. Sharon, Swathi?" Ikara turned to ask of her friends. The two stared at the menu bewildered, as if they didn't frequent this Taco Bell at least three times a week.

"I guess I'll have a soft shell taco, a salad, and a small coke," Swathi ordered. The girl behind the cash register smiled.

"What, are you on some kind of diet?" Sharon laughed. All four laughed.

"Um…gimme, a beef burrito, fajita, a hard shell taco, an apple pie, and a large coke," Sharon ordered. The cashier's expression displayed her opinion of Sharon's high-caloric order.

"God," Swathi s laughed. Ikara shook her head.

"And she wonders why she can't fit in size 6 anymore," Ikara smiled.

The girl behind the register smiled and shook her head as she began ringing up the three orders. After informing them of the total purchase, she waited for Ikara to count out the necessary amount. "Okay, here's your change. Y'all can have a seat and we'll bring your trays," the girl stated. The three proceeded towards the table area.

"Eric, take my spot. I got the trays. I'm about to punch out anyway. It's four o' clock," Braun stated as he hurriedly removed his apron. The Mexican boy whom he had spoken to nodded as he proceeded to prepare the burritos and fajitas.

"Okay, amigo," he responded.

At the table, the three girls were laughing and talking. Swathi ran her hand through her hair as she tilted her head back, a beautiful smile on her face. As she looked around, she noticed a Hispanic couple entering the restaurant. The woman, a bronze-skinned, oval-faced Mayan with stylized hair was wearing a two-piece ensemble of a white blouse and black, split skirt, which incidentally accentuated her voluptuous curves. But Swathi did not pay attention to these attributes. She was more interested in the woman's Burberry purse and matching sandals.

"Ooh, I love that purse. I saw one like that the other day when I went to Rolling Oaks Mall. It'll go really well with the outfit I want," she stated as she stared dreamily at the woman's purse. Ikara and Sharon observed the purse as well and gave their own judgment.

"Yeah, it is nice, and expensive," Ikara laughed.

"Devonte was talkin' 'bout puttin' that type of interior in his car. I looked at him like he was crazy, girl," Sharon stated, rolling her eyes.

Swathi looked puzzled.

"When did Devonte get a car?" Swathi inquired.

Ikara laughed, "It's his wish mobile."

"Yeah, Devonte don't even got a job. His spoiled self," Sharon stated.

At that moment, Braun made his way over to the table with three trays.

"Here y'all go. I don't know who ordered what, y'all gotta sort that out. So, what's the deal?" Braun inquired as he took a seat next to Ikara.

The three began selecting their trays. Braun playfully motioned at Ikara's chicken fajita as if asking to sample it. Ikara laughed and pretended to decline his request.

"It's as if, like, you don't be eatin' these all day. Go on, boy," Ikara laughed at Braun as he reached for the fajita.

"We was just talkin' 'bout yo friend with his sneaky, spoiled rotten self," Sharon stated as she bit into her beef burrito. "But I love 'em though. You gon see 'em today?" Sharon inquired.

Braun smiled and ribbed her about talking with her mouth full.

"Probably, why? What ya'll got planned?" he inquired.

"I need him to get his momma's car so he can take me to the mall tommar," she stated in what seemed like one breath, gesturing with her head as if to insinuate that Braun should have somehow known.

"You know she has to have a new outfit for the back-to-school dance,"

Swathi stated as she crunched on a salad breadstick. Braun smiled and shook his head. He knew Sharon well and knew that she was very particular about her outfits.

"Yeah, yeah, I know. She 'ont want nobody else wit the same thang she got on. Princess, you thankin' bout actually goin' out to a dance? Around people?" Braun laughed.

He'd always playfully referred to Swathi as princess, confusing her native Pakistan with Saudi Arabia. Saudi Arabia has a monarchy, while Pakistan is a republic. Those lacking in knowledge of the Middle East assume that all Arab people are sheiks or kings or princes. The three girls laughed at Braun's humor.

"We're making her go. You're worse than Maria, you know that?" Ikara stated, playfully nudging Swathi as she sipped her coke. Swathi laughed and continued eating.

"We gon' help this princess find a prince," Sharon stated before biting into her hard-shell taco.

Braun observed her and said, "Slow down girl or you are gonna get big as a house eatin' all that. Devonte ain't feelin' no fat girl," Braun teased. The others laughed.

"You just want this fajita. But it ain't workin'. I'm eatin' all this here. And anyway, Devonte says I'm gettin' finer," Sharon stated as she gesticulated with her neck. She placed her hand to her hip and rolled her eyes. Braun laughed along with the others.

The four left Taco Bell and were now at Ikara's mother's Range Rover. Braun opened the door as Ikara got in and sat behind the steering wheel. He scanned the interior of the vehicle as Ikara placed the key into the ignition. "This Range is nice. It looks like a space shuttle inside or somethin'. navigation system, computer, look at all this. I might have to cop me one of these," Braun stated as he appraised the vehicle's interior.

Sharon laughed, "You gon' have to work double and triple time on that grill." The others giggled at her humor. Sensing the slight embarrassment on Braun's face as he smirked sarcastically, Ikara placed a consoling hand on his. She looked into his face with an assuring smile.

"Like I'mma be workin' at Taco Bell all my life. I'm gon' ta law school. So I'mma have cheddar. Legally," Braun rebutted with his head down. He sounded unsure as to whether this could happen and, sensing this, Sharon attempted to make it up to him.

"I got faith in you. I might need your legal assistance one day when I catch Devonte down bad with one of them wenches," Sharon laughed.

Braun smiled and shook his head and returned to looking at Ikara.

"I got somethin' nice for you. I picked it up yesterday. You'll find out later," he stated. He observed another vehicle pulling into the parking lot. He looked back at Ikara as he began to close the door. "Call when you make it home, alright?" he requested.

Ikara whispered that she would. The two kissed briefly. Afterwards, Ikara backed the Range Rover out of the parking lot and Braun held up a hand and pointed to his heart.

✶✶✶✶✶✶✶✶

It was clear over San Antonio. Not a cloud in sight. There was a light wind blowing this late August day. The Mexican boss and his two henchmen were walking briskly on the runway towards his white Leer jet. All three were dressed in leisure attire, Armani or Versace shirts, slacks, and alligator skin loafers. The men moved with a sense of urgency, and rightfully so.

The dealers were well aware of the recent federal roundup conducted on the eastside. They read all of the newspaper articles highlighting this unprecedented roundup which nabbed forty-one drug dealers and netted over $250,000 in drug confiscation, over $800,000 cash, and dozens of artillery, from .45 caliber Glocks, .9mm's, and shotguns, to SKS, HK's, AK47's and M-1's. But, what was more alarming to the Mexican lord was that each of his workers' connections, with the exception of Chatter, had been arrested. Certainly his callous flamboyancy and ill-advised transactions hadn't kept him below the radar. He was highly visible, and this worried him.

The drug lord glanced down at his Rolex prior to entering the Leer jet that was waiting for him. One adjunct climbed into the cockpit and spoke in Spanish in reference to their flight time arrival in Mexico City. He also discussed the remote possibilities of their being accosted by the DEA agents. After the brief exchange, the drug lord and his henchmen prepared to board the jet. No doubt the men had made arrangements for this hiatus in order to escape apprehension by the U.S. Marshals. All accounts were closed, money withdrawn from banks, and businesses vacated and liquidated of revenue. However, it had all been in vain. As the Mexican boss raised a leg to step onto the Leer jet, he suddenly heard the sound of police helicopters looming over his estate. Seconds later, several unmarked federal agent cars and vans came to a screeching halt in front of him. The agents ran towards the men, weapons drawn and barked orders. The Mexicans looked perplexed, but raised their hands and surrendered.

Chapter 18

Tariq's expression was stone-faced as he and Somali cruised through San Antonio's southside in silence. His eyes carefully observed their surroundings, which consisted of modest homes of Mexican-styled stucco, palmettos, and vast lawns. Tariq made note of the fact that these communities were not as dilapidated as the African-American neighborhoods on the Eastside.

They passed by a convenience store and Somali observed the elements which had deteriorated the moral fabric of the community. *Had these hardworking, blue and white collar Hispanic men and women been afraid for their safety, or for their children's safety? Did they depreciate the value of their homes as a result of the presence of drug dealers and gang members?*

Somali made eye contact with these bangers. There were eleven of them clinging to a 1963 Impala that was engineered with a hydraulic system. It was silver and black and its impeccable paint job glistened in the sunlight. Its chrome spinners were nearly blinding. As Somali stared at them, one of them, a stocky Mexican with a du-rag pulled nearly to his eyes threw up a gang sign. This prompted two others to hold 40 oz. bottles of beer to initiate the same. The others simply held their girlfriends close and stared on with indifference.

The scenes as they approached Martinez's residence were practically identical to this encounter. Hispanic male and female gang members were posted up along the avenues by stylized vehicles, drinking beer. Most of the males wore T-shirts or no shirts at all, tattoos etched across their chiseled bodies; their trousers low, slung over sneakers displaying postures of machismo as they gestured and barked in Spanish at Tariq's vehicle. This was clearly hostile territory. Tariq started to have second thoughts about the meeting as he slowed down in front of Martinez's residence.

From directly across the street, in front of a moderate, well-manicured stucco bungalow with small palmettos in the front yard, Tariq and Somali were being watched. Their observers were seven gang members. One of them was a small framed kid with piercing eyes. His name was Eduardo. The others looking on were El Gatos, Manuel, Lisa, Tina, Toro, and Miguel. They were all unknown to Somali and Tariq. However, Braun, Devonte, and Phil had been well acquainted with them months earlier during the mall incident.

Tariq and Somali exited the vehicle. Their eyes swept the vicinity. Small Hispanic children were playing in the street or running and riding their bicycles. They were enjoying the summer afternoon. Some found refuge under the shade of trees like the large palmetto that sat in the middle of Martinez's modest yard. The sunlight trickled down in beams through its branches.

Tariq closed the driver's side door behind him and straightened his tie as he glanced around cautiously in the direction of Eduardo's gang. He and Somali proceeded up the driveway and approached the large Spanish-style wood door. After exchanging a meaningful look with Somali, Tariq braced himself. He cleared his throat and knocked on the door. A little Mexican boy screamed and ran playfully into the street to retrieve a ball. This startled Tariq, but also captured his attention. All the while, Eduardo, with a beer in his hand and being massaged by Lisa, stared on.

After a few moments, the sounds of footsteps could be heard approaching. A female voice called out from behind the large wooden door.

"Who is it?" she inquired.

Tariq glanced at Somali once more as his anxiety and uncertainty increased. *"What are we doing here?"* he asked himself.

"Ma'am, we are here to speak with your husband," Tariq responded. There was silence. Shortly thereafter, the door opened and there stood Officer Juan Martinez. He towered over the two O.B.U. members and gave them a look of curiosity before he greeted them. "Gentlemen?" Martinez greeted as he looked between Tariq and Somali.

"Officer Martinez, I'm Tariq Galla and this is…"

"Somali Qusta," Somali greeted, scrutinizing the man.

"We are from an activist organization here in the city. If you don't mind, we would like to have a word with you," Tariq informed.

Martinez continued eyeing both men carefully. His curious wife, who stood a few feet behind him, inquired as to whether there was a problem. Juan turned briefly to make eye contact and assured her there wasn't.

"Sure, certainly, come right in," Officer Martinez invited them in, although his expression betrayed his cynicism. The two O.B.U. members entered the living room. Both surveyed the elegantly-decorated abode with its charming Mexican artistry and carpeting. Officer Martinez waved a hand to invite the men to take a seat, which they did. Both bore strained expressions in anticipation of the difficult task at hand.

Officer Martinez took a seat, neurotically rubbing his hands together. His expression had shifted to skepticism and nervousness when he heard the mention of an activist organization. It triggered thoughts of the O.B.U. men bringing forth some civil suit in the event he was somehow found guilty of second-degree murder. After he took a seat, he gestured for the men to present their business.

"Mr. Martinez, we are here on behalf of the victim of whom you and your partner have been indicted for the use of excessive force in his murder. We need some confirmation. I feel you are an honest man and you can be open with us. We need you to tell us exactly what happened that night," Tariq stated. He clasped his hands together as he studied the man's expression. The question appeared to cause Mr. Martinez some discomfort.

"Uh…hmm! You gentlemen wouldn't mind something to drink, would you?" he asked nervously. Tariq and Somali declined. They were anxious to get this interview over with.

However, Martinez arose and excused himself. A few minutes later he returned with a beverage for himself. After clearing his throat, he stammered as he attempted to answer the question. Somali repeated the question in curt tones. "I'm afraid my being an officer of the law, and thus versed on the law, I don't feel it appropriate to answer such questions without the presence of my lawyer," Martinez responded.

The two O.B.U. members exchanged meaningful glances. They were poised for such an evasive tactic. Thus, Tariq had planned an attack on the man's moral fiber, with the hopes that during the trial Martinez would betray the code and implore the truth.

"We understand, Mr. Martinez," Tariq stated after a brief pause, then smiled. "Mr. Martinez, let me ask you something. How long have you been on the force?" Tariq questioned. Martinez was not certain where Tariq's line of questioning was going and looked perplexed.

"Two years," he responded.

"Two years? And how long have you been partnered with Officer Kupchek?" Tariq further pressed.

"Mr. Galla, I feel that this line of questioning is leading back towards what I've already told you. I will not answer anything related to this case without the presence of my lawyer. Is this conversation being taped or something?" Martinez inquired.

"I can assure you that it is not. And my line of questioning doesn't have anything to do with the case," Tariq assured Martinez in the hopes of calming him down. Martinez took a sip of his beverage. It was becoming more apparent as the minutes passed that Martinez was hiding something. It was at that moment Somali removed some paperwork from a satchel he was carrying and presented it to the nervous man.

"We feel that it is imperative you read this," Somali stated bluntly. Officer Martinez stared down at the paperwork in confusion. "You see, your partner, Officer Kupchek, has a long, troubled history, especially in regards to minorities. As you read on, you will see he has lost the force thousandsof dollars in civil suits on several occasions. He has been involved in questionable testimonies against minority defendants when there were overwhelming evidence to support the defendant's innocence. He was criticized for racial slurs against blacks and Hispanics such as yourself. And, in his thirteen years on the force, he was dropped from lieutenant back to patrolling twice for unprofessional acts and scandals. Twice he shifted the weight on fellow officers who were terminated in exchange for the lesser penalty of a demotion. That's who you're teamed up with," Somali informed with conviction. The two O.B.U. men had done extensive research into the thirteen-year trek of the racist and corrupt officer.

Martinez flipped through the documents and read the court and precinct files on his partner. He shook his head in disbelief. Tariq and Somali exchanged meaningful glances again. They knew they had Martinez on the ropes. He'd been hit with hooks of racist profiling, jabbed with insubordination and traitorous facts, and now it was time for the knockout blow.

"Everything is right there in black and white. For the record, Kupchek has been heard by several of your fellow officers making racist comments in reference to the tragedy of those nineteen Mexican immigrants who died on the back of that tractor trailer a year ago," Tariq added. The purpose of bringing this incident up was to hit it home to Martinez and drop him to the canvas. His seventeen-year-old female cousin was one of the victims who had perished on the back of the tractor trailer as a result of dehydration, hypothermia and suffocation.

The incident occurred on May 14, 2003 during the transportation of some 70 Latino immigrants, from Harlingen, Texas, near the Mexico border, to Houston. These immigrants had migrated from various regions such as Mexico, El Salvador, Honduras, and the Dominican Republic. Their deaths caused public outcries of justice for immigrants by the Latin community.

Activist groups, such as the Salvadorian organization 'Crecen' and 'Mexicanos en Accion' spoke out publicly during a rally in 2005 commemorating those who died. Also, the National Network for Immigrant and Refugee Rights was extremely vocal after the deaths. It pressured Congress to pass a comprehensive immigration package and stated that "The deaths of these immigrants should be placed on the U.S. government."

After hearing the last revelation by Tariq, Martinez slowly folded the documents. His face was now a mask of sorrow.

"My little cousin, Alma, was on that trailer. She died of hypothermia," Martinez stated solemnly.

Tariq was engulfed in sympathy for the man. He and Somali were reminded that Martinez was directly affected by this tragedy.

"I'm sorry to hear that, Mr. Martinez. We had no way of knowing…" His words were interrupted by the wave of Martinez's hand as he rose and gave the folder back to Somali. After a moment of silence, Somali cleared his voice to speak.

"Mr. Martinez, I want you to think about something. I know that as an officer for the San Antonio Police Department you are probably sworn by some oath or code of loyalty. But, if this black youth were killed unjustly, we feel that it is the moral thing to do what is right. You should ask yourself this question: If it were you, putting him in the heat along on a wrongful death case… murder? If it were you, do you think he would abide by this oath or code of loyalty? Think about it," Somali stated.

Officer Martinez listened intently and seemed to be under his spell. Martinez nodded and his eyes darted as his mind reflected over the document that he read and the words that the two O.B.U. members had spoken.

After he finished speaking, Somali started to rise to his feet.

"We're not going to take up any more of your time. So we'll go now, Mr. Martinez. But we appreciate you for allowing us your time," Tariq stated, rising also and extended his hand.

Officer Martinez rose from the sofa and put on a complacent smile that belied the indecision in his eyes as he extended his hand. After firmly shaking hands with the officer, the two O.B.U. members let themselves out of the house. They left Officer Martinez to flop down on his sofa in anguish. He gulped down the remainder of his drink and stared off into space as if in deep thought.

✶✶✶✶✶✶✶✶

The Barbara Jordan Center was packed nearly to capacity. It was the last Saturday before the first week of school and kids from ages thirteen to young adult were there to enjoy themselves before returning to the chalkboards and textbooks.

Monotonous in itself, compounded with the biased curricula used in today's school. Many African American youths lose interest in what is being taught in school and have dropped out. The strobe lights flashed as the young teenagers danced to the powerfully rhythmic tunes of Destiny's Child's, 'Make Me Lose My Breath.' The congested dance floor was one big gyrating organism as young females in provocative outfits performed the latest dances with boys in oversized jeans and San Antonio Spurs or Dallas Cowboy hats and jerseys. Some boys wore gold teeth and jewelry, which glistened under the flashing lights.

Walking along the outer wall of the dance floor, Ikara was dressed in a white T-shirt and faded blue jeans over white and pink Timberland boots. She held onto Braun's hand as she led him across the floor. Her hair was freshly styled and her face was lightly made up with a hint of rouge and clear lip gloss.

Following closely behind the couple were their friends, Devonte, Sharon, Swathi, and Piye. Piye and Swathi were not there as a couple. However, Swathi, who decided to ditch her eyewear tonight was attempting to initiate a conversation with Piye. Out of courtesy and respect for Ikara, he casually responded to her overly-enthused advances.

The entourage of six stopped along the way to mingle with other 'wallflowers' when Swathi and Piye were caught in a precarious one-on-one intimate situation. Piye looked uncomfortable and looked around the dance hall as he fidgeted with his 'peach fuzz' of a goatee. He stole glances at Swathi in anticipation of further attempts at bonding.

Swathi moved her arms innocently. Her face was aglow with a gorgeous smile. When she glanced over at Piye, he registered uncertainty in her face. In that brief moment, a few African American boys smiled and briefly said hello to her as they passed by her. They shied away from approaching her when they noticed Piye standing near her. It was presumed from their reaction that they thought Piye was her boyfriend. Ikara, Braun, Devonte', and Sharon were fully engaged in a conversation with Marquis. Marquis is the rather studious Afro-centric young brother from the park that they often go to. As usual, he was adorned in cultural colors: red, black, and green. His black shirt was adorned with the slogan, 'Grab Education,' which was coined by the legendary Reggae group Steele Pulse.

"What's happening, guys? When did you get here?" Braun shouted.

"I've been up in here. I was over at the DJ stand. I was trying to get them to circulate some 'Roots or Dead Pres," Marquis shouted. His eyes were aglow and a wide grin was spread across his face. Braun knew that Marquis's request for the DJ to play culturally-conscious rap music was in vain.

"Ah man, come on, man. You know nobody is trying to hear no going back to Africa. Everybody is trying to have fun, man," Devonte laughed. Marquis shook his head and spoke to a passerby before turning his attention back to Devonte.

"You all are never trying to hear it, D," Marquis stated.

Devonte laughed, "Man I'm going to get you guys some plane tickets to the 'motherland'. And you bet you all will not come back. Man, I'm feeling Destiny's Child. Man, have you seen Beyoncé in that video?" Devonte asked lustfully. He lost himself in the moment, but was brought back to reality by Sharon, who slapped him on the shoulder, much to the amusement of the others.

Meanwhile, Swathi mustered up the nerve to make another attempt at conversation with Piye. "I really like this song. Do you like Destiny's Child?" she inquired with a warm smile. Her voice was almost inaudible, causing Piye's face to contort as he asked her to repeat herself.

"What?" he shouted as several youth passed by them to enter the dance floor at the exact moment the song ended. This allowed her words to be heard clearly.

"I said, I like this song. Do you like it?" she shouted, and abruptly had to lower her voice. This caused her slight embarrassment, which she played off with a smile as she ran her hand through her hair. Piye smiled as he looked away and answered indifferently.

"It's alright," he stated. Swathi nodded and her expression displayed her dissatisfaction with his nonchalant response. She nevertheless planned to pursue him further.

"I think you should play football. I mean, for the school next semester. You're so big and strong with big muscles," she smiled.

Piye laughed at her attempt to be congenial. He felt compelled to be sarcastic. However, upon turning around to respond, her radiant beauty under the flashing strobe lights totally consumed him. He was momentarily entranced by her eyes. His emotions were gripped and he became uncomfortable. He was Nubian and his emotions had been distorted by his father's unethical and perversed view of Arabic peoples, due to the situation in the Sudan. But Braun's incessant rationalization and morality over the years began to eat away at this perverse standpoint. And now, in this instance, as he looked into Swathi's doe-like eyes, he began to question his father even more. Neither Arabs nor Europeans were inherently evil, especially not this beautiful, innocent, and intelligent Pakistani girl who stood before him. He wanted to embrace and kiss her. She recognized the look in his eyes which evidenced these emotions. At the last second, he fought off the emotional shift and once again looked away before responding.

"Play football? Because I'm big and black, I'm supposed to play sports?" he stated sarcastically without looking at her.

"No, I didn't mean it like that," she stated with a nervous laugh.

"Yeah, I know. Anyway no, no, I'm not playing football. I don't play any sports. I keep in shape for other reasons. I don't entertain for 'massa'. Sports are a distraction," he responded.

At that moment the DJ began spinning another song. This time it was one of a slower speed. Couples began to replace the other dancers, who were gyrating in suggestive dance moves and sweating profusely.

"Ooh, that's my song! Come on Devonte," Sharon stated as she tugged at Devonte's shirt. Ikara, Braun, Marquis, and Yolanda proceeded to the dance floor. As they passed by Swathi and Piye, Sharon said, "Come on you all." Swathi sighed with laughter, indicative of her nervousness in presenting this proposal to Piye. But after a moment, she gathered herself and awkwardly presented it to him.

"Um, look, I'm sorry. I didn't mean to offend you," she stated.

Piye nodded his head and accepted her apology without actually verbalizing it.

"So would you like to dance?" Swathi asked.

The strobe lights continued to flash and illuminate Piye's face. He turned his head and began clasping his hands together as his arms swung back and forth. He secretly desired her and wanted to dance with her. He wanted to let down his defenses and get to know her as a person, but visions of how his father would react to his becoming involved with an Arab crossed his mind.

"Look, there are plenty of others in here you can dance with. Kick it with one of them, okay? Look over there. Dance with him. You all got the same ethnic thing going on," he stated as he gestured in the direction of a Pakistani boy dressed in hip-hop fashion. The boy was eyeing Swathi as he sipped a soda. The pain was instantly reflected in Swathi's innocent eyes. Piye regretted the racist implication. He turned and walked away from her and left her with a dejected expression. She was devastated.

The slow song ended and the six friends made their way off of the dance floor, each couple held their partner's hand as they neared the concessions. Piye was there alone as he bought something to eat and drink. Looking around the vicinity, Braun turned to Piye and inquired as to Swathi's whereabouts. With his back still turned, Piye dryly responded, though his eyes were filled with guilt.

"I don't know. I guess she probably got interested in someone else. You know," Piye stated as he bit into a bear claw. The expression on Braun's face evidenced cynicism. He sensed that Piye had, without tact, rejected Swathi's advances and ran her off. Ikara, who stood behind him, was obviously thinking the same thing.

"Where's Swathi, Piye?" Yolanda inquired as she looked around. Piye remained silent. After a few moments of observing his silent friend, Braun turned sharply and announced to Ikara his intentions to find Swathi.

As Braun made his way through the gyrating bodies and flashing strobe lights, Swathi stood alone outside besides Ikara's mother's Range Rover. She was staring out at the passing traffic. Her eyes were reddened and her face solemn. Every so often, her dainty hand would reach up to wipe away a tear, which she was doing just as Braun arrived. With a concerned expression on his face, Braun approached her timidly. He observed her from behind as she wiped away another tear, noting that she was completely oblivious to his presence. He was struck with a wave of compassion that was quickly superseded by the anger he felt at Piye for causing her distress.

"Swathi, what's wrong?" he spoke out in a compassionate tone, startling her. Swathi wiped away a tear, then attempted to disguise her pain with a smile. She ran her hands through her silky black hair as she briefly looked Braun in the eye. She was slightly embarrassed by what she perceived as being overly sensitive and looked away. She cast her gaze downward as she declared she was okay.

"I'm okay really, it was so silly of me, really," she stated. At that moment, Sharon and Ikara approached. Braun and Swathi had similar expressions of concern on their faces. Braun's caught sight of them through his peripheral vision.

"What was silly? I don't understand. Did Piye say something to hurt you?" Braun inquired.

"Are you okay? What happened?" her friends inquired with concerned expressions. Swathi feigned a laugh as she shook her head and held up a cautioning hand.

"I'm okay. I'm okay. I was just in over my head. No need for everyone to feel sorry for poor little Swathi. I'm just supersensitive. That's all. You know me. I cry during PG movies," she stated. Her humor was an attempt to curtail her friends' sympathy. Each smiled, but still with an expression of concern. It was obvious that she was hurting.

"What did he say to you, Swathi?" Braun inquired.

Swathi remained silent for a moment before responding. Her voice cracked in the middle of the sentence and became a squeak in between words as tears once again began flowing down her beautiful face.

"He said I should talk to someone of my own race. I didn't know he was like this," she reported.

Braun was incensed now. Sharon and Ikara shook their heads. Both were familiar with Piye's overzealousness towards the Nubian cause and his stance against Arabs or anyone resembling their ethnicity. Neither of them had expected him to extend this distorted hatred toward their friend. This beautiful, loving, and spiritual flower would never deliberately hurt anyone. They too were outraged.

"Swathi, Piye didn't mean that. He's going through a lot. You have to…" Sharon and Ikara's words were interrupted.

"It's okay, really. I understand. It's okay," Swathi stated, wiping away a tear.

It was all that Braun could stand. He made it a point to rectify the situation, and to force Piye to make amends through a sincere apology. He turned sharply on his heels and stomped back in the direction of the building. His mind was racing with tactful ways of how to confront Piye. His anger at Piye's delusional ethnic spite clouded these tactful approaches. As he made his way back through the mosh pit of young hip-hop enthusiasts oscillating to another fast paced R & B song, his anger grew.

"Piye! Piye!" Braun shouted out to him. Piye was already undergoing rational pleas from Devonte, who stayed behind for that purpose. He looked up with an expression of guilt and examined Braun's contorted visage. "Piye! Man, I'm telling you, you go out there and apologize to Swathi right now! This racism has to stop, man. That girl has never hurt anybody! She just wanted to get to know you and now, I'm wondering why!" Braun stated. He was breathing erraticly. He knew Piye's temper and was somewhat intimidated by his Herculean size. However, he stood firm.

Studying his friend's expression, Piye saw his seriousness. Curious onlookers gathered at the spectacle. Devonte maneuvered between the two in anticipation of Piye moving on Braun, Piye shook his head. Staring off in embarrassment at the spectators, he set down
his soda. He rose from his seat and maneuvered past Braun.

Outside, Ikara and Sharon were still consoling their friend as Piye strode up. He slowed down as he observed Swathi wiping away a tear. He had no idea that his thoughtless and hurtful response to her advances had caused her such pain. He felt even guiltier and unsure about his apologetic approach. But it was imperative. Piye's hulking frame was spotted first by Sharon as he approached from behind them and she rolled her eyes.

Piye spoke out to Ikara timidly.

"Ikara, I want…I want to speak with her alone," he requested. Ikara, who was sensitive herself, was fighting back tears. She looked at Piye with sorrowful eyes. Without responding to his request, she turned to her friend and asked her if she was okay with speaking to him alone. Ikara looked one more time into Piye's eyes and motioned for Sharon to come along. She complied and gave Piye a disdainful last look. This one he didn't see.

There were a few seconds of silence as Piye observed Swathi, who looked away. He didn't exactly know how to approach her. He wished that he could relive that moment and tell her how much he had really been attracted to her and how much he was drawn to her personality. He hated himself for hurting her and for allowing his distorted views of Arabs to affect him to such a degree that he would maliciously attack this beautiful, innocent soul.

"Swathi, Swathi, I'm sorry," he stated. Swathi simply nodded without looking at him. Her head hung slightly. Her flowing hair obscured her face as she leaned against the Range Rover. "Swathi, look at me please," he pleaded. Hearing these words, Swathi's initial apprehensions of his apology being predicated solely on Braun's request changed. She heard sincerity and hurt in his voice, which compelled her to slowly look in his direction. Piye moved in closer and stared deeply into her eyes before speaking. "I didn't mean that. I swear I didn't. You're beautiful, and I don't mean just in appearance. And I don't want you to be under the impression that I hate you," he stated with compassion.

"But my people, you hate," she replied timidly, dropping her head once again.

In that instant, images of his father's ranting about the 'evil' Arabs raping, murdering, and pillaging innocent people during their invasion of Africa crossed his mind.

"Swathi, no, no, I don't hate your people. I'm just…I've been raised on so much hate and my people suffered so much," he stated.

Swathi interjected, "My people have suffered too."

Piye nodded his head and looked away before returning his gaze.

"I know, Swathi. I'm sorry. My hatred gets displaced sometimes. I hurt people who have never done anything to me. Because of people oppressing my people, I say stupid things. Things I regret. I do things I regret, like hurting you. Please, Swathi… forgive me," he pleaded again.

While he spoke, Swathi leaned on his every syllable. Her eyes intensely examined his and her expression showed signs of forgiveness.

"I forgive you, Piye and I understand," she responded. Her eyes still glazed over.

Piye nodded and looked around uncomfortably. The situation was awkward. He smiled in hopes of lightening the somber mood.

"So, can we go back inside now? Where everyone's having fun, you know, this is a dance," he smiled. Swathi laughed. She ran her fingers through her hair as she looked at him.

Piye extended his hand to her. "Will you stay on the dance floor with me the rest of the night? We have to make up for the time out here when we could have been in there," he requested.

Swathi's face glowed and her wide smile exposed her pearly white teeth.

"Umm, okay," she laughed. She placed her hand in his and in that brief moment the two held meaningful eye contact. It was spiritual. The two began walking back in the direction of the center.

Chapter 19

Tariq pulled up behind a late model Chrysler LeBaron that was parked in front of a squat wood and brick bungalow. It was painted yellow and had sparse shrubbery and yard ornaments throughout the front lawn. This quaint little home was surrounded with an aged steel fence with a sign on top of it which read: "Beware of dog". The dog made its presence known the second Tariq closed the gate behind him, barking and rattling its chain in suspicion.

Tariq proceeded with caution down the brick walkway which led to the house's front steps. He squinted from the bright sunlight until the shade from the tree in the yard next door blocked its rays. The block was a rather quiet one. Few incidents were reported on this block of blue-collar workers, one of whom was the man in a welder uniform from the day the federal agents raided the area. He waved at Tariq as he knocked on the wooden door.

A few seconds passed and footsteps could be heard approaching on the clapboard floors. "Who is it?" a woman called out in a cautious voice.

"Mrs. Smith, this is Tariq Galla. I'm with the O.B.U., ma'am. I'd like to come in and have a word with you," Tariq introduced himself. She unbolted the locks and opened the door. However, Mrs. Smith eyed him cautiously through the crack of the chain-locked door for good measure. After observing this middle-aged African-American man, with a complacent expression, adorned in African garb, she relaxed and allowed him inside.

The inside of the house was decorated with vibrant colors that matched the paintings on the wall. There was a painting of a black cameo of an African-American woman with braids encased in a gold frame; a portrait of an African family; and a large portrait of an African looking Jesus Christ. This was the largest picture at the center of the room. Underneath it was a picture of Mrs. Smith with her son, Jamie Smith.

After a brief but thorough observation, Tariq took a seat on her burgundy leather loveseat. The interior of this home reflected this woman's persona. Her clothing was stylish and she wore a freshly-styled perm. She was young, mid-thirties, and seemingly independent. She appeared confident, to a degree. After such a tragic occurrence, her spirituality seemed broken. Tariq empathized with this sister.

"Can I get you something to drink, Mr. Galla? I keep some brandy for special occasions, if you'd like?' she offered and broke a smile that belied the still-curious look in her eyes.

"No, thank you, Mrs. Smith. I'm not given to alcohol. I haven't touched it in years, but thank you," Tariq declined. Mrs. Smith then took a seat on a recliner, withdrew a cigarette and lit it. She released a funnel of smoke as she let the cigarette hang loosely in her limp hand and dropped the ashes into an ashtray atop the coffee table between them. Her eyes began to express speculation as to the reason of his visit.

"I know you're probably wondering why I'm here," Tariq stated.

Mrs. Smith raised her eyebrows to confirm this.

"Yes, it did cross my mind," she smiled as she dumped more ashes into the ashtray. The scent of cigarette smoke mixed with perfume filled the room with a pungent odor.

"It's about the case involving your son, James," Tariq informed. At the mention of her son's name, Mrs. Smith expression changed to one of suppressed sorrow.

"The case involving my son? I don't understand," she responded.

Tariq shared with her the paperwork surrounding Officer Kupchek's notorious past. Mrs. Smith reached for the paperwork and shook her head as she released a funnel of smoke.

"I don't see how this is going to do any good. White cop shoots another black boy in a drug area. They're just going to make my baby look like he was at fault in that court room," she stated. She sighed as she ran a hand across her forehead. She opened the folder and mumbled unintelligible words.

"Mrs. Smith, these documents are Officer Kupchek's malfeasant past of corruption. It is evidence that may bring justice when revealed," Tariq informed her. He hoped to change the woman's pessimistic outlook on the outcome of the trial. As she read certain excerpts, she shook her head. She was still in disbelief as to how a black youth's death at the hands of a white cop in a volatile area, a white cop sworn to preserve and protect the community, would be unjustified in the eyes of a probably predominately-white jury, a jury completely in favor of the anti-crime bills and war on drugs systematically aimed at a people whom they racially oppress.

"It's still going to be the other officer's and his word against this. There were drugs and they'll presume he was dealing. They aren't going to take into account and won't care that he was a good student with a good future. And there was a gun found in the car," Mrs. Smith stated in despair.

"It still doesn't give the police the right to shoot him in the back. He was unarmed. And that's all that matters in this case," Tariq retorted.

Mrs. Smith rose to her feet in distress. She clutched the folder in which she had replaced the paperwork. She released a deep sigh and walked over to the picture of her deceased son. She touched the glass, and in a dispirited tone, began indirectly rambling about him, for whom she had high expectations. "James was a good student in school. He always made the honor roll. He would run in to show me his report cards. He said he wanted to be an engineer like his father. He idolized his father. He wanted to be just like him," she started while staring off into space. It was then that Tariq noticed the picture of a man in blue-collar uniform. "But then he was killed in an offshore accident. James was only nine years old. He was devastated. His father was his whole world. And now he's gone," she stated. Her chest heaved and tears began to roll down her face. "I don't know what to do. My baby, my baby," she repeated over and over again.

Tariq felt slightly guilty for reopening up these disheartening memories. He stood up from the loveseat to console her.

Mrs. Smith, I'm sorry. I didn't mean…" His words were cut off by hers.

It's okay. I'm okay. Here you go Mr. Galla," she stated handing over the folder back to him. Tariq examined her in silence. She removed another cigarette from her Virginia Slim pack and started to further discuss her son.

"Are you sure you're okay, Mrs. Smith? If you want me to leave I'll…" With an ambiguous hand gesture, she once again cautioned him. She blew out a funnel of smoke before retaking her seat on the recliner.

"It's just still hard for me. First, I endured the death of my husband. I loved him so much. After he was killed on the rig, it was so hard on me. I had to go out and find work. I had a diploma but no skills. So I went to technical college for nursing," she said.

"How long have you been in the nursing field?" Tariq implored.

Mrs. Smith tapped her ashes into the ashtray and replied, "Over six years now. I'm right here at St. Jude on East Southcross," Mrs. Smith informed.

Tariq's eyes registered admiration for the woman. He realized she was a strong woman who, in a time of crisis, had regrouped and laid a foundation for a promising career.

"That's commendable, Mrs. Smith," he complimented.

Mrs. Smith nodded. Her eyes glazed over once again as she reflected on her son. She shook her head and picked up the picture of him.

"James was my peace of mind. He was my everything. I still imagine him walking across that stage to receive this diploma. I imagine him walking through that door," she stated, struggling to fight back the tears.

"Mrs. Smith, I can only imagine your grief. And to learn of James' academics only reinforces the injustice that was carried out by the officer. Along with other concerned citizens, I am going to make sure this officer is prosecuted," he stated.

Mrs. Smith nodded. "I know my child would have been something special. I want this officer to pay. I want retribution. It's the only way I can have some peace and closure, Mr. Galla," she declared.

Tariq felt extreme sympathy as he stared into the young woman's eyes. Her eyes told of great burdens and a lack of inner peace from the two voids she now had to contend with, the loss of a devoted hardworking husband and the son whose righteous path in life was detoured by the excessive force enacted by the police. Tariq reached out and clasped her hand.

"We are going to do everything we possibly can in this investigation to see that the prosecutor convinces the jury to make him pay," Tariq remarked.

"Do you think this information will make a difference? Will this Hispanic cop tell the truth?" she asked.

Tariq dared not give off his pessimism. However, he had to inform her of the circumstances.

"A fellow member of our organization and I made it a point of interest to persuade this Hispanic officer. We were able to get him to read these same documents in order to have full knowledge of just how racist and corrupt his partner is. We hope he will do the right thing. We also intend to stress James' academics and how he aspired to make something of his life by going to college. It is important to let the court see that this act was a malicious attack on James' rights and that he never posed a threat to anyone. The main issue is that he wasn't armed. Justice will be served," Tariq stated in confidence. Mrs. Smith broke a smile as she squeezed his hand.

"Thank you, Mr. Galla. I really appreciate what you and the O.B.U. are doing," she stated graciously.

Tariq smiled. Then he rose from his seat still holding her hand.

"It's a pleasure, Mrs. Smith. If there is any way we can be of further help, just let us know. Read over the information and you can mail it back to me, or if you'd like, you can bring it to me at my address. Maybe you can have dinner with my family," Tariq stated as he reached for the doorknob. "Take care of yourself, Mrs. Smith," he said. He proceeded out of the house, closing the door behind him.

✶✶✶✶✶✶✶✶

Somali was having a conversation with another member of the O.B.U. Both were dressed in traditional African garb and sporting kufis. The guest, a senior citizen with nearly all grey dreadlocks and bifocals carried a satchel with documents which pertained to an upcoming meeting. The two were laughing as the man patted Somali on the shoulder, and he paused when he reached the door. "Make sure Brother Furuq has his presentation ready. I know he's been busy. But this is important too. I want everything in order for these visiting organizations," the brother ordered.

"I'll get on him, Brother Yoruba," Somali stated, returning the pat on the back. The elderly gentleman then proceeded out of the house.

Turning on his heels, Somali walked through the kitchen. He stopped at the stove where his wife was preparing a traditional African dish of okra, spiced meats, and bread. He rubbed her arms and kissed her on the cheek before inhaling deeply as the tantalizing aroma perforated the kitchen. "Everything smells good. Okra is just like I like it. What type of spices did you use in the meats?" he inquired as he took off his kufi. His wife laughed.

"Special African blend mixed with some paprika," she informed. "What was Brother Yoruba talking about?" she inquired.

"The meeting and other issues. The police case. He just stopped by on his way to another meeting," Somali informed.

"Well, everything is almost ready. Tell Piye to make sure he washes his hands. He's been out there playing with Phil's dog. I don't even know why Phil's mother gave him that dog. I don't like them old dogs," she stated as she took off her mittens. Her face contorted into a scowl to emphasize her dislike for pit bulls. Somali laughed.

"I'll tell him," he responded, then took off down the hallway to Piye's room.

Piye stood in front of his mirror with his shirt off, observing his physique. He was startled by his father's abrupt announcement. "Son, dinner is almost ready and your mother says don't forget to wash your hands," Somali smirked.

"Okay, pop," Piye responded.

"Are you ready for Friday?" Somali inquired, while motioning at Piye's bed. Across it was an orange and black dashiki and a pile of paperwork. Piye glanced over at his bed.

"Yeah, I'm ready. I'm kind of nervous about giving a speech in front of all those people. But I'm ready." His expression hinted that something was troubling him, something urgent which needed to be expressed. However, Somali did not pick up on the expression. He attempted to proceed on down the hallway as Piye fidgeted with his dashiki, but was immediately called back.

"Pop," Piye called out to his father. Somali backed up to his son's doorway. His expression was inquisitive as he anticipated Piye's reason for calling him back.

"Yes, son?" Somali inquired. Piye averted eye contact. His expression was nervous. "Something troubling you?" he pressed, studying his son. Piye nodded. His expression changed to a more subtle one.

"Yeah, matter of fact there is, Pop. We need to talk," he stated. He looked sternly into his father's eyes, causing Somali's mind to race with questions as to why Piye asked for this serious talk. He motioned with his hands and beseeched Piye to present his problem.

"It's like this, Pop. You know I'm with everything the O.B.U. stands for. I'm Nubian. You taught me that. I researched that and I know our people in the Sudan and over here too are in constant struggle. And we have been in struggle ever since the invaders infiltrated the continent. I know who the enemy is... now. I just don't see them as being the enemy, Pop," Piye stated.

Somali tried to grasp exactly where his son was coming from and whether or not he was taking on a new stance. "I don't understand, son? You know who the enemy is now? And you feel that I'm delusional, maybe, as to who the enemy is?" Somali inquired, looking at his son with scrutiny.

Piye swung his arms back and forth as he looked up at the ceiling. He shook his head as he began explaining without looking at his father. "I'm not saying you're delusional, Pop. What I am saying is that, in some cases, the people we see as the enemy, simply because of their ethnicity, really aren't the enemy. The enemy is anybody who's counterproductive and obstructive to the progress of the people. And that could be another black," Piye stated.

"I'm more than aware of this, son. Remember, I was there during the 60s. I've seen whites marching alongside blacks with Dr. King, Jr. And in the late 60s and 70s I attended funerals of Black Panthers killed by Karenga's United Slaves. So where are you going with this?" Somali asked.

Piye smiled as he thought about Swathi for a moment. He began to speak, but averted his father's eyes. "I met someone and she really made me see..." Piye began. But his words were interrupted by Somali's laughter.

"You met someone? Oh, let me guess, a white girl?" Somali asked.

"No, Pop. She's isn't white. And even if she was Pop, we can't continue misdirecting hate. That in itself is counterproductive because we lose focus,"

Piye explained.

"So, now you are going to tell me about how to fight in the struggle? I was knee-deep in it before you were born, son. The only way to defeat an enemy is to hold everyone as suspect who fits the description and stamp them out if given the slightest indication. It's what the soldiers had to do in Vietnam. They couldn't discern the difference between the Viet Cong and the South Vietnamese. In daytime, they would be saying 'good G. I., Good G. I., me no V. C., me no V. C. But at night they would ambush. So in many instances they eliminated anyone who fit the description," Somali responded.

Piye shook his head. He was ashamed by his father's ideology. It was an ideology that had been deeply rooted in hatred and delusion. They were distorted views that were superseded only by their ineffectual methods for combating the agents of repression and a lack of real militaristic format.

"Vietnam, huh? So you're adopting the same ideology the racist government used to attempt to wipe out an oppressed people? The same ideology used by a government that allows cocaine and heroin into the country to poison our people or banish us in prison camps? The same heroin the U. S. soldiers in Vietnam used and distorted their judgment. That's right, high on heroin, Pop. They were high on dope. What's your excuse?" Piye stated in defiance as he scrutinized his father. "I'm going to wash up for dinner," Piye demanded and brushed past his father. He left him standing there in the threshold of his bedroom door with a rather bewildered expression.

Ursula and Catrina were showcasing some of the top-of-the-line interior furniture to a potential customer, a middle-aged Caucasian lady whose modest attire did not correlate with the 2004 Mercedes Benz she arrived in. Her pompous flair with words certainly made up for this inconsistency. They were examining a rack of Persian rugs when Ursula waved a hand above the fabric to give a marketing critique. The woman seemed to be appraising the fine fabric work, and began informing the two interior designers of her very own Persian rug collection. She had a number of Persian rugs throughout the interior of several of her homes.

"I think it would go splendid in my oak wood floor beach house. There are so many beautiful patterns in this hand-woven material. It's funny, but I'm actually out buying fabrics for a home that we thought we would have to collect insurance on," the woman stated as she examined another rug.

"Ooh! This is nice," she added. Ursula and Catrina wondered what she meant by collecting insurance.

"Collecting insurance on the house? For what?" Catrina inquired.

"My husband and I own a beach house in Pensacola, Florida. There was a terrible threat of losing it to the hurricane that was due to hit. However, it dwindled into a tropical storm. And, here I am shopping," the woman informed.

Both Ursula and Catrina bore expressions of sarcasm bordering cynicism. *Why would people buy houses on cliffs or along beaches knowing there was a great chance of losing the home to natural disasters? Insurance scams, maybe? Perhaps.*

Moments after the upscale lady explained the insurance situation, the doors opened and in walked a distinctive a young woman, dressed in African looking clothing. Her beautiful brown skin was shining with perspiration. Her smile exposed her white teeth as she exhibited relief at the air conditioner's frigidness, as compared to the humid and desert-like temperatures outside.

Excusing herself from the tour of exotic rugs with the Caucasian lady, Catrina made her way over to the young woman who was examining some of the fine fabrics of the interior furniture on display.

"Hello, how are you today?" Catrina chimed with her hands behind her back. Her heels and suit, compounded with the effects of her spectacles, gave her a very professional appearance.

"I'm fine, how are you? I was just browsing through the fabric displays," the young woman responded with a courteous smile.

"Are there any certain fabrics you might be interested in? We have a collection of Amritzar, George Smith." Catrina asked as she examined the sister's African attire.

She didn't speak with an accent and this aroused her curiosity more.

"No, I'm not looking to redecorate. Home interior is my field. I'm graduating from St. Philips next semester and I just wanted to come in here and get the inside track on the business," the young sister informed. Catrina nodded.

"Oh, you are at St. Philips? I presume you're studying our culture also?" Catrina inquired. The sister smiled and nodded in confirmation.

"I have a sister in Community Alert People. Her name is Joyce Green," Catrina added.

"She's involved with the New World Learning Center. I met her earlier this year at the ceremonies for the children," the young woman acknowledged. Before Catrina could respond, Ursula approached and the women exchanged greetings. Catrina explained proudly the young lady's academic achievements and aspiration to be an interior designer. Ursula and the young lady were already well-acquainted with each other, as both were members of O.B.U. However, both simply smiled as Catrina introduced them, without interrupting her. "We've been acquainted for some time. I'm in the O.B.U.," the young lady informed. Ursula laughed as she placed both hands onto the young sister's shoulders and hugged her.

"Catrina, this is Sister Vontreece. Vontreece, this is my consultant, Catrina," Ursula smiled. "I got a call about an hour ago from a potential customer interested in refurnishing a condominium in Universal City. She'll be here within the hour. So please advise her on that. If she has any questions, I'll be in my office on the computer going over some things with Sister Vontreece," Ursula instructed after handing some brochures to Catrina. She proceeded to escort Sister Vontreece towards the back.

Ursula and the young sister were now inside of the office where Ursula would often go to browse the internet and chat with interior designing enthusiasts abroad. She would also get and share business tipswith other decorators online. She explained the business to the young sister and showed her the sites she should go to access more information.

Vontreece was very attentive and listened carefully to Ursula and paid attention to the interior arrangements on the screen. She also watched as Ursula maneuvered the interior designs with the mouse.

"See how the color patterns of the floor's rug contrasts with the walls? This is bad coordination. Now, if we implement this pattern, which is bolder but still in accordance, it gives the room its proper coordination of color patterns," Ursula explained.

"How about we delete this and use this softer tone? It doesn't throw off the effects of the base color pattern. Does it?" Vontreece inquired as she used the mouse to implement her own scheme. Ursula's expression registered her compliance.

"I'm impressed. That's very good coordination, Vontreece," she responded. The young sister smiled proudly. Then Ursula began maneuvering the mouse as she searched the computer's screen.

"I want to thank you Ursula for spending time with me. And thank you for believing in me and pushing me to pursue my dreams," Vontreece stated. Ursula smiled while continuing her search and responded without looking in her direction.

"Well, Vontreece, I'm just proud that you've retained focus and believed in yourself. You can go as far in this business as you like," she stated, looking proudly at her young apprentice. Vontreece smiled. Her eyes were full of enthusiasm. "Now, I'd like to show you some other aspects that I know you'll find interesting," Ursula assured as she returned her attention back to the computer. She pointed at the screen and maneuvered the mouse as she explained further details of the interior design business.

For the next thirty minutes, Ursula explained the business side of the interior design industry. She discussed the advantages and disadvantages about the business and the importance of marketing. Ursula stressed the importance of staying abreast about the latest trends and the many different types of quality fabric available.

"It's a lot to remember about the financial and marketing aspects of the business. But right now, just focus on the designing aspects. We'll go over some more of that at a later date. Okay?" Ursula stated as she closed the laptop. She motioned Vontreece towards the door and stated, "There's a designing trade show coming up next month on the 15th and I'd like for you to attend, okay?"

"I'll be there. If I'm not too exhausted from all the classes I'm taking. Thank you, Sister Ursula," Vontreece replied. She proceeded out of the room as Ursula briefly watched the young O.B.U. sister through the glass window with pride. Her eyes glazed over with pride for her young O.B.U. sister. She returned to her seat behind the computer.

★★★★★★★★

Tariq was wearing his spectacles and diligently researching a legal case in his study room. Since the police killing of young James Smith, he had been painstakingly searching through federal and state law books in hopes of finding cases similar to this one. This research, along with O.B.U.'s personal investigation into Kupchek and Martinez, had been consuming nearly all of his time.

After jotting down notes, Tariq set down his pencil upon the desk. He removed his spectacles and pinched his tired eyes. It was then that he heard the front door open up and he knew it was Ursula. He thought to himself as he reclined back in his seat. He released a sigh and stared over at the bookshelves, his mind racing with depressing the images that had been called to mind, due to the emotions he experienced in dealing with the Smith case. As he sat there meditating in that brief instance, he replayed the images in his mind. His mind replayed the images much like a semi-auto, which in many cases would discharge suddenly without provocation on black and Hispanic motorists. He thought about the images of crying mothers as they were called to the scene; the shouting officers with weapons drawn; and terrified expressions of black and Hispanic youth's moments before they were assaulted or hit with a barrage of bullets. It was disheartening.

As Tariq shook his head from the sickening images, he caught sight of his loving wife Ursula in his peripheral vision. She stood there for only a moment, but long enough to observe the disconcerted expression on her husband's face. She entered the room. Tariq attempted to place a smile on his face to conceal the disturbance. However, his eyes defied this attempt and revealed his soul.

"Oh, it's nothing, honey. How was your day?" he responded before the two kissed.

Ursula set her purse upon the desk and glanced down at the law books as she began to respond.

"It was okay. Sister Vontreece stopped by. I'd told her to come by so that I could show her the ropes. She's a very resilient girl. I think she'll go far in the business. What's this you're researching?" she inquired while looking down at the law books.

Tariq put his spectacles back on his face and rubbed his hands together. He looked down at the law books himself as he released a sigh.

"A lot of legal stuff about different excessive force claims. All are federal in that book. The law has a lot of leeway when it comes to what's classified as excessive force, and what is done within the line of their duty to subdue a perpetrator or suspect. I just don't think justice is going to be served, especially if Martinez doesn't do the right thing. Even with his testimony in favor of the prosecution, it's a long shot," Tariq explained.

Ursula's expression evidenced her struggle to grasp the legal protection of officers in cases where it was clear they acted irrationally.

"I just don't understand. It's evident the boy was unarmed and he was shot in the back," she argued.

Tariq nodded in agreement to her assertion. However, he was aware that an officer on duty, patrolling in a high crime area in pursuit of a known drug dealer, outweighed the fact that the victim was not the suspect and was unarmed.

"Well, from a logical standpoint, that would be enough to convict. But not under the sometimes illogical judiciary in regards to young black boys being gunned down in our communities. You know, I went to see his mother today," he informed.

Ursula folded her arms as she anticipated the report of the outcome and expressed concern.

"So, how was she? I mean, I know she's probably still struggling to cope. I can't imagine losing a child. What it's like to go through that?" Ursula asked sympathetically.

"She's doing as well as can be expected. She's a strong woman. I brought the paperwork on Kupchek's criminal past. And I explained to her the potential ace in the hole with Martinez, provided his conscience plays a part," Tariq explained.

At that moment, Ikara and Caleb crossed each other in the hallway and playfully bumped into each other the way siblings do. They garnered the brief attention of both Tariq and his wife. Then Ursula inquired further into Mrs. Smith's opinion concerning the chances of justice being served in the case of her son's murder.

Tariq explained how he perceived Mrs. Smith's reception. He also described the emotions he experienced at seeing another distraught black mother with a loss of a child and her loss of confidence in the system--the police force as well as the judiciary system. And, furthermore, loss of trust in the establishment responsible for creating laws that enable police to harass and profile black youths in our communities.

He further illustrated the woman's heartfelt reflections of the son she gave birth to. The son who was cheerful, an academically-talented child who strove for a college education, and was a prospect for a career in the NBA. She talked about the emotional void she was never able to fill when she lost her husband who was fatally injured on an oil rig off the shores of Galveston, Texas.

"As she explained to me the situation with James, there was so much passion and so much truth. She showed me pictures of him, his past report cards, trophies in basketball and the college brochures he received. I know he wanted to go to Texas. They cut his life short through racism and fear," Tariq explained.

There was a moment of silence as Ursula mentally envisioned James' mother, who was stripped of the possibility to hold her son again. She was only left to reminisce and reflect over pictures and memories. She was desperately trying to get Tariq and anyone else who listened to see that her son had had potential.

"It was blatant injustice that his superiors didn't strip him of his badge years ago. We have to do everything in our power to assure that justice is served to Mrs. Smith this time. More importantly, that her son's death won't be forgotten in the history books as another statistic, but will serve as a precedent and deterrent to all police officers who abuse their badges of authority," Tariq stated firmly.

Ursula stared deeply into her husband's eyes. And she could now see that his diligence in the Smith case was superseded by a deeper goal. No, he wasn't just fighting for the justice in Mrs. Smith's cause, but for Paul Childs, Amadou Diallo, Dante Dawson, Tim Thomas, and the hundreds of other slain young black men, gunned down or brutally beaten to death before their time at the hands of the police.

Chapter 20

The bright lights at Judson High School stadium illuminated the football field. The atmosphere was electric and the crowd was full of energy, dressed in their respective team colors. The Judson Rockets were dressed in their red and white home jerseys and tugs. Their rivals, the Stratford High School Spartans from Houston, Texas were donning their green and white colors. It was a thriller thus far, with the home team Rockets maintaining a lead of 26-21 with 1.08 seconds remaining in the game.

The second half had been hard-hitting and tense. Both teams' defenses stymied the other with little action in terms of offensive production. However, the Rockets had substantial success running the football and pounding off tackles or running sweeps gaining significant yardage. Each time penetration was made into Spartan territory, their defense would stiffen.

Neither team had driven into the other's territory to score. The Rocket's first score of the second half came off of a turnover by their star strong safety Devonte Johnson. He had already racked up nine solo tackles, reacted to a tipped, a errant pass, and caught the ball in stride. He maneuvered past defenders and sprinted 41 yards before being pushed out of bounds at the Stratford third yard line. Two plays later their tailback took it in from the one with 10.08 seconds remaining in the 3rd quarter.

This made the score 19-7, but Stratford would score with 7.01 seconds remaining when the Rockets gambled on 4th and 1 from the 41 yard line. After the Spartan defense had stacked the line and prevented the first down, the quarterback on the next play heaved a 41 yard strike to his receiver who caught the pass over his left shoulder at the pylon and electrified the Spartan crowd. They kicked the extra point to make it 19-14. After that score, there would be a 7 minute lull until, with 1 second remaining in the 3rd when a Spartan receiver hauled in a slant pass, 63 yards for a touchdown.

After turning the ball over on their 27 yard line, the Spartan defense began to wear down as the Rockets pounded the football, running dives, pitches, off tackles, and counters, until they scored on a thrilling quarterback keeper to go ahead 26-21. But Stratford's quarterback completed passes of 14, 9, 11, and 5 yards to put them in good field position with 1.08 left. A strange turn of events would take place after Stratford's quarterback threw an errant pass that was intercepted by a Rocket cornerback. As the cornerback weaved through and around tacklers, the quarterback himself stripped position, at the Judson 33 yard line. The crowd was aghast and on their feet. The atmosphere was tense, but then the defense stiffened. Limiting a first down run play by Stratford's leading tailback to 3 yards, then covering a pass play that, if caught, would have put the Spartans at the Rockets 18 yard line. So now it was 3rd down and the Rocket's defense had gone to a nickel coverage.

The quarterback was under center barking out plays and looking down the line, checking off by pointing. His receivers were poised, looking straight ahead as to not give any signs to their predetermined patterns. Devonte and his defense continued to show blitz. When the ball was snapped, the defensive line pressed while the young sophomore quarterback showed composure. He stepped back into the pocket and effortlessly sent a bullet spiraling seconds before being hit. His target, a wide receiver slanting across the middle, caught the ball in stride, but he didn't hold it long. Moments after the wide receiver caught the ball, he was knocked off of his feet from a blindsided hit by Devonte, causing him to cough up the football. As the ball tumbled across the field back towards the Stratford sideline, there was a mad scramble by both teams to recover it. It was a recovery that the Rockets had been successful in securing and ignited the crowd. The referees signaled no catch and instantly caused the previously joyous Judson sideline to protest. Their head coach flew into a rage as he pleaded his case to the unyielding official. Stratford would retain possession at the 30 yard line with 11 seconds remaining.

Now 4th down and seven, the Spartan offense reset. Three receivers out wide, the quarterback operating out of the shotgun. The Rocket defense once again showed signs of blitz and as the quarterback checked off, Devonte made a feigned charge to the line. His hands flinched and his muscles tensed as his body suggested his intention to safety blitz. The quarterback received the snap high, but controlled it. There was pressure coming from his blind side by the left defensive end, but the charge was picked up by a tight end. He remained poised in the pocket until it collapsed by the onrush of Devonte' in his safety blitz and defensive tackles. The cornerbacks had blown coverage down field, which was a critical error. Releasing a high arching spiral, the quarterback hit his receiver just as he was stumbling at the back of the end zone. There wasn't a cornerback or safety within seven yards of him and he rolls out of the end zone cradling the ball.

The Stratford sideline exploded in cheers, as did the fans. The Rockets fans, cheerleaders, and team players stood in silent awe as the officials signaled touchdown. On the Rocket's side line the coach gritted his teeth and shook his head. He, no doubt, was still seething over that 'no catch' call by the officials.

Several of the Rocket's team players sank to the turf on the side line in anguish, as others with helmets off looked on dejectedly in disbelief towards the jubilant Stratford side line. Devonte jerked off his helmet. His face showed disgruntlement as he stared up at the scoreboard while he walked back to the sideline. No time remained and the pending extra point was irrelevant. The score alone had put the Spartans up by 1 at 27-26 and this score was final, leaving a proud, and once-exuberant Rocket's crowd in silent shock as their team trudged to the middle of the field. The cheerleaders looked on in silence and the crowd dejectedly poured out of the stadium.

✷✷✷✷✷✷✷✷

Ikara and Braun walked side by side through the hallway at Roosevelt High School. Both of them were dressed impeccably in the latest fashions and cradling several textbooks.

Braun waved at several students who passed by while he and Ikara stopped to chat near a wall. Braun glanced down at his watch and commented on the approximate time afforded them before the bell would ring.

"It's almost time for the bell. I hate this class, American History, His-story. Mr. Fitzgerald seems more than excited every time he reads these lies that glorify his people," Braun sighed as he stared off in the direction of several students congregating across campus. He smiled and affectionately rubbed the side of Ikara's face. "Say, you were really into it the other night. I was checking you out while you were out there," he stated. He reflected fondly over her dance line performance the past Friday night at the Roosevelt game. Ikara smiled and blushed.

"Yeah, I thought we had that game. I hear Judson lost too and Devonte took it pretty hard," Ikara laughed.

"Yeah, Sharon was crying into her pillow for D. Man, he can't take losing," Braun commented. The subject switched to Piye and Swathi's emerging relationship. Though not an item, Swathi confided in her friends her desire for the relationship to take on new dimensions. After a brief pause, Ikara posed a question which revealed her curiosity into Piye's real intentions towards her friend.

"Does Piye ever, like…talk about Swathi? Like, as in them becoming a couple?" she inquired earnestly.

Braun smiled and shook his head.

"Piye…how can I say this? Piye is real reserved. He's not open 'bout girls. His conversations are centered around Nationalism, weights, and healthy foods, and stuff. He has said she is gorgeous, though. So I guess he is feeling her. But he has never really said anything about them hooking up," Braun rambled. He studied Ikara as he revealed his confusion at exactly what Ikara was perhaps expecting to hear. "Is she feeling him like that?" he asked, releasing a slight laugh.

Ikara smiled and looked away as she cradled her books to her bosom.

"Um, yeah…she is. He's all she can talk about. She's never really been involved in a relationship. You know she's bashful," Ikara stated.

"I know," Braun responded. At that moment, as if conjured up by the mention of his name, Piye appeared, clutching a folder in his hand. His expression was complacent as he stopped alongside the couple. He acknowledged Ikara first, then turned to Braun.

"You got all them notes Mr. Ruiz gave us Friday? I hope you do, man. I need them," Piye asked. Braun proceeded to retrieve the notes. As he did so, Ikara felt compelled to ask about Piye's feelings about interracial relationships. She also had an ulterior motive for initiating a conversation with him, which was to make a personal inquiry into just how serious his intentions were towards her friend. However, after her deceptive inquiries, Piye did not grant her this opportunity. Feeling uneasy about this particular subject matter, he diverted with an ambiguous answer and hurried away after thanking Braun for the notes.

Ikara stared at Piye as he maneuvered through the rush of other students and a smile creased her face that belied her eyes which bore the look of an unfulfilled inquisitiveness. Braun recognized the look, and his intuition told him that she had notions to ask Piye exactly the information she had previously asked of him, and he laughed.

"Do you think he sensed you were coming at him about Swathi?" Braun asked. Ikara laughed at his uncanny sense of perception.

"Maybe, and how did you know I was about to ask him about Swathi? Are you reading my mind?" Ikara smiled as she leaned forward towards Braun. Her eyes were wide as she stared into his.

"That's right, so you better not think about anybody else or I will know," he teased.

"You know I only think about you," she giggled. Braun stared into her eyes, admiring her beauty and realizing just how much he loved her at such a young age. As the two leaned forward to kiss, the bell rang. After disengaging reluctantly, the two walked through the mob of students.

✶✶✶✶✶✶✶✶

It was another busy corporate day at Tariq's Global Marketing Telecom Services. Men and women in business suits walked through the large office carrying portfolios and sipping coffee. Others conversed on cell phones or diligently tapped away on the keys of their computers.

Tariq was conversing on his cell phone as he sat at his cubicle. His face was serious. He removed an ink pen from his top pocket and jotted down notes onto a legal pad near his computer.

Adjacent to him was Somali, who was leaning forward towards the computer screen as he made entries. His face was a mask of concentration until a sleek, thirty-something sister in a pastel suit approached him with several documents. He glanced up into her beautiful caramel-toned face and smiled. His eyes evidenced curiosity as he diverted his gaze towards the paperwork she'd extended before him. "This is what you requested. All of the products translated from English to five other languages, French, Russian, Chinese, Hindu, and Spanish. It'll only be a small fee," the lady stated in a whisper as she leaned forward to pat him lightly on the shoulder. Somali smiled and accepted the paperwork and acknowledged her with a thanks as she began to prance away. Her curvaceous hips swayed with each motion.

"Thank you, Mrs. Williams," he stated, and stared back at his computer screen. He placed the documents that she presented him down onto his desk and began tapping once more on his laptop keys. He paused and tapped several more entries before gathering up the papers into his portfolio and rising to his feet.

At that moment, Tariq hung up the phone and turned in his seat to read the marketing display on his computer's screen as Somali walked up with the documents.

"Read these, it's an open door policy, so to speak, on the web," Somali informed. Tariq shifted in his swivel chair and began scanning the document before requesting Somali to continue.

"Open door policy? What exactly are the functions?" he inquired. Somali folded his arms then leaned back against the front of Tariq's cubicle wall as he began to brief him.

"Online businesses such as ours can operate as open-ended software platforms that can accommodate thousands of other businesses," Somali explained.

"Innovative websites can now exchange functions and other data to a greater extent. That's good," Tariq commented.

"Take your time and look over these," Somali stated as he unfolded his arms. Tariq nodded and placed the portfolio next to his computer. Somali made a move as if to leave, but then suddenly paused. His facial expression was of deep contemplation. He turned back to Tariq with a raised index finger, suggesting he was preparing to present a noted point. "You know this isn't related to the business so I'm not gonna take up too much of your time with it," Somali began.

"Well, shoot. What's the deal?" Tariq encouraged him.

"Well, I had a…talk, so to speak, with Piye. He really gave me something to think about. He let me know that this racial hatred I've been lugging around in my heart for years is counterproductive to our movement. And, he's right. It has clouded my judgment. It made me shut out those who could have been beneficial to our cause," Somali explained. A smile emerged across his face. His eyes shone with age and wisdom glowed as he reflected over his young son's irrefutable logic. Tariq nodded as he envisioned the headstrong, Piye giving his father advice concerning racism.

"And what made him finally arrive at this conclusion?" Tariq inquired.

Somali smiled, "He met this Pakistani girl," Somali informed.

"Ooh, that'll do it every time," Tariq laughed and patted him on the shoulder as he turned to walk away.

"Read those and get them back to me when you're finished,' Somali instructed. He then returned to his cubicle as Tariq began typing more entries onto his desktop computer.

November 2004

The sky was overcast on this mid-November day, giving an even bleaker backdrop to the Alamo. Blocks away, its dreary grey concrete was obscured from the hundreds of concerned black citizens who had gathered in Martin Luther King Park Jr. Members of O.B.U. and other political black activist groups had arrived here to be heard on the issue of police brutality. Once again, there was an early morning assault on a young African American male whom officers claimed "fit the description," was assaulted by several white police officers after being pulled over on East Houston Street. Fortunately, the youth, who was only sixteen, wasn't seriously injured and suffered only minor abrasions and a busted lip. Unfortunately, the unmerited assault was not caught on tape.

The demonstration featured such reactionary groups as NBPP (New Black Panther Party), N-Cobra, and O.B.U. Things were tense, but controlled. Some carried signs with anti-police attack slogans and held them up high as if to taunt the police whom had gathered in the park as well. They were there allegedly as a 'security measure' to ascertain indifference, and listened intently to the issues presented by O.B.U. member Brother Yoruba. He was on the platform speaking and his firebrand tone incited momentary applause and 'right ons'.

For the last half hour, several members from different organizations had taken the podium, voicing their disappointment in the ever-increasing racial profiling of black youths by the police. They expressed concern for the racial profiling taking place in their respective communities within San Antonio, as well as abroad. They asserted their personal or organizational platform ideology for rectifying the situation. Some ideologies were rational, while others bordered on anarchic.

Many of those whose 'ultimate' solution to these vicious attacks reflected anarchy were from the militant NBPP members, mostly comprised of young black men and women in their twenties and early thirties. Several of their representatives made statements that had put the police on hand that day under duress. As Brother Yoruba prepared to leave the stand, one of these radical members prepared to receive the microphone from him. His body language and facial expression showed his eagerness to make his voice heard.

"And, in closing, we will continue to work in conjunction with others in the community on this proposition, in order to secure the safety of our children from this blatant racist profiling." After Brother Yoruba's speech, there was applause. The entire constituency shouted in agreement to the issues and solutions he conveyed. Ikara, who joined her parents in this cause, clapped as she stood next to Braun. Beside them were their friends Piye, Yolanda, and Marquis. Ever the young militant, Marquis sported a shirt with the image of a cop inside the cross hairs of a rifle's scope.

"Greetings, my fellow brothers and sisters and concerned parents and youth alike. I'm Brother Kabil of the New Black Panther Party and I just want to expand on some of the things that Brother Yoruba stated. They are real and the time is here for us, as a community to take a stand," Brother Kabil exclaimed. The constituency listened attentively and was still energized by Brother Yoruba's firebrand speech. "This vicious attack the other day by our oppressors on this sixteen-year-old brother was more than unjustified.

He was a high school student with a superior grade point average and no criminal record. A liquor store was robbed and witnesses reported the robber as being six feet and two hundred pounds. Ladies and gentlemen, I know this young brother well. I know his people. He is a good boy. But this is not the point. The point is, while witnesses reported the perpetrator of this crime as being six feet, two hundred and forty pounds, this young brother, ladies and gentlemen is only five feet six and one hundred and forty pounds! How, then, could he have fit the description? It was just a simple case of a black youth driving a nice car, which was, in reality, his mother's, in a black neighborhood. This scene plays out all over the nation and results in humiliation, injury, and death without cause. We cry out for justice from the very same system which sponsors these terrorist acts! It's time to stop crying! Stop pleading! Stop dialoguing with our oppressors! And use whatever tactic or resource necessary to deter these types of incidents from occurring in the future!" Kabil spoke in incensed overtones. The militants and radicals of the crowd were nodding, clapping and giving a show of support with upheld fists. One such group, thoroughly supportive of his obvious violent reprisal implications, was Wild Bill and his gang, who were there in large numbers making disdainful exchanges with the police.

As Brother Kabil stepped down from the podium amidst cheers and shouts from the contingency, he was warmly embraced by activists, including O.B.U. member Tariq Galla. Tariq was dressed in traditional garb and a fitted hat of orange, black, and green design. As the applause began to die down, Tariq held up an open palm and looked down at the notes he had prepared. His wife Ursula held an anti-police assault sign and stared in anxious anticipation.

Tariq looked out over the crowd for a moment as he thought about the speech he had prepared. He briefly made eye contact with followers as well as the oppressors, the police and infiltrators alike.

"Before I give my presentation, I would like to first acknowledge that it is unfortunate for all of us to be gathered here once again. It brings to mind one of the statements that the young Brother Kabil just made. And that is that perhaps it is time to stop dialoguing. Chmm!, Ah, many speakers here today brought out valid points and solutions to this problem. I can't say that I agree with them all, but there were definitely insightful plans of action," Tariq stated. As he spoke, the crowd listened attentively, some nodding with expressions of sincerity. Others like Wild Bill and various members of his gang stood there with their arms folded.

Switching directions was precisely Tariq's intention as he stood behind the podium. It was not that many of the implications in which Kabil and other speakers had made did not mirror his own feelings, but rather for other reasons. He was doing it for himself, having a dialogue with the police who were on hand. Their expressions were blunt and their eyes were shielded behind their police sunglasses.

Tariq felt the same way many older members felt: that inciting words of reprisals would only lead to the police becoming paranoid. Paranoia could lead to hiked-up racial profiling instead of decreasing it. Also, uncalculated and overly-emotional rhetoric, such as Kabil's speech, could force lawmakers in the legislature to impose acts that would not benefit the community. In retrospect, the police tend to use these threatening statements as justification for their actions in the event of another unmerited slaying of a minority youth.

Tariq and the elders felt that subtlety was the only measure that would suffice. History taught them this when dealing with civil rights issues. An organization can ill afford to draw negative attention from the government before it is able to take a militaristic stance. Premature radicalism was the undoing for many black activist groups of the 1960s, 70s, and early 80s.

After a brief pause for effect, Tariq continued onto another course in his presentation. "However, I feel that at the present time, for the sake of unjustified ramifications or provoked confrontation between ourselves and those who have been sworn to preserve and protect, we should keep our emotions in check." His presentation was interrupted by several people in the crowd who obviously protested his diversionary tactic from the previous speaker's militant stance. Looking out over the protestors, he decided to call on a William Johnson, otherwise known as Wild Bill. 'Ah, yes, Brother William. You have something you want to add to the platform?" Tariq inquired.

"Yeah, I do have something to add, Brother Tariq. I agree with Brother Kabil and Brother Yoruba, man. They have a point. It's time we handle our business, man. They fucking,…oh, excuse me, messing over us, man. I'm down with Kabil. He is in the hood," Wild Bill stated with conviction.

"Yeah, man, Kabil is 'in' the hood with us. You know what I'm saying. Is keeping our emotions in check and keeping their feet off our neck, man?" added Bull.

The officers on hand exchanged meaningful glances when Tariq held up a cautioning hand.

"Okay, okay this is an open forum and everyone is entitled to express their opinions. This also means that everyone is entitled to their own agreement or disagreement. We are dealing with issues that are detrimental and, as activists, myself, and others from our organization and similar organizations have to come up with rational solutions," Tariq stated.

Wild Bill's expression was cynical.

"You disagree with Brother Kabil and brother Yoruba. So what are you going to do, man?" Wild Bill inquired.

Tariq looked down at his notes and back in the general vicinity of Wild Bill before averting eye contact. He had never seen Wild Bill so angry, and it made him uneasy.

"Brother William, it's good that you should ask this because here I have drafted up exactly what we should do." Tariq stated and held the written draft up as he read. Clearing his throat, he spoke into the microphone.

The draft was a proposal of action from a much different perspective than Wild Bill or any of the other revolutionary minds had anticipated. Instead of initiatives for reprisals of violence against the police, he instead had called for civil class action lawsuits, not only for actual physical assaults, but also whenever citizens suffered mental anguish from constant harassment. He suggested that citizens arm themselves with recorders or camera phones; not with weapons. He believed in having the tangible evidence of abuse, be it physical or psychological, to present into a civil claim.

"Ladies and gentlemen, this is how we protect ourselves and our youth from wrongful assaults and reprisals. It's not violence. Exercise your rights. You do have them as an American citizen. When your rights are infringed upon, you petition the courts in civil action, which we plan to do in order to compensate Mrs. Smith and the young man who was recently assaulted. In the future, this will help in the event of other such malicious attacks. We live in a democracy, ladies and gentlemen, and we have to do things in a democratic way," Tariq finished his impassioned speech amidst lukewarm applause from the constituents. He passed the microphone to another sister, who was herself part of the O.B.U. However, as the applause died down, there was another last second attempt at defiance by Wild Bill.

"I have one more thing, Brother Tariq," Wild Bill stated. All attention was now drawn to him and the people anxiously anticipated his comment, including Tariq.

"What is it, Brother William?" Tariq inquired.

"When that Constitution was written in this democratic country, it wasn't written for us, man," Wild Bill stated. And with that, he and his gang began to maneuver away from the podium and ultimately out of Martin Luther King Jr. Park. He left Tariq dumbfounded for a brief moment, before straightening his dashiki and descended down the steps of the podium.

Chapter 21

Braun walked up the walkway to his house with a yellow bookbag strapped across his back. It had been raining all week and today, this chilly day in late December, was no exception. The sky was a dismal grey and the light droplets that had been pitter-pattering on his windshield as he drove home from school were now a constant downpour.

As he reached the front door, the sky momentarily illuminated with lightning. He fidgeted in his pocket, looking for the key before opening the door, hurrying in, and shutting it behind him. His senses were immediately bombarded with several pleasant aromas from the kitchen. His grandmother was an ardent gourmet chef and had prepared a large meal. From the smells that filled the kitchen, he detected blueberry pie, steamed vegetables, and fried chicken. And, of course, there was always the overwhelming aroma of her special buttermilk biscuits.

As he cut through the kitchen, he was met by his grandmother. Her warm smile embraced him as she removed her oven mitts.

"Hey ma mah," Braun chimed out in the name he'd always affectionately referred to her by. She was the only mother he had ever known.

"Boy, you are soaking wet. Go on in and get out of them wet clothes before you catch a cold," his grandmother stated as she observed the droplets of rain running down his face.

"I'm not that wet, Ma mah. I practically ran up the steps trying not to get wet," he replied as he kissed her on the cheek. He removed his bookbag as he proceeded down the hallway to his room. Before he reached the threshold, his grandmother called out to him. She paused as she was lifting the lid on one of the pots. She had suddenly remembered something.

"Oh, I forgot to tell you, you have a letter on the table," she shouted.

Upon hearing 'letter', Braun immediately wondered who sent it. *Was it a letter of recommendation? Could he have gotten a letter from a university in regards to a track and field scholarship? Or academic? Perhaps he was being too speculative. Was it from Ikara?* She surprised him every so often with little romantic letters. He smiled as he took off his slightly dampened shirt and used his towel to remove the still present droplets of water from his face and hair.

He returned to the kitchen and passed his grandmother en route to the refrigerator. He opened it to retrieve a quart of Tropicana orange juice.

"Everything is almost ready, so you can go wash up," she informed as she stirred a pot of cream potatoes.

Braun opened up a cabinet, retrieving a glass as he responded.

"Alright, ma mah," he replied as he poured the glass of orange juice. He walked over to the table where the letter was waiting. He sipped his beverage then picked up the letter. His eyebrows furrowed and his eyes squinted as he read the return name and address. It was his friend Phil, writing from the Bexar County jail.

Braun opened the letter as he sat down at the table. It was one of several letters Phil had written him that month. He had collected more than twenty letters from his friend during the course of his two months of incarceration.

Phil's letters were laced with anger, misplaced albeit-anguish, penitence, and expressions of physical intimacy deprivation. These emotions, of course, were typical of the average psyche of someone recently incarcerated and disenfranchised from society. He was now faced with having to physically and psychologically readjust to a closed, controlled society.

Of course these were merely base emotions and it is also common to feel an unceasing sense of loneliness, self-pity, abandonment, defenselessness, and oppression. These emotions, combined with the aforementioned, can and most often does, lead to anti-social or destructive behavior for those languishing in prison. However, through his writing, Braun could not easily detect this trait in Phil.

Though Phil's letters did exhibit these emotional states, penitence was perhaps his strongest emotion. Already in the process of escaping from the drug trade, Phil had made plans to stay on the straight and narrow following his incarceration. His level of consciousness had risen and he now fully understood that his distributing drugs in his community, contributed to the psychogenic disruption of his fellow African Americans mind. His actions made him genocidal.

But his now awareness was not the only key factor to his psychological torment as a result of his dealing. He was feeling guilty for abandoning his mother, brother, and little sister and it was eating away at the fibers of his conscience. As Braun read this particular letter, this thread was more evident.

After Phil's introduction, he informed Braun about the recent developments with him such as: getting into another altercation with a fellow in–

mate; updates from his lawyer regarding the worst case scenarios regarding his case; the rift between the others who were also indicted on the federal drug case; and who else the feds had on their indictment list. Each letter's contents would disclose similar revelations.

The letter would eventually shift to that of sentimental concerns, induced by Phil's distance from family, friends, and certain love interests. He always inquired after his mother, siblings, and relatives. Other than his mother, siblings, and an aunt, few people came to visit him. Braun paid several visits to see Phil, but they were emotionally strained. He once brought a female acquaintance. Phil was always requesting that Braun or Devonte orchestrate correspondence between him and other females. The two would put forth the effort, but most of the young black sisters would refuse or promise they would and then never deliver. Braun's eyes swept over the letter, his mouth moving as he read silently.

Dear Braun,

What's happenin' main? Same ole here. Meditatin'. Tryinna keep these fools out my mix. Had to show one a week ago. He got his licks, I got mine. All that matters. I ain't no punk!

Man, lawyer ain't tawkin' good. Givin' me the run down on RICO's stature still. Tawkin' 'bout sentencin' ranges and all that. And tryinna get me to some medium security facility. Shit! Man I ain't tryinna do no mo time period! Max or medium. But I ain't snitchin! Everybody turnin' over. Big Mo, Dorele, Jo Jo, Lil G... all rattin', Dog! You know the feds got Carlos Vasquez too. They knew how he getting' it in the states, connections in Mexico, everything! I'm through wit the game, dog 4real. Say, main. If you can, I need you to send me some change. You know mom gotta take care of my lil sister and brother with the money I left. You feel me? Handle that. And I..."

Braun read the remainder of the brief letter, then folded it and returned it to the envelope. He didn't know much about the law, but he understood terminology such as Feds and RICO. The length of sentences were difficult, if not impossible, to anticipate.

As he folded the letter into the envelope, he shook his head in anguish and placed his fist underneath his chin. He battled to fight off the emotions which were inducing tears to form in his eyes as he thought of Phil's situation.

He thought about how he would probably never return to support his little brother and sister. *What would be the outcome of their lives now if their mother relapsed into her drug habit?*

"Are these enough potatoes for you, baby?" Braun's grandmother called out. Her voice broke his dejected trance. Looking over at her without really observing the tray, he responded with a half-smile creasing his face that belied the pain in his eyes.

"That's fine, Ma mah," he responded and left the table.

✴✴✴✴✴✴✴✴

The rain that had been coming down steadily the past several days had ceased now. It left behind a cold snap in its wake which made the temperatures this mid-autumn day quite chilly. Although the sun beamed brightly in the picturesque blue sky, people walking by were wearing long sleeves and windbreakers.

A flock of black Orioles flew overhead as Tariq and Somali walked side by side. They were in front of the Garvey House on 646 Holmgreen Road where a traditional African spiritual ceremony had been held. There had been a large turnout. Children in African garb paraded past as adult brothers and sisters conversed over topics which varied from community awareness to food preparation and dieting. Tariq acknowledged several members as he and Somali stopped to converse one-on-one in front of his car.

I wonder if Kabil gave my message to Kalib Shereef." Tariq inquired as he looked around at the contingency.

Somali clasped the portfolio he held before him.

"I feel he may have sensed the nature of your intentions to meet with their Minister of Defense. I think it would have been more effective if you would have just admonished Kabil yourself," Somali asserted. Of course he was speaking in reference to that picket at Martin Luther King, Jr. Park a few weeks ago, in which Kabil had given the strongest implication of taking on armed resistance against the police department. This was a move that most members of the O.B.U. were adverse to, and as a group failed to admonish Kabil, the young radical NBPP member.

"Admonish Kabil? He's headstrong and full of radical romanticisms just like the way he perceived the 60s Panthers to be. A lot of the political agendas are directly contradicting the original Black Panthers. Brother Bobby Seales even expressed this. I think it best to get their minister to stress to Kabil and the others how imperative it is not to incite further tensions with the police department at this time," Tariq explained.

Somali nodded his head in agreement to Tariq's assertion.

Brother Tariq, Brother Somali greeted two young sisters in passing. Both wore traditional orange garb, and their hair was braided and in dreadlocks. The two O.B.U. chairman acknowledged the two young sisters and gave them both accolades for their scholastic achievements.

"She has done a commendable job. She didn't let her pregnancy stop her from achieving her goals," Somali stated.

Tariq averted his attention as a San Antonio police cruiser paused at an intersection. He stared at the cruiser as he spoke.

"The court hearing, as I've seen, is really going in the officer's favor. The chips are stacked against Mrs. Smith. She's been there for every hearing and twice I've had to console her. The reaction from Kupchek, his attorneys, and some members from the police force indicated that they feel this case was laughable. They seem to believe that there will not be an indictment of Kupchek; at least that is the impression I get from each hearing," Tariq reported.

Somali studied his friend's expression as he spoke. He could almost feel the passion emanating from him. He was like a prize fighter losing on all cards and desperately in need of a knock out in order to win the bout. Somali empathized with him and Mrs. Smith.

Looking away from Tariq, Somali released a sigh of anguish. A gust of wind blew, scattering autumn leaves across the street from a nearby tree and rustling Somali's dashiki.

"You can't let it distress you, my brother. You're doing all you can. We're doing all we can. If we can't get a conviction on wrongful death, we'll just shoot for civil suits in that case and the other. And hopefully we'll get results, even if it becomes a drawn out process. But we'll fight," Somali stated. He then reassuringly patted Tariq on the back. "I have to go check on the progress at Sadiq's restaurant. Maybe I can get a free sample of some Caribbean dish, Texas style," Somali grinned as he patted his stomach.

Tariq smiled, "You just ate okra and chicken Texas style. You better watch that stomach." Somali laughed and opened the door of his vehicle. The smile vanished from Tariq's face as his eyes continued to reflect his pessimism pertaining to the case. He glanced once more in the direction of the police cruiser that passed by before getting into his own car.

✶✶✶✶✶✶✶✶

A car's driver stepped on the brakes to avoid hitting a kid who'd gone after a football. Hearing the sudden short screech of the tires, Braun and his friends, Piye, Devonte, and Marquis looked up from Braun's front porch. The kid, wearing a Dallas Cowboy's football jersey, retrieved the football and galloped across the street where five more boys of elementary school age waited and cheered him on.

"Kendrick! Watch for traffic! That football isn't that important!" shouted Piye across the street.

"Go 'head and put that Scarface in there, man. I'm tired of screw. I'm ready to hear some Brad Jordan," Devonte stated. Marquis stood over him with a pair of clippers as he carefully lined his hair and gave him a professional razor lining. Braun switched the CD to the one Devonte had requested.

"What do you think the Cowboys are going to do this week, Marquis?" Devonte inquired.

Marquis continued to line his hair with precision. His eyebrows furrowed and his eyes remained focused and without stopping what he was doing, he responded, "I don't know. After last week? Man, they had Pittsburgh. Vinny be making bad decisions."

"You can't blame that loss on Vinny. The Steelers got the number one defense in the NFL. Vinny did better than most quarterbacks could against them. Defense just didn't come through at the end. We are going to smash the Bengals, though," Braun asserted.

"Man, Dallas cornerbacks are weak. Carson Palmer might torch that shit," Devonte laughed. He was not a Cowboy fan, but rather followed the Tennessee Titans. He used to be a fan of the now-defunct Houston Oilers.

"You want me to cut a star in your head?" Marquis joked. He paused as he held the buzzing clippers inches before Devonte's face. Devonte laughed as Marquis feigned a serious expression.

"Man, I did not say anything about Dallas when you cut my head. I don't know how you let yourself get off into that, Marquis. You Muslim," Piye stated.

"I don't know. I've been a Dallas fan since I was a little kid. And being a Muslim didn't change that. There is nothing wrong with watchin' sports as long as you don't let it consume your life," Marquis rebutted. There was momentary silence and nods of agreement. Then Piye switched subjects.

"Anyway, what was Phil talking about in his letter? Are the Feds still putting pressure on him, huh?" Piye inquired.

Braun's expression changed as he reflected on the letter. The emotion he felt at that moment seemed to seize him once more.

"He was just talking about his case. His lawyers are trying to get a deal. He is still gettin' in fights and stuff. Telling how everybody ratting, like Dorele, Jo Jo, and Lil G. Everybody is rolling over on Carlos Vasquez," Braun reported. Ironically, a song entitled 'Snitch Figga' by Scarface, emitted from his portable CD player. Instantly Devonte laughed and made the comparison.

"How it is, everybody wants to play...nobody wants to pay," Devonte stated.

"That's why it doesn't pay to play. Oh yeah, he wants you to get back his rings and necklace from Kejuanna," he added. Devonte laughed and moved his head slightly, which caused Marquis to pause and look at him with an expression of sarcasm.

"His rings and necklace man, Phil is tripping. How am I going to get his rings back? I told him that Kejuanna messes with anybody rolling. Now he acts like he is surprised she won't come and see him. Chicks aren't nothing. He hasn't been asking you about Tammy?" Devonte inquired. Marquis turned off the clippers. "That's it?" Devonte asked Marquis. Marquis shoved a mirror before his face as he got up. He swiped at the hair that fell onto his shoulders. Braun extended a broom in his direction before responding to his inquiry.

"Yeah, he has been asking about Tammy a lot lately. Now he made a bad decision not choosing her instead of them gold diggers," Braun stated.

"Are you talking about the Tammy who works at Taco Bell with you? She's nice. She don't look like the type to go for dope dealers," Marquis commented. Devonte finally noticed the broom Braun was handing to him.

"Come on, man. I wasn't going to leave the hair down there," Devonte' retorted, pretending to be upset. Braun smiled and responded to Marquis' assertion as he flopped down in a porch chair.

"She doesn't go in for drug dealers. She's liked Phil since before he got in the game. She wanted him to get out of it, but he wasn't trying to hear that. I told her he wanted her to visit, but she isn't putting her life on hold for him," Braun stated. Piye's eyebrows rose.

"Can you blame her?" Piye responded. Braun shook his head briefly as he stared away. Piye flopped down in one of the other chairs as Devonte examined the other CDs Braun had displayed while nodding his head to the beat of one of Scarface's songs.

"Face be goin' off, main," Devonte stated. Piye looked over at Braun, then averted eye contact. His expression revealed he was thinking seriously about some issue.

"Any word when the trial is going to be?" Piye inquired.

"He was talking about how the judge keeps setting the date back. There are a lot of them, you know," Braun explained.

"I can't wait to see all these so-called gangsters snitch on the Mexican," Devonte stated as he pushed buttons on the CD player in search of a song.

"Yeah, so much attention is being drawn to their case, petty crimes, houses getting shot up and stuff, that the media can't even focus on the police murder case. They are too busy profiling us," Marquis stated.

"Everything is focused on police putting out more laws to lock down the hood," Piye stated. At that moment, a car pulled up in front of a house adjacent to Braun's. The driver of this compact sedan was a female, although the tint of the windows obscured their view of her. Her passenger exited and walked up the driveway. She was smiling as she waved in the boy's direction. She looked studious even though she wore a loose fitting outfit, which her curves accentuated and caused Devonte to linger on with his lustful leer.

"Mm, mm, mm! I wish I could lock that down," Devonte' stated.

Marquis smiled, "Do you have to have all these sisters? Sharon isn't enough? Come on man, you are the reason why sisters are saying there aren't any good black men. Break out of that player stuff, man. What if you have a daughter? Do you want her to meet somebody that wants to 'lock down' every sister he sees?"

Devonte could only smiled, "I can't help it, man. I'm weak for that. Like Soldier Slim said, "I'll pay for it." Devonte pretended to dance like he was at a club.

"Sharon doesn't have to worry about that one there. She is out of his league. She's a Delta Sorority woman at Baylor University studying pre-med," Braun informed.

"Uh, oh. She's older than fourteen and intelligent?" Piye stated in humor. Braun and Marquis laughed as Devonte feigned being appalled.

"He looks shocked, like, man you know you only go at tennis shoe chasers," Marquis added and bent over in laughter.

"Come on, man. Let's go riding or something. It's boring around here," Braun suggested. Devonte reached into his pocket retrieving his car keys as Piye playfully put his arm around his neck. "Let me go put my CDs inside," Braun stated then began gathering up his CD.

"Bring that face, man, and you better have some gas money," Devonte smiled.

"Gas money? Your head is looking like Steve Harvey's barber did it and you are asking me for gas money? Shh. You owe me," Marquis stated as the two neared the Acura. Braun closed the door behind him and made a dash down the steps.

"Go by the Stop-n-Go first," Braun suggested as he opened the back door.

"Yeah, so you can get me two bear claws and a twista," Marquis added. Devonte' gave him a sarcastic look and climbed in behind the driver's seat as Piye laughed and closed the door behind him.

✻✻✻✻✻✻✻✻

The sun had set and the lights of the San Antonio central business district were illuminated. The skyscrapers and high-rise office buildings dominated the skyline for miles around and the headlights and noises of cars reverberated through the night. Cars honked diesel engines fumed; systems blared; honky-tonk music played in cafes and bars; police and ambulance sirens roared; and rotary blades of police taskforce helicopters buzzed. These were all the routine sounds and sights of a typical San Antonio night.

Miles from these sounds and sights of the bustling downtown area, nestled away in the quiet suburbs of his Live Oak home, Tariq sat on his couch. He was dressed in a dark green silk robe and slippers. In his hand he held a remote. His eyes seemed distant and tired. And rightfully so, since it was a busy day at the office, he had a lecture at the community center and had helped his son with homework. The images on the television screen were upsetting him.

A shadow appeared to his right and he glanced in that direction. Seconds later a figure, sleek and curvaceous, eased down beside him and curled up with her legs underneath exposing smooth chocolate skin and well-pedicured toes. It was his wife Ursula, who ran a gentle hand across his shoulders.

"What are you watching?" she inquired as a commercial played on the television screen.

"The news," Tariq responded dryly.

"No wonder you look so depressed," Ursula smiled in hopes of bringing a smile to his sullen face. It worked. However, the smile belied the true feelings in his eyes and after a moment, he responded.

"No, that's not making me depressed. Of course, there are always depressing topics. But uh, I was just reflecting over certain issues, like the case, the state of the people and the tension. And I just can't block out the demonstration that day in the park. Wild Bill made a statement and it still bothers me," Tariq stated. She continued to massage his shoulders as she looked into his eyes with an expression of concern.

"What part of what he said disturbs you?" Ursula inquired.

Tariq's eyes glazed over as he stared into space. He looked over at his wife before responding.

"He emphasized that since we no longer resided in the neighborhood, we could no longer identify, so to speak, with the condition. Implying that he felt my plans--our plans--were not reflective of theirs. That we were outsiders. He made me almost feel guilty that I decided to move my family to a more safe residential area," Tariq asserted. Ursula inched closer to her husband and touched his face so that he could look at her.

"Wanting a better life for our children is nothing to be ashamed of. Not wanting our children to be subjected to drugs or hit by a stray bullet, how could that be wrong?" Ursula retorted.

Tariq looked down as he spoke and explained to her that it would be extremely difficult for her to be able to relate to Wild Bill or others who shared his feelings. In his words, "Wild Bill's street ethics forbids him from disenfranchising himself from his gang or gang activities; thus his ethics are anti-progress and anti-political in concept. That is, a war being fought could only be done in the 'trenches' and not with 'distant strikes' from technological warfare. The 'trenches' were his eastside neighborhood and the enemy was the police. His militaristic intelligence or lack thereof called for armed resistance on the set battlefield. Tariq was considered the technological bomber that dispersed napalm."

"Wild Bill and many like him don't have the knowledge of the law or our civil rights. A war with the police department or government for that matter can only mean armed confrontation. They're mad. They're oppressed. They're depressed. And they just want to lash out. They don't want to strategize, or can't strategize. He feels that our talk of civil reprisals is just that, talk. Since we're not from the 'hood', then we're just smoke-screening for the organization," he explained. After he finished, it dawned on him that Wild Bill and the others were right, to a degree. He knew countless self-proclaimed black activists who were of the burgeoning class, who simply did just that. Their concerns were not of the people. War, whether from a political stratagem or militaristic perspective with the police, was not on their agendas. The politicians focused on bamboozling their fellow African Americans with double talk and promises in order to win elections or the financial support of the people.

Ursula listened intently as Tariq spoke. Her facial expression showed her comprehension of Wild Bill's stance.

"I see, more or less, he feels that we're just campaigning so to speak. That we're trying to draw the spotlight to the O.B.U. And that our intentions are not genuine. But that's a narrow way of assessing things from their point," Ursula replied.

Tariq smiled, "They're young and they're a product of their environment. The neighborhood breeds combativeness. He feels it's the only way to fight oppression, meet violence with violence," Tariq reasserted.

"But they must realize that there's no winning that way," Ursula stated matter-of-factly. Tariq's eyebrows rose as he considered her statement.

"At this point, I don't even believe winning is an objective with Bill. Tensions are growing in the case of James Smith. He had the support of not only working class citizens, but even the dealers and gang members like Bill. Not to mention the constant harassment, and now this other sixteen-year-old gets beaten to within an inch of his life. It's heating up out there on the eastside. I just hope this situation doesn't reach a boiling point."

Chapter 22

The sun was shining brightly at its apex, despite the chilly 46 degrees temperature outside. The sky was strewn with beautiful light blue clouds. It was picturesque in contrast to the present signs that the dead of winter was here, with the leafless trees and dead grass that turned brown in front of the houses and buildings.

A car passed by in front of Mr. Gonzales' Stop-n-Go as Braun and Piye conversed and walked inside. They were well dressed and appropriately for the weather. They were hunched over with their hands shoved deep within in their baggy fit jeans as they fought off a gust of wind that had just blown. Their squinted faces obscured by their beanie head wear and chins down turned into their jacket's huge zipper neck linings.

As usual, Mr. Gonzales was behind the counter dusting off while his son did inventory on the shelves behind the counter. They heard the cowbell on the door ring and the two paused momentarily from their tasks to acknowledge the two with smiles. Though if the smiles were received by Piye as reflexive to their warm greetings towards him, it would be deemed delusional on his part. For it was incidental due to Braun's presence. As the door closed behind them, Mrs. Gonzales peeked out from her position beyond the threshold leading to the back. Mr. Gonzales gave Piye a quick disdainful leer, which did not go unnoticed by Piye or Braun.

It had been quite some time since Piye accepted that those of other nationalities were not all oppressors. He had also stopped getting into confrontations with Mr. Gonzales and his son. But, he never apologized and therefore, was not embraced or trusted by the Gonzales family. His expression after receiving the disdainful leer evidenced his feelings about finally making amends for all past racial expletives or hostilities towards them.

The two boys proceeded down the aisle in search of their favorite snacks.

They opened the refrigerated box to retrieve their twisters. As they did, Mr. Gonzales maneuvered behind the counter and made eye contact again with Piye. This prompted Piye, with a twister in hand, to make a move towards the counter. Braun just retrieved his twister and was in the process of commenting on the upcoming Dallas game, when he saw the exchange of glances take place, including Piye's reaction. He reached to grab Piye's arm before he followed pursuit.

Mr. Gonzales watched as Piye approached the counter. He carefully and cautiously eyed him in anticipation of what could be concealed underneath Piye's large Starter jacket.

Braun was uncertain as to whether or not Piye was about to cause a scene. He shook his head and looked away as Piye reached the counter. But what would happen next would take both Braun and the Gonzales' aback. As Mr. Gonzales and his son scrutinized the often racially antagonistic Piye.Piye spoke out in a soft tone, timidly fidgeting with his hands as he struggled to look Mr. Gonzales in the eyes.

"Look, I know that in the past things have been kind of strained between us. Uh, I know I said a lot of things that offended you all. Those things don't reflect how I feel today. So, I would just like to apologize. And I hope you can accept my apology," Piye stated with compassion as he extended his hand to Mr. Gonzales. His expression was sincere and his eyes shone with emotion.

Mr. Gonzales' expression was of utter surprise. Initially, before Piye made eye contact, he was uncertain as to the legitimacy of his approach. His expression had been cynical. But now he and his son were convinced that Piye;s apology was sincere and they both openly accepted his apology. Everyone, including Braun, smiled. Their eyes were filled with joy at hearing Piye's sincere apology.

It took a brief moment for the apology to really register, but finally Mr. Gonzales shook Piye's hand firmly. He clasped his arm with his other hand as his son came over to pat Piye on the shoulder. Piye released his grip on Mr. Gonzales' hand and leaned across the counter to embrace him. It was a melodramatic scene and a special display of ethnic harmony, one that most definitely should be played out every day all over the country.

The two boys walked down the block while taking bites into their snacks and washing it down every few steps with their beverages. The scene still played in Braun's mind. He was proud of his friend. He was excited to know that the one aspect of his friend, his racist ideologies, which he had possessed since he became old enough to grasp the concept, were finally gone.

"You know at first I thought that it was all about Swathi. I know she's gorgeous. And I felt that you still harbored them racist feelings, but just kept them concealed because of her. But I see you are real with it. That's straight," Braun stated. He looked over to check him out and observed how his statement might have affected him.

Piye was looking away observing a dark pink Integra with tinted windows. It sped by with its sound system thumping, sending vibrations through them. He returned his focus to Braun as he sipped his twister. "Yeah, it's like this, a brother at the Garvey House told me this, and you know, he is right. I know that everybody is their own individual person. And I try to judge them…I mean, treat them you know…according to how they treat me. And don't judge just because of race. The brother told me that and I'm applyin' it," Piye stated. Braun nodded and shoved his hands deeper into his pockets as he looked away.

"Good rule. Good rule," Braun responded.

The two walked across the lot of a service station. Braun looked across the street with his eyes squinting as if in the process of making a statement. But just as he was about to speak, a banged-up grey primed Delta 88 whipped into the lot. The occupants wore ski masks and brandished weapons. The passenger gripped a sawed off shotgun and leveled it at Piye.

The two boys froze in a shock. They were paralyzed and their faces were masks of horrified confusion. The wielder of the shotgun barked out, along with other parties inside the car, "Give up, nigga! Out tha pocket, nigga! You thank we playin'! Niggas move!" the occupants shouted out. The voices were disguised in gruff tones and sent shockwaves of terror through them. Then came laughs from inside the car, as the ski-masked passenger withdrew the shotgun. He and the others began removing their masks and revealing their identities. Wild Bill was the driver, Red Dawg was the shotgun wielder, and Lil Gun, Bull and another member whose street name was Midnight rode in the back.

Piye's chest heaved and his twister bottle shook nervously as he brought it up to his mouth. The gang members continued to laugh as they got out of the car. Red Dawg, his gold teeth glistening, patted Piye on the shoulder as he passed, which incited Piye to violently jerk his arm away.

"Come on main, we's jis funning, Dawg," Midnight stated as he climbed out of the backseat. Wild Bill smiled and took a sip of his beer, folding his arms as he sat down on the front end of the car's hood.

"Yeah, they's just fuckin' round, main," he stated as he looked at Piye and Braun. Piye's face was contorted in anger. He was seething at first and tried hard to control himself from verbally castigating them as he watched Red

Dawg enter into the service station with Lil' Gun. Bull was drinking a 40 oz. bottle and came around to stand perpendicular with the boys. Though smiling at first, his eyes changed after recognizing the anger and emotional shock on their faces and felt compelled to seriously rectify their obviously apathetic move.

"Piye, Braun, hey main, we ain't mean to rile y'all, feel me? It's all good, main. Come on, dog," Bull stated as Piye shrugged off his attempt at an apology, and looked off, shaking his head. Wild Bill spoke out with his arms still crossed as he looked away.

"Say main… Braun I know y'all wasn't really feelin' that shit Brother Tariq was runnin' tha other day in the park was y'all?" Wild Bill inquired. Braun, still slightly shaken and upset, did not respond. "All he was sayin' bout non-violent approaches…shit! Thought I's watchin' an old 60s King speech," Wild Bill stated in humor.

"I have a dream that police will stop kickin' our ass," Midnight said in his best Martin Luther King Jr. voice. Wild Bill and Bull laughed. Braun's eyes averted, as he was highly against the demeaning of Dr. King Jr., a man who was anchored in the struggle both strategically as well as on the front lines. Anyone ignorant of the man and his humanitarian works, courage, and integrity was made self-evident by the gang member's comments.

"I don't know. Umm, Brother Tariq 'been' in the movement ya know. I mean, we can't just take to the streets killin' police," Braun asserted.

"How come we cain't?" Wild Bill stated without blinking. His blank expression belied the smile which exposed his trademark missing front tooth. Both Piye and Braun stared at him with expressions of disbelief. It was now more than ever before that they realized Wild Bill was deranged and obsessed with killing. He even romanticized his own demise in the streets, in the cause of a war against the police department, believing it was inevitable. The boys remained silent for a moment before Piye spoke out.

"You serious? They'd slaughter us, Bill. They'd declare martial law," Piye remarked. Wild Bill smirked, shaking his head as he looked off. At that moment Lil Gun and Red Dawg came out of the service station holding bags and 40 oz. bottles of beer while bickering amongst themselves over some trivial issues. "So what we spose ta do? Jis let the police keep beatin' us down? Shootin' us in tha back? Main, I'm down ta ride, dawg," Bull stated, then turned up his 40 oz.

"Main, you a stupid lil nigga, main. I told you don't bet everything. Nigga took ya fast. You ain't no cold blooded poker playa," Red Dawg exclaimed as he set his bags into the front seat of his car. Lil Gun argued in defense as he patted his chest. His eyes wild as he followed Red Dawg. "Just pump the gas, nigga," Red Dawg stated as he cracked open his 40 oz.

"Yeah, pump the gas, nigga. No card playin' ass. Know you wasn't ready fo' no five card stud," Midnight heckled.

"Fuck you Midnight! Yah blue black ass nigaa! This nigga don't need no ski mask. He could rob a sto' and go stand outside, and police pass right by his black ass," Lil' Gun shot back. The rest of the gang members laughed.

Braun refocused his attention on Bull and began shaking his head as he reflected over his statement. "That's suicide, Bull. A no-win situation." Bull could give no reply. As Lil' Gun replaced the gas hose on the pump, Wild Bill unfolded his arms. His keys rattled as he made a move around the front of the car. He paused and turned to address Braun's assertion.

"Sometimes it ain't about winnin'. Know what I'm sayin'?" he declared. Red Dawg extended his beer towards Braun and Piye and they declined. Red Dawg opened the car door, laughing as Lil Gun climbed into the backseat. The .45 caliber Glock pistol became visible in his underwear lining as his Starter jacket rose. Wild Bill pointed a finger across the hood at the boys, signifying that they should think carefully over the statement he'd just made. He climbs in behind the driver's seat and closes the door leaving the boys to continue looking on as the Delta 88 pulls out into the traffic.

✳✳✳✳✳✳✳✳

It was another beautiful but chilly day and the park-goers were out in full bloom. They were enjoying the sunshine, which took some of the bite out of the 49 degree temperature. On a bench, cuddled closely together and dressed seasonably warm were Braun and Ikara.

Ikara wore a pink beanie to match her jacket and Timberland boots. She clasped her blue mittens together as she cheerfully commented on the way the cranes swarmed in the pursuit of bread crumbs that Braun was at that moment tossing out. Now empty-handed, he was affectionately placing his arms around her.

"They're such beautiful and graceful birds. I love feeding them," Ikara stated as she folded her arms together. Braun stared down at her and smiled. He adored her, and not just her physical beauty. She took time out to reflect on nature and to enjoy the beauty of the earth with all of its colorful flowers and mysterious creatures. She loved nature. She loved its beauty and had a spiritual concept of life. This was something that most people from his environment--neglected. Wild Bill and his gang--didn't possess concept. Their mindset was capitalistic. Their actions were primitive. "They are. Ya know, you possess a lot of qualities that I just don't see in most girls where I'm from," Braun stated in a soft tone of voice as he looked out over the park. Just then, a gust of wind blew and stirred around the squawking cranes. Ikara shivered slightly. Her eyes squinted as she stared up into Braun's face.

"And what qualities might that be?" she inquired.

Braun smiled as he gazed into her brown eyes.

"Like… you have spirituality. A love for nature, too. In these days even females try to be hard, yah know everybody's on some thugged out, 'I'mma get mine's, type of trip. Nobody wanna just…be themselves. It's like…they afraid," Braun stated as he reached into his pocket to retrieve another plastic bag of bread crumbs. "Everybody's concept is messed up. Everybody is self-destructive. Then they blame other sources for their state of being other than themselves. Then…they become suicidal. Maybe not exactly puttin' a gun to their head…but delvin' into thangs that they know could put' em in St. Mary's," he finished emphatically. His last statement came out loudly due to him straining to hurl the bread crumbs a significant distance.

As Ikara watched in silent awe, the graceful white cranes swarmed around in the air, squawking noisily. Then, like dive bombers, they would swoop down and snatch pieces of bread crumbs the same way they would spot fish in the ocean or lake from a mile up and swoop down to trap them in their beaks.

Ikara's eyes swept the vicinity of the park, observing the dozens of park-goers on this chilly but bright sunny day as she reflected over the explanation Braun had just given her. She looked down and responded.

"You know, what you just said sounded a lot like what my father often talks about," she stated. Braun examined her.

"Really?" he responded.

"He's… always sayin' how there's so much exploitation on television. The video images and how everybody tries to be like that. They put themselves in a position to be profiled and blame the whites. I agree with some things he says. I don't know. He wants to help people. Our people. But maybe some of our people don't want his help." Her last statement sounded dejected as she looked down. Braun nodded in agreement and folded the empty plastic bag back into his pocket.

He responded, "Funny you say that. We ah…ran across one of the gang members who was at the park that day. Remember the one who ridiculed your father's platform? Well, he was really talking crazy the other day." Ikara stared into his eyes with enthusiasm, and in anticipation about the news she inquired, "What was he saying?" Braun shook his head as he reflected over the deranged look in Wild Bill's eyes and the sinister smile of the man who had no concept of life or death.

"He's jis like… losin' his grip. Talkin' bout startin' a war with the cops. If they start that everybody in the neighborhood and other black neighborhoods gon' be affected," Braun stated. Ikara placed a hand onto his chest as she looked up at him, but remained silent. Braun shook his head, then placed his hands into his jacket pocket as he looked away. A half-smile creased his lips as his eyes shifted. "I love my hood. But I feel trapped like I'm doin' a prison sentence. Graduation is right round the corner. But it seems like it's takin' forever to get here. Guess it's 'cause of all the messed up stuff that's been goin' on. All I been thankin' bout lately is college. The big campus. A new environment," Braun stated. His eyes glazed over as if envisioning the university campus which he spoke of.

Ikara stared up at him quizzically.

"That's all you've been thinking about? College? You mean you haven't been thinking about me lately at all?" she stated in humor as a smirk pursed her lips.

Braun smiled and recognized his girlfriend's attempt to bring him back from the brink of despair.

"I was goin' off again, huh? Of course I be thankin' bout you. You know that?" he replied as he touched her face.

"You better be. And you better not be getting any ideas about runnin' around with none of them college women on me, either. Talkin' bout you can't wait to get to college," Ikara said. As she talked, Braun laughed and affectionately embraced her and kissed her on the cheek.

"None of 'em could take your place with me," he assured softly as he stared into her eyes. She held his gaze. The two began kissing, after which Ikara displayed a devilish smile.

"You know, I bought you something the other day at the mall," Ikara said.

"And you just tellin' me? What is it?" he inquired curiously.

She smiled playfully.

"Well, it's not exactly for you. But…it's for only you to see," she stated tauntingly. Braun was overcome with suspense. Tell me," he stated as he attempted to control his laughter. She whispered into his ears, instantly changing his expression to one of unbridled lust at hearing she had bought a pink bikini.

"And umm, the house is empty now. But at six o' clock it won't be," she whispered seductively. Braun's pulse rate quickened and his chest heaved slightly as he thought about her beautiful caramel body, silky smooth skin, and perfect curvaceous form, parading around the room and putting her impeccable figure on exhibit just for him. She would allow him to slowly remove that bikini and make love to her.

"Six o' clock? What time is it now?" he inquired in a lustful pant. Ikara laughed as she sensed his sexual surge.

"Almost three. Um, hmm. So…," she laughed and started to speak, but was unable to complete her sentence before laughing uncontrollably when Braun reached down to pick her up. After setting her down the two shared in laughter and then walked through the park past the squawking cranes and through the scattered populous of park goers.

Tariq and Somali were just finishing their Caribbean-influenced dish and were now rising from their table as the owner, Sadiq, who was dressed somewhat lavishly in black a leather jacket, pants, boots, and fitted hat, made his way over to their table.

"Brothers enjoy your meal?" Sadiq inquired as he extended a hand towards Somali.

"Yes, yes, it was delicious, Brother Sadiq. How is it going?" Tariq asked, while wiping away a remnant of sauce from his mouth as he looked around the quaint restaurant. At that moment Somali tipped a waitress, an African-American sister of brown skin tone and short hair, who smiled genuinely then maneuvered away towards another table where an elderly gentleman with salt and pepper dreadlocks was enjoying his meal. The music of reggae icon Bob Marley played softly in the background. The elderly man, incidentally, was one of only five patrons dining in the restaurant that was built to accomodate fifty people. The recognition of the scarcity of patrons was the primary motive behind Tariq's inquiry.

Sadiq briefly observed the interaction of the waitress with the elderly gentleman, and then turned to face Tariq and Somali. "How's it going? Well…," he responded with a wave of the hand around the restaurant. The gesture, compounded by the cynical expression on his face, was self-evident of his displeasure with the lack of patrons frequenting his restaurant. "…Look around. Empty, empty tables everywhere. I try to cater to people. Give them a taste of Caribbean culinary, ya know. Exoticism of the Caribbean. But apparently, the people would rather spend their money with vultures and ingest unhealthy saturated fats pushed into their mouths by these turban-wearers and rice-eaters. They're stealing all of our business," Sadiq spoke with passion. His words dripped venom as he pointed across the avenue in the direction of a Pakistani restaurant.

As Sadiq spoke, Tari and Somali exchanged glances. No doubt both were not completely in agreement with the paranoid delusion of his assertion. The two had on many occasions suggested that the cuisine of Sadiq's restaurant may not be appropriate for the community in which he'd established it. The blacks were more apt to go for 'soul food' or fast food and preferred to eat fried chicken, red beans, pork chops, pizza and tacos, some of which could be ordered at Hamburani's. In their assessment, Sadiq's business venture was simply a bad investment.

"I don't know if they're actually stealing business, Brother Sadiq. I think it's just a case of black businessmen selling out to them. I don't believe these people actually come over here with the intentions of knocking the American black businessman. They're just trying to live the American dream," Tariq stated with a wide smile aimed at lowering Sadiq's guards as he pats him on the shoulder.

"You might wanna try coming up with some good soul food, my brother, like hog maw and fried chicken. Mix it with the West Indian cuisines to attract the people. You know, not too many brothers and sisters know about Caribbean dishes?" Somali added with more humor. Sadiq however, didn't seem to find any humor in the least. Instead of humoring them with a smile, he looked away shaking his head.

"I don't know why you brothers can't see things for what they are. Brother Tariq, I understand you've always had a more…liberal, way of ah…black activism. But you, Brother Somali, I'm surprised at you. You seem to have had scales placed over your eyes. These suckas have cornered the market. It's not just about my success or lack thereof in this restaurant, it's bigger than that. Nah, nah…it's bigger my brothers. Other brothers who opt to open up their own business in close proximity of these foreign suckas lose revenue, also. We…won't…buy… from our own. We're always eager to make the next man's pockets fat. That is the problem, my brothers. We have to support each other and I'm certain this Mr. Hamburani is dealing in narcotics, just like the vast majority of those suckas. His dealings further debilitate and degenerate our people," Sadiq finished. He was seething.

Tariq and Somali both examined the man in scrutiny. He was berating foreign entities who were merely trying to sustain and enjoy the economic freedoms of this democracy, simply because of his bad business decision.

"Dealing in narcotics? Mr. Hamburani? Brother Sadiq, come on. Those people are hardworking citizens. You're stereotyping them just like the imperialists do to our people when we achieve success," Tariq chastened.

"I'm not being delusional or stereotypical, my brother. They're given political as well as economical backing to finance these business ventures by the government. The same government that refuses to grant us reparations for all of the backbreaking labor our ancestors did! And I'm delusional? I'm not supposed to be upset when these camel-riders come over here and extort our people? Take food out of black men's and women's and children's mouths?" Sadiq ranted on. This was routine with him and the two O.B.U. brothers decided it was time to make an exit. Somali looked sympathetically at the man with a smile, however, and patted him on the shoulder as he made a move past him.

"Lighten up, my brother. It's Kwanzaa. It's time to celebrate our heritage and not berate others," Somali stated as he reaches the door. Sadiq simply looked at him. Tariq stopped short of the door and turned back to the man as he dusted himself off.

"Why don't you come by and celebrate the Mishumaa Saba? Get some inner peace, my brother," Tariq offered. Sadiq simply smiled and nodded in response as Tariq stepped outside. Tariq shook his head in disgust as the door closed behind them.

Chapter 23

School hours had now ended. Having just had a discussion on activism of the 1960s, Braun, Piye, and Marquis decided to stop by the O.B.U.'s African–centered bookstore in order to obtain more factual data than what was presented to them in their Americanized school. It was nearly five o' clock as Braun coasted to a stop in front of the bookstore on East Commerce. The bright rays of the sun shone brightly down on the glass windshield. The rays glistened off of the glass and chrome, caused Braun to squint slightly as he got out of the car. The sun was quite distant during February and no longer possessed the sweltering heat as it did in the summer. In fact, it was quite chilly at 39 degrees and dropping. Braun was sporting a Spurs jacket as Piye wore a black leather jacket with a hoodie, and Marquis, with a thick black hoodie underneath a long Starter, were well-prepared for the cold temperatures.

The three boys made their way into the bookstore and were warmly greeted by two members of O.B.U. All three frequented the bookstore and thus were on a first name basis with the librarians.

"Marquis…Piye…Braun, how are you young brothers? Just getting' off from school?" greeted a balding dark-skinned brother with glasses as he tapped on the keys of a computer. He was wearing a green dashiki adorned in black, red, and green beads. The other assistant, who was checking call numbers on books and relaying them to the other gentleman, acknowledged the boys with a smile and an upheld fist, symbolizing Black Power.

"Khari…Sundiata," the boys acknowledged nearly in unison. The three paused before the desk and made visual examination of the displays. They were mentally jotting down articles of interest. The bookstore was sufficiently equipped with tapes, jewelry, Afro-centric gifts, incense, African inspired clothing, games, videos, cards, and children's books. It had everything that an African-American seeking knowledge about his heritage would need. He tapped an entry onto the computer first, then Sundiata looked up into the boy's faces. His hands gestured as to their particular business there this day.

"Ah, you young brothers looking for something in particular?" he asked.

"Yes, Brother Sundiata. We were just talkin' bout activisim in the 60s. The Panthers, R.N.A… and we just wanna do a little research on the matter, ya know," Braun informed.

"Yeah, we's kinda…relatin' the situation today with them. It's the same repression, brutality…but less activism. Less militancy," Marquis stated. Sundiata smiled proudly. He was always enthusiastic about the Afro-centric conscientiousness of these young brothers. For the millennium, an era where the level of conscientiousness is perhaps at an all-time low, it was noteworthy to him. He grew up in the 1950s when blacks took to the courthouses, schools, and streets in order to obtain civil liberties and the 60s when 'Black Power' and 'Power to the people' were the slogans; and it was common to see brothers of African descent in dashikis getting involved in community activism at young ages. Huey Newton and Bobby Seals were barely out of their teens when they formed the Panthers. He was dispirited by the youth of today. He believed they were culturally displaced with no motivation to return; and given to materialism to such a degree that no semblance of Black Pride, awareness, or strength was evident. Individualism had become the mass mentality. In an article written by Phil Johnson it had been accredited, along with fear and ignorance, as being "A granite rock wall that barricades us from acting in concert with our needs." Sundiata, along with the O.B.U. in general, called for a new era of awareness. He called for an end to spiritual, cultural, and genocide of the people.

"Well, you know we have everything on that subject. Ah, of course the Panthers, S.C.L.C. etc." As he reflected, looking up at the ceiling to recollect the many black activist organizations of the 60s era, his words were interrupted by Marquis.

"S.C.L.C.? What's that other organization with similar initials?" he inquired, trying to recollect the organization from the recesses of his mind where many articles he'd read were stored.

"S.N.C.C.," responded Khari. Sundiata nodded in agreement as Marquis pointed his finger at Khari.

"That's it," Marquis stated emphatically. Sundiata began to explain to the boys exactly who the S.N.CC. was and what political role they played in the 1960s Civil Rights Movement.

S.N.C.C. stands for the Student Non-Violent Coordinating Committee. They were activists in the north whose political agenda included challenging segregation laws in the south, which they contested adamantly with Freedom Riders. One of their key members—a native of Trinidad, Stokely Carmichael—

was a renowned Black Nationalist and coined the slogan 'Black Power'.

Carmichael, who later changed his name to Kwame Toure—paying homage to early proponents of Pan-Afrikanism, Ghanaian Kwame Nkrumah and Guinean Sekou Toure— were diligently entrenched in the Civil Rights Rights Movement. After enrolling in Howard University in 1960. He joined the S.N.C.C. and helped to organize the Lowndes County Freedom Organization. The organization chose a Black Panther as its emblem in 1964, and two years later that emblem would be adopted by the Black Panther Party for Self-Defense.

Though initially supportive of Dr. King' Jr's non-violent approach to racist segregation, Toure began to become increasingly frustrated at the beatings and murders of activists. He espoused a different format of self-defense tactics, self-determination, political and economic power, and racial pride. The S.N.C.C. even changed its name to Student Nationalist Coordinating Committee.

The mid-60s, in contrast to the early phase of the civil rights movement, became synonymous with black empowerment and uprisings. Civil unrest in urban communities and an all-out war against black activist groups were met with armed resistance. This was a tactic that had proved fatal to these black organizations.

Today, the real threat of armed resistance against the police, though ill-advised anyway, was not even an issue. Other than idle talk by suppressed minorities and occasional confrontation by gun-toting street gangs--whose motives are not liberation, but rather in most cases, escape from incarceration--the police are quite safe. Resistance starts with ideologies. Ideologies become blueprints, which are carried out by revolutionaries. On a higher level, youth in the African-American communities of today neither possess the ideology, the motivation to draw up a blueprint, or efficient numbers of conscious youth to construct a stable activist front. Much less revolutionary front to the magnitude of the Black Panthers or Black Liberation Army of decades past. And this was a fallacy Sundiata and other O.B.U. members hoped to eradicate.

"You should find what you're looking for on those aisles right there." Sundiata pointed the boys in the direction of the shelves books containing information on the radical 60s.

The boys each scanned the shelves. Marquis came across a particular book that caught his eye and removed it from the shelves. It was entitled 'Agents of Repression' published by South End Press. 'Agents of Repression' gave in-depth information about dozens of radical organizations in the 1960's and early 1970's, including J. Edgar Hoover's diabolical Counter Intelligence Program (Cointelpro), which caused 95% of the to disband. Using infiltrators, calculated police terriost raids, trumped-up charges, arrests, and other schemes, the FBI successfully neutralized forward progress of these militant factions.

"*Agents of Repression.* Kabil was talkin' bout that book at a NBUF meetin' in Houston last June. That book got everything in it," Piye informed. Marquis began flipping through the pages while reading certain sections, as well as viewing the grim real life photos that were shown throughout the book.

In that brief moment of examination the boys discovered many facts that none of them had had previous knowledge of: the split between the Panthers as Eldridge Cleaver descended from Huey's Oakland chapter; the execution of the Black Panther and the Party's Chicago chapter leader Fred Hampton at the hands of the Chicago Police; and George and Jonathan Jackson. These were all brothers in the struggle in California for the liberation of the people. George, of course, was accused of killing a guard in the infamous Soledad Brothers case; and Jonathan went down in history for organizing a daring rescue attempt of George at the Marin County Courthouse. It was a rescue mission that resulted in the death of a judge, but also cost him his life at the young age of seventeen.

"Now that's what you call dyin' in the struggle. Jonathan Jackson was only seventeen years old. Can you believe that?" Marquis stated. His face masked of pride as he stared at a photo of young Jonathan standing with Angela Davis. She was a renowned sister in the revolutionary movement with credentials as an instructor at UCLA, who possessed an adamant ideological stance on communism.

"Oh yeah? That's when he and some mo' brothas tried to rescue George at the Martin County Courthouse. Sad he had to die though," Braun asserted.

"Didn't a judge or D.A. or somebody get killed in that?" Piye inquired as he continued to browse through the pages of one of the books from the bookshelf.

"A judge, that's what I'm readin' about now. Man, need mo' brothas like that today in the struggle," Marquis replied. Braun was in silent disagreement for a moment, but felt compelled, as he scanned the shelves, to respond in tactical disagreement.

"We have 'em. A similar incident was about to happen in Jasper, Texas. Brother Quanell X from the Houston Black Panther chapter along with members from the Dallas and New York chapters were there at the court proceedings in arms. Major arms, ya know. Talkin' M-16's and stuff. But if somethin' would have jumped off, what the outcome was gon' be? It had 200 Texas Rangers and County deputies on hand, ya know. Woulda been a massacre. And you know after ery'thang was over, the Panthers woulda been profiled," Braun enlightened.

The incident which Braun spoke of was in connection to one of the most heinous race crimes of our times. James Byrd Jr., a black man, was dragged behind a truck by three white men. Byrd was chained by his legs to the rear bumper of the truck and dragged until his body was torn and dismembered. This incident brought the small lumber milling community of Jasper to national notoriety and revealed realities of race hatred prevalent in what was an apparent Ku Klux Klan stronghold.

Braun referenced how the Klan had taken out a permit to hold a tactical rally at the courthouse in an effort to refute their involvement with this heinous crime, albeit they did this in their usually insensitive and racist rhetoric of white power reinforced with racial epithets. But to their surprise, these racial slurs were met with oppositions from the Panthers, which were led by Quanell X of the Houston chapter and Khalid Abdul Mohammad of the New York chapter.

The rally became intensely heated with the Panthers—including Quanell X---having to be restrained by police. But the 200-plus law enforcement agents were not enough to restrain these revolutionaries as a whole. The Panthers were armed and secured the perimeters in the courthouse square. Much to the shock and awe of the huge number of citizens present, the Klan fled and revealed their cowardice .

It was the first time justice had been served in a white-on-black crime in a racially prejudiced town. It was openly admitted that blacks were hanged in the courthouse square. Two of the three assailants in this malicious hate crime were sentenced to death, while the third received a mandatory life sentence.

After Braun's assertion, the other boys nodded in agreement. Marquis closed the Cointelpro book as Piye flipped through the pages of another book. He nodded his head in approval. He found the book of his interest, which was entitled 'Stokely Speaks: Black Power Back to Pan-Africanism'. It was an in-depth insight into Kwame Toure and the S.N.C.C.

"This one of the Stokely's books on Pan Africanism. I'mma check out this one. What is that you got, B?' Piye inquired of the book Braun held in his hands. Braun turned the book to its cover revealing the title, 'Soul on Ice', by Eldridge Cleaver.

"*Soul on Ice* by Eldridge Cleaver, I'm familiar with that one too," Marquis stated then clasped his book down by his side. "Ya know, Khari's pop was with Eldridge when the Panthers split," he added, which caused looks of reverence.

"Y'all ready?" Braun asked as he read the preface. The boys acknowledged that they were indeed ready and proceeded back towards the front. As they walked, the three took inventory and made comments about some of the Afro-centric articles on display in Voices, such as replicas of tribal masks worn by Dogons, jewelry with African queens, and medallions. Braun made reference to buying one of the pieces of jewelry as a gift for Ikara as Piye examined a tribal mask and Marquis sniffed incense.

"You brothers made your selections? Sho' you right. What is this? Oh…'Agents of Repression'. Hmm…lotta information in this, in-depth information. Tells ya how infiltrators of the FBI messed the Panthers around. Still got many infiltrators today. They politicians posin' to be in our best interest," Sundiata stated. Braun placed the African queen cameo necklace down on the counter before Khari.

"Nice piece, I like this myself. Gift, huh?" Khari inquired as Braun handed over to him the necessary amount required to purchase the necklace.

"Yeah, for my gal," Braun responded. Sundiata at that moment was handing back the Cointelpro book as Piye slid his book before him. At that moment two more patrons entered. A small teenage boy with dreadlocks and a girl who appeared to be his girlfriend. Both were wearing burgundy Texas Southern sweatshirts. The two acknowledged each of them, then continued on to browse the shelves.

"I see you found one on ole Stokely. Prolific brother, uh…rode with the Freedom Riders through the south in the 60's. Trynna fight the racist Klan law makers in Mississippi. Went to jail for it too," Sundiata informed them as he tallied the purchase. After doing so, he handed Piye the book as Khari made his own assertion. Though much younger than Sundiata at age forty-one, Khari was well versed on the radical 60s. His father was a member of the Panthers.

"And he was young. All of 'em was young. My pops was only eighteen. But this a new generation. Most of y'all peers ain't interested in reactionary movements. Everybody blingin'. Or murderin' over colors or neighborhoods. Blocks they don't even own," Khari stated as he looked over Sundiata. Khari was often castigating the youth of today. He idolized the revolutionaries from his childhood vantage point growing up in the late 60s in Oakland, and had very little optimism about the new generation developing into what those radicals of that era personified.

"Yeah, well…these young brothers on the right track. Might become the next Huey, Eldridge, and Seal. Yes sir," Sundiata stated with a toothy grin.

Each of the boys smiled. Their eyes reflected their pride in being compared to these men of valor. Braun held up his book as the others turned to leave the store and backpeddled as he bid farewell.

✷✷✷✷✷✷✷✷

Tariq, dressed in a dashiki and an African fitted hat sat behind a table alongside dozens of other members of O.B.U. Another special meeting had been called to order to address certain issues pertinent to the black community. This particular meeting was called in order to address the issue of social security, which was of great concern to the African-American working class citizen.

Social Security was designed to facilitate a basic safety net for the sick and elderly workers. The Bush Administration created an agenda that aimed to disrupt social security and promoted an economic conflict between banks and insurance giants.

As it stands today, the United States government has a 9.1 trillion dollar deficit and this is perhaps due to the fact that politicians constantly debate about how much to cut back on social security. They primarily target the sick and elderly in order to garner more money to use as expenditures to further the war in Iraq, a war that has cost the U.S. billions of dollars.

Tariq sipped his coffee, then interlocked his fingers before beginning to address the news at hand.

"I feel, and I'm quite certain many of you feel, that this restructuring of social security is not only an injustice to the working class people, but it also undermines the people's knowledge of the government's capability to financially extend wealth in regards to social security," Tariq stated. There were several comments of agreement to this assertion.

"Certainly, I'm in agreement with Brother Galla. The government misappropriates tax payers' funds in order to back the war in Iraq and other political agendas instead of extending sufficient funds towards the elderly and sick. Free healthcare should be a right," reinforced Sister Qusta, the wife of Somali Qusta. She spoke passionately as she swept the contingency with her eyes.

There were statements of agreement to her assertion, which coincided with her political beliefs and support of Communism. This, as a part of its government's creed, guarantees free health care for all its citizens. A luxury like this, however, is not afforded to U.S. citizens under the Democracy.

The Bush's Administration, however, was not the first to attack social security. It was enacted under President Franklin Delano Roosevelt as a part of his 'New Deal'. The 'New Deal' was the first such assault of this system of financial support on the working class people. It was enacted on May 12th, 1981 when President Ronald Reagan submitted his first budget to Congress. This budget proposal included cutting Social Security benefits. Fortunately, Congress rejected this reform proposal.

However, this overt attack on the Social Security system did not cease. It arose again in the late 1990s as the ruling class politicians incessantly tried to convince people that Social Security was not economically sustainable and is destined for bankruptcy. It was purported that trust funds would be completely exhausted by no later than 2042.

After Sister Qusta's assertion, Brother Yoruba explained the trillion dollar economy and the lie of the bankruptcy theory.

"Sister Qusta is very right. The rich, ruling politicians of this nation, whom you and I both know could care less about the sick and the poor, have propagated lies that, uh, this trillion dollar budget of trust funds will run out eventually. But, uh, as we have been educated to the system of social security, we know that it is a contributory system. Much like investing in a stock, these politicians are propagating these lies in order to cause panic. A panic that will, uh, legitimize their ultimate gutting of the system completely," Brother Yoruba explained.

After comments in reference to Yoruba's speech passed throughout the contingency, Brother Sundiata held up a hand to signify that this particular session was over. He began to clear his throat and wrapped one hand around the other as he stared down at a referendum. "Uh, we're gonna, excuse me, uh, bring this meeting to a close. But I'd like to first assert what everyone here should be familiar with concerning the 'advocates' who have been fighting along the battle lines with us on this issue. As you know, the AFL-CIO (American Federation of Labor and Congress of Industrial Organization) has opposed this program proposed by the Bush Administration. But in looking for allies in this fight, we have to be conscientious. You have these members of the Democratic Party posing to be allied with us, who were the very same ones presiding over the cutting of welfare benefits. So keep an open mind. And

uh, as I always stress…let's cover our own backs." After Sundiata's closing comments the meeting adjourned and members of the constituency stood and turned to embrace or shake hands with their faction members.

✶✶✶✶✶✶✶✶

"…We will stand firm and we will not falter. Justice will be served! And we will see to it that it does. This was a malicious, brutal attack on this young man's civil rights. And not one police officer has been indicted. Or even corrected. It's preposterous…" Those were the inflamed words spoken by the San Antonio head of the NAACP. His suit and tie complemented his clean-cut look. His eyes, behind his spectacles, were inflammatory, reinforcing his assertiveness as he pointed his finger away from the news cameras which filmed him.

Another image flashed across a news channel. The image of an elderly woman pointing back towards her broken-down door, a result of forced entry by the police using a battering ram and weapons, an entry she insisted came without warning.

"They jis…I was in nair cookin' an' all a sudden, boom! They knocked my do' off the hinges and was yellin' an shoutin' an' stuff. I was scared for my life."

Yet, another news broadcast showed a solemn white police officers as he pointed to 'evidence' he felt justified the police reconnaissance in the urban black community. This evidence consisted of bullet holes in signs and gang writings on walls, which were being removed by black volunteer workers at the moment. He held a plastic bag containing rock cocaine, and stated that boarded up crack houses were havens for "dangerous criminals who'll take even the life of an officer if cornered."

"…People who are not out here in these streets do not know the task that we, as police officers, have in preserving and protecting the community. This is a potentially hostile environment. There are gangs with automatic weapons and no value on human life, including the lives of myself and my fellow officers. As you can see… bullet holes there…the sign, graffiti right here on the wall. This clearly states 'death to police'. And none of us as officers can ever be certain when we will be violently accosted. And precautionary measures in most instances are very necessary."

Another news coverage featured an African-American man dressed in a blue shirt and coveralls. As he spoke, many other concerned black citizens converged around him. Some were holding signs with anti-police slogans and nodding their heads and pumping their fists for the cameras, as others murmured their dissatisfaction with the police.

"I saw the news coverage of the cryin' police officer. But you in the media have to have an open mind. He was simply using the criminal visuals to justify their acts. Demonize the community so they can get away with terrorism. That's what it is. Terrorism. He was makin' them seem like the victims. The oppressed. When it's our young black people being persecuted.

Beaten, shot in the back, and all without provocation. Our elderly women's houses ransacked. And there's no justice. Where is the justice?" The man pleaded with a dejected expression and his arms open. "…No justice."

These news reports aired days and weeks apart and were witnessed by activists, militants, and even the minority criminal element in the black communities. One of these criminal groups,which witnessed the news coverage and was thoroughly frustrated and disheartened at the constant harassment and injustice in the police trial procedures were Wild Bill and his gang.

Walking down a back street of boarded-up houses, an abandoned building and a vacant lot with several trees, Wild Bill and four of his gang members passed around two 40 oz. bottles of beer. Though the sun was out on this chilly late February day, a brisk wind blew, causing Lil Gun to shove his hands deep into his pockets and hunch his shoulders. He tried to shield himself from the arctic wind that easily penetrated the black hoodie he wore.

The others were more equipped for the biting cold as they donned thick lined half-trenches or Starters over hoodies and sweatshirts. This was, perhaps, more to conceal weaponry of .9mm pistols; a cut off stock Winchester 30/30 rifle; and sawed off .12 gauge pump shotgun, Red Dawg's choice weaponry. He had secured his shotgun in the lining of his trench Starter.

With a black ski mask rolled up, but pulled down near his eyes, Wild Bill gestured as he looked around the vicinity, making references to the obvious urban neglect of his community. He claimed it was the result of misappropriated funding. As he spoke Bull passed one of the 40 oz. bottles of beer to the closest member to him, Rocco. Bull's hulking stature appeared even larger inside of his thick hoodie and half-trench, which concealed the cut stock Winchester 30/30.

"Main, they be fuckin' off all that money our people pay on taxes, main. Parkin' Benzes and Lexuses an' shit in front they houses. That's why I been hittin' 'em e'ry chance I get, know what I'm sayin," Rocco stated as he dapped his burglary partner in crime, Wild Bill. At that moment Red Dawg reached into his pocket and pulled out his cell phone. In the process, a bag of rock cocaine fell to the pavement.

"Shit! What this nigga want, man?" he stated to himself as he kneeled to retrieve his crack rocks.

"Spose ta hit 'em e'ry chance ya get. I'm down wit runnin' off in one of dees bank, though. Where all the money at, man," Bull asserted as a late model car passes.

"Niggas hit a bank downtown yesterday mornin," Lil Gun announced. "Man, save me a swig, man," he added as he reached at the bottle Rocco held. There was a pause, then Wild Bill commented.

"I saw them fools. Niggas got Starter hats pulled down like people cain't make out who dey is. Right after that they went to interviewin' this fuckin cop. All that shit like that justifies in they eyesight, them beatin us down an' shit. Shootin' us in the back. And getting' away wit it," Wild Bill stated. His words dripped venom as he caught sight of a moving vehicle in his peripheral vision.

"Thank police gon' beat that charge, main?" Bull inquired as he received the beer bottle back. Wild Bill held up a cautioning hand as he continued to peer through the houses onto the street behind. This caused the rest of the gang members to take notice of what alarmed him. A San Antonio police cruiser rolled to a stop in front of a boarded-up crack house.

The driver of the police vehicle, a tall, medium-built Caucasian with a crew cut, sporting shades got out of the vehicle. He unbuttoned his holster strap as he looked around the vicinity. He closed the car door behind him and proceeded to walk around the front of his car as his partner, an African-American of stocky build and light complexion. He, too, took inventory of the surroundings. Speaking into his radio, the Caucasian officer led the way up to the house.

The officers proceeded to check around the front of the house, stooping down and picking at pieces of plastic. It was obvious to onlookers that the officers had been tipped to drug activity being conducted from out of the house and were hoping that their random stop would catch the perpetrators in the act. But now, seeing that the house was unoccupied, decided to do a little inspection anyway and thus proceeded inside. A shadowy figure moved in haste alongside a house. Another figure in a bandanna posted up beside the closed gas station directly across the street from the police vehicle. Crouching next to a stalled car, Wild Bill had his ski mask down and he took position behind a tree while cocking his .9mm. Berretta as he eyed the crack house.

Wild Bill ran several houses down, then jogged across the street in order to post up alongside a house on the same side of the street where the cop's vehicle sat. His legs spread far apart, he rocked slightly as he steadied his 30/30 Winchester rifle. Red Dawg hid behind bushes alongside a house twenty feet behind Wild Bill's vantage point. He talked to himself as he steadied the pump shotgun in the direction of the house, while Rocco, from the other side of the old gas station, kneeled on one knee. His .38 revolver was cocked as he steadied his arm.

The wait was intense as the gangsters watched the jacket-clad police officers move about in the house. Lil Gun's breathing became erratic as he psyched himself up. His hands fidgeted as he thoughts about the repercussions they would face as a result of murder or attempted murder of a police officer. He thought about the extensive time he would spend in Huntsvll or the lethal injection table. Beads of sweat ran down his nervous brown face as he had second thoughts, but there was no backing out. Red Dawg nodded as one officer came into view. His gold teeth glistened in a villainous smile through the mouth hole of the ski mask. He glanced often at Wild Bill, who stood motionless, his eyes a sinister leer as he pressed up against a tree. Across the street, drops of sweat ran down into his bandanna despite the cold, obvious effects of too much alcohol consumption. Wild Bill's trigger finger twitched nervously on the release and the 30/30 wavered in his hand. Then, the intense moment reached its climax as the black officer appeared at the doorway, his hand clutching what appeared to be a crack pipe while his partner once again transmitted over the radio. His hand leveled on his semi-automatic pistol.

"Pipe's warm... razors everywhere... fresh urine on the toilet seats. Uh... water on the floor in the kitchen and three rocks. Looks like they knew we were comin' and were in a hurry to get out," the black officer stated as he took his two steps outside the house. The gangsters were all tense. Each had a weapon leveled at the officers who continued to converse. Then Bull inhaled deeply.

The loud thunderous crack of the 30/30 caused the officers to recoil. The black officer dropped the paraphernalia and quickly reached at his semi-auto with the first cracking shot from Bull's 30/30. Perhaps distance compounded with nervousness and inaccuracy sent the first shot from the 30/30 awry, knocking a large chunk out of the frame of the wooden house, sending shards of shredded wood in its wake.

Several shots followed and the Caucasian officer retreated backwards into the house as the black officer received a gunshot wound to the upper leg and lower torso. The impact of the bullets caused him to buckle as he crumpled to the ground. He was bleeding profusely from the spiraling .9mm Ruger bullet. It had severed his femoral artery and the splay of buckshot penetrated just below his bulletproof Kevlar vest.

The rounds of gunfire were deafening. Buckshots peppered the doors of the vehicles; .9mm. missiles of death busted out its windows and knocked shards of wood from the house, as .39 caliber revolver bullets splattered the cars headlights and kicked up dirt from the ground. Wild Bill re-cocked in precision as he side-peddled backwards, just missing the black officer's body. Seconds seemed like minutes. The crackle of the rifle, barks of the police's semi-automatic from the house's window; glass busting and clinking on the pavement from both the police vehicle and the vehicle Lil Gun crouched down as he fired his entire seventeen rounds from his black .45 semi-auto, and the six thunderous roars from Red Dawg's Marsburgh reverberated through the air as the five gangsters fired indiscriminately at the officers. The white cop, was on his back inside the house, radioed in for back-up as two shots from Wild Bill's .9mm Ruger busted out the remaining pane of glass on the window. The bullets sent shards of glass sprinkling over the officer.

The officer's breathing was labored as he shouted into his radio. With an empty weapon beside him, he became apprehensive of the possibility that the gunmen could be approaching his partner, causing him further anguish.

"Officer down! Officer down! 400 block of Utah! Requesting backup and mobile unit!" The officer shouted as glass continued to flail him from the hail of rifles, shotguns, and pistols. The gunshots and glass caused him to shut his eyes tight and grit his teeth in fear of what seemed inevitable. Then the gunshots tapered off and finally ceased with one reverberating echo of the 30/30.

The officer slowly opened his eyes as the deafening gunshot echoes faded into the whistling of the wind. The dogs in the vicinity barked and rattled their chains. Then he slowly scuttled his boots across the glass-filled floor to arise in an upright position next to the window as the sounds of police sirens became clearer.

Peering around the edge of the window pane, the officer observed his partner. He was motionless, but nevertheless breathing. Then his eyes swept the vicinity. The gunmen seemed to have vanished into the air. Gone without a trace or even an inkling as to who their identities were. But he was relieved nevertheless and began painstakingly maneuvering towards the door. The officer squinted his eyes at the sun's glare as he stepped out into the yard, looking into the direction of the speeding patrol units as their lights flashed and their sirens blared. He knelt down over his fallen partner and assessed the severity of his wounds as the other officers leapt from their vehicles.

Chapter 24

Two miles away, in another neighborhood, a cowboy in a plaid shirt, hat and denim jeans with chaps was riding a bull. The crowd was going wild and cheering as the cowboy stayed on the bucking bull a full eight seconds before being hurled into a security fence. He managed to avoid the fury of the bull's horns as rodeo clowns in outlandishly-colored outfits rushed to his aid. It was the annual rodeo event and people from many parts of Texas were in attendance. Everyone was dressed in their urban cowboy attire with big silver buckles and cowboy hats; eating popcorn, hot dogs and drinking. But elsewhere in San Antonio, specifically the predominately African-American communities on the eastside, there was a different kind of scene, one of despair instead of joy. The faces of youth and elderly alike, were masked with anguish. Based on recent events, it was understandably so. It had been several days since the ambush of the police officers by Wild Bill's gang. And henceforth, the black communities suffered ramifications. These ramifications came in many different forms, from more patrolling; to crackdowns on gang members hanging out in numbers; curfews; to simply stopping someone, anyone, who even remotely looked suspicious,--young black males,--and interrogating them. These interrogations ranged from pat searches to name profiling for arrest records. Many of the citizens had become victims of this alleged security crackdown.

Scenes of teenage youth being frisked and interrogated by officers became common. Police justified these security measures and displayed hi-tech Kevlar vests for the news cameras. Gang members scattered at the sight of police vehicles. They tossed their drugs, beer bottles, and in many cases, weapons. These atrocities can be compared to martial law in a sense. The police used ambush to justify suspending the rights of the African American citizens. Violations of the curfew resulted in dozens of arrests. As the news broadcaster was currently reporting, he looked complacent. Then in closing added: "The streets of these eastside neighborhoods are perhaps safer than they've been in years."

Many felt the backlash of Wild Bill's gangs extension of their political ideology and listened with utter disgust at media representatives who propagated lies and misinformation about the militaristic police presence in their communities. Braun felt the same way, and was conveying his disconcertment of his community's plight to his fellow co-worker, Eric Fluentes.

"It's that crucial, homie?" Eric stated as he removed his apron.

"It's that crucial. We, like, live like hostages…ah, a third world country or somethin'," Braun further explained as he removed his apron and then slapped hands with Eric.

"Later homie. Hey, why don't you come by the crib, homes. Maybe we can go kick it or somethin', sometime. Hey, I'll show you how I hook up these bikes alright homie?" Eric offered with a sincere smile on his face.

Braun turned back towards him as he punched the clock.

"I just might do that, homie," he responded. Eric's smile widened as he nodded and pumped a fist. He then returned to preparing tacos and fajitas.

"I'm outta here, Tammy. Oh, and Phil keep askin' about you," Braun informed as he passed by her at the register. She smiled, but averted eye contact as she tapped the register keys. It was obvious her uneasiness about the proposal and the guilt at not honoring her word to write him. "Look Tammy, I know that you tried to get him out the game an' all. He made a mistake. Look at his situation from all angles, know what I'm sayin'. And like I said, he plannin' on leavin' it alone. Guess he jis got caught up, but…," Braun's sentence was interjected.

Tammy sighed, "Braun, you know how I feel about him. Braun, I'm confused. And he doesn't even know how long he'll be away. And I jus' can't put my life on hold for him. Especially when I don't know if he's actually gotten his life together. I have a future. I'm going to college. I need someone who wants a future also. Not an image," she responded. Her expression was pleading.

Though Braun was empathetic with the plight of his friend, he was also understanding of Tammy's stance. And he respected her decision. She was focused in life. Ambitious. She wasn't like many young sisters, intrigued by images or lifestyles of boys whose ignorance, compounded by materialism, would jeopardize her life and ambitions.

Braun nodded to Tammy's impassioned reasoning. After carefully examining her eyes and reading the confusion in them, he looked away and responded.

"Yeah, I…I feel that, Tammy. And I cain't say that I totally disagree wit you. 'Cause most girls risk everything for images. But you smart. Know what I'm sayin'. But I gotta say this, Phil's my boy. Grew up wit'em. And, he was influenced by a lotta reasons to go into that lifestyle. But I think…I know that the real reason wasn't about image. He felt obligated to take care of his lil' brother and sister. And his mother. He loves 'em. Tammy," Braun explained.

In doing so, Tammy's expression began to change as she looked away. It was evident she was taking the information into consideration. "I don't expect you to put your life on hold. Phil don't expect you to put your life on hold. And I respect that you want a more focused man. He respects it. But he considers you his friend. I do too. So… as a friend, do that. Just write 'em. Ya know. Let 'em know you at least thank of him… as a friend," Braun implored. He knew that he had reached her and had gotten her to look at things from Phil's perspective. He had touched on her sympathetic nature. Then with a smile, he bid her farewell. "See ya tommar, Tammy." He retreated out of the restaurant, leaving her standing there, meditating over his words a moment before two patrons approached for service. She quickly refocused and put on a gorgeous smile. She welcomed them and began to take their orders.

Braun's car coasted to a stop in front of Phil's dilapidated house, which, like several other houses on the block, was in need of painting. This was another problem he would have to rectify, he thought to himself as he put the car in park. He had stopped by Toys-R-Us on his way home from work and now collected the two items he had purchased from the passenger seat.

Braun's eyes swept the vicinity as he walked up the cracked concrete walkway leading to the steps of Phil's mother's house. The block was quiet, save for the distant barking of a dog and low thumping of a car system. Only an elderly man walking up the street and a middle-aged woman retrieving her mail, disrupted the silence of the post-ambush condition that had been induced by constant police harassment.

He rang the doorbell and waited with the two gifts secured under his arms. He stood anxiously as he anticipated the little girl and boy's reactions to these gifts. He made it his personal business to see to it the children were happy, and not just on holidays. His concern for them wasn't seasonal. After a lapse of perhaps a minute, the door creaked open and there stood Phil's mother. She was conservatively dressed and her hair was done. This was a contrast to her pre-rehab time. Her face ignited in glee at seeing him and she began to open the screen door.

"Hey, Braun, baby. How you doin'?" she chimed as she hugged him. After the embrace her eyes fell on the two gifts. "Oh, you don't have to keep buyin them gifts like this, baby," she laughed. They have enough toys and stuff now.

Come on in, that's why that pill-head boy be so late doin' his homework, now. Playin' them video games. You see where he at?" she stated as she closed the door behind them. Phil's little brother was thoroughly into playing a PlayStation video game, but threw down the controls and rushed in to greet him.

"Braun!" shouted the little boy, as Braun set down the toys atop the dining room table. Braun hugged him, then playfully nudged and prodded him. "Ooh! This is the game I been talkin' 'bout, mamma!" he shouted ecstatically as he removed the video game cartridge from the bag.

"Now, don't be on that all night and ain't got yo' homework. You heard what mamma said," Braun chastened. "'Sides, can't get good enough to play for the Cowboys if you play video games all day," he added humorously. The little boy laughed then rushed back into the living room with the cartridge.

"You want sometin' to eat, baby? I know you probably hungry. Jis gettin' off from work. I got chicken, red beans, and corn bread with mustard greens," she offered as she fidgeted with her hands. Her expression evidenced her receptiveness to Braun's concern for her children, and her eyes showed the loving incandescence of a mother towards her own child.

The offer sounded appetizing to Braun, and even though he had been eating practically the entire day at work, he didn't want to refuse her offer. "Red beans and chicken? You know I want some, Mrs. Tina," he responded with a smile. Phil's mother walked into the kitchen to prepare his meal.

The two were now seated at the table. Braun bit into a spicy breast piece. Its crispy skin crackled with each bite. His expression was a testament to its tantalizing effect on his taste buds. He nodded his head and signaled to Mrs. Tina his approval.

"I'm glad to hear Jalena made the honor roll. I's really hopin' she was here," Braun stated as he wiped his mouth with a napkin.

She smiled, "She should be here in a little while. She should have been back. My sister has her. Know she spoils her rotten. And she loves her auntie. 'Spose to be getting her li'l braids done. My baby."

"Braun! I want you to come watch me play. You wanna play? I can beat you. I know how to make the karate man go…and make him fly like this. And your man won't win. Come look," Gary shouted as he played the new martial arts-based game Braun had bought. Phil's mother smiled as she shook her head. With his mouth full, Braun responded, but his words were barely audible.

"Let me finish eatin', Gary," he laughed. Mrs. Tina ran a finger through her hair as she looked at Braun.

"Braun, I… I really wanna thank you, baby. It's been rough…and… sometimes I jis don't know which way to turn. But you, Mr. Galla, and a lot of people been helpin' me. And I thank y'all. I'm getting my life back together. Slowly Sharon's lettin' me help fixin' hair at the salon. I'mma be okay. You almost finished? It was good, huh? Mrs. Tina can cook. I haven't lost that," she stated. She tried to exhibit a look of high-spiritedness. But he recognized her concealment of the despair she was actually experiencing. It was evident in her eyes, despite the smile. She then arose from the table and accepted the tray from Braun and walked into the kitchen as she continued to talk with her back to him. "I hope Phil ain't been worryin' you 'bout me and the kids. Or writin' one of them lil' gals," she laughed.

"No, Mrs. Tina. I don't thank of y'all as no worry. Y'all family. But yeah, he be askin' 'bout 'em. The girls," Braun smiled. As he did so, he thoroughly observed her. The effects of a psychologically abused woman who fought up and down battles with drugs and depression, and the loss of a husband and sons to the penal system. She had been subjected to humiliation and degradation, but with spiritual strength had fought back to regain her stability. She was still fighting, and was uncertain of how long she would retain this stability.

She laughed at Braun's confirmation and shook her head as she looked at him. It was at that moment the gate outside could be heard opening. Peering out of the window as he finished wiping his mouth, Braun's eyes lit up and a wide smile crossed his face. Seeing his car parked in front of the house, Jaleena had made a beeline for the steps. Her shoes clip-clopped up the concrete walkway as her pigtails flopped. Mrs. Tina saw her sister's vehicle and walked out of the house to greet her. "Yavonne, hold up fo' you go," she yelled. Braun stood at the doorway and waved in acknowledgement of Devonte's mother.

"Hey, Mrs. Johnson," Braun called out to her. She responded with a courteous smile and waved as Mrs. Tina approached.

"Hey, momma," Jaleena chimed in her squeaky voice. Mrs. Tina kissed her on the cheek as she rushed past her, eager to greet Braun. Much to her mother's amusement and Braun's as well, he had become a surrogate brother of sorts. And they were an extension of his own family. Practically leaping into his arms to hug him, Jaleena began explaining enthusiastically to Braun her experiences of the day spent with her auntie as the two retreated inside.

"…and then we went to see the fish at the 'quarium and I got this. I'm glad big head Gary didn't come so he ain't get none," she stated, sticking out her tongue at her brother as she waved a Hershey's candy bar around. "And my auntie say I look like 'Lisha Keys with my hair braided," she stated. Gary, peering from his position in the living room, shouted out a snide remark.

"Girl, you don't look like no Alicia Keys. Braun don't care bout dat no how. C'mon play the game wit me, Braun," he practically demanded. Braun rose from his position, looking in Gary's direction and sensing their competition for his attention.

"And he don't wanna play dat ol' stupid video game with you. Come on, Braun. I wanna show you the straight As I made on my report card," she stated. Rolling her eyes and moving her head in defiance to her big brother, she coaxed and began to pull Braun in the direction of her room as she bit into her candy bar.

"Okay, okay," Braun stated, in the midst of laughing. He glanced back at Phil's mother who had just returned back into the house as Yvonne drove away from the curb. She smiled in recognition of the children's competition over Braun and shook her head as she returned to the kitchen.

✶✶✶✶✶✶✶✶

The dinner table was set at the Galla family's modest home. This evening, Tariq, his wife, and children had invited dinner guests: their close friends, the Jinnahs. The seven dined on some Afro-Centric meals as they talked. They covered topics from the trivial to economics and world crises to cultural, which, incidentally, was the chosen topic at the moment.

Nawaz cut a piece of his fish, after sampling some of Ursula's well-spiced cucumbers—was one of the Galla family's favorite dishes—as he listened to his wife comment on information given moments earlier by Tariq.

"I find that interesting. If it is always important to reach back to help others, especially those who are less fortunate. And we should always connect with the suffering of our ethnic people. Learn and teach them also. Is good," Mrs. Jinnah explained as she stuck a fork full of okra into her mouth. It was seasoned with pepper, causing her to pant and feign fanning herself. "Is hot," she laughed. Ikara and Caleb exchanged meaningful glances.

"Mm hm. In our native language we call it Sankofa., which means to go back and retrieve history," Tariq informed the Jinnahs. At that moment Caleb reached to grab a dinner roll off of Ikara's plate, only to have his hand playfully slapped. After which, he received a look from Ursula who hadn't found his playing in front of the houseguests the least bit amusing.

After cutting her eyes from Caleb and returning a more pleasant expression to her face, Ursula began to speak. "Speaking of history, you have a lot of history yourselves. Do you try to educate your daughter about

Pakistan? I mean, I understand she grew up over here," Ursula inquired as she cut into her fish.

Nawaz chewed his food rapidly as he studied his wife, anticipating her response to Ursula's inquiry. "Oh, yes. Swathi…she has always been interested in learning about her family's history," she responded.

"We fly back to Pakistan periodically. She's receptive to learning our culture. But she is not too receptive to practicing any of zem. Especially our customary dress. You see, she is American. And it is not, er…cool, as you say. She dresses like them…," as he points at Caleb and Ikara.

"Zee hip-hop…what chu call it, right?" Mrs. Jinnah joked. Ikara and Caleb laughed. Tariq smiled as he chewed a slice of fish. Then he began to speak as he looked in Nawaz's direction.

"Hmmm. It's funny you should say that. You refer to her as being an American. Explain this to me," Tariq asked. As he awaited Nawaz's response, he ate another helping of okra, chewing rapidly as he looked at Nawaz quizzically.

Nawaz wiped his mouth first before taking a sip of his beverage. Nawaz responded to Tariq, "American is an adjective to describe simply the country in which we currently live. The government we live under as citizens you see," Nawaz explained.

Tariq, with hands overlapping the other, nodded and smiled in comprehension of Nawaz's implication. He suggested that his reference to Swathi as American only described her regional citizenship rather than ethnicity, a point he'd often stressed to many urban black youths and adults as well, who'd flatly denied being African, and considered themselves Americans, not as in their implied citizenship, but as their ethnicity. This misguided and un-nationalistic view stems from a complete detachment from their true cultural identity.

"That's interesting. Because this is what I try to instill within our people. The youth. That we are Americans by citizenship. Not ethnic background. We're Africans. And when presented with such a question of our nativity, they should respond as such. Unfortunately, unlike your people, ours have lost touch with their cultural identity," Tariq responded.

Ursula lifted a bowl of fruit and offered it around the table. As everyone selected their fruit, she expanded on Tariq's comment.

"But they seem to regain it when they're faced with troubles from our law enforcement agencies and courts. And I'm not mentioning names," she stated.

"You know, I always ask Swathi about Pakistan. She gives me the impression that she's really into the cultural thing. She's always like, telling me of the hidden beauties there. The customs, ya know," Ikara asserted while plucking grapes from the stem. Nawaz smiled. "I'd like to visit there. Someday," she finished.

"Swathi. She is a very impressionable girl. You too are such good friends. She speaks very fondly of you. You interested in visiting Pakistan? Is it okay if she flies to Pakistan with us, Mrs. Galla?" Nawaz inquired and chucked as he wiped his mouth. Ikara placed a hand over her face as she smiled and motioned her head, pushing back her long flowing hair from around her ears. Ursula laughed as she retrieved an apple from the bowl.

"I don't think she can stay away from her little boyfriend that long," Ursula stated with humor.

"Mom," Ikara stated as she feigned shielding her face in embarrassment. There were laughs around the table. Then the Gallas and their house guests continued dining on the remainder of this well-prepared African meal.

✶✶✶✶✶✶✶✶

The sunlight was shining in beams through crevices in the clapboard windows of Wild Bill's orange crack house. Despite the arctic chill in the air outside, it was a beautiful day, and the morning dew glistened on the ground like sparkling diamonds. The serene silence of the morning was disrupted only by the barking of a pit bull and the grinding metallic sound of a garbage truck compactor.

Blocks away at the police precinct, police officers with special response tactical units stormed out in force, brandishing submachine M-13s. Geared in dark blue tactical wear with Kevlar vests underneath and safeguard face shields, the officers filed out in precision into an awaiting van, as detectives clad in grey suits boarded unmarked vehicles. One of the detectives—a balding, stocky Caucasian man—secured his weapon into his holster as he transmitted instructions before boarding a van.

Inside of the gang's house, Wild Bill was just arising from a slumber, sitting up on the side of a sofa as his eyes focused. He was awakened perhaps by the barking of the dog or the sound of the hydraulic compactor on the garbage truck.

Across from Wild Bill on a worn mattress was another one of his members Lanky and Midnight. The lanky street kid who dealt from pillar to post. He was shifting and his eyes were squinting from the beams of light shining directly on him until he, too, awakened. He sat up on the mattress. His face was a mask of delirium.

Bull was already awake, sitting upright on a tattered recliner while his hands fidgeted at a pack of Kools cigarettes. His trusty 30/30 Winchester was propped against the wall. As the garbage truck appeared outside the window, he observed the workers exiting the vehicle. They ran to retrieve garbage from the yard across the street. Then, as Rocco appeared from down the hall, passing Bull and Wild Bill to flounce down on a beer crate in the corner.

"Throw me one, man," he sighed as he rubbed his face. Bull removed a Kool 100 from the pack and tossed it to him. He lit his own cigarette before placing the lighter into his pocket causing Bill, after a moment, to stare over at him, disoriented. "Give me the lighter," he requested. Bull blew a funnel of smoke as he looked at him.

"Damn! Want me to smoke it for you, too?" he stated sarcastically.

"Jis gimme the light, nigga. Got no time for playin' early in the mornin', man," Bill responded disgruntled.

Bull laughed as he reached back into his pocket to retrieve the lighter. At that moment, Red Dawg—who just exited his modest, well-manicured partially-bricked home—walked briskly across the street. His shoulders were hunched from the brisk winds that penetrated even the half-trench coat he wore as he puffed on a cigarette. His Long Horn Beanie which bore a steers head was pulled down nearly to his eyes, which were chinked as he observed his surroundings.

Wild Bill leans forward on the sofa. His eyes were glazed over and his expression was one of deep meditation induced by anxiety. Midnight leaned back against the wall and placed a hand across his forehead and started beating on the wooden floor as he nodded and rapped some unorthodox lyrics he had been reciting in his mind.

"Nigga Midnight with this rap shit early in the mornin'! You ain't gonna get no contract wit Scarface, main," Rocco laughed.

"Already got a contract out on me fo' bangin' up fools like you," Midnight stated. "Man, I'm hungry as a motha fucka, main. Gotta call this nigga Red Dawg tell 'em brang over some eggs and bacon and shit. His momma cook, main. And some Florida orange juice," Midnight laughed.

"The pen spoiled you, nigga. Ain't nobody brangin' you black ass nothin' out here, man," Wild Bill stated. At that moment, as he neared the house, Red Dawg caught sight of a vehicle moving through a vacant lot between houses on the back street. Turning his head towards the blur, his vision caught the tail end of the vehicle, a San Antonio police cruiser. Then a second and third followed, causing alarm. He mentally made a note of it. However, he didn't see the other police vehicles that had preceded it, nor the police van which was parked alongside the corner block of the street he was on. The detectives were inside of their vehicles with headsets, communicating with the special response team, which was exiting the van on the next street. The lead detective's binoculars were trained on Red Dawg as he made his way up to the boarded up house. He looked around suspiciously before tossing aside the butt of the cigarette he'd been smoking.

"Wonder what the fuck time it is?" Wild Bill stated. At that moment, a shadow was seen crossing the lawn causing Rocco to crane his neck in order to peer out of the window. He leaned back after seeing Red Dawg's face. After a rapid knock, Wild Bill authorized his entrance. Red Dawg opened the door and looked back over his shoulder as he closed it.

"Bill, Bull, what up Midnight? Rocco…say man, shit heatin' up on the real, man. I jis seen three S.A. cruisers, main, comin' up Nevada Street," Red Dawg stated in a panic. His expression displayed anxiety as he rubbed his hands together in an effort to warm them. His comrades' demeanors changed instantly from early morning delirium to being fully alert and alarmed.

"Three cars?" Midnight blurted out as he rose from his lying position to sit erect. He rubbed a hand across his face while his eyes darted in their dark sockets. Red Dawg unzipped his jacket as he walked past Midnight to slap hands with Wild Bill. Then, flouncing down next to him, he reached under his leg to retrieve Bill's .9 mm. Ruger in which he'd sat on. As he began to speak, Bill accepted the gun and stood up.

"Yeah, man. Know the papers talkin' bout they got leads and shit to the shootin'," Red Dawg informed, drawing alarmed expressions on the faces of the gang bangers. This also caused Midnight to shake his head in disbelief.

"Leads? You read this, man?" Midnight inquired.

Bull reached for his Winchester 30/30 as Wild Bill, with pistol gripped in his right hand, stopped in his tracks.

At that moment on the street directly behind the crack house, the taskforce officers in black uniforms,were scurrying. With submachine guns and face shields, they took up positions beside trees, cars and houses. Their weapons were trained on the house as the lead team captain waved several others through the weed -covered, littered backyard of the house.

Wild Bill, with an expression of concern on his dark face continued to stare quizzically at Red Dawg, who continued to explain what he'd read. Rocco jumped to his feet, removed his 38. caliber revolver and peeked out of the window at nothing. There was a serene calm and seemingly nothing amiss as the motley crew of sanitation workers continued on with their morning task of collecting garbage.

Rocco receded from the window and retook his seat on the crate. He shook his head then looked down at his .38 revolver. "Man, you got me edgy as a motha fucka," he stated. His tone was nervous and beads of sweat were forming on his forehead.

"Three police cars this time of mornin'? They only roll deep like dat when a warrant din been served. I don't like this shit. We might need ta raise up," Bill stated. His eyes stared blankly as his mind formulated possibilities as to what business the San Antonio police had in the immediate blocks, including worse-case scenarios concerning their reactionary assault on the police three weeks prior. Perhaps these scenarios had crossed his comrade's minds as well, as each bore expressions of concern. Then the sound of police cruisers and tactical vans screeched to a halt and sirens blared, which sent each of them in motion. Bill cursed aloud as he led the way with .9 mm Ruger upraised. "Back do', man!" he shouted out. But as he made two steps down the hall, the back door burst open and in poured two ATF agents in black gear and face shields. As the two task force members moved in swift precision to either side of the doorway, Wild Bill started, firing several rounds from his .9 mm.

In the dimly-lit corridor the muzzle flash from the Ruger illuminated the black silhouetted figures. Its .9 mm spiraling missiles of death belted home on the third task force member's Kevlar vest. He crumpled to the ground as rapid bursts from the other agent's submachine M-13s rang out, their bluish-white muzzle flashes blinding. There were dozens of rounds exploding nonstop in the mere nine seconds.

Several high-velocity bullets tore through Wild Bill's torso. His own rounds bucked from the Ruger as his blood splayed on the walls and hallway. His body thrust up against the hallway wall violently before slumping to the floor. He never relinquished the .9 mm Ruger, which he still clutched firmly in his lifeless hand that twitched as his eyes stared blankly.

The bursts of rapid gunfire had abruptly halted the other gang member's routes. Red Dawg trailed behind Bill and was struck by two of the M-13s high velocity rounds. One bullet entered his side, lodged inches from his spine, and the other severed his clavicle and spun him down hard against the opposite hall wall. And the bursts continued. The others, who halted after Bill and Red Dawg had gone down, were in sheer panic. Indecision and terror were etched across their faces as they cowered from the deafening barrage of rapid fire muzzled flashes echoing the hallway. They recoiled in horror at Red Dawg's agonizing screams of pain over the expended rounds of M-13 ammunition.

Then, as Bull entered, with 30/30 cocked and ready, and with an expression of desperation enveloping his face, a task force member stepped over Red Dawg and appeared in Bull's range as Midnight and Rocco opened the front door.

As Bull's 30/30 barked out, belting home in the Kevlar vest of the task force member, Rocco and Midnight released shots in the direction of the police vehicles and officers stationed outside of the crack house. There was immediate retaliatory fire from the officers and detectives behind the vehicles. And Rocco, suffering a wound to the abdomen, was the first to fall as Midnight who was hit twice, continued firing a .44 Bull Dog until another shot hit his thigh which buckled him to one knee. Raising his weapon in the direction of the officers, he took a final shot before he was struck in the head. He collapsed face-first to the ground. Inside, Bull was overwhelmed by the charging task force members. His body jerked violently as it was thrust against the wall. He slumped to the floor amidst penetrating high velocity bullets. The room was filled with bluish smoke and the last shot echoed over the click-clanking of the expended shell. Then there was calm.

As the police helicopter buzzed above, inside, the taskforce members were making reconnaissance through the carnage. They hovered above the bodies of Bull, Red Dawg and Wild Bill, guns trained on them, anticipating one last reactionary move. But there were none forthcoming, as none of the gang members moved.

Outside, the officers had rushed to the bullet riddled bodies of Rocco and Midnight, shouting and aiming their pistols and M-16s. Midnight lay motionless. Rocco grimaced in agony from his abdomen wound as detectives violently tightened handcuffs onto his wrists. It was all over. The fierce fire fight had left in its wake seven casualties. Four were pronounced dead on the scene: Midnight, Wild Bill, Bull and the agent whose vest did not protect him from Bull's high powered Winchester 30/30. The survivors were Red Dawg, Rocco and the first officer who'd received minor injuries after being struck by two of Wild Bill's .9mm bullets. Red Dawg and Rocco would later stand trial for the death of the task force member, and be sent to death row in the U.S. Maximum Security Prison at Terre Haute, Indiana.

Wild Bill and his gang had been labeled 'urban terrorists', terrorists who 'maliciously' and without provocation ambushed law enforcement agents. It had taken several weeks but informants had finally come forward and revealed information crucial to the investigation, and they'd tracked down their most wanted suspects.

"As you can see, the task force members are exiting the house now. There is no way of discerning how many were in the house and ah, there was a firefight though it cannot be established how many casualties. But one of the suspects is confirmed to be dead and another one appears to be wounded has been apprehended. I'm receiving word now that there have been casualties within the house… and two other suspects are confirmed dead…there also are two officers down inside of the house…one is also confirmed dead and another… oh, there he is now. He appears to be okay."

The police helicopter news man continued reporting accounts of what had been the bloodiest armed resistance against police in San Antonio's history. The broadcast was shown, not only in San Antonio, but on CNN World News: the shouting shirt-and-tie-clad detectives with guns drawn; the black-clad taskforce units exiting the smoke-filled house and walking outside onto the winter-browned grass and dirt in front of the house; and Rocco being lifted onto an ambulance gurney as the taskforce officer, stripped of his shirt and Kevlar vest exposed, was being held erect by officers as he grimaced in pain. The swirling blades of the police helicopter rippled the shirts of the officers and danced around dirt and leaves as the twirling red and blue lights of police sirens gave a melodic backdrop to this war-torn scene.

Chapter 25

April 2005

The scene on this beautiful April day varied around the city. White-collar businessmen and women entered buildings downtown dressed in suits and carried briefcases or dossiers as automobiles whizzed by; children of different ethnicities ran and played in suburban communities as parents washed expensive vehicles or manicured their very spacious lawns, which were occupied by elaborate homes; and urban dwellers in projects, apartments, and housing areas coped with existing poverty and repression in conventional and unconventional ways. There were scenes of youths on porches drinking beers or in backyards fighting pit bulls, yelling and cheering as these animals tore at each other, or playing games of basketball. There were teenage boys in sweats or shorts, their sweat glistening off of their brown bodies.

But there was another scene this day. One that took place in the Mexican barrios which differentiated it from the normal scenes played out every day on news broadcasts of domestic violence, drugs, and profiling of Mexican gang members with elaborate tattoos and stylized cars. These images created a stereotypical view of the Mexican community. Today the atmosphere was quite different. Celebratory. It was fiesta time. And many of the Mexican citizens in the city were en route to the festivals, including gang members. They boarded their vehicles as families exited modest homes in cheerful moods. One family consisted of a wife and husband with their two children who excitedly ran to board their SUV as the husband opened the sliding door.

Fiesta is the Spanish word for feast day or holiday. In origin, fiestas either are celebrated for religious or political holidays. Such as for a particular saint or holidays like Easter and Christmas, or the day Mexico gained its independence. All Latin American countries hold fiestas. Mexicans in both Mexico and San Antonio, hold extremely colorful fiestas.

These fiestas usually begin before daylight with a shower of rockets, the percussion of firework displays; and the ringing of bells. The vendors set up booths where they sell candles, drinks, and souvenirs in their Zocalo (public square). Men and women in elaborate commemorative Mexican dress dance to traditional music as children and other spectators clapped and cheered along to the sounds of the horns, tambourines and shakers. Their faces were joyful. This was the scene in the barrio. The Mexican people of the community (including Ikara's friend Maria, who was, at the moment laughing giddily as she performed a dance to the music) came together for great food, music and dance in a celebration of their way of life.

Teenage boys dressed in track and field tank tops and shorts showing off their sleek and toned physiques replaced the scene of the fiesta. Spectators from Roosevelt High School sat in the bleachers observing the team and speculating about the prospects for the team this spring. Braun, with his hands on his sides, walked with his head down. He was focused on the physical feat ahead of him, which was to qualify for the 100-meter dash.

Breathing in and out in a lung exercise, Braun stretched. He grabbed his right leg, then left as he glanced over in the direction of the bleachers. A smile widened across his face as he locked eyes with Ikara, who smiled in return. A female trainer raised her right leg to loosen up her muscles so that cramps or other injuries would not occur during her practice events, which were the 200-meter dash, 100-meter dash, and 400-meter relay.

Braun jumped up and down several times, and then jogged in place for a few seconds to further loosen his leg muscles. Then he briskly walked over towards his fellow track teammate, who were, at the moment, lining up behind the starting line. Each was slightly perspiring under the late afternoon sun, shaking out kinks and stretching before taking position. Braun slapped hands with Marquis, and then the two kneeled down.

Ikara was now on her feet. Her smooth caramel skin shone as the muscles of her well-conditioned legs flexed on her way down the steps of the bleachers. As she fidgeted at her shorts, she eyed the boy she loved and hoped that he would win or at least qualify for the event. His three previous years on the track team consisted of him being first leg in the 400-meter relays, hurdles, and 1500-meter race. At 5'10, 167 lbs., his well-defined and long legs carried him over long distances. In all of his track meets, he finished in second or third place. However, in most of those races he lead most of the way before losing ground at the end. This outcome was attributed to his lack of conditioning. Braun always settled for silver or bronze medals.

The hurdles was the event that had gotten him recognition from college scouts. He came in first place for each event the previous year. And he was anxiously anticipating letters from major universities, with Texas A & M being his first choice. This prestigious university, of course, was his father's alma mater.

Braun was tense and nervous. Over the course of the previous weeks he'd been working on his short distance speed. He and Marquis timed each other. Marquis clocked in at times of 11.41; 11.27; and 11.15 seconds, while he Braun improved from 11.82 seconds the first week of practice, to 11.52. This was an improvement, but still not nearly fast enough to qualify for a spot in the 100-meter event.

As their track coach walked by, clipboard and stopwatch in hand, Braun stopped after reaching the 100-meter finishing point. Braun stared down the track. His muscles twitched and a bead of sweat tricked down the side of his face. The coach gave the signal to set. Marquis glanced over at Braun briefly then stared ahead. Ikara was now jogging in place, continuing to focus. Then the signal was given for the boys to go.

Braun got a good jump out of the starting block and continued to control the race through the first 60 meters. No one was within a yard of him as his long legs pumped like that of a gazelle. Thigh muscles rippled and wavered with each stride. His face evidenced determination and strain. As the other track competitors reached the 75-meter mark, the gap began to close. Now at the 85-meter mark, Marquis was neck and neck with Braun on his right, while another runner had overtaken him.

There were cheers for different runners as they approached the finish line, with Braun finishing behind Marquis—who came in second – with a time of 10.98 seconds, a great qualifying time. As the runners yielded several yards past the finish line, the track coach seemed pleased. He looked down at his stopwatch at the winner's time, 10.12 seconds.

Braun, with hands now on his sides, breathed in and out as he returned back past the coach, who nodded his head in approval of his performance time.

"Great time, Braun. You'll be participating in the 100-meter event Friday," the coach congratulated. Braun was thrilled, though his exhausted expression didn't evidence this as he simply waved a hand in acknowledgement before taking a seat on a bench. He immediately reached for his Gatorade bottle as Marquis joined him. He too reclined with a sigh of fatigue.

"Man! That's it. You in the event, man. Shooo! You made me have to really push it. 10.98? That's determination. I hadn't never clocked in that fast myself," Marquis stated as he stretched his legs out before him. Braun continued to chug down Gatorade. He spotted Ikara as she sped around the track during her 200-meter dash. Her well-toned leg muscles rippled with each stride. She was out in front and as she approached the finish line amidst cheers, there wasn't another girl within a meter of her.

"Yeah, I was real loose. I was breathin' good and I was getting' a good stretch with each stride, ya know," Braun responded, wiping away the sweat that had trickled down his face. His eyes never diverted away from Ikara, who was walking with her head down and hands on her sides. Girls who participated in the running event or were in the process of practicing other events were congratulating her. She raised her head and breathed in and out deeply. Her eyes closed as her chest heaved. She retrieved a jug of Gatorade from a trainer and began to walk around the track towards the boys.

Marquis's eyes diverted to the other participants in the events, mostly the girls. He nodded his head in the direction of the field where a dark-skinned sister with finger-waved short hair was soaring through the air over a cross bar.

"Doretha got some ups, huh? Told her I'm surprised she don't be dunkin' in the basketball games," Marquis stated.

Braun laughed right at the moment several other girls on the field waved in their direction. The two boys acknowledged them as the sound of track cleats approached to their left was heard.

"Let me out. Here comes Ikara, B. Hey Ikara, I saw ya. Tryinna get that scholarship too, so you can follow Braun to A & M?" Marquis teased.

Ikara shook her head as she stifled a laugh and ran her fingers through her hair before sitting down next to Braun. Marquis trotted away.

Braun removed the leg wrapping from his leg and grimaced in pain. His muscles retracted in his hamstring, the result of not stretching enough or perhaps a vitamin deficiency or dehydration. He stretched his right leg out and gripped his hamstring muscle as Ikara stared in concern.

"You're cramping up, you know you should spend more time stretching. And I bet you haven't been drinking water or taking vitamins, either," Ikara chastised as she motioned for him to lay on his back. He laid back on the bench and she stretched his leg so that the muscles extended would stop contracting.

"That feels good," Braun stated. His eyes were closed. Ikara was now massaging his hamstring.

"Mm hm. You were just real tense. I see you qualified. I toldja you could do it." She gave accolades, which brought a smile to his face as he stared up at the sky above.

"I saw you, too. Marion Jones, you might better slow down fo' dey come check you for steroids," Braun laughed. Ikara laughed as she continued to massage his leg.

"Yeah, every time we excel too much we just had to have taken steroids. I think it's sad the way they did her," Ikara responded as she finished massaging his injured hamstring. She once again ran her hand through her hair. Braun sat back upright on the bench and wiped sweat away from his brow with a towel.

"Well, they've done us worse. Ya know, I was just thinkin' bout what Marquis said befo' he left," Braun replied as he watched some of the boys complete their triple jump routines. "Oh, about me coming to Texas A & M behind you?" she inquired.

Braun's eyes darted in their sockets as he reflected on the possibilities of entering Texas A & M and a smile creased his face as he glanced briefly at hers.

"Yeah, well …that too. But basically just the proposal of me goin' to Texas A & M. My dad's old school. I have a chance to finish what he started. Like walkin' in his footsteps which stop at this green door. But I'm goin' through the door," Braun stated. He smiled as he went into a reverie, picturing his father from the pictures he had seen of him. He was honored to be his father's son. He was a revolutionary from the new emergence of social conscientiousness during the mid-80s when such profound groups as 'Public Enemy'; 'Poor Righteous Teacher'; and 'X Clan' opened youth's eyes to their African culture and the repressive state of the current condition of the black people here in America. They informed the masses about the covert operations of the FBI. They recalled to consciousness the reactionary 1960s by dubbing prolific speeches from brother Malcolm X on many of their tracks.

Ikara looked compassionately at Braun, trying to empathize with the emotions he had to be experiencing and wanting to so desperately embody the spirit of the father he had never known. She imagined this man to have had great spiritual strength. And through Braun, she had actually known the man himself.

"Your father had to have been a strong, caring man. And I imagine he was a lot like you are today. But you don't have to follow in his footsteps," she stated as she examined his expression.

He nodded in agreement to her assertion. A smile appeared on his face at knowing her implied statement evidenced her content with his own strength of character. Then, as they heard the sound of the whistle, both turned their attention towards the boys' coach as the hurdlers finished their heaps.

The boy's track coach began clapping his hands and patting the hurdle runners on their backs as they passed. Then, with a wave of his hand in a circular motion, he pointed both arms in the direction of the locker rooms as he once again blew the whistle, signifying that this day's track practice was now officially over. Ikara leaned over to briefly massage Braun's shoulders. She grabbed their towels and Gatorade jugs and the two proceeded to walk across the track alongside other track members.

✷✷✷✷✷✷✷✷

In the wake of an ever-prevalent repression and oppression in the black community and the nationally known fact of Native Americans seeking and being rewarded reparations for their injustices-- namely the malicious slaughtering at the hands of the U. S. Calvary and the stealing of their ancient tribal lands--activists in San Antonio began organizing in the community towards the vitality of reparations.

This call for reparations had been on the black activists' slate for several years. They educated through writing articles, conducting radio and television interviews, and speaking at college campuses. These activists also sponsored community discussions and traveled throughout Texas teaching about reparations, and participated in the Millions for Reparations rally in Washington, D. C. This eventually led to activist brothers Oscar Vicks and Robert Wade forming the San Antonio 'Millions For Reparations Committee'.

Reparations for African descendants was an issue for black activist groups across the nation for many years, motivating these activists to eventually effect a movement designed specifically for the purpose of connecting local reparations movements to the national and international movement. This movement evolved into 40 chapters, nationwide N'Cobra, which stands for the National Coalition of Blacks for Reparations in America. It was established in late 1987, with chapters in Ghana and London as well. San Antonio would form its own chapter of N'Cobra in June of 2005. The chapter headed by Oscar Vicks and Robert Wade would sponsor yearly events that would include community discussions, museum tours, history presentations, fundraisers, and support of black businesses, as well as food drives.

At one of their monthly meetings, Tariq, his wife and other members of the O.B.U., met for a discussion of the reparation subject. Tariq, dressed in a green dashiki and fitted hat, held the floor. His facial expression dead panned as his eyes diverted to make contact with each of the constituents as he spoke.

"The overall wealth or the national budget of this country, was founded to a great degree on the exploited labor of African slaves and their descendants. And this fact is rather ironic, considering that racist imperialists of today contribute to the social degradation, repression, and poverty of our people still," Tari stated. There were nods of agreement from the constituency at the close of his assertion.

Somali's wife, in traditional African dress and braids, spoke out. Her finger was upraised in gesture of her presentation of a valid point as she stared down at her notes.

"I'd like to also point out that civil litigations need to be seriously taken into account on an international scale. Excuse me, to a greater extent in the form of lawsuits, which may be imperative from our perspective here in the United States. Yes, lawsuits against these major corporations who were founded on the exploited labor of our ancestors," Khadija stated. She then retook her seat amidst claps and comments of agreement.

"Sister Khadija is indeed correct. And this has been an open slate for discussion with N'Cobra. We believe it is imperative to bring these corporations before the federal courts, the world courts, if need be. Banks, oil companies, all of whose annual revenues can probably be traced to the labor of our people. Free labor. No overtime, time and a half, just exploitation. Unpaid wages that are generations overdue. And we feel it is time for back payments!" These were the inspiring words of Brother Sundiata as he looked up at the constituency through his bifocals.

"Indeed. Indeed. Thank you, Brother Sundiata. That was interestingly put. We have a task. Make no mistake about it. We have a task on our hands dealing with these imperialists. And obtaining our political agenda, be it through campaigning or through the courts of this nation, will not be easy, especially considering a new phase of political warfare against our people. Of course, I'm speaking of the Bush Administration's antipathy to the welfare programs. Not of course to imply that our people are inclined to take handouts. No, but the fact is there are many underprivileged African-Americans, which is mostly due to economic repression and racism by our government, and they cannot find sufficient occupation and thus are depending on these programs. Now, in relation to reparations, if the government is campaigning against welfare, how much more will they campaign against demands for millions of dollars in reparation?" stated Brother Yoruba. To this very logical revelation there were nods and expressions of serious contemplation.

"Of course they'll lobby against it. They wouldn't be the imperialists they are if they didn't. But it is up to us as a people, to fight now for this right, as our Native American brethren fight for theirs," stated a light-skinned sister with dreadlocks. Her words were impassioned as she slapped the back of one hand into the palm of the other. Her eyes were afire as she stared around the room. Tariq shifted in his chair as he examined her. His fist rested under his chin. "…we as African-Americans are the only people not to be compensated for our generations of labor, abuse, and genocide. Yet, we, as a working force, help through our tax dollars to finance reparations for other people--in many cases, in foreign countries! It's a slap in the face. We are discriminated against on many scales of corporate America, but our meager wages are garnished by taxes expended to help finance the very same companies who, in the past, used racism as a pretense to exclude us from the workforce, and built up the very same police force which have oppressed and brutalized us! Murdered even! So yes, I'm totally in agreement with Sister Khadija and Brother Sundiata. Civil suits…boycotts…international assistance. Whatever it takes to be compensated for the exploited labor of our people so that we, as a generation of people today, can finally make vast strides in an equitable sense," she finished. Everyone was moved by her speech.

Tariq took a sip of his beverage and glanced down at his watch.

"Thank you, sister. Sister Nzinga from the Houston chapter of the National Black United Front, which as you all know, will be on our agenda as we journey to Houston for our annual excursion during the Pan-African Cultural Festival later this month. In bringing this meeting to a close, I'd like to add…"

✴✴✴✴✴✴✴✴

Braun and his friends Piye and Devonte, walked side-by-side down the hallway. It was their final period that day. Braun stopped to place books in his locker as he spoke on what was, perhaps, the hottest topic of the day: the San Antonio Spurs and their prospects of winning a third championship in five years.

"I been tellin' ya'll that. Detroit got too much defense and clutch shooters. They have been in the big games. E'ry time it look like they finished, they sprang up. But the road stops here. Too much Ginobli and Big Timmey," Braun stated. Devonte nodded to his assertion. Then, his attention was diverted as two African-American girls passed by, who were dressed conservatively, yet appeared respectable. Their youthful beauty was enchanting as both smiled in the boy's direction.

"Hey, Braun. Hi Piye," the girls greeted, both intentionally playing off Devonte as he appraised them devilishly.

"Oh, it's like dat? Ya'll know ya'll frontin'. I know I'm all up in there.

Come here, Tonya," Devonte said. The girls laughed as they exchanged meaningful glances. Then, as he approached, one of them held up a cautioning hand as she turned her head and pretended to ignore him, causing him to laugh. He playfully placed his arms around her.

"Move, Devonte! Stop, boy!" she giggled.

"Catch ya later, D," Braun stated as Piye made a signaling-off salute.

"Hold up, ya'll. Stop trippin'. Why you 'on't be returnin' my calls? Look, check dis out…" Devonte began whispering in her ear, causing her to blush as she rolled her eyes, looking up at the ceiling.

"I'm gone, girl," her friend stated as she strutted off and waved her hand in the air as if disappointed that her friend had given him any time.

"Love you too, Chandrika," he shouted back at her sarcastically. "I'm serious. You know that, Tonya. I'mma call you, aiight? I gotta run. Hey, ya'll hold up!" he shouted as Braun and Piye laughed.

"You play too many games, Devonte," Tonya stated. A wide smile was etched across her face. Despite shaking her head, her expression and posture evidenced her intrigue. Devonte then winked at her, as he turned to run down the hallway after his two friends. "Know ya'll ain't leavin' without ya boy. Say, I needja to run me by Chameeka's house right quick," he stated as he placed an arm around Braun. Braun sighed sarcastically as he brushed his arm away. Then the three boys disappeared down the hallway as Devonte resumed the conversation over the Spurs. Their comments echoed behind them through the hall.

Braun's car squeaked to a halt in front of his grandmother's house. The squeaking caused slight concern as he got out of the car. He looked down at his tires as if he was able to actually see the cause of the noise. He closed the door behind him, then proceeded to open the gate, while rapping some lyrics as if rehearsing for some competition.

His grandmother, who was in the kitchen cooking, turned her head at the sound of his footsteps jogging up to the door. A smile creased her face and her eyes evidenced the love she felt for the grandson. Then as the door opened, she removed her cooking mittens and walked to greet him.

"Hey, Ma mah," he greeted as he closed the door behind him. He walked over to hug his grandmother.

"I wasn't expectin' you home dis early. I just started cookin'," she stated as the two disengaged from their embrace.

"I've finished most of my classes. And ain't got no more track meets, so… the red beans smell good," Braun stated as he looked down at the envelopes on the dining room table. His expression changed to one of serious curiosity as he spotted an envelope addressed to him. The letter was partially hidden under other mail so that only his address wasn't obscured. His grandmother was already aware of who had sent the letter and smiled proudly as he fumbled through the other letters to retrieve it. She then replaced her cooking mittens and began stirring the pot of red beans and ground meat, which she spiced with her special blend.

Braun raised the letter before his face. He carefully read the address of the sender. His eyes darted as he read each word and his expression changed to one of disbelief. A smile crossed his face briefly, then vanished as his eyes continued to dart back and forth, while he opened the letter in haste. At the sound of his tearing open the letter, his grandmother turned her head slightly to watch him. She had a smile of pride on her brown face. The letter which he so diligently tore open was from College Station, Texas, the location of Texas A & M University. And after reading the brief letter of acceptance inside, his smile widened. Shaking his head, his eyes wide and his expression indicative of great exhilaration, he held the letter up and turned to his grandmother.

"Ma mah! This is it! What I been waitin' for! Texas A & M just accepted me. Ma mah! I got a full scholarship!" he shouted emphatically. His grandmother removed her mittens and walked over towards him as he continued to read the letter. He shook his head, as if in utter disbelief that his lifelong dream had finally come true. And after his grandmother examined the enclosed letter of acceptance, she too lit up with cheer.

"That's great, baby. Oh… Braun, baby. Ma mah is so proud of you!" she stated as she hugged him tightly. After releasing him, she kissed him on the side of the cheek. Then the two continued to stare in complete exuberance at the letter, which represented the doorway to his prospective future.

Chapter 26

The audience, which consisted of concerned parents, siblings, relatives and friends, clapped as a student draped in cap and gown proudly received his diploma. This piece of paper signified twelve years of achievement and diligent work in academics. The student—a Hispanic boy—accepted the diploma and smiled widely as he shook the principal's hand. It was Braun's co-worker, Eric, whose mother, father, and siblings each bore expressions of sincere pride.

The principal walked away from the podium as the recipient stood behind it. His expression was ecstatic as he briefly glanced back at his graduating class. As the applause from the audience died down, he looked up into the faces of the crowd who were waiting in anticipation of his speech. He graduated at the top of his class. His gold sash represented his accomplishment.

"I guess all I can say is that I had a lot of encouragement from my parents. And they ingrained in me the ambition to be successful and to accomplish my goals, including academically as well as in my future endeavors. That's basically it. Class of 2005, yeah!" He ended his brief speech with a shout-out to his fellow graduates as he raised up his diploma. Amidst cheers and applause, Braun strolled towards the podium and hugged his classmate. He then approached the principal, who extended him his diploma while whispering personal accolades about his exceptional academic achievements. Braun finished second in his class. He was an honor student and graduated with a 3.8 GPA. His grandmother, from her vantage point in the audience, smiled proudly as her grandson took his place behind the podium.

Braun placed his prepared notes down upon the top of the podium. He stared down at the paper as the audience continued to clap. He studied his speech half of the night and was well-prepared. But he decided it was in his best interest to bring the speech to the podium for insurance against temporary amnesia when it came time to actually recite it. He was certain that he would forget his speech once he glanced out over the expressions of the audience. And at the moment, as the applause tapered off, he sensed the very stage fright which he anticipated.

Braun cleared his throat and briefly stared out across the audience until he connected with his grandmother's smiling eyes, which were wet with tears of joy and pride. Then he looked back down at his prepared notes, shifting behind the podium as he began to speak.

"Good evening everyone. As you can see, I have prepared a speech. I'll be brief, though. Don't wanna lull anybody to sleep. First I'd like to give thanks to God, the Creator who enabled me to have the strength and will to achieve this academic success. And to my loving grandmother, whose strength and encouragement motivated me to utilize this gift from God," Braun spoke as the audience listened attentively. Their expressions were sincere. He paused to clear his throat before continuing on now with his prepared speech. He glanced up briefly into Ikara's beautiful face, who, along with her parents and brother Caleb, made the trip to Roosevelt High School to see the graduation ceremony of the class of 2005. "Chmm! I'll continue on now with what I've prepared. Opportunity should be seized when presented, especially in terms of utilizing the educational foundation afforded us in school. I say foundation because that's what education is. Without it, it is like erecting a skyscraper on marshland and expecting it to be stable. You need a foundation. And I intend to utilize this foundation to build the structure of my life. To build a legitimate career so that my children can reap the benefits and be able to understand the purpose of having a good foundation. The foundation of education and the activism of African-Americans who fought diligently against school segregation until their hard work, resulted in the May 17th 1954 Supreme Court ruling against racial segregation. Brown vs. the Board of Education gave us African-Americans that opportunity. And not to utilize it would be, in a sense, disrespecting those who fought and died for us to receive this right. I intend to utilize this right. I hope my fellow graduates also utilize it and succeed in their future endeavors. Thank you."

Braun's serious and enlightening graduation speech was greeted with applause and reverberating responses as most of the audience arose to their feet. Then raising his diploma in triumph, he kissed it and proceeded to hug the next graduate that passed by.

★★★★★★★★

Pedestrians walked along the downtown streets as automobiles passed by the municipal courthouse, which today was abuzz with activity. Citizens interested in criminal justice had gathered to hear the outcome of the high-profile case of Juan Martinez and Larry Kupchek, the two police officers indicted by a grand jury for the fatal shooting of black standout basketball star James "Jamie" Smith.

It had been a week of courtroom theatrics and high-profile cases brought before the grand jury. A middle-aged Caucasian man in a business suit paused in front of the courthouse as he read the newspaper article on these events, sipping his coffee as he read the headline, 'Traffickers tried in RICO act violations.' The small print columns that informed of the outcome seemed to unsettle him, for within these columns was a photo of a smug Jewish lawyer and his client Carlos Vasquez. He'd been acquitted. However, next to his photo was one of three black males in orange jumpsuits and steel shackles being led out of the courtroom by the sheriff's deputies. The young men's faces revealed disconcertment and anguish. One attempted to shield his identity by holding up his cuffed hands before his face. His head was ducked, his facial hair stubbly, and his hair unkempt, but his identity was still clear. It was Philip Johnson. After hours of the district attorney's legal rhetoric, video imagery of Phil and his affiliates dealing in drug-free zones, and the defense attorney's rebuttals, the seven day federal drug trafficking trial ended in guilty verdict on all accounts. The businessman shook his head as he rattled the page. Then, sipping his coffee, he continued on to his grey 2005 Lexus as a brown-complexioned sister of middle age proceeded up the courthouse steps. Her sullen face spoke of untold repression and anxiety. Her name was Cynthia Smith. She was the mother of the young man, whose murder these officers of the law had been indicted for. She was determined to see that justice was served in the case of her son.

But justice in this high-profile and racially tense case seemed to be remiss. It was overshadowed by propaganda and overzealous activists who descended on the courthouse after being interviewed by various news stations and were now seated throughout the municipal court. Some were clad in business suits and bowties, these were members of the Nation of Islam. Others wore African garb with their dreadlocks and braids flowing from underneath African fitted hats, these were affiliates of the Organization for Black Unity and the National Black United Front. There were others who had the appearances of black bureaucrats, continuously jotting down notes. *The NAACP perhaps? Journalists?* Whatever the case, these black men and women were exercising activism in a joint interest. Their faces were serious with contemplation. Their eyes scrutinized the judge and were cynical of the powers that be. The instruments of oppression represented the counter to the black activist's punches, including the judge, the defense lawyers for the prosecuted officers, racially-biased jurors, and the bailiffs. They were bulky, armed, apprehensive, and tense about the possible display of militancy by the black radicals present. Security had been beefed.

It was a fiasco. After hours of testimonies, outbursts, numerous sustained and overruled motions, and blatant racial favoritism by the judge who seemed to be overly sympathetic to the officer's rendition of the incident. Kupchek cited tension in a gang-ridden environment, calling for extra precautions, and stressing his vulnerability in pursuit of potentially armed fleeing suspect into an alley. His partner corroborated his story as the activists listened intently. The district attorney's presentation was listless at best, and towards the end of the trial the outcome--despite Cynthia Smith's heartfelt testimony and picture presentation of her son--was predetermined. The powers that be controlled the gambit. And Tariq, who was joined by his fellow O.B.U. Brother, Somali, had lost the chess opening. The artifice was Juan Martinez' conscious had failed. He testified without blinking to his partner's account of the shooting. And after the Court Clerk read the return verdict; the defense team erupted in cheer, the black activists voiced their adverse opinions and utilized their freedom of speech to express their lack of faith in the American justice system. Tariq turned to view Mrs. Cynthia Smith's reaction to this blatant misuse of justice and saw that she wept silently. She had lost her son. She had lost her husband. And now, she had lost her belief that racial profiling, exploitation, and systemic lynching of blacks had ended with the 1960s.

The outcome of the officer's trial caused public outcries in the black community. Immediately after, the lawyers of the two officers were interviewed and the news reporters seized the opportunity to allow the black activists in attendance to voice their dissatisfaction. And now, a day later, many of these same activists congregated together at the Garvey House to discuss what feasible measures to take in order to bring forth other actions against the officers. Though an acquittal had been granted in the officer's favor, these activists sought civil actions against them in a possible wrongful death claim.

The atmosphere inside of the meeting hall was tense. NOI; NBUF; N'COBRA; O.B.U. and other concerned citizens were in the audience. They voiced their personal dissatisfaction with the trial's outcome, as well as offering up legal reprisals. Tariq and Somali were in the midst of this heated meeting. And Tariq, who was in traditional garb, made inventory of the congregation as he sipped a cup of coffee. Tariq's gaze around the room as Brother Khalid spoke. There were various expressions and postures exhibited, from enthusiasm bordering on fanaticism. Their body language and furrowed brows were indicative that a boiling point had been reached.

Some bore expressions that were deadpanned and unblinking as they listened intently to Brother Khalid's speech. There were some people there that caused Tariq to feel uneasy. He had never seen some of these people before at any of the community meetings and they were not affiliates of the organizations present. Tariq believed that they might be infiltrators and he felt compelled to signal Brother Khalid for fear that, eventually, the militant-minded young brother might make an incriminating statement.

"…It's an abuse of justice. Point blank. Justified because the young brother took flight and there was a gun found inside of the vehicle. He obviously was in fear of his life. And rightfully so, and this is a democracy? Yeah. Disorganized democracy! The police departments are equipped with stun guns. This is a sufficient means to stop a fleeing person from up to twenty feet, which was approximately the distance this young brother was from the police at the time the pig opened fire!" Brother Somali pointed a finger as he spoke with anger. The constituency nodded and shifted in their seats. Some pointed and gestured in agreement at certain points in speech.

"Exactly. And I believe that, for grounds of civil reprisals, which certainly Mrs. Smith, I feel, is entitled to, this could be sufficient evidence. It wasn't a situation where the officer was surprised. Reflexes were not an issue," Tariq chimed in with conviction as he looked around the room. Then the sister sitting next to him, her flowing dreadlocks shaking as she searched the room, spoke out.

"Right. Reflexes were not the issue. The cop wasn't surprised in an ambush. He chased a fleeing black boy and shot him in the back at close range! And I feel that we should do whatever is necessary to assure that Mrs. Smith at least gets monetary compensation for the murder of her son at the hands of this racist cop!" Sister Khadija, who lost a brother at the hands of the police, spoke passionately, receiving remarks of agreement from the congregation of activists.

"…What we have here is the system's way of legal lynching. In the 40s and 50s lynch mobs could come into our communities throughout the south and enact vengeance upon black men with no legal repercussions! And that's what we're seeing here today. The police beat, cripple, maim, and kill without any legal repercussions!" ranted Sadiq. His index finger was extended as his eyes focused around the room. Agreements were shouted, and the sound reverberated around the room. Most of the members wore expressions of disdain. Tariq was mentally exhausted and thoroughly dejected by the outcome of the police trial, but attempted to comment. But the disgruntled responses and shifting in the chairs by members drowned out his attempts and prompted Brother Yoruba to use his microphone in order to bring some semblance of order back to the meeting.

"Okay, okay. Let's try to keep focus and be level-headed in this. We're beginning to maybe become riled up in here like one of those lynch mobs," Brother Yoruba stated. He made a stab at humor as he rolled his hands around one another, staring through the bi-focals upon the bridge of his nose as his head scanned the audience. Then as the noise level began to decrease, Tariq started out, impassioned. His eyebrows were furrowed. His eyes were sad. After pausing for effect and glancing down at his notes briefly as the group levels its focus on him, he continued his speech. "…The line has been drawn. But we have to go into this battle with a solid strategy. We have to be unyielding in our fight for our rights. We will petition the courts. And we will bring our artillery to their doorsteps. Meaning, we're going to get mass media attention. Get the whole world in on what's happening. And maybe finally garner the international support and federal intervention we need to put an end to this racial profiling. Now, at this time, if there aren't any resolves, we'd like to bring this meeting to a close."

✶✶✶✶✶✶✶✶

Swathi wore shorts which exposed her well-toned legs and sat Indian-style on her mother's sofa as she talked on the phone. Her long hair flowed onto her face and she had to every so often push the strands away from her face as she leaned forward. Laughing giddily as she spoke, her eyes revealed a certain dispiritedness. A dispiritedness that her friend Ikara—who was on the line along with Sharon—perceived and made her best attempt to lighten.

"Yeah, that was funny. I couldn't believe she wore that. But…at least she did have someone who was interested enough to bring her to the prom, unlike me," Swathi said. On the other end of the line, Ikara, who was, at the moment, flicking through channels with the remote, looked sympathetic as she tilted her head. A smile creased her lips as she began to explain Piye's reason for not taking her to the prom.

"Come on, Swathi. Don't do this to yourself. You know if Piye could have taken you he would. He promised her long before you two became close. You want him to go back on his word to her?" Ikara stated. Swathi remained silent for a moment. "Yeah," she responded, though not serious.

Sharon and Ikara both laughed.

"Listen to you," responded Ikara.

"No, I'm just kidding," Swathi rectified.

"And Piye told you it was okay with him if you went with someone else,"

Ikara stated.

"I know. But I didn't want to. I wanted to go with him. And…I don't know. I don't even know how he feels about me. He's so…I don't know… an introvert. I mean, this is my birthday and he hasn't even called me," Swathi stated.

Sharon laughed, "Swathi. It is only eleven o' clock. You know how boys are on weekends. He's probably still in bed."

Swathi's eyes darted as she listened to this reasoning. Her eyes momentarily looked at the elaborate clock on their living room wall. She then smiled and sighed, "You're right. I'm just anxious to see him. Today, I mean." Now lying flat on her stomach, she looked out of her window as if she expected Piye to appear at any moment.

There was a brief silence, and then Sharon informed her two friends of her departure after getting a call from Devonte. Both hint jokingly towards her early morning rendezvous with him.

"Didn't your mom just leave for work?"

"Mm hm." Ikara said.

"You two were just together last night," Swathi added. On the other end of the phone, Sharon squirted on perfume and gave herself the once-over in the mirror.

"Well, I got it like that. Soo…I'll get back wit ya'll, um…much later," Sharon responded.

Swathi placed a hand over her face and laughed as she shook her head. After Sharon hung up, Ikara commented on her friend's sexual activities, there was another pause of silence from Swathi, who was once again looking out of the window with her eyes glazed over as if in deep contemplation, which prompted Ikara to inquire about her silence.

"Swathi. Why you so quiet? I know you're not still frettin' over Piye not callin'?" Ikara inquired.

Swathi paused and then responded, "Ikara," she called out, now resting on her side.

"Swathi, I think Piye really likes you. But I also think that it goes past a friendship. But maybe he's just…I don't know. Why don't you just ask him?" Ikara suggested.

Swathi laughed and as she laughed, the sound of an automobile engine could be heard outside of her house, causing her to sit up and attempt to peer out of the window as her father—who was, at the moment, dressed for a day at the office—walked through the kitchen. He straightened his tie, then peered out of the window, too. Then as the driver of the vehicle got out,

Swathi's expression ignited in elation.

"Oh my God…oh…my…Ikara, you won't believe who just drove up, it's him… I'll, I'll call you back," she stated excitedly, eager to go to the door. But she realized that—in her own mind—she was not adequately beautified enough at this early hour to receive him. She ran a hand through her hair and then looked down at her bare feet. As Swathi went through the anxiety surrounding of Piye's unanticipated visit, Ikara smiled to herself in her home, glad that now maybe her friend could get some confirmation to the question in which she just presented.

"Uh, no. I mean…yes. Could you get that, dad? I have to go…" Her words were met with Nawas's nodding and gesturing for her to go liven up, which she hurriedly did. Nawaz shook his head and smiled as he sipped his orange juice. The doorbell rang and he proceeded to answer. He, too, was anxious to meet the young man.

Piye stood outside, looking nervously around the vicinity. Behind his back he held gifts, a pink teddy bear and chocolates for Swathi's birthday. As the door opened, he was caught off-guard at seeing Mr. Jinnah's face instead of Swathi's. He became more nervous until the friendly, sincere smile of Mr. Jinnah put him at ease. Piye found the words to finally formally introduce himself.

"Ah, Mr. Jinnah" he greeted, then unconsciously extended the hand which held the bear. Laughing, he withdrew it and placed it underneath his arm before extending his hand again. Jokingly, Mr. Jinnah pointed at the bear.

"I thought this was for me, no? How are you doing, young man? I presume you are here to see my daughter, correct?" Mr. Jinnah inquired as he shook his hand firmly. Mr. Jinnah then patted him on the shoulder as he invited him in, where he was met with another surprise. Coming down the hallway was her mother, who was followed closely by Swathi, who excitedly peeked over her mother's shoulder. All four stood before each other, the mood was euphoric. Then, Swathi, after examining her parent's receptiveness to Piye, formally introduced him.

"Mom, Dad, this is Piye. He's the one I've been telling you about," she informed them excitedly. Mr. Jinnah smiled. His eyes were bright as he once again patted Piye on the shoulder as Mrs. Jinnah extended her dainty hand, after which the two parents dispersed. However, as Piye presented birthday wishes and the gifts to a now thoroughly happy Swathi, her parents watched them exchange meaningful glances. Their expressions were exuberant at their daughter's glow.

✶✶✶✶✶✶✶✶

For twenty-four years the Organization for Black Unity has sponsored an educational excursion from San Antonio to Houston. This excursion, which is called 'Ujmaa' (cooperative economics) is meant to reinforce one of the organization's seven principles. On this particular day in late May, with the weather conditions less than picturesque due to scattered showers, the followers of the O.B.U. were nevertheless enthused about making the 200-mile trek.

Adorned in a variety of attire, from T-shirts with O.B.U. insignias to dashikis, the constituents of the organization—including children—were preparing to board the charter bus to Houston. Among these constituents were Tariq and his family, accompanied by Braun, Marquis and the Qusta family. All were enthusiastically speaking about the predetermined stops during the excursion as they boarded the bus.

Riding the long stretch of highway to Houston, Braun and Ikara sat together and pointed every so often out of the window at points of interest, or commented on sights in the distance which were commonplace in the plains region of Texas. Through cow towns, pastures, rolling plains and ranges, the constituency laughed or held discussions centered around the excursion. They were anxiously anticipating the reception of the fellow brethren who awaited them in Houston.

There were warm receptions upon their stop at the Shrine of the Black Madonna Pan-African Orthodox Church. Most of the elders of the organization, such as brothers Yoruba, Somali, Sundiata, and Tariq, exchanged ceremonial hugs and handshakes and discussed the general purpose of the day's agenda. They were pleased at seeing so many of the young members, which was imperative if substance from the Nguzo Saba was to be made self-evident.

The Nguzo Saba, or Seven Principles, of the organization's creed consisted of, first, a want to see the division of black people come to an end; second, a want to see the black community move collectively to develop black-owned and operated businesses; third, a need to develop a sense of black culture; fourth, a need to control the education of black children through the creation of African-centered institutions; fifth, a need for institutions to be built for the constructive educational and cultural development of the community; sixth, a want to see a cadre of young men emerge with the purpose of protecting the legal and moral character of the community; and seventh, a want to see an African based value system come about that will prepare them for a more collective and productive way of life.

After their reception, the travelers were led by the Bishop of the Orthodox Church to the sanctuary, where he gave a brief overview of the Shrine Church and the meanings of the symbolism used in the paintings on the wall. The travelers, were enthralled at this enlightening tour. They commented and pointed at the elaborate, cryptic paintings and symbols.

From there the O.B.U. excursionists were exposed to the Shrine's bookstore. They shopped and browsed the culturally educational facility before touring the black Holocaust and black scientist/inventors exhibits. The travelers were inundated with actual accounts of the many atrocities the African-American population has had to withstand in nearly 400 years in a socially-repressive land, thousands of miles away from the motherland. They also learned how they overcame systemic flaws to becoming prominent inventors. Blueprints of the common inventions of the day in which were not credited to these African American inventors in the American school systems' text books.

Each of the youth, while touring the Black Holocaust, Black scientists and inventors exhibits, bore expressions of enthusiasm, including Braun and his entourage. They commented on various facts and shook their heads in some instances when horrific facts pertaining to black suffrage were presented. But they also bore expressions of great pride when facts about inventors or revolutionary fighters in the struggle were highlighted.

From there, it was on to the Houston headquarters of the National Black United Front, where they were welcomed by its national secretary and lunch was served by the O.B.U. members. The travelers and members of the NBUF dined on Afro-centric dishes of well-cooked okra, chicken, and fruit before the tour of the Buffalo Soldiers Museum, where the youth and adults alike were educated about the valiant black fighting soldiers of the old frontier. They were soldiers who risked their lives fighting in the wars of the United States. The 38th, 39th, 40th, and 41st regiments were included, along with the 9th and 10th Cavalry. The enthused group watched a video documentary after viewing authentic articles and memorabilia of these honored black soldiers.

After building with other black activists and youths, Tariq, acting as spokesman for the O.B.U., gave a signing-off speech before the group prepared to board the charter bus back to San Antonio. The members of NBUF proudly listened to their fellow brother and nodded at his assertions. They were primarily centered around the advancement of the people through the growing organizations which were paving the way for the youth.

"Brothers and sisters. On the behalf of the O.B.U., we would like to extend thanks to you. I hope that, for some of our new excursionists, those who made the trip for the first time, it was a very enlightening experience. I myself enjoyed it, as I'm sure did everyone. And we're hoping to do this again for a twenty-fifth consecutive year. Peace, brothers and sisters. Looking forward to seeing you at the festival in the upcoming months," Tariq signed off with the wave of an upheld fist.

The travelers began boarding the charter bus and waved back at the members of NBUF. Most were talking about the enlightenment of the day's events, while some bore expressions of fatigue, They were obviously anxious to get back to their respective homes in San Antonio. As the bus lurched forward, he took his seat next to Ikara and held up a fist in salute to two brothers and a sister that stood outside of the building, adorned in all black; the three NBUF members returned the salute.

Chapter 27

It was time to celebrate. The celebration, however, came in the wake of hostile tensions between the police department and the urban black community. The Spurs had won the NBA championship and the parades were in full bloom, followed by trophy presentations and autograph signings at the Alamo Dome. Both events were witnessed firsthand by Braun, Ikara, and their friends. They thoroughly enjoyed themselves. Braun was proudly displaying his autographed shirt from Tim Duncan as Devonte' shook hands with other members of the basketball team. It was an exhilarating feeling and Braun was all smiles as he hugged Ikara.

This had been the scene several nights prior, and the excitement was still hovering in the air. The thrill of the moment was still evident on Braun's face as he walked hand-in-hand with Ikara along the River Walk, downtown. Of course he was sporting a Spurs black jersey with Tim Duncan's number.

There were many tourists here on the River Walk this beautiful June day. They were snapping pictures and conversing over some dish they'd eaten at one of the outdoor restaurants along the River Walk, or the other sights of interest such as the Alamo.

Braun and Ikara both observed the tourists as they boarded a river touring boat. They would often indulge in the quaint resort of the city while enjoying each other's company, the food of the outside restaurants, and the boat ride. It was Ikara's favorite activity. And it was evident on her face, though her eyes were concealed behind her brown-tinted sun shades as she pointed towards points of interest, causing Braun to crane his neck along with the other boat riders.

The ride churned through the winding river around the downtown area. The tourists were enthralled with the beautiful scenery and historical sites that were the essence of San Antonio, this old west town with strong Hispanic-influenced cultures and architecture. Then the boat riders got off the boat, each off to another predetermined adventure on their tourist agendas. Braun and Ikara went to their favorite Mexican eatery along the River Walk.

Ikara wiped sauce away from her mouth, along with the remnants of the egg, cheese, and beef burrito which she'd just eaten. Braun sipped his beverage as he looked around the vicinity at the patrons, then, setting his glass down, he smiled.

"I's just thankin' bout somethin'. Somethin' Phil said one day. He'd talkin' 'bout for the right price he'd ride bulls in the rodeo," Braun laughed as he cut a glance in the direction of a Caucasian man in a ten gallon hat. His entire persona was urban cowboy. "…I just thought about that because of…" He nodded his head in the direction of the man, causing Ikara to glance over her shoulder. Instantly she had to contain her laughter.

"Yeah, I can see him in his hat and spurs," she replied. Braun laughed and shook his head before biting into another piece of fajita. Ikara finished her burrito, then looked over at him meaningfully. Her eyes were aglow and a smile remained on her face as she chewed. Braun sensed the lingering stare and looked up at her as she chewed rapidly.

She laughed while ducking her head. Her eyes averted momentarily as her initial response was almost inadvertently blurted out. But then she tactfully switched directions.

"Swathi's birthday was the other day. And she was really down at first because she hadn't gotten a phone call from Piye. But it was only 12 o' clock. And I was like, Swathi, he's still in bed," Braun smiled. Nevertheless, he somehow sensed that this was not what she'd been thinking about at the moment he'd caught her observing him in adoration.

"Yeah, he told me he got her somethin' nice. My boy, Piye. Never thought one day…ya know…Swathi is Pakistani and…you know how he is…was," Braun stated as he wiped remnants of sauce from his mouth.

"But it's good though. He's changed. Swathi's so in love with him," she smiled. After a brief pause, she once again switched gear. "You know…I've been thinking a lot lately about this separation. You know, you going off to college and everything. And I'm… just…"

Her rambling was interrupted by Braun. "I'm gonna miss you too. And believe me, it's hard. Wish you were goin' wit' me," he replied.

Ikara smiled at his uncanny way of anticipating her thoughts.

"And you know I wish I was there on campus with you. All those sorority women. I'm warning you, Braun Erickson," she smiled.

Braun laughed as he took a final bite of the fajita. He assured her that she was fretting over nothing. Then there was a brief pause. Ikara once again stared at him. But her gaze was troubled. And once again he caught her stare and studied her quizzically. Staring down at her plate, she began to speak. "I really enjoy being with you. Doesn't matter the place or time," she stated.

"I enjoy every moment we're together too," he responded as he examined her. There was something in her voice and eyes that kept telling him she wanted to say more.

"Braun, where do you see us being...I mean...after you go off to college? Because, I know sometimes people go in different directions. And I was just wondering how..."

Braun interjected, "Where do I see us being? Different directions? Ikara, where is all this comin' from? I mean, all I can think about is you. College ain't gon' change that. Sorority girls or nobody else gon' change that. I mean..."

"I missed my period," she stated as she looked down at her plate.

Braun was stunned.

"Excuse me?" he implored. His heart raced as visions of he and Ikara bringing forth another life into this world flashed across the screen of his mind. And in that instance he envisioned a daughter, a little African princess who would be a reflection of him and Ikara. But this vision was darkened by practical questions, such as how could they, at such young ages with their prospective education and careers not even having been situated, take on the responsibility. They had no financial stability or experience with raising a child.

Ikara continued, "I took the home pregnancy test the other day, Braun, and I'm pregnant," she confirmed. Her doe-like eyes searched his soul. Braun averted eye contact as his mind tried to grasp the reality of what she had just told him. Then a smile, which belied the astonished look in his eyes, slowly etched itself across his face. He was at a loss for words.

"And I'm scared, Braun. What will my parents think? How are we gonna tell them?" she asked. Braun's expression was empathetic. Leaning forward initially, he then maneuvered around to the other side of the table with his chair, sat next to her, and cradled her in his arms. He whispered in her ear and then placed her head to his chest as he stared off blankly.

✶✶✶✶✶✶✶✶

Tariq's Lincoln coasted to a stop on the corner of a busy avenue in the heart of the eastside, where small businesses, liquor stores, and service stations outnumbered residential housing. He was accompanied by two of his O.B.U. brothers, Somali and Sundiata. As the three got out of Tariq's vehicle, they looked around the vicinity and noticed a few pedestrians walking down the busy avenue, giving them quizzical looks. *Perhaps it was their Africanized garb?* Certainly not. In fact, the pedestrians probably did not notice the three O.B.U. men, but were instead looking at the smoldering, burned down building that the car pulled up in front of. Tariq closed the car door behind him, and walked cautiously around the front of the vehicle. He carefully examined the charred remains of what had been Sadiq's Caribbean restaurant. It had been cordoned off with yellow tape. According to the whispers amongst the fireman on the scene, arson was suspected. Sadiq the owner stood in front of the store with his hands on his hips as he shook his head in disgust. Tariq, Somali, and Sundiata approached Sadiq, whose face was dark and rigid with anger. He spoke aloud, "I spent many years working as a fry cook in many different restaurants after finishing college so that I could become an entrepreneur. I spent all of my savings to open up an Afro-centric restaurant, and now it is all gone.

Tariq extended his hand to Sadiq and said, "Brother Sadiq, what's the verdict on this?" Tariq punctuated the question with a wave of the hand at the charred building.

"The verdict? Everything's gone. Everything I worked hard for. Saved for. Gone. Investigators come over and ask all these cynical questions as if to imply I burned down my place for insurance," he stated in disgust. A grimace appeared on his face.

Somali and Sundiata shook their heads in unison.

"Figures. We're always a suspect even when we're actually the victims. Any clues? I mean, who could have done this?" Somali inquired.

"No chance of faulty wiring?" Sundiata added. Sadiq ran his hand across his head as his eyes turned almost snake-like, staring across the street at Hamburani's, the Pakistani establishment.

"No chance, no chance at faulty wiring. No, this is arson and I can't prove it right now, but I'm almost certain this sucka Hamburani had somethin' to do with this," Sadiq stated with conviction.

Tariq looked over in the direction of Hamburani's small restaurant, which served up Mexican dishes as well as hamburgers, fries, and even his own special Pakistani cuisines. He had a difficult time rationalizing Hamburani's motive for possibly wanting to eliminate Sadqi, whose Caribbean restaurant certainly wasn't making nearly the revenue of Hamburani.

"I don't understand. What are you basing your suspicions on?" Tariq inquired.

Sadiq looked cynically over at him, then at Sundiata and Somali.

"Brother Tariq, I know it's been a considerable time since you lived in this neighborhood. And I don't know whether you've been keeping abreast of the situation. But there's a power struggle going on my brother," Sadiq stated.

Tariq was well aware of the situation on the eastside with foreign enterprises. But he was in disbelief of any actual power struggle. Most often these foreign entrepreneurs, as in many cities in the U.S., simply buy out black business owners.

"A power struggle?" Tariq inquired.

"So you're saying the motive was to eliminate the competition?" Sundiata asked.

"All fingers point at this sucka. That's why it is imperative to take back our communities. Drive them out! Sucka can't even look me in the eye. I sense it. Been thinkin' 'bout confrontin' him. I've just been restraining myself, damn! Lost everything. Every damn thing!" Sadiq yelled.

"We must weigh the situation from all angles. We don't want to be hasty, brother," Somali stated.

"Your insurance should cover it, so let's trust the investigative work of the authorities," Tariq added.

Sadiq's expression turned blank. Shaking his head once more, he once again glanced over at Mr. Hamburani.

"Hmm. Entrust it to the authorities? The same authorities that we plan to demonstrate against I suppose?" Sadiq responded.

Cars rolled by temporarily blocking the view of the Pakistani's store. Then, Hamburani, who'd been outside moments earlier, disappeared, through the restaurant's door.

Sadiq's statement registered with Tariq and as he briefly glanced into the similar expressions of his comrades, his eyes told of the lack of faith in the police investigation himself.

✶✶✶✶✶✶✶✶

The house was relatively quiet, save for the humming sound of a window fan. Braun relaxed back on his grandmother's sofa. His eyes stared blankly in a state of deep meditation. Perhaps he thought about his prospective future in college, which would be effectuated in a few months. *Or maybe his thoughts were centered on this revelation which he'd received earlier from Ikara?*

Over the past several days he had been in deep contemplation over the prospects of having a child. *Was he ready? Could he handle the responsibility of being a father at the young age of eighteen? And,what about Ikara? Her future? Would she be able to finish her senior year in high school now? And how would her parents receive the news?* Though he really loved Ikara, and the promise of a child being brought forth into this world with her was blissful in its spirituality, he was nevertheless insecure.

Braun removed his hands from behind his head and leaned forward. A smile covered his face that belied his eyes, which revealed concern. Then these eyes' peripheral vision caught sight of his grandmother's car coasting to a stop in front of the house. He had not yet revealed Ikara's pregnancy to her. The woman who had raised him as her own. The only mother he'd ever known. And who he'd affectionately referred to as ma mah.

His grandmother's voice was heard as she spoke to elderly neighbors across the street. Her voice was rather youthful in its pitch, as was her gait. In her mid-fifties now, Agnes's appearance belied her age. Only her mannerism and deep-set eyes told of the emotional pains of her past uncovered this illusion. Moments after hearing her voice, the sounds of her soft leather nurse's shoes could be heard walking over the clapboard porch. Old and weak boards, well-worn from years of rain and inclement weather, squeaked as she reached the door. As the screen door ricketed open, the knob on the oak wood door turned and there stood his ma mah. The expression on her dark brown face was surprised at seeing him up at 6:45 a.m.

"Braun, I'm surprised to see you up wit' the chickens," she chuckled as she closed the door behind her. Her white nurse's uniform accentuated her womanly, heavy-set hips and thighs.

"There's nothin' wrong is it, baby?" she inquired.

Braun smiled, then responded.

"No, everything okay, Ma mah. Jis' went to bed early," he responded.

His grandmother laughed as she walked over towards him. Braun laughed in spite of himself as she leaned over him to kiss him on the cheek. The scent of her perfume remained in the air even after she had gone into the kitchen.

"You must didn't cook nothin' this mornin'. Why didn't you fix you somethin' ta eat? Ma mah not gon' be round you forever," she stated as she retrieved a skillet from one of the cabinets. After a brief pause of laughter, Braun responded to his grandmother's inquiry.

"I ate, I ate a bowl of cereal. Waddn't really that hungry," he responded as he looked down at his hands.

"Sho' you don't want me to fix you some deviled hash and eggs?" she inquired as she went to the refrigerator. In doing so, she observed his contemplative posture through the reflection in the mirror on the far wall, causing her concern. She walked back into the dining room area looking over at him quizzically as she placed a hand onto her full hips. Braun attempted to right himself as he observed her concerned expression. "You sho' you alright, baby? 'Cause you been actin' mighty strange lately," she further inquiried. His grandmother had read him. And at that moment he saw no further reason in hiding the facts surrounding his dilemma. So after a moment of reflection, he looked up into her eyes.

"I jis…thankin'. I uh, kinda been thankin' a lot lately. College. You. A lot of thangs. My future. Then…then I talked to Ikara the other day," he started. Agnes's expression remained concerned as she eased over towards him.

"You talked to Ikara and? What did Ikara say, baby? She didn't say anything that upset you, did she?" she inquired. Braun was silent momentarily. Then, averting eye contact, began to reveal to his grandmother his cause for being in deep thought the past several days.

"We went to River Walk the other day. Ate at one of them outside restaurants. She likes eatin' there. Says it's to her, like bein' in some exotic country or somethin'. And we was talkin' and she hit me out of the blue with news I wasn't prepared for. She told me… she told me she was expectin'. She is pregnant. And I really don't know what to do, ma mah. I mean…I'm goin' off ta college and…" The rest of his thoughts were interrupted.

"Baby, Braun, has she told her parents, baby? You're just babies. Ikara's only a child. Why haven't you been told Ma mah this, baby?" his grandmother pleaded.

"I's, I's jis…I ain't know how you's gon' react. She scared. She ain't told her folks yet. And…I kinda wanna be there anyway when she do tell 'em. I ain't hidin' from 'em. And I'mma do what I have to. Face this responsibility," Braun stated.

Agnes smiled as she shook her head slightly. Her eyes registered pride after hearing Braun's proclamation, which in itself evidenced his maturity. She felt pride in the fact that her grandson, was determined to take on responsibility; he had become a man. She reached out to cup his chin and turned his head to face hers in order to look into his eyes and said, "And you're doin' the right thang, baby. What a man is spose' to. Remember what I've always told you--always have respect for yourself and others. Go on to her parents and you tell them how you feel. And that you are man enough to face this responsibility. Ma mah support you, baby," his grandmother stated passionately. She then released his chin and smiled as she stared at him affectionately. Braun smiled as he averted eye contact. His face was still full of thought. Agnes then patted him on the knee as she rose from the sofa to head down the hallway, leaving him to meditate about the situation.

Tariq stood before his dresser's mirror, placing on his tie which he seemed to be having difficulty with. This prompted Ursula, who found this amusing, to walk over and offer assistance. *Perhaps it was due to his rush for work? Or having an agenda mapped out and anxious to carry it out?*

"Take your time, honey. What's the big hurry?" she inquired.

Tariq smiled as he stared straight forward into the mirror.

"Ah, I've got to run an errand before I go to the office," he informed. Ursula made the necessary loop, then tightened his tie. "Thanks. What would I do without you?" Tariq said, then kissed his wife on the lips. Ursula smiled.

He walked past her down the hallway, glanced in at Ikara, who was primping in the mirror.

"Breakfast is all ready. Just have to fix your toast. Did you want cappuccino?" she inquired. Tariq was standing at Ikara's threshold and signaled his agreement with her offer.

"Yes. Yes, that's fine, honey," he replied. He then turned to observe his daughter as he straightened his shirt and placed his dossier underneath his arms. Ikara turned away from the mirror and slowly walked to her closet. Her face was sullen, and Tariq, in that brief instance, recognized this, and examined his daughter as she stood with her back exposed to him, fidgeting with her pink shirt. "Going somewhere this early, pumpkin?" Tariq inquired.

Ikara's expression remained neutral when she responded to her father. "No, just…wasn't sleepy is all. Can't figure out what I'm gonna wear today," she giggled. But the laugh belied the look in her eyes. She was anxious. She and Braun had talked that morning. The two had agreed it would be best to inform her parents of her pregnancy while in each other's company.

Tariq repositioned himself at the threshold. His eyebrows furrowed as he scrutinized his daughter. "There's nothing wrong, is there? Because you haven't been yourself lately. Anything you want to talk about, honey?" Tariq implored.

Ikara fidgeted and tried to maintain her composure. Tariq tried to ascertain the real emotional state of his daughter. At this precise moment, Braun's car coasted to a stop in front of the Galla family's large brick dwelling. Putting the car in park, he cut off the engine. His eyes briefly scanned the vicinity and no one was moving about at this early morning hour. The serene calm made him just that more nervous. His anxiety grew as he contemplated the immense situation. *How would her parents react? Would they now resent him?* He thought to himself, releasing a sigh as he looked down at the dashboard. Thoughts of how Ikara's parents would react raced through his mind and made him apprehensive. Then he slowly got out of the vehicle.

Inside of the Galla home, Tariq sipped on his cup of cappuccino as he placed the newspaper onto the table. He read a caption which, judging from his expression, had gripped his full attention. Then, as he prepared to take his seat at the head of the table, the doorbell rings.

Hearing the doorbell ring, Ikara turned sharply. Her worried face now registered even more anxiety for she knew who the visitor was. Tariq looked up quizzically from the newspaper. And Ursula who was scrambling eggs in the skillet, looked curious as to whom this visitor could be at the early hour of 8:27 a.m. Tariq proceeded to arise from the table after taking one last sip of his coffee.

Outside the door, Braun stood in silent reflection, wishing that he could fast forward his life through this dilemma. He had to brace himself. This had to be done. It was imperative. He had to do the right thing out of respect for himself, Ikara, and her parents. As he shook off the jitters, the large oak wood door suddenly opened and there stood a rather surprised and somewhat curious Tariq.

"Braun? How're you doing, son?" Tariq greeted. His tone evidenced his curiosity as to Braun's unexpected visit. Braun recognized the tone and expression. Intuition told him that Tariq's curiosity extended well beyond the early visit in and of itself. He perceived that Ikara's parents had detected something peculiar about her social and emotional state as well.

"How are you doing, Mr. Galla? Uh, I, I need to come in and talk to you, if it's okay?" Braun spoke softly.

Tariq observed him.

"Hi Braun. You're by early. Is everything okay?" Ursula greeted as she set down Tariq's breakfast tray on the table.

Hearing her mother and father's greeting, Ikara stood by the threshold of her room and listened intently.

"Everything's okay, Mrs. Galla," Braun responded. She watched him momentarily, her eyes registered deep concern. Then she called out to Ikara, startling her.

"Ikara?" she called out.

"Yes?" Ikara responded.

This further added to her parent's suspicion, for both knew that she had to have heard Braun's name mentioned.

"Braun is here," Ursula informed her.

Her parents exchanged concerned glances as Braun looked down at the floor.

"Have a seat, son," Tariq offered. As he did so, Ikara hesitantly made her way down the hallway. Her doe-like eyes glanced back and forth between Braun and her parents. Her hands were nervously fidgeting like a small child anticipating being spanked or scolded.

"Mrs. Galla," Braun calls out. She paused and stared at him quizzically as she untied her apron. It was then that Tariq noticed his daughter. Her dejected spirits and the look of guilt in her wide eyes in the presence of the boy whom she always spoke about, sent up red flags. At this moment his intuition told him exactly the purpose of the young man's early morning visit.

"Yes, Braun?" Ursula implored.

Braun lowered his head. Clasping his hands together after rubbing a nervous hand across his face, he looked up between Ikara and her parents.

"I need both of you here. I think...there's somethin' I,-we have to discuss with you," he informed.

Tariq glanced at Ikara, who stared at the floor, before looking at his wife. Closely observing his daughter, he got her attention and motioned for her to take a seat on the sofa. She did so timidly. Her mother joined as well and examined her daughter with curiosity.

"Ikara? Baby, what's wrong? What's going on, Braun?" Ursula plead while reaching out to hold Ikara's nervous hand.

Tariq remained silent and stood with both hands in his pockets as he stared blankly into Braun's face.

"Mr. and Mrs. Galla, this is kind of hard for me. Um, I have respect for you both...that's why I'm here this morning. Uh, I've been wanting to come forward with this...but I was afraid," Braun stammered.

"Afraid? Of what, Braun? You know you can talk with us if there's a problem," Ursula stated. She continued to look between him and her daughter. Tariq still remained silent, as if awaiting for the inevitable confirmation. Braun lowered his head once more, then released a sigh and stared blankly at the wall.

"Ikara and I... had sex...and, and...she's pregnant," Braun finally stated. At this point tears began to roll down Ikara's face as she quivered. She was muttering words that were unintelligible and the only decipherable phrase was an apologetic assertion.

"Momma, I'm sorry...this wasn't planned...please, don't be mad at me and Braun," Ikara quivered. Ursula drew her near. The shock of the revelation, however, was superseded with the emotion she felt at her daughter carrying a child for this young man whom they loved and considered a son.

Tariq grappled with emotions himself. His baby girl. *Pregnant at seventeen?* It was an emotional state no one could adequately prepare for and one he had deep dread for. He was becoming angry and experiencing anxiety. There was no malice in his heart for the young man who, at the moment, was staring compassionately at his daughter.

As Tariq stared at his sobbing daughter, he was stricken with a loss of words. Braun attempted to console Ikara and Tariq intervened. Staring teary-eyed into Tariq's eyes, Braun anticipated an admonishment. But there was nothing forthcoming. Instead, Tariq whispered to him his personal appreciation for his facing the situation as a man. "You've done the right thing, son. You've done the respectful thing," Tariq assured him. His eyebrows were furrowed, but somehow, in his eyes, Braun found solace. After a brief meaningful exchange, Braun then joined Ikara on the sofa. The two consoled each other in an embrace as Ursula continued holding her hand.

★★★★★★★★

"We'll have to bring that up at the next meeting. Things are definitely getting out of hand," Tariq stated as he walked away from his O.B.U. brother, Somali. The two held a one-on-one conference at Somali's home. With the meeting now over, both men—who were dressed in casual attire save for the Kente cloth hat Tariq wore—bid their farewells as Tariq walked across Somali's well-manicured Johnson grass.

"I just hope things at this state can be quelled, my brother. Give my regards to the family," Somali stated with an upheld fist. Tariq aptly responded with a return salute. After acknowledging a motorist passing, he walked around the front of his vehicle.

Coasting in silence though the degenerative streets of his old neighborhood, Tariq's expression was somber. His eyes held evidence of empathy as they beheld visuals that caused strong emotions within him: young derelicts consuming alcoholic beverages and falling victim to the systemic plot of conveniently placing liquor stores throughout the community; the crack addicts; the boarded-up dilapidated houses; and the pillar to post street dwellers. Then there was the element of street gangs. Even though Wild Bill and the core of his lieutenants primarily ran these streets, most of them were deceased, awaiting trial, or on the run. There seemed to always be some tension in the air in the neighborhood. And as he looked into the dark disgruntled faces of denizens he passed today at this twilight hour, he saw evidence of just that. However, at this moment, the tension seemed to be derived from another source: young black clad men skulking in the vicinity of Hamburani's restaurant. The men looked menacingly at the Pakistani man who appeared to be quite nervous as he exited his 2004 Yukon. Tariq studied the tension-filled scene then veered his vehicle across the avenue where a group was congregated.

A middle-aged black man with neatly lined hair and stern eyes, attired in a welding company uniform, emphatically lectured to a group of gang members. Tariq was well-acquainted with the man. He was a blue-collar worker who was active in the community and vocal at rallies. He stood up in the face of the oppressor. His last stance, which took place a year prior during one of the federal drug raids, had landed him in jail.

Tariq coasted to a stop in front of the group. He put the car in park as his attention was gripped by the verbal assaults that were being directed across the busy avenue at Mr. Hamburani. Mr. Hamburani disdainfully waved off the youth as another—who was in closer proximity to him—walked by, pretending to throw a bottle in his direction. This action caused him to flinch. The scene was unnerving to Tariq. Flashbacks to the racial profiling of Middle-Easterners post-9/11 were being conjured up in his mind.

Tariq closed the car door as he further examined the obviously hostile display. He turned his attention towards the man who was currently lecturing the gang.

"Mr. Carter, what's going on here?" Tariq inquired.

Mr. Carter extended a hand in greeting. He looked over in the direction of Mr. Hamburani, who was in the process of retreating inside of his restaurant.

"You betta run inside you rag head motha fucka!" shouted the youth. His back was exposed to Tariq, but he nevertheless recognized the voice. And as the young gang member turned in his direction, he made facial recognition. It was Keith, the kid affiliated with Wild Bill's gang. His face was contorted in a mask of hatred.

"Brother Tariq. How's things goin' with the O.B.U.?" Mr. Carter greeted him.

"Making strides. What's going on? What's that all about?" Tariq inquired, with a wave of the hand in the direction of Hamburani's establishment. All of the young men, including Mr. Carter, stared over in the restaurant's vicinity.

"Just everyone's eyes are finally opening now, Brother Tariq. These brothers right here and there see now, that the system, these foreign entities, imperialists in corporate America and the police department are working in conjunction against them, against us. And that as long as we continue to fight each other… plunder each other…kill each other…and poison our communities with drugs we'll be helping their cause," Mr. Carter explained.

Tariq reflected on the man's reference to "foreign entities" and "working in conjunction" (with the system and the police) and he wondered if this reference was directed at Hamburani. Mr. Carter was a level-headed man. Rational. *So could he now be considered irrational in his apprehensive stance against Mr. Hamburani? Caught up in the misdirected hate and melodrama spawned by the young radicals in the community who believed Hamburani had burned down Sadiq's restaurant? Possibly irate at the police investigation?*

"I don't understand? What does all this have to do with Mr. Hamburani?" Tariq inquired. There were expressions of cynicism bordering on sarcasm on the faces of the young gang members, suggestive of their opinion towards Tariq's liberal stance.

"Main, Hamburani burnt down Sadiq's bidness, main. Ery'body know dat," stated a dark-skinned kid with a black Texas A & M hat turned backwards.

"Yeah, man. And police interrogated Sadiq like he done it! Grilled 'em and e'rythang. But ain't questioned Hamburani or any of these other foreign mafuckas!" seethed Keith. Tariq looked back and forth between the two gang members quizzically.

Mr. Carter spoke, "And this in itself is questionable. Considering there were two witnesses. Mrs. James, whose house is diagonal from Sadiq's restaurant, and Derrick Jones who was on his way to work at the approximate time of the blaze, both gave corroborating versions of an Arab-looking teenager jogging from behind the buildin' lookin' around suspiciously. And both clearly stated that who they saw looked like Hamburani's nephew. Other people round here say they saw 'em earlier in the same clothes Derrick and Mrs. James described him in," Mr. Carter explained.

Tariq listened carefully as Mr. Carter explained. He weighed out the evidence.

"Did either of them go forward to the police with what they saw?" Tariq inquired.

"Right after the blaze, Mrs. James states that she called the police and told them about what she'd seen. And Derrick explained to firefighters and the police. But neither of their eyewitness accounts were mentioned on the news. Neither has their descriptions been used to profile a potential suspect in the papers. The police seem more intent with playing the insurance fraud card against the Brother Sadiq," Mr. Carter retorted.

Tariq's eyes darted in their sockets as he reflected over the details that Mr. Carter had just relayed. Then without really focusing eye contact with either of them, he began to speak. "Let's not get too paranoid. We have to thoroughly investigate the…" His words were interrupted by a still-disgruntled Keith, who continued to skulk back and forth as he looked menacingly over in the direction of Mr. Hamburani's restaurant.

"Investigate! Man, what mo' evidence we need? Two people, man…two people! Both say they saw this turban head mafucka snoopin' round Sadiq's bidness, main! Din all a sudden his shit go up in a blaze? Come on, man! I say we burn his shit down!" Keith ranted.

"Burn all these mafuckas shit down! They done took over this mafucka. Assaultin' people and shit! Police ride wit' em," another gang member stated.

"Because they help to socio-economically restrain us. Keep us in our current situation. They're mercenaries," stated Mr. Carter.

Tariq did not like the tone of this conversation. It was the same irrational tone he'd recalled hearing from Wild Bill and Sadiq, a tone evidencing their politics had become overridden with vigilantism spawned.

"Circumstantial evidence. Come on. Mr. Carter, Keith, 'Two Gun', listen to yourselves. Circumstantial evidence is what the system uses every day around the country to legally lynch our people. Let's not form a lynch mob here," Tariq pleaded. His arms gestured for the group to calm down. Keith walked away, kneeling down as he stared down the street, while the others—save for Mr. Carter—looked down at the ground.

"I agree with your assertion, Brother Tariq. And I too feel that more has to be sorted out. To be just. But when is the system going to start investigating us justly? And not shooting us in the back unjustly or showing indifference towards our establishments being robbed, vandalized, or burned to the ground? Think about it, Brother Tariq," Carter stated emphatically as his eyes scrutinized Tariq. His words caused him to once more avert eye contact as he reflected on the brief speech he'd just heard from him.

Chapter 28

Ayouth of approximately junior high age approached the passenger side door of a Honda hatchback. Underneath his arms he held two books and a folder. The driver of the vehicle—an African-American woman with reddish-brown hair and glasses—popped the locks on the door as she waved to two gentlemen standing just beyond the boy. These gentlemen were Tariq and Nawaz. Both were attired casually and bearing proud smiles as they waved to the lady. The vehicle pulled off shortly after the boy closed the door behind him.

The community center's tutoring session had come to a close at this hour. And only a few students remained in the parking lot as vehicles belonging to their parents or guardians arrived and departed. Most honked or acknowledged the two activists and other volunteers who were boarding their vehicles too.

Tariq patted Nawaz on the shoulder as the man attempted to walk towards his own car, causing him to pause. "Uh, I need to talk to you about something, Brother Nawaz," Tariq informed. His eyes were serious. As Nawaz studied his serious eyes, Tariq slowly removed his hand from his shoulder. He released a sigh before running a hand over his head and averting eye contact as he scanned the parking lot.

"Sounds urgent. What is the problem, Brother Tariq?" Nawaz inquired, while folding his arms before him.

"There has been for a period…tension, as you know, in the black community, due to police assaults and as you also know, there's some ah… animosities between the blacks and the foreign entities who they feel are taking over the community," Tariq explained.

Nawaz's eyes darted in their dark sockets momentarily before locking with Tariq's.

"Yes, er…I am well aware of this. But have things somehow worsened?" Nawaz implored.

"Fact of the matter is…yes. Unfortunately it has. There seems to have been a certain black-owned business burned to the ground a few days ago. And the youth gangs and political black activists in the community are seething. Screaming foul. Because they feel Aswan Hamburani might have sabotaged Sadiq's establishment to eliminate competition. The police believe differently. They seemed to believe it was an insurance scam. And my personal beliefs? Well… I don't know," Tariq explained. His mind raced with possible scenarios. *Could Sadiq have deliberately set fire to his own establishment? If so, what would be his motives?*

Nawaz looked quizzically at his partner. Then after a brief pause he responded, "I understand now how this tension has escalated if these people believe Hamburani would do such thing. I know him well, Brother Tariq. This is not his way. He is a good man. But you yourself don't really believe he is responsible no? I detect your beliefs that perhaps this man did indeed perhaps sabotage his own establishment, correct?" Nawaz inquired.

"It's a possibility. And a possibility that I took into consideration from the start," Tariq stated.

"But why? What reason? Was his business not doing well?" Nawaz further inquired.

"His restaurant specialized in Caribbean cuisine. We don't have a strong West Indian population here. I understand his desire to bring cultural cuisines to the region. But there just wasn't many patrons frequenting his establishment. Certainly not in comparison to Hamburani's. This fact pretty much cancels out a motive of competition elimination on the part of Hamburani. I think he realized it was a bad investment. And just figured he'd collect on insurance. But I feel there was another hidden agenda," Tariq stated.

Nawaz once again folded his arms and stared at Tariq quizzically.

"Hidden agenda? I don't understand?" he replied, dumbfounded.

Tariq looked off into the distance at the traffic. His mind raced with his ideological perceptions of this hidden agenda theory. "Sadiq, like many others, does not want any foreigners in the community. He feels that foreign entities are advocates of the system that represses our communities. And Sadiq wants to take action. He hasn't the political backing or the gumption to take the steps. So he's created mass hysteria, hoping the black youth gangs will lash out, out of pent up anguish and ignorance," Tariq explained.

Nawaz's expression registered disconcertment at hearing this revelation. He could not fathom why racial hatred between two peoples who had suffered similar persecution would arise in light of the obvious root of African American repression—the government.

"These implications, Tariq, are hard for me to accept. Why, why would this man think this way? This is poisonous ideology. Our people entered this country to have opportunities at a future. Not to prevent others from progress, Brother Tariq," Nawaz stated. His tone was sympathetic, as if trying to get consolation from Tariq, whose expression, after hearing Nawaz's plea, registered guilt. Tariq's guilt was on behalf of those whose racial hatred was hidden underneath his nose under the guise of Afro-Centricity. He felt compelled to apologize on their behalf.

"Certainly, Brother Nawaz. And it's self-evident. Most who are affiliated with our Afro-Centric structure are not against you or your people and respect your people's pursuit of capital in this democracy. But as with all people, there are bad elements. Those like Sadiq, whose racist ideologies contribute to the media misconception of how nationalism is defined," Tariq shakes his head in disgust after his passionate speech. He looked away as Nawaz continued to examine him. Then with a smile that belied his eyes, he patted Nawaz on the shoulder as he extended his right hand. "Take care of yourself, my brother." Nawaz smiled warmly, though his eyes still reflected concern. Then Tariq walked past him to his vehicle. He left Nawaz there, momentarily reflecting over the conversation that had just transpired.

The lights of an approaching vehicle illuminated the surroundings of this quaint cul-de-sac. They highlighted expensive cars and elaborately-manicured hedges in spacious lawns and profiled finely designed brick homes with cobblestone or brick driveways. The vehicle coasted to a stop. Its lights turned off and its driver exited. Looking around the vicinity with dossiers underneath his arms, he proceeded up the driveway to his home. The Galla residence.

Tariq closed his elaborate oak wood door behind him. The house is relatively silent, save for the swooshing sound of the air conditioning system. Was everyone asleep at this hour? Only 4 o' clock? Hmm. He thought to himself as he proceeds into the living room area. It was then that Ikara, talking softly on her cellular phone, appeared from nowhere. She nearly bumped into him.

"Oops. Excuse me. Hi dad," she stated, after bracing herself against him. Tariq smiled, then kissed his eldest daughter on the cheek as he walked down the hallway, fidgeting at his tie.

"Hi, pumpkin. Where's your mother?" he inquired as he paused in the middle of the hall. Ikara, with the phone cradled between her face and shoulder, and the remote control aimed at the television set, pointed an index finger in the direction of upstairs. The study? Tariq ponders. His eyes darted briefly. Then he refocused on his daughter, smiling to himself before turning to proceed upstairs.

Ursula was sitting at the desk inside of their walk-in library. Set before her are pamphlets and interior designing magazines which she was, at the moment, browsing through. She was jotting down particular fabrics or furniture that appealed to her sense of design. She didn't sense Tariq standing there observing her as he removed his tie. She looked up from her work as his shadow passed in front of the light source illuminating the desk.

"Oh, hi, honey," she greeted in warm reception as Tariq leaned to kiss her on the lips. She then refocused on a page with elaborate rugs and an elegantly designed kitchen. Tariq picked up one of the brochures and thumbs through it. But his eyes revealed the fact that he was not really seeing the photos but was, rather, buying time in his own way before opening up to his wife. "I was thinking about re-ordering several of the fabrics and outdoor furniture in these. See anything in there you like?" Ursula inquired. A smile was etched across her face as she continued to browse the designing magazine. Tariq's eyebrows were raised as he smiled that belied the deep contemplation in his eyes crossed his face.

"Well, you know, interior designing is your field of expertise. I'm just a layman. I'd probably have a green wall with a red sofa or something," he joked. Ursula laughed. Then, glancing up into his troubled eyes, the smile slowly vanished from her beautiful face. The expression evoked by Tariq's light humor was replaced by a look of concern.

"Something's on your mind again. What is it?" she inquired.

Tariq's eyes averted from hers. His face twitched as he placed his hands on his hips. "Everything's...everything's wrong. I just feel like tensions in the old neighborhood are getting out of hand," he responded. Ursula's stare showed that she was reflecting back over the dilemmas in the urban black community.

"Oh, I see. There hasn't been another police incident?" she inquired.

Tariq shook his head to the contrary.

"No. No police incidents. Thus far I should say. They've been calmer since the acquittal," he responded. He then began walking towards it as Ursula continued to examine him quizzically.

"Then, what's going on now? I mean, I know that the police aren't the only social problem. But..." Her sentence was interjected.

"No, the police are never the only social parasite. And definitely not in this instance. You know Sadiq's restaurant was burned to the ground and I never mentioned this to you before, but I have my suspicions," Tariq informed as he looked out of the window into the dark void of space and the woodlands which encompassed the terrain behind their home. He also looked at the lights of the city in the distance that sparkled in patches through the branches of the trees.

"Suspicions? About what, honey?" she further implored.

Tariq then turned slowly to face her.

"My suspicions about the fire. And that Sadiq might have sabotaged the place himself. For more reasons than one," Tariq stated with conviction. He stared in the direction of his wife.

"I don't understand, baby. Why would Sadiq burn down his own business? He saved for years. And he went to business college…" Her words were interrupted by her husband.

"He wasn't making any revenue. It was a bad investment. We don't really have a strong West Indian population and the business was going under," Tariq said. He paused for effect as he walked over to a bookshelf and ran a hand over a book's binding.

Tariq turned to her. "Sadiq's hatred towards foreign business owners taking over, incited him to create this hysteria. He's using the already tenuous situation with the police and the mistrust of these foreign business owners to incite a potential riot. He knows the youth gangs are volatile at this point. And he's trying to ignite the spark," Tariq explained.

Ursula's eyes were wide. Her expression was filled with terror at hearing this revelation. "A race riot? Tariq, you don't feel you're being a little too suspicious in this situation? Sadiq is…well…overzealous at times, but inciting a riot?" Ursula responded. A smile of sorts crossed her face , though her eyebrows were furrowed and her eyes registered unadulterated fear. *Fear, perhaps, for the potential of Tariq's theory being true? Or fear that her husband had become paranoid?* Tariq recognized the expression. Her tone was self-evident of her skepticism.

"I'm not being delusional. And Sadiq is beyond being classified as overzealous. We're not dealing with a person vigorous in helping the people, solving problems or being politically active in regards to stamping out the repressive predicament of the people. No. You've seen him at the community awareness functions. He's rabid. Disturbed. Everything he speaks is racist in content and I just don't sense real nationalism in him. I think he just uses black organizations to back his causes and business ventures. And he adds fuel to the fires to these misguided militants whose agendas are just as racist as the Klan," Tariq spoke in incensed tones.

"I didn't know Sadiq was this narrow. Are you sure? I know you're emotional about…" Her words were once again interrupted.

"Things are out of hand. I was down there the other day. It looked like a mob scene forming. Sadiq has everyone turning against these people. They're decent citizens just trying to have success with their businesses. Feed their families. Live the American dream. Sadiq and others like him have always wanted to stop them from living the dream. And now they're using the fire to persecute them," Tariq stated in disgust. As he spoke, he shook his head, looking down at the floor as one hand rested on his pocket and the other gripped the bookshelf.

Ursula shook her head. Her eyes were filled with sympathy for those such as Mr. Hamburani who were being persecuted. With that empathy was also embarrassment. She was embarrassed to know that her own people were persecuting another ethnic group which had endured hardships and oppression much the same as her people. Her mouth began to move as if she were in the process of responding. But before she was able to, the phone rang.

The phone was closest to Ursula. She answered it on the first ring. "Hello? Oh, Brother Qusta…what's this? What's going on in the news?" Ursula inquired. Her eyebrows furrowed. At the mention of news, Tariq's face registered confusion. On the other end of the line was Somali, in his house robe and slippers, glancing back in distress at the images on the T.V. screen. As he spoke his words were anxious and urgent.

"…A youth has been shot on the eastside. And the motive…I don't know…this is bad,"

Somali stated. As Ursula listened, Tariq had already flicked on the television set, scanning channels past Hispanic programming until he reached the news broadcast. He felt bewilderment now as images of Sadiq's burned down restaurant were shown, as it had been filmed live. The restaurant was still ablaze as the fire department struggled to contain it.

"…This was the scene of the blaze that destroyed this place of business late Thursday night.

Detectives called to the scene of the shooting have been told by witnesses that the incident could be linked, explaining that allegations against Mr. Hamburani in connection with the blaze that destroyed the black-owned business, might have prompted this black teen male to confront him. The teenager, a sixteen-year-old whose name is being withheld at this time, allegedly accosted Mr. Hamburani with a broken bottle. Fearing for his life, Mr. Hamburani retrieved a semi-automatic handgun, shooting the youth once in the abdomen. When the police and ambulance attendants arrived at the scene, the youth was pronounced dead. No charges at this time have been brought forth against Mr. Hamburani in connection with the fire or the shooting..."

Tariq was stunned. He felt numb at hearing this broadcast. In that instant, his heart went out to the young victim and his loved ones, along with a deep loathing for the man who indirectly, through false propaganda, caused the youth's death.

For approximately a half block radius around the downtown police precinct, hundreds of African-American protestors had gathered. Many were irate and chanted anti-police slogans, while others chanted and cried out for what they deemed a blatant injustice in the Hamburani shooting incident. Many felt the incident could have been handled less violently and they believed that charges should indeed have been brought forth.

Around the perimeter of the precinct, police officers in full riot gear barricaded the building--sticks and shields in hand, legs spread wide apart, and menacing eyes concealed behind shades and face shields. As incensed radical brothers and sisters approached, shields and sticks were extended to push them back. Protesters were knocked to the ground. News team vehicles screeched to halts. The reporters and cameramen scurried out of the van with cameras equipment, then rushed in the direction of the protest. They tested their microphones as cameramen adjusted their headsets and camera straps.

"...Ain't no justice! It's just us! We're harassed by these police who have sworn to preserve and protect, but all they do is brutalize us! It plays out all over the nation!" ranted a very disgruntled Mr. Carter as he pointed in the direction of the police officers. His words, though shouted, were almost unintelligible amidst the reverberating chants and angry outbursts.

"...They've turned our communities into police states!" shouted Khadija. Her face was a mask of insolence as she turned her head this way and that. Her flowing dreadlocks swayed as she pounded her hand into her palm to emphasize her assertion.

"...And the only protectin' these bastards do is of the non-black presence in the community! Protect their freedoms and give them legal leeway to kill young black men!" Sadiq yelled at the top of his lungs.

Tariq, along with Somali, was trying to calm down the crowd. He looked disdainfully in Sadiq's direction, then continued to gesture with his hands as he stood between police barricades and demonstrators.

"Brothers, sisters...let's bring some order here. Let's get some order. How can we be heard or our demands even be taken into consideration if we can't present ourselves in an orderly way? Let's calm down...get some order here,"

Tariq pleaded.

The chants and shouts began to simmer, but there were still outbursts by those such as Sadiq, Mr. Carter, and Kabil, who were dressed in all black with berets, as they pointed cautioning fingers in the direction of the police. And still the cameras rolled. Reporters hurried to interview these activists and militants, as they were anxious to cover this unprecedented affair. But across town, in the heart of the Eastside, there was another story unfolding. As Tariq's cellular phone rang, dispatchers inside of the police precinct were frantically issuing orders for units patrolling neighborhoods on the Eastside to respond to a disturbance.

A youth of approximate junior high school age jogged down the street holding perishable food items. His clothes were shabby and his hair unkempt. His face was determined as he glanced back at the sound of shattering glass. Then he passes Brother Khari who was kneeling down beside a parked car. His expression was of terror as he held the cellular phone close to his face. His spectacles were pushed to the bridge of his nose and looked around the scene in dismay as he reflected upon two fiery balls of flames.

"Brother Tariq? Brother Tariq!" he shouted into his cellular phone as more shouting youth and gang affiliates run past. Some were carrying Molotov cocktails and others had spoils from their pillaging. Tariq's facial expression evidenced the fact that he was having an extremely difficult time hearing Brother Khari. "Brother Khari? What's the problem? You sound distressed." No sooner had Tariq spoken this statement than the sounds of police sirens blared, as the squeaking of rubber-soled police tactical boots moved frantically to patrol units. The officers' expressions were that of utter delirium as semi-automatic pistols were shoved into holsters. The officers received transmissions of a possible riot situation on the Eastside. And as Tariq shouted for Khari to repeat his report, a police helicopter rose above. Its deafening rotary blades caused Tariq and the other protesters—who, behind blue blockades, were still being pushed back by the police batons— to look up.

"Brother Khari!? I'm having trouble understanding! There's a police helicopter and it seems units are being dispatched! What's going on?" Tariq shouted while urging him to confirm. At that moment there was an explosion, causing Brother Khari to flinch.

"They're rioting on East Commerce! It's crazy! They're burning down everything, Brother Tariq!" he reported. Tariq's face was pallid as he stared speechlessly. As the confirmation of the incident was broadcast over the police unit radios, several news teams went into action. Tariq stared over at a very guilty expression on the face of Sadiq, who, only for a brief second, held eye contact, then averted his gaze. He continued to fake enthusiasm as he pumped a demonstration sign.

Smoke billowed from two buildings as a news helicopter soared high above the East Commerce section of the Eastside while covering the chaotic scene below. Foreign business owners fled their establishments as they were assaulted, accosted, and chased away by vigilantes. Some were exiting their stores only to find that a Molotov cocktail had engulfed their vehicles in flames.

There were shouts and screams of agony and confusion, along with the laughter and chants of the youth gang vigilantes who had declared anarchy. They were flustered by the injustices of the system and directed their hatred towards people who had probably had to endure just as much hardship and oppression as they had.

"…As you can see below, total mayhem has erupted on the corners of East Commerce and South Olive Street. Several buildings have ignited and you can see the flames that have engulfed this vehicle here… units have been dispatched to the scene, as well as ambulances…this is in the wake of escalating tensions in the neighborhood, heightened by the recent shooting death of a teenager at a Pakistani owned establishment. As you can see, there is a young male jogging into a liquor store with what appears to be a weapon…"

As the news cameras filmed, the sounds of police sirens could be heard approaching above the reverberating swoosh of the helicopter's rotary blades. The scene of the young man brandishing the weapon was viewed firsthand by Braun and Piye. The two had been on their way home after a day at the mall with Ikara and Swathi. They were shocked and dismayed to see cars aflame, people running and shouting, and smoke billowing up into the air. It was surreal.

The young man who went into the store wielding a pistol happened to be Keith, without a ski mask or any other form of disguise. The store's owner had since fled and the aisles had been ransacked. Keith hopped across the counter and pried open the register as two youths flashed by. One stopped after noticing him. His hand clutched a bottle with liquid and oily cloth.

"Keith! Come on, man! Cops is comin'! We bout ta torch this bitch!" The youth shouted as his chest heaved. The sun glistened off of his sweaty brown face as he looked frantically around the vicinity. Keith hurriedly stuffed the money into his pocket and then jumped back across the counter. He slipped down and crashed into the glass doors in his mad dash as shots echoed in the distance. The shots were exchanges from a .9mm. semi-automatic—which was fired from behind a store counter by a Pakistani store owner—and the gang member fired his .9mm Berretta in the general vicinity of the store before being shot in the leg. He stumbled away, cursing at the leg wound.

In yet another scene a gang member—'Two Gun'—holds a .38 caliber revolver to Mr. Hamburani's head as his wife pleaded for him.

"Rag head mothafucka! You killed my cousin, bitch! I'mma blow yo head off!" Two Gun ranted while pointing the barrel of the .38 at Hamburani's head. A loud explosion was then heard.

Braun and Piye exited the vehicle amidst several people running past with looted items. The cries and pleas of the Pakistani woman compelled the two to attempt to assist. They jogged in the direction of the mayhem as they shouted. But their assistance wouldn't be needed, as Keith and the two other gang members ran towards the scene ahead of them, screaming at Two Gun and hustling him away from the scene as the flashing blue lights of the shrill police sirens could be seen in the reflection of the windows of a parked car.

As the gang members fled, Piye stopped to check on Mr. Hamburani and his wife. Braun observed another scene of distress on another corner and ran to assist. As he reached the scene, he saw several youth accosting a Korean woman and her daughter. They attempted to flee in their vehicle and a police cruiser screeched to a halt feet away from Piye.

The Korean woman screamed as one of the youth tussled for her purse. The tug-of-war ended with the youth punching the woman full in the face, causing her to relinquish her grip. The force caused the kid to stagger backwards and stumble to the pavement. As the approaching police unit neared, another large youth jerked him to his feet. Items fell from the purse as he hustled along. One of the items that fell out was her cellular phone, which Braun scooped up to return to her when he approached the car's window. When the woman saw Braun, her eyes were enlarged with terror and she cried out in her native tongue.

Braun responds, "It's okay. It's okay. I'm not gonna hurt ya'll. I'm tryinna help you. You okay? You okay?" Braun peers into the car, noticed blood on her cheek and wiped it away. Her daughter realized that Braun had good intentions and stopped screaming. A block away, Officer Jackson and his partner were quickly approaching the scene. Officer Jackson spoke into his police radio as he observed gang members fleeing into alleys and around buildings.

When the police cruiser pulled up to the Korean woman's vehicle, Braun was still standing next to the car. The police got out of their vehicles with their weapons drawn.

"Freeze! Step away from the vehicle with your hands up! Move it, now!" shouted the officers.

Braun was still preoccupied with calming the Korean woman down. Braun was startled by the officer's shouts and inadvertently jerked away from vehicle and turned in their direction.

As the other officers questioned Mr. Hamburani, shots rang out causing the Pakistanis and the police officers themselves to move quickly. The officers took cover besides their vehicle while looking frantically around the vicinity. Fires continued to cause small explosions, and shouting looters continued to run through the streets. On the other block, the Korean girl's screams had resumed. But this time it wasn't for her mother being assaulted. There, sprawled on the pavement and bleeding profusely from two gunshot wounds, was the young man who had come to assist them.

Piye sensed danger and began to slowly jog towards the scene. His chest heaved and his eyes became wide with terror. There was a lump in his throat. His heart raced as the anxiety welling up inside of him strained his run. It was as if the wheels of time were churning to a stop. And as he neared the spot where his friend's bullet-riddled body lay, the smell of smoke, the screams, the running looters, and the police sirens vanished.

Officer Jackson's partner lowered his head and shook it in anguish as Officer Jackson himself stared on. His eyes were entranced as he continued to aim his semi-auto. As his partner refocused, his eyes sympathetic, he spoke out, "Oh Jesus. Oh no, that's…that's a cellular phone he's got in his hands, Jackson. Jesus," His partner stated while running a hand over his face. His expression was remorseful. Piye reached Braun as both Korean mother and daughter exited the car crying. They explained to Piye what happened as they pulled at him.

"He was only trying to help! He was only trying to help!" Their words, however, fell on deaf ears as Piye, tears now streaming down his face, dropped to his knees beside his friend. Braun's eyes were closed and he was motionless. His white T-shirt was now turning a crimson red from the entry wounds the large caliber weapon had made. Still firmly clutched in his right hand was the cellular phone. Piye, sobbing uncontrollably now, slowly reached to pull his friend close to him as Officer Jackson stared on in dismay. Dropping his head in guilt, Officer Jackson reached for his radio and called in for medical assistance.

"I need an ambulance at the corner of East Commerce and South Olive St…," Officer Jackson sighed as he signed off. Shaking his head as he stood up, he then replaced his semi-auto back into his holster as Piye rocked his friend in his arms.

Hours had passed since the sparking of the riots. The steps in front of the precinct were now empty. The protesters had long since returned to their respective homes. And on the Eastside the sun was setting. The brilliance of the fiery sphere had now gone beneath the horizon, giving way to twilight.

The scene was like a third world country: cars charred; broken glass, and spilled perishable items looted from stores strewn about in the streets; and gutted out stores smoldering from the pipe bombs and Molotov cocktails. Police and National Guard units patrolled the streets, ordering many off of the streets and in some instances hauling gang members and other looters from their homes in handcuffs. One happened to be Keith, who, along with "Two Gun" and several others of Wild Bill's gang, was placed in the back of a police unit, as a truck with M-16 wielding National Guardsmen rolled past.

It was dawn. A police helicopter soared above the central business district and captured the brilliance of the lights of the high rise buildings and the neon lights of the bars and clubs on the streets below. All seemed quiet. Normal. But elsewhere another event was taking place that wasn't of the norm.

The hour was 6 o' clock a.m. and it had been predetermined that a candlelight vigil was to be held at this hour in the light of the chaos and bloodshed that had taken place just hours earlier on the Eastside. In front of the Alamo dozens gathered. Men, women, and children. People of all different nationalities, ethnicities and creeds. Whites, blacks, Mexicans, Koreans, Protestants, Catholics, Muslims, and Buddhists. They gathered in a spiritual congregation to bring some peace and sanctity in the wake of this travesty. It had been a brutal and racially-tensed week. A week that had seen several people lose their homes, businesses, and even their lives due to a very pandemic disease that plagued practically every city in America: the epidemic of oppression, ignorance, and racial hatred.

The lights of the candles flickered as the people held hands, many with eyes closed, tears streaming down their faces as they sang spiritual songs. It was a time for comforting. Healing. Silent prayers had been said. And people who had for years held disdain for each other were now holding each other's hands firmly. The power of love and God were evident on their faces. The vigil would last for hours. Late participants arrived as others left. The circle grew smaller with the passage of time until the candles were all burned down and the potpourri of people was gone.

Five days later, debris and charred vehicles remained on the eastside. But

God had once again allowed the sun to rise, now peeking above the horizon and revealing the grey bricks of this ancient mission. It was dawn now over the Alamo, and everything, despite the weeks of travesties, seemed peaceful.

A little girl dressed in a black dress and white gloves walked in silence. Her face was sullen. Her name was Jalena and she was Phil's little sister. In her hand she held a white rose. Just behind her were others, adults who were also dressed in all black. They were mourners at City Cemetery No. 4 to pay their last respects to a young man who had been loved by the community. He was a shining lantern through the pathway of education, peace, and humanitarianism, as well as nationalism. He was a lantern that, through vindictive oppression, was snuffed out forever, never more able to shine down its light.

The little girl bent slightly to place the white rose upon the silver casket which rested above the gravel pit. Tears formed in her eyes, but she wiped them away and was led away by a very distraught and thin woman. It was her mother, who stepped back behind the circle of mourners. Braun's grandmother shivered as she stared in the direction of the grave. Her expression was solemn. Her eyes were distant. She was being consoled by Piye. Piye's eyes were reddened and his head was bowed as he held his arm around her. Next to her, also consoling her, was Tariq. To his right was his wife and daughter, with Swathi and Sharon close by. Both were distraught. Tears streamed down their faces as they touched Ikara's black dress sleeves. Ikara slowly released the grip her mother had on her hand and maneuvered towards the casket with her own white rose and a picture of them together. Tears flowed down her face and her lips trembled as she set the rose down. After a moment, she was led away by her mother and father. The ceremony began to dissipate and the mourners made their way from the grave site. They severed themselves from this morbid scene of sadness and the surreal dreamscape that was punctuated by uncontrollable sobs from family members and friends. But despite this grey hour in their lives, the brilliant sun continued to beam down through the tree branches upon Braun's casket. Next to it, as some mourners perhaps may have noted, were two additional elaborately-designed headstones of granite and bronze. Both were weathered and dull from the passage of time. The one to the immediate right read Lakiesha Erickson and to its left, Eddie Erickson.

www.ingramcontent.com/pod-product-compliance
Lightning Source LLC
Chambersburg PA
CBHW021035030726

47496CB00006B/1550